DIRE:HELL

by Andrew Seiple

Cover by Andrew Halbrooks

Edited by Beth Lyons

ISBN: 069212134X
ISBN-13: 978-0692121344

DEDICATION

With thanks to Stuart Slade, for writing the Salvation War

CONTENTS

ACKNOWLEDGEMENTS

This book would not have been possible without my many and skilled beta readers. Thanks again, guys!

CHAPTER 1: SKYJACKING

"And lo! did the bringer of the one true game arrive in the Inferno. And finding the ground offensive to tread upon, she lifted her gaze to the skies..."

--Excerpt from the first chapter of the first book of the Chronicles of the Shared Lie

I'd heard once that the road to Hell was paved with good intentions. But now that I was looking down on it, my spectroanalyzer confirmed that it was pretty much just bricks.

The specialized visual mode was the only way I could even make it out at the minute. I hovered within the grinding fury of a fiery sandstorm, one of the many that churned and writhed above the barren landscape that we'd been transported to a few days ago. In lieu of white, puffy clouds, it had these things, all gravel and ash and howling hot winds. The grit was doing a number on my armor's outer layers, and I winced to register each scrape and scratch that flickered across my heads-up display. I'd need some serious downtime with a buffer after this was done.

But I didn't have a buffer. I didn't have much beyond what I'd brought with me during my unplanned trip to Hell. I had *access* to plenty of raw materials, but I needed shelter to build the tools to build the other tools to finally build the tools I needed to refine materials and repair my armor.

Hopefully, if this plan worked, I'd have all that and more before too long. The alternative was a slow, grinding death as my devices wore out. And my friends too, for that matter.

"We have movement," one of those friends spoke through the crude radio comm I'd rigged up. Alpha. My first true minion, a captured software entity, now trapped in the shell of an android. He'd proved his loyalty and competence many times over.

"Which direction?" I radioed back.

"From your position? Seven o'clock."

I turned, switching to voltaic vision, tracking electricity, ignoring the static frizz and fuss of the storm...

...and there it was. Vast, monstrous, something like a cross between a manta ray and a bird. I measured its bulk, and smiled. I'd seen aircraft carriers smaller than this monstrosity. It was one of many that traveled the skies here, occasionally swooping down to feed.

I'd mentioned the "aircraft carrier" comparison earlier to another of my friends, and it had triggered a wild, thoroughly insane idea that had been too bizarre to pass up. From that seed of an idea had sprung an even more bizarre plan, that lead to my current state of sandblasted stealth.

"Confirming the vector," I said, sliding to the side as the unthinkable bulk of it shuddered past. It spread wings wide to catch the thermals, vast pores on its side pulsing open and wheezing to adjust the air within it, spraying its surroundings with the equivalent of organic jets.

A lesser pilot would have been blasted away by the gusts of foul wind.

But I am lesser at nothing. I am Dire, and I stood resolute as the clouds of ash whirled and howled anew around me. My gravitic thrusters were able to compensate, and for three solid minutes I watched the thing cruise by, using my voltaic sight mode to trace the vast nerves in it, and the organic electricity running throughout its scaly body. Oddly enough, some of the big patches of bio-electricity seemed to be shifting around physically inside its body. Moving organs?

"...what did you say?" a voice came over the radio, educated, dry, and wavering with stress.

"Huh?" I reviewed my last words, about confirming the vector. "Oh. No, she wasn't talking to you, Vector. Just referring to the vector of approach." The static rose and flared as I explained, and my words were evidently lost.

"Come again?" Professor Vector asked. "Can you repeat that?"

I sighed. Radio was such a clunky medium, especially *here*. What passed as an ionosphere was different; the storms were hell on the waves, and it gave out at the weirdest times. But given what we had on hand, it was the best solution for the least resources.

"The target's coming down for a look-see!" Delta broke into the conversation.

"Recon. Call it a recon run," Gamma sighed.

"Does it really matter?" Beta added. "The end result is the same."

"It's hard to read an expression, but it seems nonplussed by the empty spike." Epsilon reported.

My Greek Chorus. Four androids, spawned of Alpha's code. Like their progenitor they were powered by mighty remote servers, normally. Due to current circumstances they were dependent upon backup arrays within my armor to function while in this dimension.

Which made the next stage of the plan all the more tricky. If I mistimed it, if the armor took too much damage, then they'd cease functioning. And five of our best assets would be rendered into empty shells.

They wouldn't be dead. Technically, hopefully, their cores were still intact back on Earth, taking care of business and getting the hell out of London. But still, losing their help at this juncture would be troublesome, and it would be hard on them as well. Ideally they'd make it back intact to sync up with their other selves.

I shook aside my worries and stared down, easing toward the edge of the storm.

Below me, the sky leviathan was coming down to feed.

The plain we were on was a volcanic, barren waste with steel spires poking up from blackened stone. Each spire had 'branches' covered with steel spikes.

And each branch bore screaming fruit.

Men and women of all ethnicity and ages. They hung impaled by the spikes, writhing as their blood flowed down gutters in the spires and gathered at the ground below before running through channels carved by erosion in the stone into a vast bloody river.

A road ran along it, meandering on its banks, going from spire to spire.

But today something was different.

Today, the great sky beast found that the first spire it came to had been stripped of food.

It didn't like that. The creature snorted through several of its mouths, a rumble like a thunderclap that shook the storm around me. The thing's heads writhed on its body as its wings beat, pulling up as it looked around.

We'd taken days, stripped the tormented souls bodily from two of the spires, leaving only one bearing its gory fruit. All in preparation for this moment.

So naturally, the damned thing turned in the wrong direction.

"Fuck!" I shouted through the radio. We needed it by the spire, or this was all for naught.

Fortunately, I am a super-genius. And I'd foreseen this sort of stupidity.

"Khalid!" I yelled, "Plan H!" A big burst of static interrupted my transmission, and I tried repeating it, but the storm's interference twisted and stole my words. *If it weren't for bad luck, I'd have none at all.*

I was tempted to jump directly to the endgame, but no, no, I trusted my friends. I had to, or we were all screwed. So instead of giving in to my instincts, instead of rushing down there and taking matters into my own gauntlets, I stayed above it all and hoped. They were smart, those two. Even without my command, they should be able to figure it out.

And they did.

Light burst in the sky above, crackling and green as the chemical flare rose and dropped near a full steel spire a little ways off. The beast paused mid-turn, wings beating as it came about in slow motion, heads transfixed by the glare. It lumbered through the sky, until the flare guttered and went out half a minute later.

"Come on you stupid bird-thing, come on..." I whispered, holding my breath as it paused.

It moved toward the spire full of prey again, and my breath eased in a sigh. Almost there. Almost to phase two.

The creature got in position, hovering fifty feet above the spire, as its wings beat to hold it steady. Definitely some sort of lifting agent in there, probably gas like Vector's autopsies had suggested. Given time and a machine shop we could have used that, but we didn't have either, so here we were.

"Aw man, here come the tentacles," Alpha radioed. "This is like the worst sort of hentai."

From my angle I couldn't see the countless feeder tendrils slurping out of the thing's belly, sliding down toward the spire and the twitching forms that it craved. But from previous observation I knew what would happen. Each tendril would find a person, tug them free, and pull them up into its digestive system.

Over the radio I heard the damned souls scream as a fate worse than eternal impalement came for them, meter after meter of ropy tendrils and slavering maws.

I'd asked Khalid if these things were like flying shoggoths. He'd told me no, shoggoths were far worse and to please avoid tempting fate any further.

"We're going!" Alpha called, and I knew what was happening, knew that even now, they were doing something any observer would consider mad.

Each of my friends, android or flesh, was leaping out from the bodies they were hiding amongst, grabbing tendrils, and riding up to be devoured alive by something that made that sand maw from Star Wars look like chump change.

And damn it all, the creature *noticed*.

I watched its wings beat faster, watched as long necks craned and heads peered down below it as a low rumble shook its writhing flesh.

"Going in early!" I radioed, and I twisted my lips against my skull, peeled them back into a grin.

Finally!

I burst from the clouds of ash and gravel, arrowed down toward the thing so quickly that the air boomed in my wake, shuddering across the plains...

...and drew the creature's attention as all of its heads snapped towards me.

"CRETINOUS CREATURE! HORRIFIC HARPY!" I roared, my voice booming out in a screeching howl that rivaled its own sullen croaks. "FACE DIRE AND FALL!"

It accepted my invitation, sliding around as it turned to bring its front half to bear. I pulled up short, cape snapping in the wind as the sonic boom rolled past me and over its bulk. Must have shaken the poor bastards on the spire below something fierce.

"We are in!" Khalid called.

"Right, disabling the crushy bits... now!" Delta confirmed.

"There's a lot of them," Beta observed, with the unnatural calm that he normally exhibited. "We may need repairs after this."

"Why the hell am I doing this, this is crazy!" Vector sobbed.

"Inject it already!" Gamma snapped. "Focus! Find the veins or whatever and get that stuff in its blood stream!"

"Technically it doesn't have blood—" Pedantry pulled Vector from his panic.

"Give it here," Epsilon said. "Doctor, I've injected the agent into its circulatory system."

And then I had to tune out the radio, as the beast breathed fire at me, and I got busy dodging.

Fire! I hadn't known it could do that. We'd never gotten this close to a live one before. "So. Fire-breathing, you guys," I spoke into the radio as I dropped from the sky for a few seconds before restoring the thrust, gripping my controls, and spiraling up at an angle. "Literal dragon-style plumes of fire."

"We are a little busy," Khalid called. "Fortunately my salve is proof against its digestive acid!"

Khalid was also known as the Last Janissary, an immortal alchemist and hunter of the supernatural whose career spanned centuries. Also, he was very upset that he'd ended up in Hell, even through such a non-traditional method. It really didn't sit well with his religious beliefs.

I didn't blame him. I didn't like the place either, and religion had nothing to do with it. Big bird-tentacle-monster things with fucking fire breath had more to do with my dislike.

Tendrils snapped out to meet me, and I twisted to avoid them. Sluggish, slow, used to dealing with prey that couldn't do more than squirm, they were ill-suited to oppose me. On the flip side, *damn* were there a lot of them.

"—need to get into the lift bladders!" I heard Vector shout through the radio. I wished them luck with that. My part in this plan was to be a distraction, on the other end of the creature. And so I played keep-away, slapping back the occasional tentacle that got lucky.

Unfortunately, my own luck wasn't so good.

One appendage got in under my guard, snaked around an ankle, and twisted at exactly the wrong moment. A turn that was supposed to bring me up around the edge of the creature instead arrowed inward—

—straight into the mass of tendrils around one of its feeder maws. My viewscreen filled with squirming snake-like tongues, and even as I tore handfuls away they levered me straight into a mouth the size of a garage door.

CRUNCH!

I lay still for a second, checked my HUD. Watched green lights flicker... and fade.

And I laughed.

The crunch hadn't been my shell, my eight-times-forged fortress of ceramic-steel, titanium, impact gel, and circuitry. It hadn't been the crumpling of my armor, or the shredding of the vulnerable body beneath.

The crunch had been the splintering of countless shark-like teeth, as for the first time in their enameled existence they encountered something that wasn't made of flesh and bone.

I turned to watch blackened, stained fragments falling to the ground below, and wondered how stupid this thing was. Could it feel pain from that?

Evidently not, as more tendrils sought me out, drew me further in, and the mouth smacked down five more times, shattering teeth, bruising flesh, and carving open wounds into its gelatinous flesh.

"ENOUGH OF THAT," I admonished it, as I ripped free from its tongues and caught the upper palate before it could close again. "CEASE YOUR MASTICATION OR LOSE YOUR MAW, YOU

MALODOROUS MISANTHROPE!"

It paused. I have no idea if it understood what I was shouting, or if it was starting to feel the pain from the abattoir I'd made of its mouth, but for whatever reason it evidently found its mouthful of villain to be unpalatable.

The walls of its maw contracted, and I knew it would next try to spit me out. "NOPE!" I declared, digging my hands full on into the roof of its mouth. I hated to damage it, we were trying to take it intact, but this thing had a *lot* of mouths. I figured it could do with one less. Or Vector could fix it. Probably.

As it turned out, I was half-right. The thing *did* try to spit, but from the back of its gullet came a horrific spew of half-digested people...

...and acid.

The wall of greenish juice slammed into me, flowed past me and out, and chemical warnings started to flicker on my HUD. Whatever it was, the substance was doing a number on my outer, steel layer.

Good.

I tracked the rate of damage, checked the spectroanalyzer, grinned to myself, and started counting. "Five. Four. Three. Two..."

FOOSH!

A few days ago, back on Earth, I'd had to tussle with acid-spitting mutants. I'd armored myself against them, with a reactive base layer. When exposed to acid, it would burn away slowly, emitting a cloud that violently neutralized any acid it came into contact with.

Instantly the thing's mouth filled with fizzing, roiling clouds of white goo, like Elka-Seltzer hitting Roja-Cola. I felt the entire creature shudder as what had been a casual spew of vomit turned into a rocket going the other way. The chemical reaction shuddered and juddered back into its body...

...and I went with it, abandoning my hold to go full thrust with the gravitics. Switching through my sight modes while my base layer burned away, I searched for my friends—

—and found them.

It was smooth sailing most of the way, through a mostly-empty stomach-like sack, past a few fleshy valves, and through a few thin walls of connective tissues. All the while the thing screeched and roared around me, twisting and writhing at the weird sensation I'd unleashed upon it. Oh, that wouldn't kill it, I was pretty sure. Not enough reactant to neutralize *all* the acid in its body or cause an explosion. Just enough to tickle something this size and keep me safe while I traversed its inner tubes.

With a final, slurping *rip* I burst through the last barrier, into a pinkish corridor, open and whistling with air, lined with feathery material and honeycombed with quivering strands of connective tissue, each as thick as my arm. And there in the emptied space, looking wild-eyed and holding up glow-lights at the sudden intrusion, stood the boarding party.

They took in the sight of me, dripping with juices, cape lost back there somewhere, tarnished by acid and pulling myself free of the rent and bloody wall.

"Uh, hey," Alpha said, waving.

"HEY." I waved back, then gave one final shove, twisting free. Minor damage to the outer shell, no systems damaged according to my HUD. Good.

"I kinda feel like this is a Here's Johnny moment," Delta said.

"Never mind that," Gamma insisted, "aren't you supposed to be on the outside, Doctor?"

"SHE HAS ALTERED THE PLAN. PRAY SHE DOES NOT ALTER IT FURTHER." I stood, brushing off gobbets of flesh. "BESIDES, THE DAMN THING'S FASTER THAN IT LOOKS. TENTACLE-WISE, ANYWAY."

"You made a Vader reference? Here? Now?" Vector pinched his nose. "Oy. Come on, we're not far from the main nerve cluster."

The wind whipped back and forth as we moved, whistling through the tubes and structures of this thing's organs. Were these its lungs? I didn't want to ask Vector, the man got pedantic whenever his primary field of study was involved.

And most of it would be wasted on me, to be honest. Sharp as my mind was, it couldn't hold information about biology, or process thoughts on organic structures worth a damn. I'd done that by my own hand, I figured. But that was past business, and I had a future to see to, so I turned and led the way deeper into the abomination that we'd boarded like an airship.

We were perhaps a thousand yards deeper into the thing's airways, when my sensors detected motion. I raised a fist up, and heard the group behind me clatter to a stop. "MOVEMENT. KHALID?"

"I know little of these beasts, save for their purpose."

"VECTOR?"

"Parasites, maybe."

"PARASITES?"

"These creatures are part of the local ecology, huge, and don't have any internal defenses once you get past the maws and acid. It stands to reason that smaller scavengers would flock to them, to— "

A split-second's warning was all I had. I twisted and threw my arms to the right. The corridor wall on that side burst and shrieking maggot-lampreys, each twice as long as a man was tall threw themselves at me, multiple jaws biting and slimy bodies twisting.

What the heck *was* it with the critters in this place having multiple mouths?

My fist collided with the first one, kept on going as ichor sprayed, striking through the soft bodies of more behind it, but they were many and momentum kept them going. My foot slipped on smooth organ-meat, and I went down.

Khalid was there, blade flashing as he danced around them, carving with strength and dodging with grace. For centuries he'd been fighting and studying swordplay, and every ounce of it was on display here, as the Last Janissary whirled and cut down hellspawn three at a time with every stroke.

I stood, armor smoking because of *course* these things were acidic, and laid into them as well, raw motor-driven strength and titanium gauntlets letting me strike with as deadly an effect as his alchemically-forged blade. To the side I was aware of my Chorus, moving with a synchronicity unmatched by any living thing as they coordinated their defense with the local close-range network they'd cobbled together down here. To the parasites, it must have been like fighting one fast, strong, fearless beast with five independent bodies.

Vector, thankfully, cowered in the corner and stayed out of it. The man was vital to our plan, too vital to risk in a situation he was ill-suited to help with.

Besides, I rather liked the guy. We'd pledged to change the world for the better, if we could only get back to it.

As it turned out, the parasites didn't have much stomach for slaughter when they were on the wrong end of it. They withdrew back into the blood-smeared wall. The flesh where they fell back looked different, I noted. Blackened, pus-smeared, unhealthy. They'd burrowed in here, made a nest long ago, by the looks of it. How many more nests were in this great beast? I couldn't say.

Eventually we'd need to investigate that and deal with them. First things first, though, and I turned to gesture back down the passage. "WELL, THAT WAS FUN. VECTOR, KEEP METAL BODIES BETWEEN YOU AND THE WALLS."

"I'm starting to dislike this place," Delta said. "Something to do with the ten-foot leech maggots or the way acid blood scores my finish, can't quite put my finger on it."

"They call it Hell for a reason," Alpha said, head moving back and forth as he fell back to the rear and searched the darkness beyond our lights. "You're not supposed to like it."

Khalid shook the ichor from his blade "Then the sooner we are done with it the better. Doctor, if you will?"

I nodded in acknowledgment and resumed my stroll.

Twice more we were attacked, though none of the worms were as large or as numerous as the first bloom. A few times we passed areas full of what looked like muddy bones. "The parasites dump their waste here, probably," Vector commented, and I could have lived a full and happy life without knowing that I'd been trudging through worm shit.

Finally, the corridor became a vast chamber, the size of a football stadium. In the center the smooth floor rippled and rolled as unknowable organs churned. My sensors registered heat rising from it, palpable and oppressive, though within human tolerances.

"VECTOR?" I asked.

"This is the spot. Most of its vitals are combined in this... heart... for lack of a better term. It should suffice." He patted the rucksack he'd been carrying all this way. It shifted as the thing inside it moved.

"THEN WHAT ARE WE WAITING FOR?"

"I need to check to see if the serum's made its way this far," he explained, getting to his knees and crawling out onto the membrane. "A sample from the center should do."

I floated alongside him the whole way, waving the others to take up guard positions in a semicircle at the edge of the chamber. There were literally thousands of tubes connecting to this room, and danger could come from any one of them. It had been a struggle to get this far, and I doubted the rest of this would be any easier.

To my absolute astonishment, I was wrong.

Vector jabbed a knife into the center of the membrane, took a sample from the wound with a needle built for horses, and ran the goo through a few vials of chemicals. "We're good," he declared, and opened up his rucksack.

Inside, a thing of pulsing flesh, wires, and electronics wheezed air through its breathing holes and twitched barbed tendrils restlessly. Vector reached in, and batted tendrils away as it tried to latch into his arm. With a smooth motion the biologist dumped his experiment onto the membrane, right where the cut he'd made oozed blood.

The reaction was instantaneous. Tendrils sought the wound, burrowed down into the flesh. I gave it a few minutes as it writhed and rocked, then nodded in satisfaction as the LEDs that Epsilon had built into the side of it flickered and turned green.

"We're online," Epsilon reported. "Mapping neural networks and flight mechanisms."

The chamber shook around us, and I grabbed Vector, held him steady as the great bird-beast felt its violation, felt its control going as the tendrils of Vector's home-brewed parasite robbed it of its own body. Something rumbled outside, distant, forlorn. I knew that it screamed, and I laughed to hear it.

Let it scream. All of Hell would scream soon enough, if it barred my way.

Finally the spasm was done, and I deposited Vector back onto the floor below. He immediately checked over his experiment, fussing like a parent with a child. Minutes passed before he looked up, and offered a wan grin. "We're good."

"GENTLEMEN, LADIES," I turned, to regard my friends. "WE HAVE ACHIEVED TOTAL CONTROL." I spread my arms, in triumph, gesturing at the grisly walls of flesh surrounding us. "FEAST YOUR EYES UPON OUR NEW VILLAINOUS LAIR!"

CHAPTER 2: INTERNAL AFFAIRS

"From her high vantage point did the great teacher look down and see the first players. And lo, did she deem them worthy of characters."

—Excerpt from the first chapter of the first book of the Chronicles of the Shared Lie

Through the vengeance of a petty, malicious supervillain that I'd thoroughly humiliated and defeated, I'd been sent to Hell. Literally.

Fortunately, I'd been joined on the trip by an alchemist with lifetimes of mystical lore, the best metahuman biologist in the world, and five of my automated minions. So we weren't exactly in a hopeless situation. It was a troublesome situation, but far from hopeless.

That said, it wasn't going to be an easy trip, even if we did manage to make it through. But we'd agreed that we'd handle it one step at a time and avoid despair.

Which was really fucking hard at the minute, as I wearily trudged through every inch of the creature's inner workings, mapping out every twist, tunnel, and turn I could, slaughtering any parasites I came across.

Around the other quadrants of the beast my Greek Chorus was doing the same thing. But unlike me, they didn't have to worry about fatigue. I'd been locked into my armor for days, unable to emerge because of the air quality of Hell, enduring painful sleeping positions, the increasing rankness of my own sweaty skin, and no real way to eat anything. I had water, at least, from my internal hydration mechanisms and reservoir and about a day of nutrient paste left. But I had no real way to get new food until Vector had a chance to treat me... which he couldn't do until I'd shed the armor.

I was pretty goddamned tired. Vector probably felt like crap, too.

But as bad as we had it, the Janissary had it worse. His alchemy kit had a bit of water in it that let him get by, but no food. And the facesucker symbiote that kept his lungs from turning into black jerky drew from his body's reserves. He'd lost weight visibly since we'd arrived. I would have shared the paste with him, but again, no way to get it to him without decanting from the armor.

So I worked without complaining or shirking. Khalid was withering before my eyes. The sooner I finished the job, the sooner we could see about fixing that.

When in Hell, let no friend fall further. That sounded like a good quote. I checked my memory for sources, found none. Then again, I hadn't exactly done much reading on the place; theology wasn't my bailiwick at the best of times.

"Doctor?" A burst of radio static, as Alpha called.

"Here."

"We've got a potential safe room. Vector's cleansing it now. Give it ten and come on back to quadrant three."

I sighed in relief. That lasted about all of three seconds before a chittering swarm of maggot-young charged me from out of the darkness. "OH NO YOU DON'T, YOU LITTLE SQUIRMERS!" They scored my boots something fierce before I was done, but they squished like all the rest.

I gave it another twenty minutes, instead of ten, just to make sure I wouldn't have to return and do this whole thing again. No clue how fast hell-worms breed. That was a fact I really didn't want to introduce into my eidetic memory. Come to think of it, this whole trip would probably be grounds for serious therapy later.

"Suru, make a note," I whispered to my digital assistant. "When we get home, she needs to kidnap a psychologist."

"Confirmed, Doctor," Suru whispered back. "Please be informed that the calendar is inaccessible. GPS synchronization is—"

"Failing. Yes, she knows. Endure, Suru. Endure." That was more for my benefit than hers, really. Suru frankly wasn't that smart. I kept her around more out of sentimentality than utility.

Finally, the area was reasonably clean. Probably could have done a better job if I gave it a few more hours, but it would have yielded diminishing returns at best. I activated my gravitics and wound my way back through the lungs of the beast, great winds flowing and blowing around me. I passed roomlike cavities as I went, organic caves that went from bathroom-sized to house-sized and back again, as the creature breathed. Not quite what we were looking for. Hopefully the safe room was in a more stable part.

It was. I stared at the chamber, easily as big as a high school gymnasium. Black junk lined the walls, and bones poked through them. It looked scabrous, hideously unhealthy...

...and unlike most of the tissues we'd been crossing over or wading through, it looked *dry*.

Vector glanced up from where he was spooling out bundles of gauzy tissue from a makeshift chemical bath. "There you are! A little help?"

"WHAT'S THE PROJECT?"

"You can fly. I need you to hang drapes, basically." He gestured, hands full of bunched membranes that did look sort of like curtains. Curtains made out of mucus and jellyfish goo, but curtains nonetheless. They overflowed the twisted swatch of cured hide that he'd turned into a cauldron and filled with chemicals and compounds. As I watched, more filmy material oozed out, and he pulled it free, holding the bath steady so it didn't spill.

"DO WE HAVE NAILS NOW?"

"I've synced the curtains to the beast's tissue. They should adhere with a bit of pressure. If not, I'll think of something."

It took more than a bit of pressure, and it was fairly slow going, but finally we got the two entrances walled off with shimmering whitish-yellow curtains of goo. Khalid helped where he could, his eyes weary above the slimy symbiote that covered his lower face. Finally Vector declared it done, dumped the bath into a rounded corner, and called Khalid over. A quick conference and Khalid handed him a few vials. Vector poured them into a hollow in the 'floor', stirred, and dropped in a few tablets. "There. Give it about half an hour."

We gave it a full hour to be sure, sitting and resting. I watched my HUD, smiled as the atmosphere got more breathable by the minute, and toxins were flushed out.

"WHAT WAS THIS PLACE?" I gestured. "NOTHING IMPORTANT?"

"One of its hearts, I think. Though it's hard to tell exactly. Beaky's fascinating. Instead of dedicated organs, he's got—"

"BEAKY?"

"Well, it needed a name, and no one had anything better." Vector glared, and pushed his spectacles up his nose. "As I was saying, most of its organs are general purpose. In the event of traumatic injury, given a few months of recuperation, other organs will convert over to the missing or damaged organs to help pick up the load."

"BEAKY."

"I suppose you have something better? Gloomy sounding, starting with D? That sort of thing?" He smirked. "Tough. I already named it Beaky."

"He's right you know. Called dibs and everything," Alpha said.

"TREACHEROUS MINION!" I boomed at Alpha.

"You knew this day would come, Dire!" Alpha boomed back. "Haha! I've been lying in wait all this time, just to ruin your chances at giving your lair a cool name!"

"Our lair," Delta corrected. "And what's wrong with Beaky? She's got a lot of beaks."

"I thought it was a 'he'," Gamma said, glancing to Vector.

Vector shrugged. "Actually I'm uncertain. I haven't found a means of reproduction yet. That study will come later, once we have more free time." Vector grinned like a kid who'd found himself locked in overnight at a candy store. "I could spend decades on this specimen, and according to Khalid this is just one creature among billions..."

"BILLIONS?" I turned to Khalid, who sat in the Lotus position, hands on his knees. "ARE YOU SURE YOU ARE NOT EXAGGERATING?"

Khalid tilted his head, considering. His cowl was stained with acid-spots and torn from his trip in through the maw, I noticed. We'd need to find some cloth at some point and fix that. "If anything, I underestimate," he spoke, muffled as always from his living mask. "The hellspawn are legion, in form and foulness."

"WELL, IF THEY'RE ALL AS EASY AS BEAKY HERE, THIS SHOULD BE A CAKEWALK."

"They are not the only things in this pit. Demons and Fallen Angels call it home as well."

"Wait," Vector said, leaning forward. "Isn't Beaky a demon?"

"No, it is a hellspawn."

"THERE'S OBVIOUSLY A DIFFERENCE, THEN?"

Khalid nodded, eyes watching the bubbling mess that was slowly cleansing the chamber's air. "There are generally three types of creatures within Hell, besides the damned souls themselves. The first are hellspawn. Animals and beasts most fierce, which inhabit the wilds and serve as pets to demons. They are mortal, and thus limited. And for the most part, unintelligent."

"DEMONS ARE A MORE TROUBLESOME MATTER, DIRE ASSUMES."

"Very much so. Have you heard of Nephilim?"

"NOPE."

"To simplify the tale, early on, when angels walked the earth freely with men, some took wives and husbands from mortals. The results were Nephilim, half-angel and half-human."

"ANGELS CAN DO THAT?"

"Yes. Although they were punished for that crime, and their offspring were hunted."

"HARSH."

"Necessary. But to get back to the point, demons were, to start with, the offspring of Fallen Angels and either humans or hellspawn."

"Which would seem to indicate that hellspawn were here before the fall," Vector rubbed his chin. "Assuming your theology is correct— no offense, of course."

"None taken." Khalid spread his hands. "My knowledge, to date, has been gleaned from the lore of secret histories that I have either heard or read, or experience from slaying hellspawn and demons when they emerged into Creation."

There was something missing from that list. "NOT FALLEN ANGELS?"

"No," he said, simply. "Not Fallen Angels."

The silence sat there in that chamber, with the hollow where a heart had once been and the shadows crept up around the edges.

Typically, Delta caved first. "Well what's so special about them anyway?"

Khalid looked at her. "Fallen Angels? They are still angels. Even stripped of the powers allotted them by God's grace, they are still *angels*. It is a measure of power against which no mortal can stand."

"Stronger than Crusader? Because the boss-lady tanked him pretty well. Twice."

"Angels are responsible for the workings of Creation, and all the stresses involved with ensuring it works properly. One does not simply slay an angel, even a Fallen one."

Delta waved it off. "Yeah, and we're constantly inventing new ways to bend and break physics. Whereas you're running around trying to whomp things with a sword. So you couldn't do it, but I mean, how do we know a particle beam to the face won't do the trick unless we try it?"

"I am saying that if it comes to that, we will not get the chance!"

"ENOUGH. PEACE." I gestured. Khalid was an old friend, and an invaluable resource, down here. Without his knowledge, we wouldn't get very far. "WE'LL TRY AND AVOID FALLEN ANGELS IF WE CAN." Time to change the subject. "OF COURSE, THAT GETS EASIER IF WE KNOW WHERE WE ARE FIRST."

"I have been giving that some thought. Assuming that the Damned we spoke with are truthful, we are in the fifth circle."

"Circle?" Beta looked to him.

"Hell is called a pit for a reason," Khalid reached into one of his pouches, pulled out a set of concentric rings. "The First Fallen landed here, like a meteor from above. The blast hollowed out all of Hell." He placed rings above each other, starting with the smallest and getting larger with each placement, using his fingers to separate them.

"So there's a larger planet outside of the pit that's Hell? Or is that Hell, too?" Beta persisted.

"That is where my knowledge ends. I am not even sure it is a planet, in the conventional sense of the word. At any rate, judging by the scenery and the nature of the punishment of the Damned, I believe us to be in the fifth ring; the space reserved for the wrathful and sullen."

"THE DAMNED SOULS WE PEELED OFF OF THOSE SPIRES DIDN'T SEEM VERY WRATHFUL. THOUGH A FEW DID SEEM SULLEN. DIRE CHALKED THAT DOWN TO AWKWARD CIRCUMSTANCES AND THAT WHOLE EXCRUCIATING PAIN THING."

They'd either fled, or assumed that we wanted to enslave them. It had taken some discussion to convince them otherwise, and I still wasn't sure they believed me. But that was a matter to sort out later, when we got back to the base camp.

Khalid shook his head. "Sullen can refer to a buried wrath, passive-aggression. Or it can refer to sloth, which I believe is the greater category of those punished here."

"So they're lazy?" Delta shook her head. "Didn't seem that way to me, once they got to work."

"It is a greater sloth. I believe that they are all people who were caught in a bad situation, and rather than make a choice, hesitated. And through hesitation, they allowed evil to happen."

"That's rather specific," Epsilon spoke up. "Can you explain the reasoning behind that theory?"

"Certainly. All the sources I have studied suggest that Hell operates under a sense of cruel irony, attempting to tailor punishments whenever possible and utilizing symbolism that is easy to grasp with some meditation. In this case, the spires and impaling spikes represent the dilemma they were caught upon, preventing them from acting. The hellspawn, such as the one we are currently within, represent the evil that befalls them due to their hesitation. They can see it approaching, but can do nothing, and thus they are devoured wholly by it."

We digested that for a minute.

"Okay, that's pretty fucked up," Delta said.

Alpha shrugged. "Hell."

"SO WHAT WILL BECOME OF THOSE WE FREED?" I wondered. "NOT THE ONES THAT ENLISTED, THE ONES THAT RAN."

"That is a matter of conjecture." Khalid tried to rub his beard, but recoiled when his fingers met the symbiote wrapped around his face. He rubbed his hand on his pants with annoyance. "I imagine that eventually they will be found and returned to spires. That is the constantly-agreed-upon fact of Hell, that torment is eternal and unending."

Vector spoke up. "So wouldn't, I don't know, being eaten by Beaky or Beaky's relatives, end that torment?"

Khalid shook his head. "Doubtful. The Damned are slain over and over again, here. Even being devoured by hellspawn would not end one's torment. The only things that might be able to deliver permanent death to the Damned are Fallen Angels, and even then, perhaps not all of them."

I felt my muscles ease a bit, in relief. We'd had to feed Beaky to get him down here. Foolish or not, I felt bad for sacrificing those Damned souls, leaving them on the spire when we'd saved several hundred more from other spires two days ago. Even now they were digesting in Beaky's belly, but they'd be back... somehow.

Though if permanent death was a kinder freedom, perhaps my morals were questionable in this instance. It would be worth consideration in the future. Also immaterial unless I somehow managed to convince a Fallen Angel to see things my way.

Vector interrupted my stream of consciousness. "We're good."

"Yeah, I know," Gamma said.

"No, I mean we should have a breathable atmosphere, now. Khalid, are you still up for the honors?"

"Gladly. Could you?" Khalid gestured to his symbiote.

We'd agreed that Khalid would be the canary in this particular coal mine. He was theoretically immortal, and I wasn't.

I turned away as Vector detached the facesucker from Khalid and tucked it into a pocket. I still caught a glimpse of writhing tendrils in my peripheral vision, and for the thousandth time I was glad that my armor was more or less a sealed system.

"Ah," Khalid said, and I heard him taking deep breaths, and coughing. "It smells... about as bad as I thought it would."

"It does take some getting used to," Vector said. "Slow down a bit. Let your system adjust."

Minutes passed, and I turned back in time to see Khalid nod. "I think I am well."

Vector took a blood sample, ran it through a few vials, and finally looked up at me. "He's fine. You can get out of that thing, now."

I closed my eyes. *Finally.* I tugged on the release, tapped the code, and vapor hissed as my armor's back unsealed. I took the opportunity to unhook the catheter, and hissed in a breath as I realized how sore the damn tubes had made me.

And oh, inhaling was a mistake, given the smell that rushed in. Long-rotted chicken, mixed with farts from very sick old men. My gorge rose, and I denied it, clawed my way outside, getting free of the metal casket that I'd been trapped in for days.

I will not vomit. I am Dire. I will not show weakness, even here, especially here. I told myself that until I believed it, and the smell, thankfully, faded a bit. Or maybe it was psychosomatic, my perception of it waning, or simply the appropriate part of my sinuses dying off from the stench. Either way it worked; I was fine.

The heat was the next thing that got to me. Moist, molten, and humid, something like Jersey on a summer's day. Sweat boiled up along my neck, and I stretched my shirt, trying to get air onto my breasts. "This is not comfortable," I grumbled.

"But it's liveable," Vector smiled. "Everything else is just a matter of time and effort. Though we've got other priorities, I'd say. Now hold still."

I found a somewhat-comfy spot to sit while he pulled out a series of syringes and then inoculated me. "There. Proof against the local pathogens that we've encountered so far, an adjustment that will let you eat the same things I've been consuming. And also a fast-acting relaxant."

"A what?"

"It'll make you sleep for a while."

"Hold on, Dire didn't reguest... request..." I sat bolt upright, tried to anyway. Then Alpha was there, holding my shoulders.

"It's cool. I *did* request it. I know you haven't gotten any sleep in days."

"No!" I pushed him away, then fell over onto my face. My muscles were jelly, but my anger was molten jelly. Molten jelly. I giggled at the thought. Wait no, I was supposed to be angry. "Issas outrache!" I snorted into the funk of the meat floor. Gods, it was, wasn't it? "Meet jelly?" I mused.

"We talked it over and you need a nap, boss."

I was aware of the Greek Chorus standing around me now, settling down in a loose formation, a guarding formation. My minions. My treacherous, loyal minions.

"Isssn over," I slurred. And then it was, and warm darkness was my lot in life.

I woke to find Khalid sitting next to me, and the Chorus departed, along with Vector. "Bastards," I snarled, rising to my knees, then hauling my weary self upright.

Khalid rose as well.

"If it helps, you may include me in that invective. I accepted their vote to enforce your slumber."

"Et tu, Janissary?" I was tempted to punch him, but it passed. The others I could get mad at, but not Khalid. He had helped me early on, long before Vector or the Chorus were in the picture. Even literally taken a bullet for a friend, though the gesture had come too late.

Probably why they'd left him to be the one to greet me when I awoke, come to think of it.

Meh, we had more important fish to fry than my anger. They did have a point too, not that I'd ever admit it to them. Under good circumstances I'd usually push myself to exhaustion and beyond before I rested, and these were by no means good circumstances.

I glanced around at the chamber. A literal chamber if it *had* been a heart at one point. No sign of the guilty parties. Another thought struck me, and I gave it voice. "So did Vector ever figure out why this organ died?"

"His current theory is parasites. But speaking as a physician, my wager is upon age." He tapped the crusty wall. "This is desiccation, not corruption. And exploration of some now-sealed passageways showed clogging and other obstructions. Beaky, as they have named it, seems to be old by the measure of its ilk."

"Wonder if it's like a tree, where you can count the rings, only instead of rings you've got mouths and heads." I rubbed the sleep out of my eyes. "Seriously, all those heads are overkill."

"Perhaps. Those parasites got in somehow. Maybe the heads are a defense against whatever lays eggs within it."

"Lovely." I headed back to my suit, dug out the leads to the radio set I'd built within it. "Okay you malicious misanthropes, what do you have to say to yourself? Over."

"Kssshh, can't hear you boss, Kssssssshhh, signal's bad." Delta responded.

"It doesn't work so well when you actually say 'Kssshhh,'" I advised. "But Dire appreciates the thought."

"Sorry, they made me do it," Vector interrupted. At any rate, the Conqueror Worm is doing its job with adequate efficiency."

"Conqueror Worm?"

"It's what he calls the parasite that's jacking our ride," Gamma explained. "Not that it's got any phallic significance at all."

"Hey..." Vector whined. "I'm a supervillain. That means I get to give my things impressive names."

"So why did you settle for 'Beaky', then?" I asked.

My minions snickered. "Anyway," Vector said, "Alpha tells me it's not dissimilar to piloting an airship. I've got your Chorus up on the edges of Beaky, feeding back information as we calibrate."

"Doesn't he have the most heads along his edges?" I didn't want my minions getting pecked to death. Or melted by fiery breath, for that matter.

"Relax. I've shut them down for the minute. The Conqueror Worm's locked down his aggression."

"Alright. So we're not flying blind; we're more or less coasting with spotters, while you fiddle around with his brain and try to figure out which sequences of pokes and chemical triggers make him go in various directions."

"A bit crude, but an accurate summary."

"Dire feels compelled to tell you that your brand of science would drive her nuts."

"Biology's more of an art, really."

"At your level, maybe."

"Aw, you'll make me blush." Damn did he sound smug.

"She's very sure you have a chemical or something to fix that."

"Well yes, actually." He cleared his throat. "Anyway I'm getting back to testing now." The room shuddered. "Oooh! That's a spicy nerve..."

"Right. Leaving you to it."

"I am still trying to figure out what to make of that one," Khalid said, once I'd set the radio down.

"Oh?"

"He is a coward, but he is also our salvation. Without him, we would be without air, food, potable water, and safe sleeping space."

"In the long-term. In the short-term, Dire would have figured something out." I cracked my knuckles. "That said, anything she could do would have been a gamble. Though she's objecting to the "safe sleeping space." I gestured around. "This is *safer*. Not safe."

Khalid's smile almost touched his eyes. I couldn't quite tell in the dim light, now that I was out of my suit and only a few lamps challenged the cloying, sweaty darkness. "Then you have learned the most important lesson of hell."

"Oh?"

"There is never any safe haven. Not for long."

I sucked my teeth. "About that. We should go and check on the camp."

He lost his smile. "I hope that you take my warning to heart."

"We saved them, Khalid. They agreed to help us. They are allies, now, and Dire does not mistreat her allies."

"Everyone who is in Hell, and got there after death, deserves Hell." He folded his arms. "They are the Damned for a reason, and that reason is that they have earned it."

"Khalid—"

He sighed. "I am not saying they cannot be good people, merely that it is unlikely. And also that it would be the height of foolishness to trust or depend on them. Demons have spent time immemorial dealing with Damned souls. They know how to use them, how to tempt them, how to prey upon their weaknesses."

I felt my lips tighten. "They are abusers. Let them come for Dire. They shall find no weaknesses, only determination enough to grind their little kingdom into dust."

"Then what?" He spread his hands. "Even if this were so, even if you were to somehow deal with the vast realm, and the Fallen Angels, and the First himself, then what? The Damned must remain in Hell. What would truly change?"

"You're defending this place?" I squinted in surprise. "You spent long enough keeping its messes out of Earth."

"I do not defend it, it is a wicked realm, and I hate that it exists. But I am saying that simply wading into demons like you would gangers or Nazis or superheros is not only a losing strategy, but futile in the long term. As is showing your back to the Damned, or trusting that your compassion to them will be regarded as anything but weakness. They are not homeless on a beach, Doctor Dire. They made their choice long ago."

I really, really wanted to take a swing at him.

Instead, I took a breath of stinking air, a second, then whirled and paced, walking around the edge of the chamber, finally stopping with my back to him, hands clasped behind me. "Janissary," I said, when I trusted my voice again.

"Doctor?"

"She's come a long way, since that time on the beach. That frozen, dark, worrisome time.. She thinks that you worry yourself by thinking that she never quite left that place."

"Yes," he said simply, and I heard his footsteps approaching. I turned and held up a hand, palm out.

"Makes sense. Many villains never get over their early days. They fall, and cannot rise again, cannot overcome their initial weakness. Stuck in the past, doomed to repeat the same mistakes, over and over, often against the same foes."

Khalid halted now, his face in shadows save for his glittering eyes. Gods, he was short, I had a full foot on him. But his presence filled the 'room'. "I would not accuse you of the same weakness."

"You just did." I rotated my hand to raise my palm upwards, closing it into a fist as I did so. "Do you remember Tugs?"

"I fear the name escapes me."

"Tugs, the junkie. Tugs, the murderer."

"Ah." He shifted in the darkness.

"You do remember."

"Yes."

"Then you remember what Dire did to Tugs." I brought my fist down like a hammer, into my other palm, with a meaty smack.

He nodded. "It was just."

"Then trust her to have learned the lesson about letting the wicked gain power." I strode over to him, clasped his shoulders. "Dire seldom makes the same mistake twice. The Damned start with a tabula rasa, as far as Dire is concerned. She'll aid the good, smite the wicked, and never, ever, give them a shot at anything vulnerable."

Khalid nodded again. "Then I will say nothing more on that matter."

I squeezed his shoulders. Then my stomach gave a rumbling growl, and we both looked down. I snorted laughter and he embraced me, laughing back. It felt good, the first hug I'd had outside of the armor since... well, since I lost my boyfriend.

Not that I was shopping for a new one. No, Khalid was a friend, and it was good to have someone I *could* put my back against. Without the complications that literally would arise if I put other bits against him.

"Come. Let us get you some filet of Beaky." Khalid let go of me and beckoned toward a flickering light beyond one of the wall hangings.

"We're eating him now?"

"Only parts that would have died due to damage from the parasites anyway. The injections Vector gave you should ensure his meat does not poison you."

"Still feels kind of strange." My stomach growled again. "How's he taste?"

"Horrible. And there's not enough meat harvested to properly feed us right now."

"He's okay with a fire in his lungs?"

"Technically we are no longer in his lungs. Also, it is smokeless flame, suspended on a patch that has no nerves, according to Vector. The burn will heal in short order, and his breathing mechanisms should remain un-irritated."

I snorted again, and made my way toward the campfire or whatever it was.

So, naturally, the radio in my suit chattered. I headed back to it and pulled it free from the armor once more. "This is Dire."

"Boss? You might want to suit up." Alpha sounded worried. Without a word, I slid into the back of the armor and began the startup protocols.

"Sitrep?" I snapped.

"The storm's lifted a bit, and there's smoke coming from the base camp."

We'd told them not to build fires. "How much smoke?"

"Big fire."

I ran through the scenarios where they would have disobeyed me to that extent, and the most likely option came down to outsiders. That meant trouble. That meant violence.

Well.

I knew a thing or two about violence.

"HOP ON," I told the Last Janissary. "SOMEONE NEEDS A RECKONING, AND SHE'S IN A MOOD TO DELIVER SOME INFERNAL JUSTICE..."

CHAPTER 3: FIRST CONTACT

"And the great teacher did look upon the first demons, and all but two she judged unworthy. They fell like See-are-ones against a full party."

--Excerpt from the second chapter of the first book of the Chronicles of the Shared Lie

As much as I wanted to haul Beaky along for backup, he was nowhere near combat-ready. Vector had a lot more brain poking to do before I'd trust our new pet abomination at our side. Besides, if there was something here with enough dakka to kill Beaky, I didn't want to risk our new lair and best shot at survival.

So instead I carried Khalid as I jetted toward the base camp, thirty-odd miles distant. Not far in the grand scheme of things.

Perhaps that was the problem, come to think of it. We hadn't set it far enough back from the road, and I'd fretted over that problem but seen no way around it. The geography and landmarks involved allowed no compromise.

My stomach growled again, and I clenched my teeth. This mess had interrupted the first solid meal offered to me in days. Hopefully we could settle it quickly.

Then the campsite hove into view, and I knew that we wouldn't be settling it quickly.

Two miles away, Beaky's twin, the first thing I killed when I got here, lay decomposing on the ground. Just beyond the plains broke, revealing a vast crack in the ground, too straight and orderly to be anything but artificial. It was a quarry, with chiseled steps winding down into a valley of broken stone and gaping mouths of caves scattered around the slate-gray walls. Gray like the dust that filled the air, that would fill my lungs in days if I was dumb enough to go without my armor.

A group of beasts shuffled and stirred at the edge of the quarry, low-slung and looking like a cross between velociraptors and alligators. They were gathered in a single spot. Next to them glittering frameworks shone bloody red as smaller forms writhed upon them. I zoomed in on the visual, then regretted it. I knew those people. I'd set them loose, and offered them safety in exchange for assistance. And now here they were, crucified spread-eagled on torture racks, screaming into the sky.

Someone had made a liar of me.

I swept my telescoped gaze across to the beasts, the five of them, and found that they had saddles and tack, and what looked like a few more torture racks broken down and bundled on their harnesses. Then I looked beyond them, to the smoke rising up from the bottom of the quarry. Couldn't see any more; the smoke was blocking my sight, and the angle was bad. Didn't feel like doing a direct overfly, not with Khalid slung under me and eminently squishier than my armor.

I nudged him, gestured to a likely spot a few hundred yards distant. He shook his symbiote-wrapped head and pointed at a pile of rocks a kilometer away. I shrugged and made for it. The Last Janissary could make good use of stealth and tactical advantage when it came to fighting. There was no point in depriving him of his strengths.

It felt like a long walk across the plain, with only the moans of the Damned to keep us company. "ANY IDEA WHAT THOSE ARE?" I rumbled, voice modulator dialed down, as I pointed at the riding lizards. They were all looking our way, but didn't seem too alarmed at the minute.

"No clue. Hellspawn."

"LEGION. RIGHT." I gave them a wide berth. No noise from down in the quarry, save for the crackling of a large fire. The screams of the Damned drowned out anything my ambient noise filters might have identified.

The lizards bristled crests when I got closer and snorted a bit more, but once I turned my back on them, they settled down somewhat. I watched them through the rear-view camera as I made my way over to Juno. She was one of the oldest Damned I'd freed from the spikes, a Roman from the Republic, long ago. Short, black-haired, perhaps in her thirties, she was currently bleeding into the dirt and spiked into the rack like a magician's sword trick gone horribly wrong.

I glanced around for Khalid, found him vanished. Typical. I pulled the spikes out of the contraption one by one, and her screaming faded into pained sobbing as she collapsed to the ground. Then I moved to the other two, who spoke no languages I recognized. Once they were loose and the screams faded, I turned back to Juno.

"WHO HAS DONE THIS TO YOU?" I asked her. We'd found a common tongue in Roman Latin.

"Demons," she whispered through a raw throat, then flopped an arm until she managed to get it pointing toward the quarry.

I nodded. "DON'T GO ANYWHERE."

To be honest, I'd known the answer to the question already. But this was more for show, more to ram home the point I was trying to get through her skull and the collective skulls of the rest of the Damned crew.

They were my people now, and I looked after my own.

I dropped into the quarry like a bolt from a crossbow, slamming into the ground in a three-point landing, dust flying as the 'people' clustered around the bonfire whirled around to stare at me. The ones with hands had blankets or coats or garments of some sort, and they'd obviously been using them to fan the flames into one of the cave mouths. I knew that cave. That was where I'd told my people to start mining. The rest of the dotted line fell into place.

"YOU'RE TRYING TO SMOKE THEM OUT, AREN'T YOU?"

The demons gathered themselves. Five humanoids, wearing leathers of a pale hue, broad-brimmed hats, and scarves pulled up over their faces until only their glowing, inhuman eyes showed. Various spikes protruded through holes in the patched leather, and they were tall, varying between eight and ten feet.

To the side, a catlike thing the size of a doberman stood frozen, eyes wide, tail lashing furiously. Its eyes were human and bloodshot, and somehow that was the worst of all.

The tallest demon garbled something, reached behind itself, dropped its blanket, and pulled out something that looked very much like a blunderbuss. I scanned it, smirked at the chemical mix my instruments returned. The demon garbled more words.

"ENGLISH! DO YOU SPEAK IT, MOTHERFUCKER?"

They recoiled from my shout. But one of the smaller ones raised a hand and tugged his scarf down, revealing a severely-handsome human face that didn't go with his sickly yellow eyes. "Speaka ta Damned tongues sen? Palaver worra ta tongue o' weak?"

"YES. UNTIL SHE KNOWS MORE OF YOUR LANGUAGE,

THAT SHALL SUFFICE."

"We be Low Riders, by chain and by claw, hunting escapes by order and authority of Bel gan Biss. I hight Thirteenth Chain. Boon compayans, Seventh, Third, and Ninth Chains, and Foolish Grub. Who be ye?"

"Wrong question, wrong question, faulty, fickle, foolish," The cat growled. "Ask *what* are you?"

"SHE IS DIRE. AND YOU HUNT HER PEOPLE." I raised a fist, raising my voice modulator's volume as I did so. "WHATEVER FATE YOU MAY HAVE HAD, IT IS HERS TO DECIDE NOW."

"Dire Ban who?" Thirteenth Chain frowned. But I watched his hand, as it strayed to the hilt of a blade at his waist. And the one with the blunderbuss tensed, muscles writhing like ropes along his arms, eyes never leaving my mask. The other three shared glances.

"DOCTOR DIRE." And there they were, peering over the edge of the cliff; the captives I'd freed from impalement, healed up well enough to crawl over and see what transpired. "KNEEL OR FALL BEFORE HER!" I repeated the phrase in Roman, for Juno's benefit, sweeping my arm out in a dramatic gesture.

Thunder rumbled, shot cascaded from my forcefield as the crude blunderbuss discharged its load, and they came for me with knives and swords.

I met them, with raised arms and mocking laughter. The first one to reach me came low, so I kicked his ribs in as his knife slid along my shell. The second-biggest one came behind him, trying to tackle me from the side, and I grabbed his head, knelt in a smooth motion, and crushed it into the ground. Blood sprayed, and I rose in time to meet the third one with a rising uppercut that split him open like lightning cracking a tree.

The fourth one was Thirteenth Chain, and he skidded to a halt, shielding his face as blood sprayed and spattered. He backed up and I advanced, catching him by the throat and lifting him high, all five-hundred pounds of him, according to my sensors and haptics. I lifted him one-handed, ignored his choking and the knife stabbing down, scraping and rattling along my arm.

Blunderbuss boy was ramming a cleaning tool down the barrel of his weapon, backing up as well. Then he cast the tool aside, a rag on the end fluttering as a twisted, withered, third arm snaked from his coat and slid a soda-can-sized cartridge into the mouth of the blunderbuss. It packed the canister tight with poundings of a tiny fist.

"DROP IT OR DIE," I told him.

He roared defiance, raised the blunderbuss at me—

And I blasted him with a ninety-percent particle beam set to wide dispersal.

When the golden light faded, and the cliff side he'd been standing in front of ceased cracking and sliding down the ridge, the only thing left of him were smoking boots. Rocks pinged and whined off of my forcefield, surrounding me in an inconstant halo of golden light, there and gone in split-seconds.

I turned to look at the cat-thing. The cat-thing ran.

It got all of ten bounding paces before Khalid stood up from a rock pile, and caught it square in the face with a vial full of yellow smoke. Oh, how it howled! It fell to the ground, pawing desperately at its face, warbling its pain to the world.

A clatter of metal on stone. I looked down to see Thirteenth Chain's knife broken at my feet. I looked up my arm to see him patting my gauntlet desperately. His face was way more red than it had been a second ago.

Ah, right. Air. He might want that.

I searched around, found a shovel sticking out of the fire. I took my time kicking out the smoky blaze, ignoring my Chain buddy's pats and struggles as the demon slowly lost his strength. Then I picked up the tool, and let him drop right next to the ashes. He coughed, gasped, and stared up at me, eyes blinking and weeping gooey tears.

I tossed the shovel right next to his face, and he flinched. "BEND YOUR KNEE OR DIG YOUR GRAVE," I told him.

He knelt, coughing.

"And this one?" Khalid asked, his blade at the throat of the hellcat.

"Man... most mortal?" It wheezed through its pain. Tremors still shook it, but its eyes were wide and blurred with goopy tears.

"IT'S SAPIENT. IT GETS THE SAME CHOICE."

"I know this breed. They are called Grimalkin. Capricious and sensitive, with mental abilities."

Well, fuck. "MIND CONTROL?" I asked him.

"No. But you have not been hearing its words with your ears."

I checked the audio logs. Interesting. "WE COULD USE A TRANSLATOR. YOU, GRIMALKIN!" I kicked the shovel its way. "THE SAME CHOICE LIES BEFORE YOU."

I held back my laughter as the cat painfully clambered to its feet, pushed its head down and its butt up. Swear to gods, I was tempted to flip out a laser sight and see if it went for the thing. But no, no, we had onlookers, and I had to maintain a certain gravitas for the audience.

Speaking of which... "CASSIAN! COME FORTH."

I gave it a minute. Just as I was ready to call again, the thinning smoke at the edge of the cave mouth roiled, and a short, soot-stained man limped out, holding a steel spike low and to his side. He took in the carnage with wide, white eyes that were out of place on his smoke-seared skin. Behind him, the rest of his band followed, armed with similar spikes and lengths of bloodstained steel.

"Jupiter's ballsack," he whispered, in Latin. He'd been my teacher for the tongue, and I'd made sure he taught me every choice epithet. I had the feeling they'd come in handy down here.

"JUNO AND TWO OTHERS ARE UP ON THE BLUFFS. ARE THE REST WITH YOU?"

He swapped the steel spur to his left hand, held out his right in a fist, and thumped his chest. "Yes, Lady." The effect was spoiled a bit, as that triggered a nasty cough. I watched him heave up black junk, caring less about it than I would have if he'd been living. From what I'd learned after we got them off the spires, they had a decent, if slow, regeneration factor. And if Vector and Khalid were correct, they were essentially immortal. Cassian had been hurt, but he would heal.

"COME THEN, WHEN YOU HAVE THE STRENGTH FOR IT. RETURN TO THE TOP OF THE QUARRY AND AWAIT."

"We have..." The old Roman coughed again. "We have dug out several armloads of copper."

I raised my eyebrows. By the looks of it, the demons had attacked hours ago. My Damned had only half a day or so to manage their mining. That was a pretty good clip.

"DIRE SHALL GATHER IT FROM THE MINE. NO NEED FOR YOU TO BREATHE SMOKE AGAIN. GO, REST. SHE SHALL SEE HOW MUCH YOUR LABORS HAVE BROUGHT."

It was a bit less than several armloads, really. But then everyone in the crew was fairly short. I scanned it with my spectroanalyzer, nodded in satisfaction. I'd have to smelt it pretty well to get the quality I wanted, but this would more than suffice. A few minutes of work and the salvaged jacket from one of the dead demons, and I had a sack of ore.

When I flew back up the cliff, I found the Damned gathered in a loose huddle, murmuring and shooting murderous glances at the Grimalkin and Thirteenth Chain. The Grimalkin stared back at me, paws folded under itself, tail switching back and forth with obvious curiosity. Thirteenth Chain, for his part, had his scarf back around his face. He was sneaking glances at the tethered lizard mounts, obviously weighing his chances. Khalid stood between the demons and the Damned, arms folded, his gaze as cold as the void between stars.

Were stars a thing here? I hadn't noticed any sort of day or night cycle, and I wasn't exactly sure where the dim red light that filled the sky came from. I made a mental note to ask our captives when we had less pressing matters to tend to.

First things first, though. "DON'T BOTHER RUNNING," I told Thirteenth Chain. "YOU WILL JUST DIE TIRED."

Khalid translated my words to Latin for the benefit of our Romans, and they translated for the rest of the group in an assortment of languages. Judging by the smiles, they liked my line of thought.

I turned my back on the demons, looked to the nine dead souls I'd ended up with. The first spire we cleared off, the Damned had fled the moment they recovered. Taken us for demons, or mistaken our mercy for some cruel game. Couldn't blame them, really, they'd spent a hell of a long time bleeding out with jagged steel blades through their guts.

The second spire, though, Cassius and Juno had stood together, hand in hand, and asked a simple question;

Why?

I answered now as I had two days ago.

"BECAUSE DIRE CAN," I rumbled at Cassius, here and now, as he looked from me to the demons and back again.

"Your pardon, Lady?"

"YOU ARE WONDERING WHY SHE SPARED THEM."

"I wonder if it is wise. There are stories of those who tried to fight demons, tried to kill them. The torments of the fools who try such things make the bloodspires seem tame by comparison. Leaving two alive to tell the tale does not seem wise."

Juno grabbed his shoulder and whispered something in his ear. She had to stand on tiptoe to do it. He blinked and shook his head. "I am not calling you a fool, Lady Dire. But you are newly come here. You have not heard the stories or seen what we have seen."

"THAT IS TRUE. BUT IT CHANGES NOTHING. THEY LIVE ON HER SUFFERANCE. WHEN THEY ATTEMPT TO BETRAY HER, THEY WILL DIE AT HER WHIM."

The cat was following our conversation avidly. Thirteenth Chain didn't react. Didn't know Latin? Probably. I'd have to quiz him to test his knowledge later. "FOR NOW THEY WILL SERVE AN IMPORTANT PURPOSE."

"And what is that?"

I pointed at the riding lizards. "DO YOU SEE THAT?"

"I see them," Cassius said, keeping his steel spike ready. "They do not seem friendly."

"NOT THEM. THE..." I didn't know the word for tack in Latin. "...HARNESSES."

"What of them?"

Romans. A very literal people. "EACH ONE IS IDENTICAL." I'd

noticed that, looking at them earlier. "DOWN TO THE METAL PINS USED TO HOLD THEM TOGETHER."

Juno, bless her heart, got it first. "If the demons riding them had made the harnesses themselves, they would be different."

"WHICH MEANS THAT THEY HAVE ENOUGH FREE HANDS THAT EITHER A DEDICATED CRAFTSMAN MADE THESE, OR A MACHINE DID. WHICH MEANS CIVILIZATION." I'd figured that from the roads, but the tack and the blunderbuss both supported the theory. "A SETTLEMENT OR PERHAPS A CITY."

"Caym," the cat offered. "The Bloodfont, on the Cliffs of Screaming Woe."

"You wish us to go to this city?" Cassus shook his head. "We would be captured and returned to the spires. Or worse."

"NO," I said, opening the jacket and letting the copper ore spill to the ground. "YOU MAY COME IF YOU WISH, AND YOU SHALL NOT BE CAPTURED OR TORTURED FOR DOING SO. BUT SHE DOES NOT REQUIRE IT OF YOU. DIRE WAS THINKING THIS WAS A GOOD ENOUGH FARE FOR YOUR PASSAGE THERE, BUT IF YOU WISH SOME OTHER TRADE FOR THIS COPPER, THAT IS ACCEPTABLE AS WELL."

"I am very confused, great lady," said the cat. "Are those rocks not their tribute to you?"

"NO. SHE IS NOT THEIR MASTER. SHE IS THEIR EMANCIPATOR. THIS IS WHAT THEY HAVE TO OFFER, FOR HER HELP AND SUPPORT." I would have helped them without it, to be honest, but Khalid had advised me to keep them busy and to insist on trading for any favors I did them. He was more familiar with their culture and the overall mentality of the Damned.

Though I was learning as I went. For the most part they were dour, paranoid, and nowhere near as crazed as I'd expected.

"Ah. May I trade for help and support?" the cat asked.

"NO. SHE IS NOT YOUR EMANCIPATOR." I let the empty jacket I'd been using as a carrying sling fall and went to loom over the cat and Thirteenth Chain. "FOR NOW, SHE IS YOUR MASTER."

His eyes narrowed, his ears went flat, but he did that head-lowering-butt-raising thing again. Adorable, really. I scratched behind his ears, ruffling his fur, and his eyes went wide in shock. "BESIDES, ALL SHE NEEDS FROM YOU IS KNOWLEDGE. SIT TIGHT, STAY SMART, AND YOU MAY SURVIVE THIS JOURNEY." I said that in English, for Thirteenth Chain's benefit as well.

"Lady!" Juno called, alarmed. "One of the Striges comes!"

I looked around, to where Beaky's blob was growing larger on the horizon. "AH YES. HERE COMES OUR RIDE."

They didn't believe me, up until the point I got on the radio and had Vector poke its brain to wave a tentacle in my direction, its motions synchronizing with my own waves. Finally the massive beast juddered to a stop overhanging the camp. The lizards were going nuts; I let Thirteenth Chain go and quell them as best he could.

Then the androids, minus Epsilon, came sliding down a set of lowered tentacles. Vector followed, surprisingly. "AREN'T YOU SUPPOSED TO BE FLYING BEAKY?"

"Epsilon's taking over for me. It was actually pretty easy once we located the equivalent to the amygdala. Besides, I had to come and see the new specimens."

The cat started backing away. Thirteenth Chain froze, looking from me to Vector.

"THEY GET TO LIVE. FOR NOW."

"Oh, I just need some samples. Nothing they can't regrow."

I turned to look at the demons, letting golden light play around my fist, particles snapping in the air as the charging arrays fluttered at less than a tenth of a percent. "WELL THEN! STAND FORTH AND BE BRAVE OR RUN AND DIE TIRED. WHICH SHALL IT BE?"

They stood. Khalid and Vector took blood samples and afterwards the biologist examined them carefully, taking notes on a beat-up old wad of paper that could have been a notebook at some point.

"Another mortal man," the cat whispered, turning its unsettling eyes back to me. "Those are worth a fortune in Hell, two fortunes, and yet you waste your time with Damned? I do not understand, Master."

"ARE THE LIVING THEN SUCH A COMMODITY DOWN HERE?"

"Yes! Rare as Lucifer's mercy. With potent seed for breeding and succulent flesh that puts the foul ashen meat of the Damned to shame."

"You might find my flesh less to your liking," Vector said, frowning at it sternly. "I've got a few upgrades."

"I would not eat my Master's property."

"GOOD." I forestalled Vector, before he could say something that put him at risk. "PROFESSOR, WHAT DO YOU MAKE OF THESE RIDING LIZARD THINGS?"

He looked them over. "I could use one to study."

"ONLY ONE?"

"I estimate them at about a ton each. One we could handle without trouble. Five would slow Beaky's airspeed down a bit."

"BEAKY'S HUGE."

"Huge and light. Think of him like an airship."

I gnawed my lip. That boded ill for some of the tools I wanted to construct. Well, Vector could possibly do something about Beaky's carrying capacity given time and enough chemicals. "ALL RIGHT. HEY JUNO, CASSIUS, WHEN'S THE LAST TIME YOU HAD A GOOD MEAL?"

They looked at me like I'd gone mad. I shrugged and turned to Thirteenth Chain. "WHAT ARE THESE BEASTS CALLED AND WHICH ONE IS YOURS?"

"They hight burren," He raised a long clawed finger and pointed. "Is mine. That un."

I nodded, then I charged the cluster of burren, slamming one off the cliff. The remainder started, scattered in all directions, and I mowed down all but Thirteenth Chain's with focused particle beams. The fourth one took three shots... I'd been drilling them through their heads, but evidently managed to miss anything important on that last one.

Thirteenth Chain's burren backed up, hissing, glanced around, then its pea brain somehow decided that the best option for survival was to charge *me*.

I locked my gravitics.

CLANG!

When the dust cleared, it was crumpled in a quivering heap twenty feet from me. I stood uncaring, with my arms folded. I checked the readouts, winced, and unlocked my gravitics.

That had actually stressed the stabilizers a bit, but it was worth it to look cool in front of an audience that I desperately needed to impress. And indeed, the gasps and oaths coming up from my Damned were music to my ears.

Which is why I was pretty much flat-footed when Thirteenth Chain attacked me.

I'd taken my eyes off of him for a second, and there was no yelling, no strategy, nothing in his charge but simple brute force: a mirror of the tactic I'd used to wipe out the burren a few seconds ago, really. He picked up a rock, ran at me, and tried to bash my helmet in.

After the third bash, when I'd recovered from the surprise, I knocked it from his hands, grabbed him by the front of his jacket, and hauled him up again. He scraped and grabbed at my mask with his claws, rasping uselessly at my empty eye sockets.

And unlike the last time I'd hauled him up one-handed, this time he wasn't stopping.

Why? I'd just killed his friends in front of him, less than five minutes ago, and he had kept control then.

I looked into his eyes, looked for answers.

And I found pain. Rage, yes, anger hot enough to eclipse a star, burning in its purity... but also pain.

I looked away, to the burren I'd slain. They twitched in their death throes. His burren was clambering to its feet, bleating at me and lowering its head for another charge.

Those other demons I'd killed, had they been his friends at all? Did he care more for the riding beasts?

Time to test that theory. I leveled my free palm at his burren. "YOUR ATTACK IS FUTILE. CEASE, GET A HOLD OF YOURSELF, AND CALM YOUR BURREN, OR SHE SHALL DESTROY IT LIKE THE OTHERS."

Thirteenth Chain's claws paused, shaking on my mask. Then he pulled them back, and I saw his mouth moving below his scarf as he tried to speak, couldn't. Finally he gave a simple nod, a jerk of his skull, and I tossed him in the general direction of his burren.

I turned my back on them both, crossing my arms... and surreptitiously locking my gravitics once more. I watched him through the rear cameras and he did nothing beyond calm his animal, as instructed. A second passed. Then five. Then ten. I unlocked my gravitics.

"You are a merciful Lady," the cat observed, in the silence.

"WHY? NO HARM WAS DONE. WHAT DOES A MOUNTAIN CARE FOR THE STING OF A BEE?"

I gestured to my Damned. "NOW WE HAVE FRESH MEAT. CLEAN AND HARVEST THE KILLS, IF YOU WANT DINNER TONIGHT."

They looked to each other, pulled out their spikes, and set to the task.

I pulled my Chorus into a huddle, beckoned Khalid and Vector over.

"First off, I'm sorry we didn't intervene," Alpha said. "We didn't expect hell cowboy over there to lose his shit. Then you had matters in hand, and we didn't want to make you look weak."

"IT'S ALL RIGHT. NO HARM DONE." I frowned under my mask. "HE HAD EMPATHY FOR THOSE BURREN."

"I would be surprised if that were true." Khalid asked. "Loyalty is not rewarded in Hell."

"Perhaps empathy with humans is not rewarded," Beta offered, "but we are dealing with an alien society and culture. There may be striations that we are currently unaware of."

"Demons are demons," Khalid said, folding his arms. "I have never before encountered one who acted with any sort of virtue."

"Yeah, but what kind of demons do you normally run into, Mr. Stabby?" Delta asked. "The kind evil shits summon up to go murder busloads of nuns, right?"

"Greater demons, yes. These are lesser. Far lesser."

"So maybe they don't get held to the same standards of vileness as the big guys? I mean shit, someone's got to haul the trash and groom the hellhounds, and that doesn't get done so effectively if every hellish dog groomer is always like 'muahahha, now I shall betray you, my master!' I'm just saying that some of them might be punch-clock demons."

"PUNCH-CLOCK DEMONS?"

"Y'know, demon Steve wakes up in the morning and it's like "Morning Damned souls," and they're like "Morning, Steve!" Then Steve puts his time card in the hole punch and pulls his eight hour shift of defenestrating dudes. And afterwards he goes and has a few hellbeers or whatever and unwinds with the Stygia bowl on hell-o-vision."

"DIRE IS REASONABLY SURE THERE IS NO SUCH THING AS HELL-O-VISION."

"It's an allegory."

Khalid shook his head. "The second you believe that any of these creatures can be sympathetic, is the moment they will turn that against you. Hell is *evil*. Demons are *evil*. That is their purpose in existence, and they do it well."

"THAT IS WHAT FAITH WOULD HAVE US BELIEVE, HMMM?"

"It is what my centuries of experience and common sense would have you believe. Though my faith does support it, yes."

"AND YET EVERY FALLEN ANGEL ONCE STOOD IN GOD'S HOST, YES?"

"There can be no forgiveness for treason."

"WELL. WHAT FAITH CLAIMS, LET SCIENCE TEST. WE SHALL HAVE AMPLE OPPORTUNITY TO OBSERVE OVER THE MONTHS TO COME."

"Months?" Vector asked.

"WE'VE GOT ENOUGH METALS DOWN HERE FOR THE NEXT STAGE OF THE PLAN. WITH THE CHORUS AND THE DAMNED MINING AND SMELTING, AND ENOUGH FOOD FOR ALL OF US BETWEEN BEAKY AND THE FOUR TONS OF MEAT DIRE JUST KILLED, WE'LL HAVE TIME TO GET THE HARDWARE BUILT. OH, WE'LL NEED WATER. LOTS OF IT."

Vector nodded. "If my theory about the local flora is correct, they see storms every week or so. Beaky's built to collect water from rainfall as well, so it'll be easy enough to tap his reservoirs, especially if you can smelt some pipes or a funnel as well as a few holding tanks. If that doesn't work we can always hit up the river of blood and set up some purification works. There's enough water in blood that it should serve our needs if we're talking a scale of months."

"I'd wondered why you weren't overly concerned with water," Khalid rubbed his chin. "Let me get a head start on taking water from the blood. Alchemy is probably better suited to it than your methods, given the paucity of tools at the minute."

I nodded to Vector. "THAT LEAVES YOU TO FURTHER REFINE BEAKY, AND WHIP UP LIVING QUARTERS FOR OUR ENTOURAGE."

"We're taking them aboard?" Khalid asked.

"OH YES. DAMNED AND DEMONS ALIKE." I turned my gaze on Thirteenth Chain who was actually cuddling his stunned burren, and at the Grimalkin, who was washing itself and utterly failing to pretend he wasn't eavesdropping on us. "WE HAVE SUCH SIGHTS TO SHOW THEM!"

CHAPTER 4: SATAN'S GAME

"And she forged the alliance, forged the pact. Both man and demon would work side by side and share the truth that was the lie."

--Excerpt from the second chapter of the first book of the Chronicles of the Shared Lie

I gazed down from on high, looking down into the quarry that we'd claimed as our own. Once, it had been mined out of iron and coal, raw material stripped away to forge the tortuous blood spires to the south. But they'd left many other metals, many other resources behind.

Those were now ours, taken bit by bit by the work crews that scurried like ants below Beaky.

"There you are!" Vector called, from back towards the carved-out hatch we'd put in the massive creature's upper hide. "What are you doing?"

"WAITING. THE LAST SECTION OF PIPE SHOULD BE CLEARED IN FIVE... FOUR... THREE..."

The ground rumbled, audible even from my current perch. Beaky shifted and squawked, clearly unhappy with the noise. Then water poured from the side of the quarry, streaming out from the brass nozzle that five of my Damned crew were busy manipulating. Brass like the rest of the pipes, brass because we had plenty of it lying around and it was a shame to waste steel. The only source for good quality steel was the spires, and if we did too much damage to those somebody might notice.

"THERE WE GO." I watched it splash down into the channels we'd carved for it over the last few weeks. "THIS WILL MAKE REFINING THE ORE MUCH, MUCH EASIER."

"I'm still concerned about the organisms on the edge of the river," Vector scratched one stubbled cheek, staying well back from the edge. "There's only so much I could do to conceal them. And if Thirteenth Chain's being honest, the river will see traffic sooner or later. If they're spotted..."

"IF THEY'RE SPOTTED THEY'LL LOOK LIKE SOME FORM OF HORRIBLE, UNPREDICTABLE WILDLIFE. LIKE OUR STRIX FRIEND HERE." I thumped Beaky's hide. The Romans called him and his kindred Striges, after some form of local legend back in the Empire. For lack of anything better, the name had stuck. "SPEAKING OF THAT, DID YOU EVER FIGURE OUT WHAT MADE HIM SCURRY OFF LAST WEEK?"

"Ah, that." Vector chuckled and mopped his spectacles. "I've figured out his part in the local ecosystem."

"OH?"

"Shit."

"WHAT'S WRONG?"

"No, he produces massive amounts of shit. It's why he scurried off. It was to go take a big dump in the spot the local demons have trained him to. It evidently helps grow their crops much faster than any other type of fertilizer they can get their hands on."

"THIRTEENTH CHAIN CONFIRMED THAT?"

"No, the Grimalkin did." Three months of living with the thing around, underfoot, lurking its heart out at every opportunity and we still hadn't learned its name. I supposed I could force the issue, but it was simpler to call it 'The Cat', or 'The Grimalkin'. To me the demons were pretty much prisoners of war, and I would not mistreat or extort non-vital information from them without a good reason. If The Cat had a reason for remaining nameless, I would respect that.

Thinking of one demon put me in mind of the other. I strode to the other side of Beaky, evading the glaring, fidgeting heads that studded him like eyes on a potato. They weren't *supposed* to attack me, thanks to Vector's tinkering, but the poor dear still had instincts, and I didn't want to push the bird-beast too far out of his comfort zone. I got to the edge, enabled my tracking software, and scanned around until I found a black, moving dot in the distance. Zooming in three times revealed the familiar form of the burren, with Thirteenth Chain on its back. Still riding his patrol, still keeping to the circuit we'd agreed upon.

"Everything all right?" Vector couldn't see what I could, of course.

His augmentations were good, but not enough to compete with my engineering expertise.

Just as I thought that, my vision glitched, and my HUD flickered, a troublesome bug rearing its head once more. I needed to clean the contacts and replace some of the wiring in the upper portion of the mask, and I couldn't do that without the proper components.

Vector's enhancements weren't as powerful as my devices, but without the tools and materials to do maintenance, they'd outlast me.

We were working on that, but I could see the time coming when I'd have to start looking at gearing down.

"I said, is everything all right?" Vector tapped at my elbow.

"FOR NOW." A thought struck me. "THE FERTILIZER. IT'S BASICALLY DIGESTED PEOPLE."

"Parts of it. And that's the reason for the centralized shit-piles. The demons on shit farming duty pull out the re-forming Damned and send them out with crews who put them back up on the spires before they awaken. So it's a renewable cycle. Every few weeks the Striges get a yen to eat, then a few weeks after that they crap them out and go feed again."

"AND PEOPLE GET DEVOURED OVER AND OVER AGAIN FOR ALL ETERNITY."

"You're missing the deeper connotations, here. The full possibilities..." his eyes fairly glowed as he smiled. "This is only one cycle, one ecosystem. You've got a biological resource here that never runs out, doesn't need food or water, and revives pretty much no matter what happens to it. The demons have harnessed the Damned to grow their crops. So that makes me wonder, just what is that river of blood for? Just what greater purpose does it serve?"

"THOSE BIOLOGICAL RESOURCES HAVE FACES. AND NAMES."

"I know. I know. But I'm starting to wonder if Khalid's aloofness isn't more the way to go, here. The demons we captured... sure, the Grimalkin makes no bones about being an evil cat, but Thirteenth Chain, well, he's decent enough for a prisoner-of-war. A little standoffish, but functionally he's not too far from human. I should know, I've put him through every test I can think of that wouldn't violate the Geneva convention."

I nodded. "AND THEY HAVE CROPS. THEY NEED TO EAT. THEY NEED TO DRINK, EVEN IF ONLY BLOOD. AND THEY STAY DEAD, TOO." I turned my head, to survey the graves we'd dug for the other Chains, now mostly-obscured by blown dust.

I remembered when I had first emerged from the surgical chair, to face a brand-new world head on. Learning bit by bit, with every interaction and observation.

This was the collegiate-level version of that. I did not yet understand Hell, and here I had been thrown directly into it. Even more so than my initial foray into a strange world, misunderstanding something fundamental here meant that I stood the very real chance of getting myself and all my friends dead.

I shook off the morbid thought. "COME ON, IT'S ALMOST PAYCHECK TIME. YOU CAN HELP DISTRIBUTE OBOLS."

At Vector's nod, I grabbed him and descended from on high. Easier than traversing Beaky's innards and using the tentacle-lift. Less slimy, too.

Khalid met us on the ground, eyes keen and glittering above the pulsating flesh of his symbiote. A new one, since the old one had succumbed to silicosis a few days ago. "HOW GOES IT?"

He pulled back his mantle to show me an assortment of vials. "Better. We found numerous crystals of antimony, allowing me to craft several reagents I have been long without."

"Antimony? Toxic stuff, that," Vector remarked.

"When it is not properly purified and run through the philosopher's stone, it is. But these concoctions are quite survivable. For humans, at any rate." He fell in with us, one hand on his sword's hilt as we picked our way down onto the quarry's floor, over the slabs of stone we'd cut into loose paths, and past the newly-created stream of water that spilled from the cliff side. The caves yawned to our left and right, about half of them covered with the dusty membranes that Vector had grown as air filters. Those were used for storage and living quarters. No need to seal off the active mines, the dust raised from the inside of them was nasty enough; barring the outside dust would do little good.

We stopped at the entrance to the highest cave and waved to Alpha. We always kept one of the Chorus out front as a guard, though it wasn't really necessary. There was no way to approach the cave without everyone in the vicinity seeing it. The guards were more about appearances and keeping a sense of normality.

Although, as I ran an eye over Alpha's weathered frame my own sense of normality took a hit. He'd been worn down by the windstorms, and the dust, and the corrosive materials that the foundry-work put him through. Just like my armor and mask he'd need maintenance from tools we didn't have yet.

But though his mask was chipped and faded, there was nothing wrong with his salute. Roman style, and I snorted to see it. "DON'T YOU START, TOO."

"Ave, dictator!"

Not all of our Damned were Romans. In fact, we only had two of them, out of the thirty-three that made up our workforce. But Romans had a way of steamrolling other cultures and incorporating them without too much alienation, so Cassius and Juno had more or less established a baseline protocol that the others followed. Privately, I thought it silly, but like so many other small touches down here it seemed to make them feel better. Made them feel like humans, instead of immortal suffering meat-sacks.

"ANY TROUBLE?"

"Pfft, please. None whatsoever. Ready to handle some filthy lucre?"

"The filthiest!" Vector grinned.

Alpha went inside and came back with one of the few notebooks Vector had brought over with him and a small tin chest, the same one we used every time. I palmed it with one hand and led the way down the hill. As we went, the laborers around the quarry stowed their tools, called into the caves for their comrades, and hastened to meet us at the square-cut block that we'd come to call the altar. I set the chest down on the surface. I opened it to reveal stacks of gleaming leaden coins, each one minted with my mask.

We had plenty of the low-grade stuff left over after refining. Easy enough to work with, easy enough to spare for this custom. I folded my arms while Khalid snapped open the notebook and started reading names. As each of our Damned came up, Vector handed them a few obols, based on how much work they'd done throughout the 'week'.

Truthfully, money wasn't very useful at the minute down here. The only things to spend it on were stores that the three of us deemed non-essential, those and favors from either us or the other Damned. I knew they traded them back and forth for crafts and services, and occasionally as apologies for offenses done.

I knew that our little settlement worked better with coin, and though I was well aware of the dangers of rampant capitalism we were a long way from corporations and financial fraud and income inequality. So for now, it was fine. If it started causing problems I'd shut it down.

After all the Damned got sorted out, the Chorus lined up one by one and took their obols. Then it was down to the last two members of our little party.

"Thirteenth Chain is finishing his patrol, yes?" Khalid asked, marking off names in the notebook.

"YES. HE WILL BE IN SHORTLY. WE'LL SEND HIM ROUND THE CAVE FOR HIS SHARE."

"That leaves me, then." The Cat slouched forward, eyes glittering with amusement. "Urbi, if you would?" One of the Damned, a dusky bald woman, came up, hands out, shaking badly enough to rattle the Strix-bone beads worked into her leather wrap. She shook a lot, had ever since I'd met her. I wasn't sure if it was a nervous disorder or something psychological, but she was functional and didn't cause trouble so that was her business. She took The Cat's share, then followed him as he beckoned. I watched the other Damned stare stonily as they made their way back into the living quarters that the demons and their hired servant had claimed. Trouble might come from that someday. I made a note to keep an eye on future developments.

"THAT'S PAYROLL DONE." I snapped the tin chest shut, handed it off to Alpha. "WORK'S DONE FOR THE DAY. WE'RE AVAILABLE FOR BARTER FOR THE NEXT HOUR."

Coin was only as valuable as what you could buy with it, and between myself, Vector, and Khalid, we could provide a pretty wide range of services and goods. Though it took precious time it kept the workforce happy, and we could and had refused more ludicrous or impractical requests.

Today, though, there was something different in the air. Rather than coming up in drips and drabs to discuss what they could get for their money, about half the Damned gathered around Cassius, and they marched up together. I watched as they stacked obols on the altar, and knew that I'd either love this request or hate it.

"YOU HAVE SOMETHING BIG IN MIND," I observed.

Cassius nodded. "We do. Are you familiar with Roman baths?"

Oh. Oh! My gaze drifted to the water, streaming down the cliff. Such an obvious idea, and why hadn't I thought of it first?

Well, no matter. This way got me some of those obols back.

I smiled under my mask. Then I started haggling.

One week later, I settled into the hot water with a sigh. It had taken five or six days to make the parts and cut the stone for this hot tub.

It was worth it. It was *all* worth it.

The water had been the last ingredient required, the rest we'd put into place bit by bit, in what little spare time we could scrounge. Smoldering lava far below, redirected from the nearby volcanic fields, heated the brass tub. Vector's membranes served as an airlock, keeping the foul air of Hell out, and oxygen-producing molds flourished on the walls and ceiling, giving the place a fuzzy, dark green coating.

"We need branches," Juno told me, as she took her place next to me in the bath. "Bark is best for scouring the skin after a good soak."

"Branches would require wood. Aside from that patch of forest to the west, the one that tried to eat Vector when he investigated it, we don't have many options there." I scrubbed at my arms with the pumice stone.

"This is the best we can do at the moment." I put it aside, sunk deeper into the tub, easing my breasts back in. "What Dire really wants are towels."

"We have too little cloth for that."

"Dire asked Thirteenth Chain about cloth. No real luck, there. Everything the demons wear that isn't leather is woven from the hair of the Damned."

"Hair shirts? They wear hair shirts?" She barked laughter. "I thought we were here to repent, not them."

"Dire is also disinclined to investigate that option, if the stories The Cat told her of the lice down here are true."

"I am not sure why you wish to." She cast a longing gaze at my clothes and underthings, stacked neatly in one of the cubbies. "So soft! And the colors are so vibrant."

"And so ragged. Didn't plan on coming here. Only have the one set, and repeated washing is doing a number on those." I rubbed my chin. "Could ask Vector to see if we could breed something like flax. Or cotton."

Though I wondered if we'd have time for that. We'd spent months here already, enlisted more Damned, and built up a presence... but we would be leaving Hell before too long, if our plans worked out. If they didn't, we'd be dead.

Maybe we could leave behind a starter crop, for Damned who stumbled upon it. Which would be immediately seized by demons after we were gone, so not so great an idea, there.

I drummed my fingers on the edge of the tub.

And that was the problem, really. These were people, down here. Regardless of what they'd done to get here, they were suffering when they didn't have to.

I was in a position to do something about it.

The original plan had been to take Beaky and jet down the pit, use surprise and force to get as far as we could until we reached the exit that Khalid insisted was beyond Lucifer. Then hopefully either reason with or beat up the devil until he was no longer an obstacle.

But...

I didn't want to leave these people behind.

Khalid insisted that they had earned their fate, and while he wasn't unkind, he kept himself as aloof as he could around them. Me, I couldn't do that.

Could they leave Hell? What would happen to them? I needed these questions answered before I could make any long-term plans or promises.

My musings were interrupted when the door opened and Cassius pushed his way through the membranes. He shucked his pants into one of the cubbies and glanced toward Juno, then did a double-take when he saw me. "Who are you?"

"Who do you think she is?" Juno asked.

He shrugged. "I do not know the faces of everyone saved from the spires."

Juno waved at my armor, standing silent sentinel in the back corner of the cave.

"Ah. Lady Dire." He saluted the empty armor, thumped his chest, and eased into the water, while looking me over. "Whoever you are, you seem fair of face. After we are clean, would you like to fuck?"

Ah, Romans. "No, she will pass on the fucking, but that's a nice compliment."

"A pity then." He eased into the water, closed his eyes, and settled back. Juno laughed until she coughed.

Twenty-three seconds later, Cassius' face slowly turned into a mask of mortification. He cracked an eye open, looked to me, looked at the armor, looked back to me again. "You, ah, you are the Lady Dire, are you not?"

"Yes, she is."

"I should not have presumed to solicit you."

"It is well. She is not offended."

"Ah. Good." His face relaxed, and he opened his other eye, studied me frankly. "It seems strange, to see the woman beneath the mask."

"Had you doubts?"

"Frankly, yes. When you first descended from the heavens to pluck us loose from the spire, I took you to be one of the Muses. I am still not certain you are not some form of goddess."

"As Dire has stated before, she is not." Time to change the topic. "How fare the labor crews?"

"The work goes well, but the boredom is bad. The Damned do not sleep. But this place drains you... saps energy and encourages indolence. When we are exhausted there is little to do, and fights have happened." He sighed. "Some have taken to carving bone dice, and this is good. Gambling has started among them, and this is the way of civilized men so we must let it happen. I have forbidden the staking of debts that take more coin than one has on hand, or for services that take more than one day to repay. But my words are not always heeded. When I find people disobeying me I shut it down, but eventually fools will get into trouble unless we find some other way to fill our time."

"Plays, perhaps?" Juno asked. "Those were my favorite thing, back while I could still walk and venture outdoors."

"Your legs seem to be fine now," I observed.

"Ah, I am older than I look. I lived for sixty years in Rome. My body seems of age from when I was twenty."

I frowned. "Strange. Cassius, are you also older?"

"No. As far as I can remember, I looked this way when my life ended."

"Now why is that?" I mused. *No, focus. Problems in the camp.* "So we need something to entertain bored and exhausted people."

"Well, yes. Fucking's out, it's not much fun when you're exhausted. The baths will help for a time, but eventually they'll become boring." He paused and I watched the thoughts pass behind his eyes. Finally he came to a decision. "Also, the demons are a problem."

"What have they done?" I asked.

"Nothing, yet. But they are demons, and many whisper that they should die before they betray us. The labor crews shun them and gripe that they get the easy tasks."

I shrugged. "They get the tasks they are best suited for. The Cat has no thumbs and couldn't wield a pickaxe even if he wanted to. And Thirteenth Chain is the only rider that Burren will tolerate."

"Yes, and I know that, but the labor crews will grumble. This will come to trouble unless we do something."

Unless *we* do something. I caught that, as he threw it out there, unthinking. I was starting to sell him on my enterprise, despite his dour and suspicious nature. Good.

"Thank you for bringing this to Dire's attention." I rose from the bath, sat on the bench near the hot rocks, and let myself steam dry. "She's going to have to think on it, figure out how to best distract the idle and figure out how to do some team-building exercises." That last phrase didn't translate well in Latin. "How is your English coming, by the way?"

"It's well," said Juno. "Easy compared to Greek."

"It is the hardest thing I have ever done," Cassius said. "But I believe I am making progress. It is very hard to believe this strange tongue is descended from Imperial Latin."

I nodded. "Good. Keep at it."

Once dried, clothed, clean, and back in my armor I strode from the cave, hands clasped behind me, brooding.

We had about thirty people now, the most that we could take without obviously depopulating the local spires. The demons were strong and tough compared to any normal human, but they'd easily get torn apart if five or six people with steel spikes and grudges caught them alone in one of the caves.

"We need to humanize them," I told my Chorus, once I was back in Beaky's ready room. "It'd be good if we could simultaneously provide some entertainment. Juno's mention of plays struck a nerve... for the most part we've got people here from around the B.C.'s or a few centuries beyond. Oral traditions are going to be a thing, storytelling and the like. We've also got dice, but want to shun gambling. So what can we do with these?"

They looked at each other for a bit, and Delta sat up like she had a loose wire. "Hey, do we still have those leftover thin sheets of burren leather? The ones that aren't tough enough for clothes?"

Burren leather peeled off in sheets of varying thickness, as it turned out. We'd been using the thicker stuff for tarps, pumps, and other industrial supplies, and the thinner stuff for clothes. But the really thin stuff... I racked my memory, realized I hadn't been handling that part of the logistics, and looked to our unofficial quartermaster. "Gamma?"

"We do have a lot of the softer stuff left over. It's about as thin and fragile as paper, though."

Delta leaned forward, hands spread wide, mask quivering with barely-suppressed excitement. "So what about Monsters and Mangonels?"

I blinked. "Say what?"

"M&M. We've got dice, we've got paper, we've got cultures that respect storytelling. This'll blow their minds!"

"You're seriously going to try M&M with ancient Romans, Axumites, Native Americans, and whatever the hell those guys with the pale skin are?"

"Oh, not just them. I wanna get the demons in on this too. And Vector. And maybe Beta."

I took a long look at her. "You really think they'd be all right with this?"

"Trust me, I've heard a ton of stories from Ray about his level thirteen wizard and how he survived Cravenloft."

Ray? No, wait, Vector's real name was Raymond.

She'd called him Ray. And was spending a fair chunk of time around him, if he was telling her about his hobbies. I spent time around him too, and I'd never heard of any high-level arcanists. Just how well *was* she getting to know him, and for what reason?

Then again, she always was the most gregarious of the Chorus, the most outgoing and fun-loving. She could just be good friends with him, and I could be reading too much into the possibilities, here.

Still, *Ray*. I finished my train of thought in microseconds, taking advantage of my superpower's enhanced processing speed, and smiled at her. "All right. Make it clear that it's voluntary, to all parties involved." I gnawed my lip. "Maybe not for the demons. Make it mandatory for them. They're more comfortable with straight-up orders than suggestions."

"Why do you want me to play?" Beta asked Delta.

She grinned. "You're like the best listener we've got. And you want to go into therapy services eventually, help people with their problems. You'll make a perfect cleric!"

"I don't plan on being a priest. Especially not after seeing Hell personally. I have no desire to worship or advocate worship for a deity who inflicts this sort of punishment on people, even if they did commit evil."

"You could be a priest of a non-Christian religion," I offered. "From what Khalid says, other gods have different afterlifes."

Beta's mask moved from side to side as he shook his head. "For now, no."

"Look, the gods in M&M aren't real," Delta protested. "What I mean by being a cleric is that they're the class that gets to heal everyone, and kind of act as the rallying point for the group. You've got good empathy, and you're not pushy; you'd do a good job with it."

"Oh. That's fine then."

"Right." I steepled my fingers. "Make it happen. See if it helps with group bonding, buys the demons a little acceptance, and helps alleviate the boredom of the Damned. We really don't have anything to lose with it; if it fails we try something else."

"Right! And we're already in Hell anyway, so even if that Chick guy is right we won't be any *more* damned!"

I blinked. "What?"

"Oh, you see, there's this obsessive guy who draws pamphlets—"

The radio cut in. "Doctor, Thirteenth Chain's coming in fast." Epsilon's voice. We'd left him on watch duty.

"Any pursuit?"

"No, but I'm getting some dust clouds out on the horizon. Could be another chaingang."

"Confirmed. The rest of you to Beaky's battle stations. Dire will go down and meet our scout personally, see what bodes." I suited up, suppressing a shudder as I sealed myself back into my armor's shell. Now that I was clean, the reek of the interior was starting to get to me. Next step was scrounging up cleaning supplies and drudging it out... if we had time, later.

I made my way through Beaky's guts, and out, descending to the ground below. Thirteenth Chain stood at the edge of the quarry, holding his burren's reins in one hand, conferring with the Grimalkin. Several of the Damned, alerted by the oddness of his unscheduled return, were making their way up the cliffside paths, but it'd take them a few more minutes at least.

I landed, kicking up the ever-present dust. "REPORT."

He thumped his chest, Roman-style. "Lady Dire. Sa binding of chains hie Broken Nails Riding found and pursued me. Na reason for them to do unless I thought a renegade."

I nodded and looked toward the distant dust, zooming in as I did so. Shapes far back in the clouds, that could be burren and demons. But they were slow now, stopping.

"HOW GOOD IS YOUR EYESIGHT?" I asked him.

"Good." He pointed at the shapes. "Seven of them, riding jan-jan, and their Grimalkin. Worra stopped because tey do not know what to make of Bee-kee, or you."

I gnawed my lip, measured the distance. Five miles off, give or take, and they could see me easily. My particle beams *could* go the distance, but the dust would severely impact accuracy and force, scatter and disperse a fair amount of their effect.

I wasn't sure I wanted to reveal my full power in front of our tame demons. Or worse, run the risk of a hammer blow seeming weak, if it failed.

"YOUR ENGLISH HAS IMPROVED," I told him, weighing the pros and cons.

"I do much practice."

As I watched the shapes melted back into the dust. Thirteenth Chain hissed in amusement. "Tey scatter. Fearful tey, worra chalt-lickers."

"THEY ARE TRYING TO ENSURE THAT AT LEAST ONE OF THEM MAKES IT BACK TO REPORT." I nodded. "COME. WE SHALL CALL COUNCIL."

I made my way back down to the altar and waited for word to spread around the quarry. One by one they trickled in... my Damned, my demons, and my friends.

"THIRTEENTH CHAIN," I told them once all were assembled. "TELL ALL YOUR REPORT." He did so, and the mob of Damned started muttering, glancing back and forth. They feared the demons and rightly so.

No point in letting that go on too long. I pointed to the Grimalkin, let my finger traverse to Thirteenth Chain. "SPEAK ALL YOU KNOW OF THIS BROKEN NAILS RIDING."

"Fools. Cowards. Canny la, but tey cowards." Thirteenth Chain rubbed his chin. "Six t'ousand hellions. Twice as much hesh."

"Hesh are those who cannot fight," the Grimalkin explained.

Khalid leaned over and translated for the Chorus, who couldn't hear his mindspeech. "So weakuns like you?" Gamma inquired.

The Grimalkin narrowed his eyes to slits, and scraped three-inch-long claws along the rock of the altar, leaving gouges in the stone. "Hardly." His paid servant, Urbi, scratched his back in an obvious attempt to calm him, but The Cat's eyes never left Gamma.

No love lost there. No matter. We had bigger things to ponder. "SIX THOUSAND. HOW CLOSE ARE THEY?"

"Ten... days ride, outwards." He gestured west.

Khalid frowned. "Yet they came this far?"

"Worra hate us, ban blood feud on Iron Scream Riding. And..." he hesitated, looked to the Grimalkin.

"You have been setting the Damned free," The Cat said, claws gone once more. "Those that do not join you, flee. By now they have noticed some of those who flee and taken it as a sign of weakness against our Riding."

Infernal politics. "THEIR BORDER IS NOT FAR, THEN?"

"Ten days, I said."

I blinked. I'd taken his turn of phrase to mean that they'd been riding ten days from a specific point. "EXACTLY HOW MUCH LAND DO THEY CONTROL?"

That took time, work, a lot of cross-translation, and a sheet of medium-grade burren leather broken out of storage to make a crude map. At the end of it, glad for the face-concealing armor I was wearing, I found myself a little aghast at the truth we'd just learned.

Hell was *big*.

The Broken Nails Riding controlled an area somewhere around the size of Connecticut. And they weren't even a major player! Iron Scream, the ones who nominally controlled the region we'd ended up in, had about twice the territory, but only about a tenth more combatants. "How is it they haven't conquered you?" Cassius asked, tapping the map with a worn fingernail.

"Tey cowards," Thirteenth Chain insisted. "Even if tey were not, our allies would crush them if they succeeded."

"ALLIES. LIKE THAT CITY YOU MENTIONED, A FEW MONTHS BACK. CAYM, WAS IT? WHERE IS IT ON THE MAP?"

The place hadn't been far from my thoughts, during this ramp up. Much of the quarry's work, many of the raw materials had gone into Beaky but with Caym in mind.

The only sticking point had been getting my Damned to go along with the idea, to leave everything we'd built for them here. And now I'd just been handed the perfect opportunity to shift the narrative *and* build up the kayfabe for the main event.

You don't let an opportunity slip by.

The demons pored over the map, and eventually Thirteenth Chain's clawed finger rested on a spot a fair distance away.

"THREE HUNDRED MILES, GIVE OR TAKE." I nodded. "SOUNDS GOOD. VERY WELL, DIRE SHALL TAKE IT."

"How does one take miles?" Juno asked. "Do you mean to take a journey, instead?"

"NO. DIRE MEANS TO TAKE THE CITY."

Silence, save for the wind howling over the quarry. The Damned looked to each other. The demons looked to me, eyes wide. Vector coughed and raised a hand, but Khalid pulled it down, whispered in his ear. The Cat's eyes slid to him, then to the Chorus, who stood mute with metal arms folded. They knew a moment when they saw it. Not least because I'd altered my photogenia app to alert them whenever I was using it. And oh, it was coming in handy, calculating the best angle to stand at for the wind to buffet my cape in a properly villainous way, adjusting the tilt of my head so that the light best reflected off my mask. At its suggestion I lifted a gauntlet and clenched my fingers. "CAYM SHALL BE HERS, AFTER WE FINISH BUSINESS HERE."

"Caym has six million hellions," Thirteenth Chain said, the words oozing out of him slowly. "Six times that in hesh. You are only one."

"WE ARE FORTY-FOUR." I gestured at the crowd. "AND ONE OF THEM IS DIRE."

"Illwrack rules there, third of his name," The Grimalkin pointed out. "Eleventhborn of Buer, he has slain the beasts of Grond and laid waste to fallen Vornia."

"THAT'S NICE. IF HE HANDS HIS CITY OVER WITHOUT A FIGHT, DIRE SHALL LET HIM WALK AWAY ALIVE."

Their silence spoke for them, as the two demons looked to each other, turned, and walked away. The Damned drifted off as well, but I heard murmurs as they broke off into small knots, and saw obols trading hands. Betting on me. Betting on how it would end up.

Good.

Khalid and Vector slid in next to me, and the Chorus fell into line behind us as I strode back toward Beaky and bed. Once we were back aboard our lair and away from the rest of our allies, Khalid gave voice to his thoughts.

"You are formidable, but I do not know if you are six million hellions worth of formidable. These Chains are low on the scale, and a highborn of a Fallen Angel will be much stronger, and have more powerful demons under his command."

"DIRE'S BEEN GIVING MUCH THOUGHT TO THAT. AND SHE'S CONCLUDED THAT IT DOESN'T MATTER."

"Okay, I want to hear the explanation for this," Vector folded his arms.

"SIMPLY PUT, WE'RE HITTING DIMINISHING RETURNS IN THE QUARRY. WE HAVE THE BEST MATERIALS FROM THIS PLACE THAT WE COULD OBTAIN WITHOUT HEAVY EMPLACED MINING MACHINERY AND DOING THAT WOULD REQUIRE A TIME INVESTMENT THAT WE SIMPLY CANNOT AFFORD. UNTIL NOW, THE DEMONS HAVE NOT TAKEN NOTICE OF US. BUT EXPANDING OPERATIONS... WELL, THAT WOULD DRAW IRE. AND FIRE."

"Which would probably be easier to deal with than six million hellions," Vector pointed out.

I looked to my Chorus. This could be a good opportunity to test them, now that I thought of it. "WANT TO TAKE IT FROM HERE?"

"Absolutely," Gamma said, taking charge, about as I expected her to. "From what we've observed, the paradigm that Hell operates upon is grinding despair and wearing its prisoners and foes down with time and vast numbers. Getting into a slugging match with the forces of Hell is a bad idea. They'll always have the home court advantage; there will always be more of them, and most living things down here are not affected by standard entropy. Ten years or ten thousand, they don't care. So at all costs, we must avoid playing to their paradigm."

I nodded. "PLAYING SATAN'S GAME IS A LOSING PROPOSITION."

"Which is why in the short-term, those Broken Nail doofuses ain't a real threat," Delta said, taking over Gamma's narrative with long-practiced ease. "There's a bunch of them but they're spread out over a state's worth of turf, and even if they wanted to mobilize in our direction, any army large enough to bother us would take weeks or even months to muster. We'll be gone by then."

"Which is key to the strategy that we seem to be priming for," Epsilon took over. "Emphasizing speed, mobility, and surgical strikes. Six, six thousand, or six million won't matter so long as we control the initiative and maintain superior mobility. Because at the end of the day, we aren't an army. We're supervillains. Most of us." He glanced apologetically to Khalid and received a reserved nod in return.

"My kids." Alpha threw his hands wide, looked to me. "How'd they do? Gold star? A-plus?"

"CLOSE ENOUGH. ABOUT THE ONLY POINT YOU MISSED IS

THAT WE NEED THE RESOURCES THAT A CITY HAS TO OFFER. WITHOUT THEM, OUR RESEARCH AND DEVELOPMENT STARTS HITTING UPPER LIMITS." I flexed my fingers, feeling the motors grind a bit. "AND WE START LOSING EFFICIENCY WITH OUR CURRENT RESOURCES. IF THIS ARMOR DOESN'T SEE MAINTENANCE SOON, WELL..." We reached the living quarters, and I decanted. Still smelled horrible, every time I exited the suit. Didn't think I'd ever get used to it. Didn't want to.

"Perhaps my only objection is that we are going in blind," Khalid said, sitting on one of the hammocks we'd strung in the corners. "The odds still seem against us, even if the strategy makes more sense, now."

"Right. That's not so good," I said, sagging into my own hammock. "So here's what we're going to do about it..."

CHAPTER 5: THE COURT OF THE CRIMSON KING

"And lo, did Doctor Dire assay forth to treat with Illwrack, forgotten and despised. And lo, did she roll a one for her diplomacy check."

--Excerpt from the third chapter of the first book of the Chronicles of the Shared Lie

Caym the crimson. Caym, the great wound of Hell. Caym, the City of Blood and Iron.

The river ended here; its great, scabbed tides twisting and roiling in hues of red and black, black from the crust and black from the flies that gathered and feasted upon its relentless waves. Brass-bottomed riverboats rowed up and down the river, bearing forth demons with pikes and nets, breaking up clots, fishing out Damned and stranger creatures, and keeping a sharp eye out for threats.

No surprise they spotted us first, really. I watched them through the cameras we'd made and mounted into Beaky's edges, watched them stop their work and point skywards as the shadow of the Strix passed over them. Then we were leaving the river and journeying up the road, panicking the land traffic, the demons and burrens and carts that entered and left from the six great gates in the rusted iron wall that surrounded Caym. Damned writhed and shrieked upon that wall, their blood flowing down grooved channels that spelled out the history and legend of Caym and its rulers, a ruby-veined testament to this ancient city and its might.

The cast-iron barrels of great cannons protruded, one between each gate, covering each approach with yawning, dark maws.

Above it all smoke rose from the fires and foundries of the city to pool in a dark, spreading cloud. If this wasn't the source of the ash storms upriver I'd eat my mask.

The whole thing looked ripped straight from a heavy metal album cover.

The shadow of our lair crept up to the walls, and bat-winged demons flew up to meet us, maintaining a healthy distance but circling in a way that made it clear that they'd happily charge if we kept going.

I smiled under my mask.

"Showtime," I whispered through my brand-new vox transceiver and climbed out of the hatch on Beaky's back.

The demons whirled and circled. Long and thin, each of them had at least ten feet in height from clawed talons on their feet to horns on their heads. This didn't count their wingspans or tails, which varied from group to group. I saw an order in them, the same sort of order one sees in a cloud of birds flying close together, wing beats synchronized in a roiling swarm.

There were perhaps four dozen of them, armed with long spears and javelins. They jabbed at Beaky's heads as he squawked his rage and unleashed flame. Nimble, well-trained, and far more maneuverable, it was a good strategy for them.

But they hadn't accounted for *me*.

I strode out from between two of Beaky's heads, out of the edge of the flame clouds with my remade cape billowing in the thermals and fire reflecting from my shiny, shiny armor. I'd chromed up just for the occasion, and I could pinpoint the moment I caught their eyes as the flying fiends paused.

"CEASE," I commanded them in hellspeech, lifting a hand and splaying my fingers in their direction.

A brief whirl as several of the larger ones, decorated in slightly more ornate clothing, conferred. Then they whipped around and sent javelins whistling my way. About half of them struck true, and I let them clatter off me with no real effect. Beaky whined as a few stuck in his hide, but they were too small to do any real damage.

I returned fire with a single particle burst, and five fell smoking from the sky. "CEASE OR BE DESTROYED," I spoke again.

That got them scattering. Once they were out of sight, I folded my arms and stood there, resolute, waiting. The ball was in their court, and I doubted they had a serve I couldn't return. I stepped forward to the edge of our Strix and gazed down upon the city. Dozens of miles wide, walls that towered high enough to blot out the sun for entire districts. Just slab after slab of iron. The bloody river flowed right through the center of it, winding past high gothic towers that stretched to the skies with countless crude shacks and hovels at their bases. In several cases buildings were built tall, narrow homes stretching eight or ten stories high, criss-crossed with cables and ropes. I followed the river with my eyes... until my sight fuzzed, as I looked to the very center of the city.

The anomaly.

We'd detected it sixty miles out. A zone that played hell with our electronics the closer we got, emitting raw electromagnetic interference. Fortunately my suit was hardened against it... though I didn't want to test those defenses by getting too close. I'd built a shielded room within Beaky for the Greek Chorus. Until that thing was dealt with, they were out of action.

Which sucked, because I needed more intel on the anomaly before I made my power play, and without the Chorus to infiltrate as planned, or any spy-drones I could make that would withstand the emag, my options were limited.

Fortunately, I had friends.

"Khalid," I voxxed as I waited, "What do your magical eyes see?"

"Technically speaking, they are not eyes. It is merely a sympathetic resonance between the talismans—"

"Dire was actually misquoting Tolkien to make a joke, there. But seriously, is Thirteenth Chain in position?" Without the Chorus and their infiltration, we'd had to enlist the Chain in our schemes. Fortunately, his role was simple: ride into the city, pretend to be on business, and go get a good look at the anomaly. What he didn't know was that the 'protective ward' we'd given him was actually a charm that let Khalid see what he saw. It worked through alchemy, which evidently didn't give three shits about electromagnetic interference.

"Almost. I see a great foundry."

"That explains the smoke above it. And the city in general. Industrial age-style foundry?"

"No. Perhaps something you would have seen in the seventeen hundreds. Kilns, lots of kilns, lots of demons and Damned hauling loads from... hang on."

"What?"

"The river. The center of the anomaly is the river. There are great, grinding stones here, damming the flow and literally crushing the blood between them. Why?"

I gnawed my lip. "Mills, maybe? Powering the foundry?"

"There may be mechanisms that required power, but I have not seen them. Still, Thirteenth Chain is on the outside of the compound, looking in, and there are many buildings. It is possible that there may be mechanisms I do not see, beyond the wheel."

"The wheel?"

"The two stones are cylinders, and the force of the river's flow, I think, pushes them. Stone gears go from them to a large wheel, just below the bloodfall. There are many small demons on the other side of it, with bags. They are turning it, it seems, and doing something with the bags. Ah, they are out of sight, sorry."

I needed more intel. This thing would be a problem. It would throw off my particle beams, cause hell with my gravitics, and render my best sensors useless if I got too close.

Still, it was only one thing among a host of other issues.

About six of those issues darted up over the side of Beaky, grabbed me, and hurled me out into the open air.

While I'd pondered, the flying fiends had evidently decided to see if I bounced.

Cute, but futile. I activated the suit's gravitics, compensated for the anomaly, and straightened up in midair, dusting myself off with a complete lack of concern for the thirty other demons milling about below me, who had evidently planned to try to filet me on the way down.

Now all of them stared in shock, as I blinked the code that turned my mask's hollow eyesockets a fiery, glowing red. "YOU ARE BEGINNING TO BORE HER," I told them in their own tongue, clenching my gauntlets and letting sparking emissions crackle golden as I flared the particle beams at half-percent charge... just enough to make a threatening halo.

"Great one, forgive us," A taller one with skull-like tattoos on its face pushed forward, sheathing its spear and spreading its hands. "We did not receive word of your arrival."

I grinned under my mask. Score one for cultural misunderstandings. I'd often wondered why Thirteenth Chain and the Grimalkin had caved so easily, back in the quarry. Extensive questioning had finally answered that, and the same answer applied here and now as it did back then.

I could fly without wings, or lift bladders or other visible means.

In Hell, the only things that could do that were the greater demons and the Fallen Angels. Ergo the display of this power indicated that the user was a badass.

Which was true, honestly. But it was nice to have a clear sign of dominance, one that saved me from having to fight off entire flocks full of these poor bastards.

"TAKE HER TO YOUR LORD." I commanded them.

"Of course, my lord…?"

"DIRE."

"May we know your titles?"

"NO."

Silence for a moment. One of them coughed.

"WELL?"

"My apologies, great lord, but we unworthy ones must tell you that our Lord Illwrack, third of his name, eleventhborn of Buer, Slayer of the Beasts of Grond, Destroyer of Fallen Vornia, Eater of the Candles of Woe, Defiler of the Screaming Siren, Thrice-cursed by the Hated Fates…"

He went on for a ways. I tuned out after a few minutes, until he got to the point. "…has decreed that all who visit Caym must enter through the appropriate gate. You, of course, Lord Dire, would be entitled to the Gate of the Guest, below and to your right, third from the river. Allow us to go on ahead and—"

"WAIT. EACH GATE IS DIFFERENT?"

"Well, yes. Everyone who enters must come in through the gate that matches best their station and—"

"NAME THEM."

"What?"

"NAME THE GATES."

He rattled through them, and I shook my head. "NONE OF THOSE SUIT HER. SHE SHALL THUS TAKE THE MEANS BEST SUITED. WHICH IS ILLWRACK'S KEEP?"

"That tower of course," he said, pointing to the largest spire.

"THUS SHE DECIDES HER GATE." I slammed out of the sky, so fast that my sonic boom rippled the air, scattered the fiends, and made Beaky shriek in rage. Before any of them could react, I slowed, hit the ground in a wide plaza with a sickening *crunch* of stone, and flipped my cape back, strolling off towards the tower

I kept my sensors dialed way the hell back, down to basic optics. This close to the anomaly, they were far too sensitive to risk maximum activation. That was also my reason for steering clear of the Guest's Gate; the path from there to the tower would have taken me right past it. I honestly wasn't sure if my shielding was strong enough to handle the proximity. This? This was stressing my systems, but it was doable.

Leathery flesh fluttered in the air behind me, as the fiends landed and hurried to catch up with me, snarling at gawkers and pushing them aside. I was moving through markets, by the look of it. Demons of all shapes, colors, and sizes, paused in the act of trading goods and services, left off from their haggling and fell silent as I passed.

Our path through the market was three kilometers long, and on that walk I saw more atrocities than I ever had in my time on Earth.

There were cafes of a sort, with cooks hacking hunks of meat from screaming Damned who writhed impaled on meat hooks, eyes wedged open so they could 'enjoy' the sight of their own ribs sizzling on grills again and again. Leather workers flensed their Damned stock of living skin, working it into gloves, boots, and coats while they chatted with their neighbors, who were busy pulling teeth from their Damned and grinding them into powder with mortars and pestles.

It was the rendering vats, where people were lowered bodily into bubbling tureens of fat, that finally made me look away, as my stomach did a slow roll.

If there had been some sign of joy at this, I think I would have snapped entirely and just opened fire until the city was dust around my ears. But of the demons I saw, none of them seemed invested in it at all. They seemed not to give it any more thought beyond the barest attention required.

This torment was simply work to them. Nothing more.

I tallied the Damned held here, and made note of their faces. Those that still had them, anyway. Much work to be done, after today's errand was over. But before that...

"Any better views on the anomaly?" I asked.

Khalid responded. "I have emerged onto Beaky's back, and I am surveying it with a telescope. It is definitely a mechanism of some sort, but I am unclear as to its purpose. After the blood passes the crushing cylinders and the wheel, it flows unimpeded to the edge of the cliff and the spillgate that opens onto the great falls."

I gnawed my lip. "Matters are in hand down here, for the minute. But it's going to get hectic shortly. Look, do you have a means of getting a photograph of the mechanism?"

"I could rig up a pinhole camera. But that would take a few hours to craft."

"Not good enough. Ah, how good are you at drawing?"

"Decent, perhaps. I have not an artist's eye."

"Do a drawing, run it down to Epsilon and the rest of the Chorus. Explain what you know, see if they can noodle out some possibilities."

As I passed between the tower's gates, the floor wailed below me. It took quite a bit of self-control to keep from jumping back in surprise. Instead I looked down, down into the face of some poor man, embedded into the floor with only his face protruding.

And then I noticed the rest of the tiles. Every three feet, another face poked out. The entire floor was coated in faces. And so were the tiles in the winding staircase, big enough for a horde of ogres. I'd just crushed the head I'd stepped on.

"DISTASTEFUL," I commented. "LET DIRE GUESS, IT'S FACES ALL THE WAY UP?"

The fiend nearest me coughed. "Er. Yes, Lord."

"LADY," I clarified. I contemplated kicking in the gravitics, but the anomaly was too close. I'd risk damaging the flight system if I did that, and I couldn't give up that advantage right now. Or maybe ever, until I got the materials and tools I needed to fix it.

I ground my teeth, steeled my resolve, and trod on the faces without care of my feet. They were Damned. They would heal. I kept telling myself that, as teeth snapped, cartilage gave, and wails fell into bubbling silence.

As I walked, I weighed my various plans, and discarded A through N. No, as fun as L might be, for this guy it was going to be O at the very least.

The stairs wound up, the blood dripped down, and accompanied by my escort of fiends I came to a throne room of purest obsidian. It stood open to the air on six sides, with a massive throne just a bit north of the stairs.

On the throne, surrounded by courtiers, sat the largest and ugliest looking demon I'd seen on my merry trip through Hell thus far.

He had the head of a boar, stretched out on a long, thick neck that fed back into a squat, round body. Six limbs splayed out around him, like legs that ended in hands, multiply-jointed and straining under the skin from ropes upon ropes of thick muscle. He wore black chain vestments that ended in a sort of skirt/kilt thing, and a crown set with rubies, placed to look like falling sprays of blood.

And right there, in the center of the crown, was a fucking Roja-Cola can. Weathered, crumpled, and with the color bleeding away around the logo, the little aluminum can jutted from the center of his crown, while rubies millions of times its worth spiraled down around it.

It took an effort of will to avoid bursting out with laughter. Then the thought occurred to me; how had that thing gotten here?

Suddenly it was a lot less funny and a lot more intriguing. And then, the reasons for its symbolism, for his display of the item, came to me. My heart filled with a fierce joy, and I felt my lips curve into a toothy smile.

"A PRICELESS ARTIFACT ADORNS YOUR BROW, LORD ILLWRACK. DIRE WOULD KNOW HOW YOU CAME BY SUCH A THING."

His eyes bulged, and he snorted. The courtiers around him gasped and muttered in fear and shock. Two stepped forward; a masked, robed form with chains extruding from his eyeholes, and a flawlessly beautiful woman wearing a metal bikini, easily mistaken for human save for the bat wings on her back and her black, pupil-less eyes.

The masked one wheezed, in a voice as tortured as the faces I'd trampled to get here. "You stand before Illwrack, Third of his name—"

"SKIP IT. SHE HAS HEARD THE LITANY BEFORE."

The beautiful woman flared her wings. "You do Lord Illwrack much disrespect. Apologize now, guest."

"YOU ARE INCORRECT. SHE DID NOT ENTER BY THE GATE OF GUESTS."

They looked startled, and the leader of the flying fiends hurried forward, pulling them into a huddle. The rest of the courtiers snapped open spiky black iron fans, and whispered and muttered as they considered me through mismatched eyes.

But Illwrack narrowed his own eyes and watched me carefully, something like a smile creeping up his lips. Old, this one. Dangerous. He knew the score; he knew what I was going for. This could only end one way.

"May we ask your name, then, rude visitor?" the winged woman asked.

"SHE IS DIRE, FIRST OF HER NAME, MORTAL AND MIGHTY."

All whispers ceased. Silence filled the room, interrupted only by the faint noise of the city below.

"You didn't come in from the Slave's gate," Illwrack rasped, his voice impossibly deep and resounding. **"Or the Bargainer's gate. Or the Sorcerer's gate."**

"NO."

"Nor did you enter by the Servant's gate, or even the Traveler's gate, which would seem to fit you, woman most mortal."

"THAT IS CORRECT."

Illwrack fell silent, smiling.

"Then you entered the city illegally, since you did not choose your gate." The masked demon said, pulling a book with rusted-iron covers from his robes. The chains from his eyes fed into it, and pulled bloody links from his head as he snapped the book open. "I fear, that you are subject now to the full force of the law—"

"You are wrong, First Manifesto. She has chosen her gate."

More silence, as the courtiers looked to each other. I smiled under my mask.

"I am currently without a bride," Illwrack stated, rubbing his chin.

"Would you care to be my queen?"

"NO. WOULD YOU CARE TO EXPLAIN WHERE THAT ORNAMENT ON YOUR CROWN CAME FROM AND HOW IT GOT HERE?"

"No."

I nodded. "SO BE IT."

"Lord, please, I do not understand," the bat-winged woman turned to him, somehow managing to turn both her ass and the side of her barely-bikini'd tits to me as she did so. "Which gate did she choose?"

Illwrack looked to me, and gestured lazily with one hand. I took the cue.

"DIRE ENTERED CAYM THROUGH THE CONQUEROR'S GATE."

Oh *that* caused a stir. Half the court laughed, the other half started talking at once, and First Manifesto started shouting. Through it all, Illwrack studied me. He was no longer smiling.

"Do you come to challenge me to single combat, then?"

"FUCK NO."

Small gasps, and the court decided to fall into shocked silence again. Ironic, that, demons taking offense at harsh language. Guess the Catholics were wrong about all that swearing. "SHE BROUGHT AN ARMY, SO SHE'S BLOODY WELL GOING TO USE IT. SHE ONLY CAME TO FORMALLY DECLARE WAR AGAINST YOU."

Now the demon lord smiled. **"My army within this city numbers three million hellions. How many do you have?"**

"FORTY-TWO. AND A BEAKY."

Now he laughed, great wheezing laughs, that shook his gut and rattled his chainmail. **"You would conquer my city with an army of *forty-two?*"**

"SHE WOULD CONQUER YOUR CITY ALONE. BUT THE EXERCISE WILL DO THE POOR DEARS GOOD."

He laughed all the harder. So I simply nodded, turned, and left.

Illwrack's laughter cut out. **"I did not give you leave to go."**

"NO. YOU DID NOT." I watched him through the rear view camera as I went. This was the point where he'd try something, if I'd misjudged him. In the event that I had, and he decided to take his shot at my back, I'd go straight to plan R-2, with extreme prejudice. It'd be a pain to ride the remnants of the collapsing stair down before the tower fell entirely, but so long as I managed the dismount, I thought my chances were good.

He didn't attack. I retraced my steps, this time letting my feet only fall on the faces of those I'd already slain, albeit temporarily.

The fliers followed me as I went, their wings folded, but their hands near their spears. I walked as if they weren't there, studying their stances, watching their body language, trying to read them.

The streets ahead of me had emptied.... imagine that. We walked alone, the only noise the thumping of my metal boots on the cobblestones. It'd take a few minutes to get out of the danger-radius of the anomaly, so I activated the vox. "Khalid? Vector?"

"We're here," Vector replied. "Still trying to muddle through that puzzle you posed the Chorus."

"It's a puzzle for you, too. What are we looking at?"

"The only reason I can think of for those rollers is that they're crushing the blood so thoroughly that they're rupturing cell walls," Vector mused. "They're breaking it down to the finest of elements."

"Elements."

"Whatever they're after, it's not biological. Unless we're talking prions or viruses, and even then there's far better ways to harvest those then pressurization—"

The words left my mind as quickly as they arrived. "Whoa, stop, bad at biology, remember? So if it's not organic, then what?"

"Epsilon has an idea," Khalid said. "Although I do not see the sense in it. Blood contains iron. Very small amounts of iron."

"Iron?" I frowned. "Why would they want that? They have plenty of veins in the quarries upriver."

"Perhaps, but none around here. Yet where did these walls come from? And the cannon? And the armor and weapons they bear?"

"There has to be a better way to get iron," I said, taking a look back at the fiends behind me again. They were conferring now, and some sort of bat-thing was riding on the leader's shoulder, whispering in his ear. When had that arrived? I replayed the visual record, caught it showing up a minute ago. I was getting too far into my thoughts, getting sloppy.

"So they want iron," I spoke my thoughts aloud, walking through them. "Then the crushers are part of a refining process. Makes sense that they put the smelters and the rest of the foundry right there, it's not just for hydraulic power, it's closest to the raw material. Those sacks they've got, they're storing the iron harvested from the blood. But how are they pulling it out of the flow?"

A long pause. Then Khalid spoke, low, his voice filled with wonder. "I think I might know."

Movement all around me, and I groaned. "Give her a second."

I paused, mid-step, and craned my mask around to stare at the fliers. They surrounded me, flicker-fast, wings taut with tension, faces masks of coldness. Their spears were out now, and their spiky knuckles whitened as they gripped them.

"YOU HAVE SOMETHING TO SAY?" I asked, flicking my cloak aside. The ones nearest my moving hand flinched, expecting a sucker punch.

"You entered Caym through the Conqueror's Gate, Lady Dire," The leader who'd spoken to me before intoned.

"YES."

"You may not leave through that gate, Lady Dire."

"TRY TO STOP HER."

They did.

After the last of them was ash on a shattered pavement, I took to the sky, my outermost layer of armor scratched a bit. They'd tried. They'd died. I put them from my mind as I returned to Beaky and the first volleys of arrows started to fly up from the walls.

I stood on the edge of my demonic steed/lair combo and glared down at the city below, hands on my hips. With a grin on my face and a realization that none of my foes had any chance of getting the reference, I gleefully quoted Bugs Bunny; "OF COURSE YOU REALIZE, THIS MEANS WAR!"

CHAPTER 6: THE FALL OF CAYM

"The battle that ensued is still replayed to this day."
"The City of Caym, as it was, has been turned into countless maps and acts as the introductory module to the mass battle system."

--Excerpt from the third book of the Chronicles of the Shared Lie: Kingdom Management

One of the keystone cities in the great ring that encompasses the punishment for the sins of sloth and wrath, Caym had long stood the test of centuries. Conquered many times but never sacked, it was a prime piece of real estate, famous for its foundries and steel. Its walls stood high, clawing into the sky, studded with archery slits, murder holes... and cannons. Great cannons, fully capable of pounding Beaky into paste with a couple of direct hits.

But they'd made a classic mistake with the cannons, one perfect for our assets and strategy: they could only elevate the guns up to a certain point. We were well above that point, and the great cannons which had served Caym so well over so many wars could no more track up to fire at us than they could grow wings and fly up into the sky.

Speaking of *that*, I watched great swarms of flying hellions rise up around the tower, boiling out of barracks, heading up into the smoky clouds. Smart of them, they could use the clouds as concealment to approach without risking return fire from any archers we might have.

It was a good thing I hadn't brought archers to this fight.

I clicked through HUD options until I got to the underslung cameras. The arrows from below weren't having much effect on Beaky. The range was bad, even with the elevation of the towers, and the shafts had little chance of penetrating his hide. With his mouths shut and tentacles safely inside, there weren't too many sensitive bits to tickle. No, the arrows were little threat. They would have been better used against light fliers, like the ones we were about to get jumped by.

Speaking of *that*...

"Khalid, are you ready?" I voxed. "Crews all in their places?"

"Yes. What are they throwing at us?"

"More of those fliers that escorted Dire in."

"Ah. The Pazuzu."

"The what now?"

"That is their proper name. Light, fast, as strong as three men."

I looked down at the scratches in my armor. "Sounds about right."

"We shall load accordingly. The bulk of them will seek to approach from above."

I warmed up my particle blasters, letting crackling gold sparks seep out from my gauntlets. "Leave those to Dire. At least for the start..."

And then the swarm dropped from the sky, and there was no more time for talking.

The javelins came first, relying on gravity to do their work. They targeted Beaky's heads, striking at the presumed weak points. Beaky roared in pain and rage, jerking in midair, trying to escape the pestering bites.

But it was futile. If they'd known more about the Striges, they might have known that Beaky didn't keep his brain or anything much important in the heads, beyond the eyes— and we'd taken the time to armor those up. Each head had slitted metal plates riveted directly into the bones of the skull. It had actually made him easier to control, sort of like blinders on a horse. Fewer distractions, less stimuli to trigger his instinctual behavior.

So when the winged warriors dropped down like a tide of angry bats, Beaky met their predations with blasts of howling fire.

As for me, I shrugged off the javelins, strolling gently along as they fell around me, a few pinging off of my shell. They shredded my cape something fierce, but I didn't mind. A small sacrifice for the greater good. I focused on blasting the warriors who were trying to close with me, spreading my beams wide and at about sixty percent charge. I'd taken their measure during the earlier fights, this setting was enough to blast them well away from Beaky and shred them. They'd be wounded enough that the fall down to the ground would finish the poor bastards off even if the beams didn't.

The crowd around the top thinned, the lines peeled back and away and angled in. I measured their approach and smiled. "Khalid," I said, knowing what awaited them. "Run out the guns."

Two solid months of work. Uncountable gallons of enzymes and chemicals and non-organic braces shoved into Beaky, turning him into some sort of hellspawn cyborg. At the end of the day we'd freed up raw tonnages for cargo capacity and reinforced his sides to take recoil from extremely heavy weapons.

And then we'd given him cannons.

Those cannons thundered now, blasting out from the vents he used to exhale waste gas, throwing great canisters of leaden shot into the sky. Their accuracy sucked; they threw stinking clouds of gunsmoke into the sky, obscuring the gunners' vision, and they had a two-minute reload time.

They hit the unsuspecting army of Pazuzu like a boulder rolling over a kitten.

On the underslung cameras, I watched shredded bits of demon fluttering down below... and I watched shot from the keelward guns rain down to wreak havoc on the city below.

There was an army gathering down there; the other two point nine million that Illwrack had bragged about, I supposed. Clustered as tightly as they were, firing from the height that we were, the carnage was pretty impressive. The panic was just icing on the cake, really.

Beaky shuddered with the cannon volleys, screaming, shrieking, and spewing fire all around.

The few Pazuzu that survived the initial volleys curved down and tried to come up, under his belly, and ran straight into the arrows that the archers below were firing up at Beaky. Poor coordination, that. But then they didn't have radio, or vox networks, or any other way of changing orders in midstream. Perhaps there were horns or something, but Beaky was wailing way too loudly for such things to be heard.

Some survived. I wished them luck in injuring Beaky from below. Beaky was good at eating things below him, and if they managed to do enough damage to convince him to open his mouths, any arrows that got in wouldn't kill him.

The problem lay in the reloading time of the cannons. Two minutes wasn't long, not when you were dealing with siege artillery. But the vanguard demons they'd thrown our way were fast, and if an officer worth his salt was up there, he'd start testing them, and then they'd find out the limitations on my guns. Then it'd be boarding through the gunports, a desperate fight to repel boarders, and internal damage to

Beaky. Not so good. A losing scenario.

I eyeballed the regrouping clouds of flying fiends. Not more than a few thousand.

I'd spent three years learning the art of fear.

Time to show them the fruit of my studies.

"TREMBLE BEFORE DIRE!" I roared and jetted into the sky. With a sweep of my arm my right pauldron's missile rack cracked open and spat micromissiles that blossomed into flaming explosions among the crowd. With my left arm I tracked and fired wide spread particle beams, catching five or eight per shot, shredding them with golden light. Then I was in among them, and I snapped my weapons ports shut, barrelling through them straight-armed like the flying brick superhero of your choice. Only with rather more gore, since I was moving at Mach two. The sonic boom shook them; Beaky howled fire below, and I moved like a dervish, arms grabbing, swiping, squeezing, and tearing with inexorable force.

It wasn't entirely one-sided. They fought like, well, demons. But their weapons couldn't break my armored shell, and whenever I got a stubborn cluster, or a fighter who knew his stuff, a point-blank particle blast saw them off.

All in all I only killed a hundred and fifty three, by my calculations, before they broke and surged back into the ash clouds. I smiled and returned to Beaky's back, arms crossed. "IS THAT ALL?" I roared at the city.

Evidently it wasn't.

Smoke blossomed from half the towers around the city, and my eyes grew wide behind the mask. "Move! Drop down!" I screamed through the vox. Beaky shuddered and moved below me... but too slowly, as the first cannonballs screamed past.

Not all of them missed.

A whump, a spray of ichor from Beaky's side, and the bird-beast howled in pain and rage. I staggered, activating the gravitics to avoid falling. Wouldn't look good, couldn't look weak.

I growled, low in my throat. "Damage report?" I voxed Vector.

"He'll live, but we don't want to take too many more of those."

I nodded. "Descend, then. Plan H."

"Ah, which one was that again?"

"Get next to the walls and have him eat the archers. Drop Spitters as necessary. Cannon for any bigger threats that come our way."

"They will sight us in and adjust the cannon in short order," Khalid shouted, his voice overshadowed by Beaky's primal scream of pain coursing through the airways. Our poor Damned must be near deaf, right now, and I thanked my foresight for putting noise dampers on the vox transceivers. "We need the Tesla Deflector!"

We'd lined Beaky with copper wire and rare earths, built a crude generator in a non-conductive part of his guts. It would generate a vast, frangible forcefield that would intercept and deflect fast-moving objects like bullets or cannonballs. But we couldn't fire it up with the anomaly still active.

I ground my teeth. If it was what Khalid thought it was, I could do this, but I'd have to get close.

I looked down, measured the odds. The teeming hordes below surged forward as we descended, hellions ranging from half-human sized to over ten feet tall, studded with extra limbs, spiky bits, and fanged, screaming mouths. About half were armored; all were armed, and the casualties they'd taken earlier seemed to deter them not at all. An arrow pinged off my mask, and I shifted my gaze to the wall, saw spidery-thin demons with four arms apiece drawing, aiming, and shooting as fast as they could pull arrows free.

"They have a good vantage point on those walls," I mused over the vox. "Let's steal it. Vector, get ready to drop the Spitters there. Clearing the LZ in five... four..." I jumped off the edge, slammed to a halt in midair next to the battlements, calculated the best firing arcs and hosed down the battlements with golden light.

Above me, Beaky's maws yawned open, tentacles snapping down, a full score of them. And tangled within every tentacle was a cocoon of flesh, twelve feet around. They splatted onto the battlements, sticking and rocking wetly, fluids roiling within and spurting without.

The horde below the walls stopped, war screams fading as they watched, entirely unsure what to make of the situation.

The cocoons split as one, fluid draining away as fleshy shells burst open, and monsters never dreamt of in Hell clawed their way into the world.

Vector's spitters. As large as cows standing upright, hooded like cobras, and eyeless, because they didn't need those to see. They stood on the wall, tottered on tall legs, and shook amniotic fluid free of their scales.

For a second the hellspawn gazed up at the mutants, and the abominations of Satan gazed upon the abominations of Man.

Then some dimwit demon chucked a spear that bounced off of the first creature.

In reply it roared, and with the roar came a fountain of green liquid spraying into the crowd below, melting those caught in its direct blast.

Vector called them the Mark Sevens. I called them Spitters. They wouldn't hold against that horde, not forever, but they'd cause a lot of damage on the way down. The demons would have to take them out in hand-to-hand combat or get cannons on them, or use tricks we hadn't seen yet. And all the while they'd be contending with Beaky's feeding tendrils, cannon shots angled downward, and gouts of acid.

As distractions went, it was pretty goddamn good, I thought. Might get me half an hour. But the problem lay in the tower-mounted cannons, which I hadn't anticipated, and really should have. Of *course* they'd have smaller guns than the big ones on the walls. Flying enemies were a thing here, so the cannons were smaller, but they were still a problem.

Time to shut down that anomaly and render the smaller guns a moot point.

I turned in midair, ignoring the spears and arrows flying at me, and zoomed toward the center of the city. I arced my flight down as I approached the anomaly, slowly easing the gravitics down so they wouldn't be affected by its electromagnetic properties.

The hordes in my way objected, of course. My forcefield flared as gunners took aim at me with bell-mawed blunderbusses. Pikemen rushed to contain me when I was low enough, and I bulled through them with scattered blasts and backhanded sweeping blows.

For a moment, I wondered if it was really going to be this easy.

Then a spiked iron ball about the size of a Volkswagen crashed into my side and knocked me through a brick wall.

I rose, sending smaller demons scattering, retreating into the interior of their warren-like dwelling. A whimpering, half-eaten Damned watched me from where he'd been spiked to a stone altar. Apparently we'd interrupted the demons' meal.

My HUD was alight with damage icons. All green, thankfully. Still...

The spiked ball that had come in with me started to withdraw, and I grabbed it, riding it out. It turned out to be attached to a chain, which in turn was attached to a metal bar that filled two of the hands of a fifteen foot tall demon. He looked at me stupidly through three eyes and reached out with his two free hands to pluck me free.

I turned his three-eyed face into two eyes and a smoking hole with a hundred-percent particle beam shot, and he toppled with a deep wail. I grabbed the flail's stock from him as he fell, gave it three or four experimental whirls and sent it flying down the path I needed to follow, running along behind it... not as smoothly as I would have liked. One of my right leg's actuators had taken a nasty dent, and I had to favor it or risk the damage worsening.

I followed in the wake of the thrown flail, through busted walls, over piles of bloody gore that had been demons. With a howl, the ranks that had drawn back surged in again around me, and I fought with everything I had. The smaller ones, the human-sized ones, they could knock me about, but they couldn't actually damage me. The larger ones, though... those could. I prioritized them as targets and used the terrain to keep them from grouping up on me, but it slowed me down.

Then I was to the point where the anomaly started affecting my particle beams, and I had to switch to melee-only. Scooping up weapons from the demons I felled, I waded through a small sea of blood and fallen demons to reach my destination. Sweat coated my back, ran down my face, and my armor's environmentals worked overtime to keep me cooled. I would *ache* tomorrow, and there wasn't a thing I could do about it.

Finally, I came to the edge of the foundry and found the hordes pulling back and away. I looked around for a reason.

I found one above me.

Illwrack hung there, the limbs on his sturdy frame churning, whirling around him as if they were attached to him by ball bearings, like he was a rotary fan and they were the blades. It should have seemed funny... but it didn't. There was nothing natural or logical about their motion as he hovered there, sneering down at me. One of his arms, this one *not* turning, held a blackened hammer as long as I was tall. Another arm, also still in contrast to his churning limbs, held a spear double the length of the hammer.

"SO THE LORD OF THE CITY DEIGNS TO SHOW UP TO DEFEND IT." I flicked blood from a sword I'd grabbed earlier and banged it against the remnants of a slab-like shield I'd liberated from one of the larger demons. "COME AND TRY. COME AND DIE."

I was hoping for a monologue, or a boast, or some other piece of kayfabe.

Instead, I got a hammer to the face, a rapid relocation down the street, head over heels, and a brand new yellow damage icon on my HUD. Not for the first time I was really glad that my actual head was in the chest of my armor. The head up above was a decoy, and it had just saved me a busted nose.

I rolled to my feet, shook my armor's head like I'd felt it, and tilted my borrowed shield, exposing my gauntlet. I waggled a finger at him, beckoned him in. "GO ON. TRY THAT AGAIN."

He did, and his hammer met the shield this time. I chopped at him with the sword, which rebounded from the haft of his spear as he blocked. Then he was inside my guard and grasping for my mask, only to grunt and shift back as my rising knee crunched into the chainmail around his groin.

I'd spent too long fighting heroes and supervillains who bought into the culture. There was no monologuing here, no threats or banter, just the very simple business of both of us trying to kill the hell out of each other. Or trying to kill each other out of Hell, as the case may be. I decided to save that witticism for somebody who would appreciate it.

Finally, my armor battered and his own chainmail rent into rags, Illwrack backed off, panting. I would have pressed the advantage, but one of my knee actuators was shattered by an earlier stomp. I shuffled after him instead, raising my thoroughly gouged and nicked sword, keeping its point up toward his face. I'd cut him four times, badly. He bled black, the ichor running down his muscled body, pooling in the street around us. Could he bleed out? I didn't know. I had the worrisome feeling that I would have to find out. He was skilled, and I couldn't get a decisive blow in past his guard, whereas the only reason I was still alive was because of my armor's sheer toughness.

The demon lord laughed, cast aside his weapons, and tore the shreds of his armor from his frame. I waited for the trick, cursed my hesitation as he rose into the air, limbs flailing in that circular whirl once more.

"You fight well, woman. But your weakness is plain to any who think it through."

"DIRE HAS NO WEAKNESSES."

"Then why do you not fly? Why does the golden light not burst forth from your hands?"

"SHE DOES NOT NEED SUCH THINGS TO END YOU." I ran a few steps forward, wound up and pitched the sword at him. But my arm was stiff, thanks to damaged motors, and he dodged with contemptuous ease. I scooped up his spear from the street and tried to line up another shot, but Illwrack zigged and zagged back and forth as he taunted me.

"Foolish to come here, mortal. More foolish to spurn my offer. I would have given your sons my kingdom."

"YOU THINK SHE WOULD SETTLE FOR SUCH PETTY FARE?" I snorted, the point of the spear tracking him as I tried to gauge his rhythm. This would go either Plan F-4 or Plan T, depending on the next few seconds. "DIRE WANTS IT ALL."

"All? What do you..." his mouth gaped open, and he laughed, belly jiggling obscenely, the stupid little cola can on his crown bouncing up and down. **"You think to conquer _Hell_?"**

From around me, a thousand gasps echoed from a thousand demonic throats. I glanced around to see the army had formed a ring around us, filing in between the half-wrecked buildings and rubble our fight had caused.

"HELL ITSELF SHALL BOW TO DIRE. THE MORNINGSTAR

WILL KNEEL OR HE SHALL FALL ONCE MORE." I intoned, turning to the side, training my mask on him and lifting the spear one handed like a pointer. "YOU ARE NOTHING TO HER AMBITION. MERELY A SPEEDBUMP ON THE ROAD TO VICTORY."

"You would defeat *Lucifer*?" he howled and fury flooded his face, strained his inhuman muscles within his dark flesh, even sprayed blood from his wounds to rain upon the ground below. **"Bitch, you cannot even defeat a *lodestone*!"**

The last piece fell into place. Plan T was a go!

Illwrack charged me, and I weighed my options, calculated the effects, and deliberately missed with my stop-thrust. I pretended weakness as the demon seized me, bore me aloft into the skies above the foundry, well-within the anomaly's danger zone. Anomaly no longer, though! I knew what it was, and cold logic and science would win the day.

"A LODESTONE, YES! A GREAT WHEEL MADE OF MAGNETIC ORE, TO DRAW OUT THE TINIEST TRACES OF IRON FROM CRUSHED BLOOD!" I wriggled, got an arm loose, blocked a stray limb as it clawed at my mask.

"THE SLAVES WERE USING ALCHEMICAL REAGENTS, OF COURSE, TO BREAK UP THE IRON CLUSTERS, PULL THEM FREE OF THE ROCK. WE THOUGHT THAT WAS WHAT THEY WERE DOING, BUT UP UNTIL YOU JUST CONFIRMED IT, WE WERE NOT CERTAIN. COULDN'T COUNT ON IT." I flipped through my vision modes, got to one that wasn't affected by electromagnetic interference, and surveyed the lodestone below me. A great stone wheel, flecked with dark ore, turning on a bronze spoke in the center of the river of blood.

"And it will be your doom!" Illwrack howled, getting a claw in despite my flailing, ripping into my mask with rage-driven strength. My helmet registered a breach and whispered softly into my ear. "Dye pack deployed."

'Blood' sprayed from my helm, and Illwrack snarled with glee. **"Bleed, mortal! Add your blood to my realm!"**

And he cast me down.

Simple plan, really. Cast me into the river, where my armor would stick to the lodestone with a force I couldn't counter and let the river seep in until I drowned.

But there was a flaw in this plan.

I knew magnetics. I'd mastered magnetics. One of my earliest inventions had involved turning a busted sonic blaster into a crude gravitic system, and oh hadn't that been a trick.

This? This was just a big freaking lodestone. Whereas I? I had tools.

I plummeted, and in the microseconds I had, I did the math, checked the angles, and flicked my gravitic system to life, in just the right way. Just had to extend my field, stretch it out, and repolarize accordingly.

The lodestone had no more chance of resisting the aligned polarity flow than a toddler could stop a monster truck. Poked like a billiards ball whacked by a cue, it tore loose of its moorings in a spray of blood and whirred skyward, flipping like a coin.

I checked the math again, tucked in, killed the gravitics, and sucked air through my teeth as the 'coin' of lodestone tore past, missing me by four inches. My armor actually paused in midair, as the tug from its fields pulled on the revealed ferrous components... then it was past and I was falling again, turning to get the right angle—

—As I flipped on the gravitics, this time to repel the lodestone.

It caught Illwrack square on, and I brought my hand down, trapping him on one side of the coin as six-hundred and forty tons of lodestone flew away from me and slammed into his iron tower with a resounding BONG.

One of his arms protruded from where he'd been crushed against his own tower, for about a second. Then it peeled away and fell, spurting, to the ground below.

I stopped my fall, inches above the river. Child's play now that the lodestone was gone and the anomaly was out of range. With one gauntlet I mopped dye from my mask, and shook my head with an exaggerated twitch. "MAGNETS. YOU SOUGHT TO USE MAGNETS AGAINST A SCIENTIST." I flew back to the river bank as the demons of the foundry, who had been frozen watching my fall, scattered in all directions.

There, on the bank, lay the crown. The cola can was crumpled and torn, most of the rubies were gone, sprayed out from burst sockets, but I picked up the black iron headpiece anyway and held it aloft as I hopped the wall and settled back to the ground, walking through the army like it wasn't there. They pulled back as I went and I paid them no heed. There was a more important matter to tend to. "Khalid? Vector?"

Khalid replied. "We are here. The Spitters are dead, but we have managed to shell down some of the tower guns. Now that I mention towers... that impact was you, correct? What did you do?"

"Just some casual regicide. You were right by the way, it *was* an enormous lodestone. It's currently restrained by the central tower, so you can probably risk firing up Beaky's Tesla Deflector."

"Of course. Then what?"

"Pull up out of the army's reach and wait for word to get around that the king is dead. Then meet Dire in her new throne room. Ah, bring some of that ironbane reagent that you mentioned. We've got a few hundred tons of lodestone to get off her new tower."

CHAPTER 7: MASKS AND MALICE

"And lo, did the great teacher bring to Caym the great game. And its magnificence enthralled all who witnessed it. None could deny the allure of the Shared Lie!"

--Excerpt from the fourth chapter of the first book of the Chronicles of the Shared Lie

The hammer descended, and I grinned as sparks bounced off my mask. I could have done this part with the pneumatic press. But it felt good, to beat the last part of my new carapace into shape.

Coal-black from head to toe, wrought of an alloy forged from the bloody iron of Caym, the newest layer of my armor was but one of many local materials that had made it into my repaired suit. I had been right; the city was a bonanza of rare earths and metals that the quarry had simply lacked.

And it was all *mine*. For the moment, anyway.

I brought the hammer down again, straight on my mask, and more sparks flew. I was beating it not to temper the metal, but to test it. Diagnostic displays, wrought from the finest glass the city had to offer, registered the impacts.

No damage.

I sighed in relief. Blood iron wasn't as high-grade as the terrestrial stuff I used, but refining it and going for a microcarbon sandwich build had done the trick. It added weight to my frame, but eh, whatever. The gravitics would cope. This suit was powered by a microfusion generator, literally the same force that let stars burn. It could cope with a few hundred extra pounds.

"Doctor?" Khalid's voice echoed through the vox link. "Your pet demons wish to see you."

"Dire sometimes wishes for a pony, a box of pretty hair ribbons and a quiet farm in the middle of nowhere with plenty of room to ride. But alas, like the wishes of demons, that wish has never come true."

"They are rather insistent. They are claiming it is a matter that threatens the whole city."

I sighed into my mask. With a few strides I crossed the floor of my tower workshop and threw open the shutters on my way to the balcony. Caym spread out below me, smoke wisping up from its foundries, pressed to the limit by my decree. Demons walked the streets, going about their business and mine.

Well, all save for the fleshmarket district. I'd put a stop to *those* particular torments, over the strident and hysterical objections of the merchants. Barely a day later came the first assassination attempt. I gave them points for style, if not originality... finding a tiny demon to fit into the plumbing couldn't have been easy. But it had been no match for the Chorus. Finding and punishing the demon responsible had been a bit harder. Thankfully, Vector had been up to the task there.

"Epsilon, do we have any of that sodium pentothal equivalent left?" I glanced over to my most logically-minded minion.

"A little. I can easily make a new batch if necessary. Why?"

"Court demons are getting uppity. Tempted to whip up an aerosol version and release it in the middle of high court, and ask them their deepest, darkest secrets. Then watch how they have to face each other the next day."

"Hell seems to be affecting you," Beta said, from his perch. He was in a lotus position up on the balcony railing, looking away from me. "Do you really want to torment these creatures?"

I shrugged. "Might do them some good to see how it feels." I leaned on my elbows next to him.

"They are no less trapped in here than us. They're just following their nature."

"Which is to be evil demons," I said, but I wondered. Thirteenth Chain's compassion for the beasts he'd raised and ridden still came to mind. I drummed my fingers on my mask, chin resting on my palms.

"Oh, they're no less dangerous for that," Beta said. "But there's no need to be cruel. That's not your nature. You would get sick of it in short order."

"True." I weighed the matter, sighed again, and activated Khalid's vox channel once more. "All right. Tell those seeking an audience that Dire shall take her throne shortly."

Only two courtiers awaited me when I entered the great hall and crossed the tiled floor so recently filled with shrieking faces and now spackled over with fresh cement. The two courtiers were the winged woman, First Whisper, and the masked guy with the eye-chains, First Manifesto. They knelt, prostrate, until I hopped up on the throne and settled my cape around my armor. I'd added more spikes, which made maneuvering the cape a little dicier.

Four Damned, attired in reworked demon armor, stood silent around the chamber. Nezool, an Axumite from somewhere around Ethiopia, led this particular squad. The others were three of the ones I'd freed from the fleshmarket. They were my honor guard now.

Then I turned my attention to the two demons, as my Chorus filed in around me. All save Delta, who had taken a leave day for some reason or the other. But the five remaining were more than sufficient, I felt.

"SPEAK," I told the demons. "YOU ARE INTERRUPTING VITAL WORK. BE CONCISE."

The two rose and shared a look. Finally, First Manifesto cleared his throat, shaking blood from his mask's eyesockets. "Great lady, we fear that the Lord of Smoke and Sinew plans to invade Caym."

"WHO IS THIS LORD, AND WHY WOULD HE DO SUCH A STUPID THING?"

"He dwells below the Bloodfont, in the Wrathlands, oh great lady," the winged woman intoned. "As to why... we believe that his spies in the city think you are weak and foolish for sending the army away. Not, that is, that you are weak and foolish. But he is stupid and surely believes so." She added, flushing red and turning so that her ass jutted out at a favorable angle.

"SPIES IN THE CITY."

"It is a matter of fact that we regularly found and executed spies from the Wrathlands under Lord Illwrack's reign. And that the Lords of the Wrathlands did the same to ours, as they caught them," First Manifesto spoke up again.

"THAT'S INTERESTING, BECAUSE THE WRATHLANDS ARE PRETTY MUCH SEVERAL MILES DOWN THAT BLOODFONT." I'd scoped the area after my conquest, taking note of the sheer cliffs, forceful winds, and thin, deadly trails that were the only land route up. "AND DIRE SEEMS TO RECALL ORDERING ALL PATHS DESCENDING IN THAT DIRECTION SEALED UNTIL SHE COMMANDED OTHERWISE."

"We believe that they sent an imp, great lady Dire," First Whisper spread her hands, making her barely-restrained boobs bounce.

"INDEED." Imps were those bat-things that I'd seen speaking with the winged fiends shortly before they jumped me in the city. They were semi-sentient, and the demons used them as messengers.

I activated my vox. "Gamma, you're the one in charge of pathside security. Did any imps get past us?"

"It's possible something got by the first day or so, before I got the cameras online. Since then, no, no imps have gotten past the turrets. A few tried, but the rifles did for them."

I nodded. "Coordinate with Alpha, backtrack the camera footage into the city, see if you can link it with the network. Spies don't rely on a single messenger getting through. If we're lucky we can figure out who's dropping these."

"We don't have anywhere near the full city covered yet, boss," Alpha voxed. "Local fauna's been doing a number on the spy-eyes and crawlerbots."

"Do the best you can. It's not vital that we find these spies, not yet. If all they're reporting on is the general state of the city, that's minor. Now if they start leaking more specific intel, then we've got a problem." I turned my attention back to the demons. "THANK YOU FOR BRINGING THIS TO DIRE'S ATTENTION. ARE THERE ANY OTHER MATTERS YOU WISH TO DISCUSS AT THIS TIME?"

They looked at me blankly. First Whisper even forgot to shake her boobs for a second, I'd shocked them so badly.

"The Lord of Smoke and Sinew is mustering his armies, filling the plain below with Damned slaves and demons and preparing for the long march up, lady. We thought it might perhaps cause you a brief moment of concern for this city which you have claimed," First Manifesto intoned. "You will certainly forgive us if we are concerned."

"Hang on," Alpha said. "How did *you* find out that he's doing this?"

"Our spies, of course," First Manifesto said, his voice resembling the tone of an overworked grade-school teacher. "We've received three imps from three different agents. He has formed an alliance with three other lords, mustered four million of his hellions, and readies great siege machines to scale the Cliffs of Screaming Woe."

I looked to Gamma. She voxed back her reply. "Three imps did come up the cliffs over the last thirty-seven hours. I tracked them to this tower and decided to let them live."

"Dire did order those paths sealed, y'know."

"The trails, yes, but you never directly commanded me to shut down the airspace. And once we learned the imps were message carriers, I figured the ones arriving could only benefit us or the city. It's the ones leaving that we had to worry about. I know, I was stretching your orders a bit here. I feel it was worth the risk."

Gamma was showing more and more initiative as she developed. I weighed it, considered the situation, and found that I didn't mind. I didn't require slavish obedience from my minions, that was for villains who suffered from inadequacy. "On this occasion, you were right. Consider every future occasion just as carefully, and don't be afraid to raise the matter to others. Including Dire herself."

A tension seemed to go out of her. My Chorus *were* developing more human mannerisms as time went on.

"Now look at First Whisper," Beta voxed, barely a murmur. I turned my gaze to her, found the winged demon's eyes sliding between Gamma and myself. "That one picked up on your body language, Gamma."

"Duh. Courtier." Alpha voxed.

"YOUR EXPLANATION HAS BEEN CONFIRMED." I turned back to the demons. "DIRE'S MINIONS HAVE BEEN WATCHING THE CLIFFS. AS TO YOUR CONCERNS, THEY ARE UNDERSTANDABLE. BUT THE ARMY BELOW WILL BE DEALT WITH BEFORE THEY POSE A THREAT TO CAYM."

The demons simply looked at me as if I'd declared Jesus Christ my lord and savior. "You will not recall the army?" First Manifesto managed.

"NO," I said, simply. "BY THE WAY, HOW ARE THEY DOING, EPSILON?"

Illwrack had roughly three million troops in the city, less a few dozen thousand that our assault had slaughtered. A few hundred thousand more had deserted, after my ascension to the throne. But the three million troops outside the city, stationed around the borders of Caym's territory, were both still unbloodied and a potential problem.

So I'd declared war on all surrounding territories and set out to conquer the Ridings, the Steadings, and all the other little -ings that made up this particular part of Hell.

It had taken about a week, but we'd mass-produced two-way radios, disguised them as severed heads carved with occult symbols, and flown them out to the various commanders. Epsilon was in charge of running this particular initiative, and he responded now.

"The West caved fairly easily. The East is taking more time. There's a solid buffer of swampland between us and Tindalo, the next City-state over. Crossing it is problematic, but once we finish the conquest in the West we should be able to spare reinforcements for that front. After that it's a matter of time."

"GO TEAM CAYM," I made little victory symbols with my fingers.

"WOO."

"Woo?" First Whisper smiled, twisting as she tried shooting victory signs back.

"JUST STOP." I wanted to palm my face. Between this and the constant posing, I had the uncanny feeling she was trying her damnedest to seduce me. I found it annoying. "DIRE REITERATES, FOR THE LAST TIME; DO YOU HAVE ANY OTHER ISSUES TO DISCUSS AT THIS TIME? UNRELATED TO THE ONGOING WARS, OR WARS TO COME?"

They looked at each other again. First Manifesto cleared his throat, a rattling sound that caused red goo to ooze from his eyesockets. "There is... the matter... of food."

"YES. WHAT OF IT?"

"There is concern growing throughout the city, about the loss of our... food sources."

Demons ate the Damned. They ate other things, but their main diet consisted of Damned flesh. I'd freed all the Damned slaves upon my ascension, and oh, hadn't that caused an uproar.

It had actually been one of my reasons for announcing the war of conquest. Two million, seven-hundred thousand fewer mouths to feed, with the soldiers gone. They could forage or live off the land. It was an imperfect solution, since they'd simply eat from the Damned they found on the way, but it bought me time.

And it also made the city's reserves last longer.

"ARE THE STORES OF SMOKED MEAT INSUFFICIENT?"

"They are sufficient Lady Dire, for now. But if we come under siege..."

"THEN THEY SHALL REMAIN SUFFICIENT. VECTOR ASSURES DIRE THAT DEMON FLESH IS GENERALLY AS NUTRITIOUS TO OTHER DEMONS AS THE FLESH OF THE DAMNED. IF THE ENEMY IS AS NUMEROUS AS YOU ASSURE DIRE, THEIR CORPSES WILL BE A READY FORM OF REPAST."

First Whisper's eyes went wide, and I saw no trace of whites at all in her blackened orbs. That had shaken her down to the core. First Manifesto, for his part, reached into his tunic and drew out his book, flipping through it with shaking hands. "Lady Dire. It... as part of... this city is part of the Pax Infernum. We follow the first law, that demon shall not consume demon, save for vengeance of blood or family."

Now *that* was interesting. I drummed my fingers on the armrest of the throne. "THE FIRST LAW."

"Yes."

"YOU UNDERSTAND THAT THE WRONG WORDS HERE

COULD POTENTIALLY CAUSE YOU GREAT DISTRESS, OR LEAD TO YOUR DEATH."

"Of course, great lady."

"YET YOU STILL FEEL COMPELLED TO TELL DIRE NO. YOU STILL FEEL THAT STRONGLY OVER IT."

The thin, eyeless demon took a breath, let it out. "I do, great lady Dire."

I looked to Beta. "This is fascinating," the android said over the vox. "With your permission I'd like to speak with him later, learn about the Pax Infernum."

"Granted." Then I turned back, and activated my speakers again. "YOUR WORDS HAVE SWAYED DIRE."

First Manifesto sagged in relief. First Whisper's wings twitched, but she kept her face motionless. Would she have been relieved or upset if I'd ordered her comrade's execution?

"PROFESSOR VECTOR WILL INVESTIGATE ALTERNATIVE FOOD SOURCE POSSIBILITIES THAT DO NOT VIOLATE THE PAX INFERNUM ONCE HE HAS RETURNED FROM HIS ERRAND. IN THE MEANTIME, THE CITY STORES REMAIN SUFFICIENT. ALSO, A THING TO CONSIDER..." I looked to Nezool and the rest of my Damned honor guard, who had stood stoically through the exchange, faces unreadable behind their helms. "THE DAMNED OF CAYM ARE NO LONGER SLAVES AND CANNOT BE BUTCHERED FOR FOOD WITHOUT THEIR CONSENT. BUT IF ANY DEMON WISHES TO PAY THEM FOR THE PRIVILEGE OF FEASTING UPON THEIR FLESH, IT IS UP TO THE INDIVIDUAL DAMNED AS TO WHETHER OR NOT THEY WANT TO TAKE THAT BARGAIN."

"What? *Pay* the Damned for—" First Whisper shrieked, cutting herself off, forcing her features out of the revolted mask they'd become for a split-second.

"Boom. Right in the paradigm," Alpha voxed. "This'll cause a ruckus."

"Good," I replied. "We could do with a proper uprising before we leave. The only way we're going to make changes stick around here is with blood, enough to double that river flowing right through the city." This had been weighing on my mind for some time.

"Thank you, great lady. Shall, ah, shall we pass your words along to those who have expressed concern?" First Manifesto managed.

"OF COURSE." I waved them out. Then I rose and beckoned my honor guard forward.

"WHAT ARE YOUR THOUGHTS ON THE MATTER?" I

translated that into their various languages, after asking in English.

"I think those mule dicks are going to try to fuck you up the ass the first chance they get," Nezool said. Two of the guards froze in trepidation at his utterance. The last, an ex-navy recruit from Georgia, laughed her butt off.

"WELL THAT'S A GIVEN. SERIOUSLY, THOUGH, YOUR THOUGHTS?"

"I have seen war in Caym before, attacks from below. I do not remember if it was this Lord of Smoke and Sinew, but it takes a lot of time to repel the invaders." That was one of the older guards, a former monk from the Dark Ages. It hadn't taken long to learn his dialect of Saxon, so I understood him well enough. The Chorus translated for the benefit of his comrades.

"HM. MONTHS? YEARS? DECADES?"

"My calendar is guesswork. I tracked time by the appetites of my owners. At a guess, no more than a dozen decades, though it could be twice that amount or more." He sighed. "No sun, no moon, no stars. Troublesome."

"We are in Hell, Widdig, and you are vexed most by the fact you cannot properly tell time," Narl snorted. He'd come from roughly the same era as Widdig, but was more about raiding and axes and boats. From what Nezool told me when he recruited them, they'd struck up an unlikely friendship from having common ground, even if it had been on opposite sides of politics and conflict in life.

"At least I am not whining about a lack of alcohol all the time."

"Like you'd turn down a cask of mead!"

Joanna, the navy woman leaned in, popped her visor up, and showed a dark face about the same shade as Nezool's. "I think an army that big is gonna take time to get mobilized. These guys, they don't have the same infrastructure chains that we do, or the urgency. They take everything slow."

I nodded. "TRUE. WE'LL BE OUT OF HERE BEFORE THEY BRING ANY REAL FORCE TO BEAR. BUT THEY ARE IN THE PATH WE NEED TO GO THROUGH..." I'd offered any Damned who wanted to journey with me a spot on the Strix express. Got fewer volunteers than I'd thought, about the same ratio that recruiting from the spires had achieved. Something about this place killed people's hope, murdered their motivations.

I seemed to be more resistant, and I didn't know why. I felt it, but it was distant. Superior self-control, I supposed.

"We'll have to deal with the Wrathlands army one way or the other, boss." Alpha shrugged.

"TRUE." I took a princely three seconds, ran through various plans, and smiled. "VECTOR'S STILL OUT ON HIS ERRAND. EPSILON, DID HE EVER DEVELOP THAT CLOTTING AGENT?"

"Yes. He's got a prototype. The stuff was simple enough to make."

I took a few more seconds to call up my CAD modeler, whipped up a diagram, working from my eidetic memory on the geography we'd crossed to get here. "TELL HIM TO DUMP IT HERE." I voxed the diagram through.

"I will. But why?"

"YOU'LL SEE." I turned attention back to the honor guard. "AND THAT BIT ABOUT THE PAX INFERNUM?"

The monk nodded. "They did not lie. Of my previous owners, I have heard seven of them discussing plans for betrayal and attack on rival houses. But they have stopped short of all-out destruction several times, because of an ancient treaty among the demons."

"AMONG THE DEMONS..." I rose and paced, thinking it over. "DOES THE TREATY AFFECT THE FALLEN ANGELS AS WELL?"

Widdig crossed himself. Two seconds later, Narl followed suit. "I do not know, Lady Dire. They do not speak of the Fallen Angels often. When they do, it is with fear."

"Demons dread where angels tread. Fallen or no they're fearsome foes," Alpha said. "There ya go. Free poem. Worth what you paid for it."

I'd learned much in the three weeks since I'd seized Caym, but there was still a lot about Hell that remained a mystery. I needed more data before I could formulate a plan that had a shot at getting us through.

Joanna spoke while I mused. "That bit about Damned selling their flesh really shook them. I don't know how well it's gonna go down with the local Damned too, Doctor."

"NO? THEY DON'T WANT FREE WILL?"

"Free will we have," Nezool said. "But our bodies are different now. Every time we feel pain, it is as if it is the first time we have ever felt pain."

"He is not wrong. Nor is it merely the pain of the body that is new. My mind should have broken many times over from the tortures I endured," Widdig confirmed. "But ever and again, I returned from the depths of madness, recovering as my flesh does from mortification."

I'd wondered about that. Given the stress this place put upon its victims, there should have been a lot more madness around. I'd seen a few down here, but now I wondered if they were the ones who'd started life out that way.

"WHAT OF HUNGER? AND THIRST?"

Joanna grimaced. "It's complicated. We feel hungry all the time, but eating anything never fills us up. We feel thirsty all the time, and when we get some actual water that helps for a while."

"Lasts longer than eating," Narl said. "But water's rare. Not wasted on Damned like us."

I hadn't paid much attention, earlier. Nobody had ever complained, and back at the quarry my original bunch of Damned had tucked into the burren steaks with satisfaction. They'd enjoyed the water, too, but they hadn't seemed to need it, or cared much until it showed up.

I wondered how much of that had been stoicism, and how much had been fear that we'd punish them or take away luxuries after we had what we needed from them. I resolved to ask my Romans when I had a second.

Though I had a second now, didn't I?

"THANK YOU. YOU'VE GIVEN DIRE MUCH TO CONSIDER. ONE LAST QUESTION; HAVE ANY OF YOU SEEN CASSIAN OR JUNO?"

"They are at their *game*," Nezool said, his voice dropping down to a whisper. "Lucky Romans!"

"I'm due for my second session in the next shift." Joanna smiled, and the other guards sighed longingly, looking at her with raw envy.

"WAIT. WHAT?"

"Monsters and Mangonels," Widdig offered up. "The game of stories."

"With dice!" Jarl grinned. "My kind of stories."

"OH-KAY." I looked to my Chorus. They put on innocent poses, though the effect was somewhat ruined as I heard Alpha snickering over the vox channel. "WHERE ARE THEY HAVING THEIR GAME?"

"I'll show you," Alpha said. "You're gonna love this."

I bit my tongue and followed my minion. He led me down the stairs, into an actual fucking dungeon. The cells were empty of occupants but filled with bones. "TELL DIRE WE LET THE PRISONERS FREE."

"The few Damned that were down here, yeah. We got First Manifesto to tell us the crimes of the demons. Some got freed. The rest, eh... well, you don't wanna know their crimes."

I nodded, then glanced to the side as a demonic functionary bowed and scurried past, on his way to another errand. Many ears here, so I switched to vox instead. "So First Manifesto kept track of the crimes?"

"He kept all of Illwrack's records, pretty much. He also handled a lot of the bureaucracy and the city's works. Dude's fussy."

"Fussy?" Not an adjective I'd expected to hear apply to a demon.

"He's a perfectionist or got some hyper-OCD, or some degree of both. I got the feeling that the only reason he's unhappy about the current situation is that it's highly irregular for a mortal to do anything like conquer a city, much less fail to die when a greater demon looks at them."

"Well, he'll have to get used to that."

"Will he?" Alpha glanced over his shoulder at me.

"Will he what?"

"I mean, we're moving on eventually, right? Anything we change here, anything we do, there's no way to make it stick once we're gone."

I grinned, but no one could see my face. "Already thought of that. You're gonna get a kick out of her solution."

"Yeah, if you want the Damned in this city to stay un-tortured then it had better be a really good one, boss. I mean you're awesome and all, but this is Hell. There's like an anti-momentum here, from what Khalid tells me. Really, really hard to make any improvements that stick."

"We lose nothing by trying. This isn't Mariposa. The enemies are legion and horrible, and Dire's free to employ whatever tricks and tactics she desires to ensure her will be done." Though I kept my tone under control, I could feel heat burn its way through my chest.

Hell... offended me. It was broken.

And I could fix it, given a big enough lever and just the right place to apply pressure.

"If you say so, boss. Oh, hey, we're here!"

I stared up at double-brass doors sized for a troupe of elephants. Elephants that were standing on each other's backs. The doors dripped with frescoes and murals of demonic slaughter.

"Swanky," I voxed.

"You ain't seen nothing yet." Alpha put an arm on each door and *pushed*.

The cavern he revealed could easily hold the entirety of the tower within it. Around the edges of the room the walls had been carved into support pillars and ringed benches.

And about every bench was filled with Damned and demons, looking into the center, a sandy pit that looked all the world like an arena; probably because it *was*. The grilled gates surrounding the room, opening up into the main floor, could serve few other purposes that made sense.

In the center of the arena sat an altar. Old, blood-stained, lined with manacles, it loomed. How many had died on it? Hard to tell.

Especially with the hex-map covering it.

Delta, my two Romans, Thirteenth Chain, and The Cat sat around the altar. The Cat's servant stood next to him, rolling his dice whenever his turn came up. Chalices full of unknown liquid sat next to the players.

Delta spoke. "The door slides open without sound." In the crowd, translators listened to her English words and spoke them in dozens of tongues.

"Superior stealth," the Grimalkin said smugly in that voice I heard with my mind. "Did you expect anything less from Hoomin the Thief?"

Half the crowd ringing the arena cheered.

But Delta wasn't done. "Unfortunately, the poison dart trap that fires when you open the door isn't so quiet. Gimme a reflex save."

The cheers turned to gasps, and now the crowd was literally leaning forward in their seats, on edge and waiting to see if The Cat's character lived or died.

"I block the darts with my shield!" Cassius called.

The arena went silent.

"Huh. Well, you are next to him." Delta tapped a finger on the map. "Okay, I'll let you give him a bonus to his save, but if he fails, you'll be hit too."

"An adequate risk. Brutus the Fourth is strong against poisons. Hoomin is weak to those."

The Cat's tail lashed. "You're trying to save me now? Why? What's your angle?"

"Don't be ridiculous," Juno snorted. "There are at least six other doors we have not opened. If there are more traps we need Hoomin alive to survive this labyrinth."

"Oh, hey boss!" Delta waved. As she did, every eye in the arena snapped to me. And all of the seated spectators rose.

"YOU ARE DOING VERY WELL. CARRY ON." I threw out my arm, and they sat back down. But they were still staring at me, so I withdrew, waving at Alpha to shut the doors behind me.

"Delta?" I voxed. "What the heck is happening, here?" She could vox me and talk at the same time, I figured.

"Monsters and Mangonels. Did you not see the Mountain Brew? Well, as close as we could get it, anyway. Ray whipped it up. It's about as bad for you as the actual stuff, but demons and Damned can drink it and it's got something like a sugar buzz."

"For an *audience?*" I knew the game, of course. I'd read the books a few years back, when I was bored once. Hadn't seen the appeal.

"I blame it on the internet. It's not down here, so things are really, really fucking boring. Something like this is new and original and doesn't take much to get going."

"There are guys back Earthside who play this in prison," Alpha said. "Dice carved out of soap, I shit you not. Same principle, when you think about it."

"Huh." I frowned. "Vector's out on a mission, so I'm not surprised he wasn't there, but I thought Beta was playing with you as well?"

"Right, well, there's too much demand," Delta explained. "He picked up the notion after a few games, and he's running his own for another batch of folks. Mostly Damned, though we've got a couple of the foundry demons playing. They have more spare time now that the lodestone's gone, and we're using the Last Janissary's iron transmutation process."

That explained the whole second-shift comment, from upstairs. Well, if it kept people busy, that was fine. "Where is Khalid, anyway?"

"I think he's with the kids," Alpha answered. "Down at the new hospice—"

"Wait. What?" I hadn't heard that right.

"The new hospice, it's where he's been tending to the Damned—"

"Get back to the part about kids."

"Oh." Alpha said.

"Shit," Delta commented. "Nobody told you, did they?"

"Evidently. Not." I felt my temper bubbling, somewhere around my stomach. "Why are there kids here?"

"I don't exactly know," Alpha said. "Janissary's tending to them, along with the folks we cut out of the stairs and floors."

I felt my lips flatten together. He hadn't said a word to me. After all we'd been through, he didn't trust me with something like this?

"Going to have a talk with that one. Mind matters until she returns."

"Okay boss, but I'm pretty sure he had his reasons..."

"Then he can say them to Dire's face." I scowled. "Metaphorically speaking." I flew up the passageway, taking the time to test out the gravitics, making sure they meshed with the armor repairs and modifications. It seemed to be operating within tolerances.

I flew up from the staircase, into the back of the tower's entrance hall, and straight into a hail of arrows that tore through the new armor patches like hot knives through cloth.

CHAPTER 8: DELAYED REACTIONS

"When initiating plots of intrigue, bear in mind they shall nearly always turn to blood. This is acceptable and encouraged, for it gives those who are only interested in fighting something to do should their more clever compatriots fail."

--Excerpt from the second book of the Chronicles of the Shared Lie; The Monster Master's Methods

Layered defenses had saved me many times in the past, and they saved me now. I dove for cover back underground, yellow-grade damage warnings screaming in my ear. Thanks to my fast-processing mind, my power allowed me to examine and comprehend the icons in the space of microseconds.

The arrows had shorn through the outer armor, but the impact gel had slowed and stopped them. The shafts were throwing off unidentified energy signatures... likely magical. I'd expected to run into sorcerous weaponry and effects down here at some point. I'd also expected the city I had conquered to rise up against me at some point. I hadn't expected either of these events to hit so soon, or together for that matter.

A second more and I was back in the hallway below.

"We've got a coup," I voxed, across all channels.

"God dammit! I just got the PC's to a fight!" Delta groused.

"Bringing the cameras up... wow, how'd I miss that?" Alpha spoke up. "The guards outside the tower are dead, spiked in place to either side of the gate. The doors are barred, and there's about twenty skulky looking bastards filling the first and second floors of the tower."

"That's it?" I felt vaguely insulted, magical arrows or no. "Keep running the game Delta, we'll get this."

Then I heard it, a groaning that tore through the air, a shuddering howl that filled the corridor, and the city beyond.

"And now we've got explosives going off around the Hate Spires. Looks like they're trying to drop them into the Royal Tower. Figure a minute to impact."

"Oh. Cute." I grinned. Adrenaline rose in me, and I felt almost like my old self once more. It had been easy so far. Almost too easy. "Yeah, keep playing, Delta. Everyone else in the city, rendezvous at the hospice."

"Yeah, about that. Twenty assassins? Waiting for you to pop your head up again?" Alpha asked.

"Oh. Right." I launched a concussive missile up through the hole, let the blast wave rip through the chamber, then came up with particle blasters blazing. Three seconds later there were nothing but twitching forms on the floor, and I'd burst through the shut and barred door like a bullet through a pinata.

Outside, dust filled the air. I filtered it, glanced around. As I did so, four metal forms whirred past me, legs pumping as they raced into the cloud and down through the rubble-choked streets. My Chorus, obeying the order I'd given.

They'd left the hard job to me, and I wouldn't have it any other way.

Demons fled, screaming, seeking shelter against the massive stones and chunks of iron that still pelted from the sky as the towers groaned and collapsed inward like the fingers of Satan's hand.

Particle beams did for the first two, carving chunks out of their bases and diverting them to fall on either side of the tower. I flew to the side as they fell, letting rubble batter my forcefield while I moved to the third pillar. My shoulder pauldron snapped open—

—and nothing happened. I checked the diagnostics, and swore. One of the arrows had nicked the circuitry. I couldn't cycle away from concussion missiles and what I needed were high-explosive. My subroutines were rerouting missile functions to an undamaged sector, but it'd be thirty-eight seconds before they were available again. I didn't have that kind of time.

I checked the architecture of the tower again, and ground my teeth. No way to do this flawlessly, or without more damage.

Unless...

I snapped my shields to my front, flipped myself horizontal with arms outstretched, Crusader-style, and flew fists-first through the third tower.

Key supports gave way before me, buckled, and crumpled inward and away, falling back towards the foundry. Damned shame that, but hey, at least they'd have the iron of the tower on-site to keep them busy smelting. If enough of them survived, anyway.

My forcefield flared and snapped off as I burst out the other side, venting heat in shimmering waves. I'd taken enough damage that I couldn't risk overloading it. Hopefully I could get by without it for the next half a minute. But I had no time to spare, the last two buildings were bowed at a forty-five degree angle, mere seconds away from striking the Royal Tower.

I'd spent two fucking weeks building up my workshops, both in the upper levels and below the dungeons. Be damned if I'd lose them now to a bunch of demon terrorist wannabes!

I put rapid particle beams through the farthest building, shearing it off with its own weight. It struck the Royal Tower but shattered, ringing it like a gong. The crumpled remains of the lesser spire fell about my conquered edifice, but I was too busy to care...

...as I flew up, put my back under the last tower, and reworked my gravitics so I could pull this stunt off without crushing myself.

It wasn't a factor of locking myself in place; if I did that with the tiny surface area I presented, I'd shove myself through the tower, and it would keep falling, unhindered. It wasn't a matter of using my armor's strength to hold it up; doing that would result in the same thing, with a slightly-larger area destroyed on the tower. It wasn't of one piece, just welded together from big plates, and all I'd do was tear one or two of them off.

Fortunately, this tower was made out of iron. I had other options.

The gravitic field utilized magnetism, allowing me to more or less cancel out gravity. But when I spread it out, aligned it to key parts of the tower's structure...

...well, I couldn't stop its fall. But I could and did cause the building to twist and 'unzip' itself, collapsing in a heap, plates flying free.

One of them struck my armor on the way down, gouged a long tear into my suit, pushing me forward, sending damage indicators straight to red. I grunted as I felt pressure on my back, felt impact gel hardening, then loosening, heard the scream of metal buckling—

—and then it was past and falling away, and I judged it safe to disengage. Core warnings flashed, as one of my nuclear failsafes engaged; that plate had almost, almost clipped the fusion cell. I'd be running at two-thirds power until I could get into a workshop. Preferably the one with the lead-lined room.

"Bad news, boss," Alpha voxed. "The hospice is empty. There's signs of a struggle."

I nodded. I'd figured as much when Khalid hadn't responded. "They've taken him, the bastards. Man, what a pity we didn't slip a tracker into his gear when we had the chance."

I felt my teeth peel back in a wild grin. "Except oh *wait*, we did that." I touched down on the ground, turned my back to the remnants of falling rubble, and walked away from the ruins. My tower still stood, like a middle finger thrust up against all of Hell, and I still functioned. Walking gave my suit time to auto-repair what it could, reroute critical functions around the damaged parts. I'd lost a lot of impact gel, taken some serious knocks, but the iron wafer composite was holding up, and my adrenaline was still pumping. "Beta, get a fix on him, would you?"

Three minutes later, he replied. "Got it. Sending coordinates."

"Hey..." Alpha said. "You know how you asked me to check the cameras for arriving imps?"

"Yeah? Let Dire guess. One of them showed up earlier at the same site where Khalid is now?"

"Oh yeah. Looks like we've found our spies. Oh shit!"

"What?"

"Remember how a couple hundred thousand of the army deserted?"

"Yeah."

"Well, some of them are here. And they're kind of stabby."

I gnawed my lips, examined the coordinates. "Can you endure?"

"Probably. It's a moot point, since you finished our backup servers. They're still functional, right?"

I glanced back at my Royal Tower. "Yep. You're good. Dire's going to go retrieve Khalid and kill some idiots. Catch up as you can."

I rounded the corner, to find about fifty black-armored demons hurrying toward me, rushing out of empty market stalls, drawing weapons as they came. I flipped my cape back, leveled my hands—

—and gunfire cracked out behind me.

The first two demons fell. *My honor guard,* I realized. Not the best shots, but they were firing from the elevation of the tower and well within range. Now I didn't regret the rifled breech-loaders I'd given them. I counted about twenty shots, give or take, in the volley.

It was enough to make the charging wave hesitate, and I laughed as I strode forward. "LEAVE HER STREETS OR DIE IN THEM, IT IS ALL THE SAME TO DIRE."

Say this for Caym's hellions, they had no lack of bravery. Nor did the wave behind them. Or the wave behind the reinforcements. Finally, knee-deep in the dead, I growled low in my throat and took to the air again. Enough of them were getting through to me before they dropped that they were actually doing some damage. Not a lot but given the pain I'd already taken, every bit lost now was structural integrity I wouldn't have against someone who mattered.

Arrows flew up at me, and I put on a burst of speed, hearing the reactor conduits whine and groan. I couldn't afford to assume I was invulnerable to arrows, anymore. The enemy had already shown that they had access to magic that didn't give much of a shit about physics.

Four minutes later, after my particle blasters were starting to groan from the slaughter I'd been conducting and my circuitry's functions were as rerouted and reconstructed as they were going to get, I arrived at my destination, a large, sprawling complex of brick and marble, blackened with soot and adorned with statue after statue of fat demons enjoying their repast: basically, feasting upon people.

I knew this place. The most influential of Caym's merchant clans dwelled here. Well, the most influential of the *surviving* clans, anyway. I'd thought they'd learned their lesson after the last assassination attempt.

I supposed they had. Their lesson had been "throw everything you have at Dire and don't hold back."

It was a good lesson, really.

I surveyed the windows and arrow slits full of archers, the courtyard full of foot troops...

...and swore, as my voltaic vision picked up flickers of familiar looking wires and charged cells, there in the central part of the complex. I opened a vox channel. "Alpha?"

"Yeah boss?"

"Did you and the others get your asses captured?"

"Ah, yeah, boss."

"Dire seems to recall you reporting that there were only fifty back at the hospital."

"There were. Then there were fifty more, and fifty more behind them, and somewhere around the fifth fifty I kinda lost count."

"We tried, Doctor," Gamma spoke. "The scenario didn't allow for victory."

"Alright. Well, let's see what kind of mastermind we're dealing with, here."

I landed outside the gate, pushed them open with either hand. "WHO ABIDES HERE?"

The hellions in the courtyard flinched. Some of them held glowing spears, perhaps one in every hundred or so. Magical, and an unknown quantity. Probably quite deadly, given time. So I took the opportunity to register them as priority targets for my FoF system.

I was well within arrow shot, but easily within cover of the stone gate if it came to hostilities. But as the silence stretched into seconds and no arrows came, I knew what I was dealing with, now. My smile grew under my mask.

I took the opportunity to check on a few of the systems I'd installed for this eventuality, found their vox-link solid. I activated their channels and waited for the show to begin.

The doors to the largest building in the complex groaned open, immense slabs of brass peeling out to reveal a great hall, lined by demons of every shape and size, though most of them trended toward the obese. A feast table had been lined up, I saw, the length of it vanishing back into the depths of the hall.

"Welcome to House Garlam, Doctor Dire!" Boomed a jovial voice from within. "I'm pretty sure we've got almost everyone you call a friend down here captive, so enter with that in mind, mmmm?"

I strolled across the courtyard without hesitation. The waves of hellions parted to either side of me, weapons shaking in tensed hands. Sensible, really. I'd left the streets strewn with the corpses of their brethren.

Inside, demons pattered out of the way, peeling away like waves of bloated flesh. Above me, spiked iron hooks stretched taut, swinging slowly, tangled with Damned. Their blood dripped down onto the dishes. Quite in defiance of my decrees, since my conquest.

Eight of the Damned up there were children, and I felt my teeth grind together.

The thing at the head of the table spoke. "You do me honor with your presence, good Doctor." It resembled nothing so much as a maggot the size of three elephants put together, with a spider-like array of hairy limbs stretched out around it, and a dainty, almost delicate baby-like face hanging on a polyp above an enormous tooth-lined mouth.

The voice was the worst part of it. I wasn't sure which orifice it spoke from, since neither its main mouth nor the little baby's mouth moved as it talked. It sounded like an aged grandmother, cheerfully reading to her grandkids at bedtime.

I turned my gaze from it, to my friends, each of which had been trussed up with chains next to the creature. Khalid, Alpha, Beta, Gamma, and Epsilon. Then my eyes widened... next to them, also trussed, were First Whisper and First Manifesto.

"Allow me to introduce myself, Doctor Dire. I am—"

"SHUT UP." I pointed a finger at him and the guards' swords whipped around to ring the captives. "YOUR NAME IS NOW MIDBOSS."

I'd blatantly stolen that line, but I doubted they knew the source.

The baby's face stared at me, goggle-eyed. Silence didn't just fill the chamber, it spilled out the windows. "What?" The great demon finally squeaked.

"WHOEVER YOU WERE, WHATEVER YOU'VE DONE OVER YOUR LIFE, IT DOESN'T MATTER NOW. YOU HAVE PRESENTED YOURSELF TO DIRE AS AN OBSTACLE, AND NOW YOU'RE NOTHING MORE THAN A SPEEDBUMP IN HER GREATER PLAN. SO YOUR NAME IS MIDBOSS, BECAUSE IT'S NOT EVEN GOING TO TAKE A FULL STAGE TO TURN YOU INTO DUST."

Now the baby's face was screaming, lips peeled back to reveal rows of needle-like teeth. "You would do well to remember your situation right now! You're wounded, your armor broken, and I have so, so many lovely hostages!"

"YEAH, AND YOU CAN'T DO SHIT TO ANY OF THE ONES DIRE CARES ABOUT."

I saw First Whisper sag into her chains, for once not flashing boobs. She knew the score.

Midboss didn't.

"You little mortal cur! Step out of your armor now and surrender, or I'll rip them to shreds myself!" Spider limbs stretched out from his form, grasped Epsilon's entangled shell. "Don't think I won't!"

I sighed. "DIRE'S GOING TO TELL YOU A LITTLE STORY, HERE." I hopped up on the table and sat cross-legged, relishing the flinches the demons around me gave at the sudden movement. "JUST BEFORE SHE CAME DOWN HERE, DIRE THREW DOWN WITH A MORTAL MASTERMIND. A POWER BEHIND THE THRONE, AS IT WERE. A SHADOWY MANIPULATOR WHO SECRETLY RULED HIS KINGDOM DESPITE THE PRESENCE OF AN EXISTING GOVERNMENT, PUPPETED TO HIS WILL."

He hesitated, curious despite himself, I could tell. "Mortal mastermind? Bah. The petty intrigues of those who can achieve a mere century of lifespan—"

"ARE ACTUALLY PRETTY EFFECTIVE. THE GUY SAW THAT DIRE WAS A LITTLE TOO STRONG TO TAKE ON DIRECTLY, SO HE HARRIED HER, STRUCK AT THOSE AROUND HER, TRIED TO WARD HER OFF BY HOLDING HOSTAGE A CITY FULL OF INNOCENTS. HE EVEN THREATENED TO LAUNCH NUCLEAR MISSILES. GOING TO GUESS YOU HAVE NO CLUE WHAT THOSE ARE?"

"I must admit to no knowledge of—"

"TRUST DIRE WHEN SHE TELLS YOU DEMONIC EVIL IS AS NOTHING COMPARED TO THE WICKEDNESS OF MAN. ANYWAY, THE POINT IS, THE ONLY WAY HE COULD THINK TO FIGHT DIRE WAS TO LAYER FAILSAFE AFTER FAILSAFE SO THAT SHE'D SUFFER BY HAVING TO WATCH THOSE MORE VULNERABLE AROUND HER DIE. IT WAS A PAIN IN THE ARSE FIGHTING HIM, BECAUSE DIRE AND HER ALLIES HAD TO PLAN FOR AND COUNTER EVERY LAYER OF HIS PLAN. IT WAS LIKE PEELING A GODDAMNED ONION, ONLY IF YOU MISSED A LAYER THERE WENT BRIGHTON."

Silence now. I could see his limbs twitching with irritation. This wasn't going how he'd planned, not at all.

"The difference between he and I," Midboss said, "Is that I am actually effective in carrying out my threats." It snatched up Epsilon and crumpled him to scrap.

"NO, ACTUALLY. AND YOU DIDN'T KILL HIM, HE'LL BE FINE ONCE HE'S REBUILT AND HIS BACKUP IS RESTORED." I stood, and the demons around the room pulled out weapons, bows, swords, spears, at least half of them glowing with mystical energy. "THE DIFFERENCE BETWEEN THE MORTAL MASTERMIND AND YOU IS THAT YOU WALKED INTO HER TRAP, INSTEAD OF HER HAVING TO SPEND ALL HER TIME UNDOING YOURS."

Midboss dropped the scrap, looked to me for a reaction, and I saw the raw hide of the maggot start to ooze a black sweat.

He saw plainly that I didn't care he'd crushed Epsilon.

"A trap?" he wheezed, in that kindly-old-lady voice. "Even if you don't care for your so-called friends, I could kill you here, and—"

"ACTUALLY IT'S CHECKMATE IN ONE ON THAT, BUT LET HER EXPLAIN FIRST." I walked forward, down that long, long table, closing the distance while I fired up a targeting system I'd spent three hours coding last week. "ILLWRACK. A MEATHEAD. ALL ABOUT BEING A STRONGMAN, THE BIG BOSS. WORE A FUCKING COLA CAN FOR A CROWN. NOW WHY DID HE DO THAT?'

"It was a gift, of course. An artifact from Creation. The power and rarity of that in this place is something I expect you take for granted."

"NO. HE WORE IT BECAUSE SOMEONE TOLD HIM IT WAS VALUABLE AND HE BELIEVED IT. NOW WHO GAVE HIM THAT? WHO TOLD HIM THAT? THOSE TWO DIDN'T KNOW." I pointed at my demon courtiers. "AND INCIDENTALLY, YOU'RE DERANGED IF YOU THINK DIRE CONSIDERS THEM FRIENDS OR WOULD BE MOVED BY THEIR DEATHS."

"Then I'll kill them now!" Midboss shrieked and raised three spider legs.

I kept walking.

"Khh, fine. I'll admit, this was more of a gamble on my part. Still, I'm out nothing from that," he sulked.

"NA NA NA, LET HER FINISH HERE. SO ILLWRACK? HAD NO RECORDS ON TRADE. NO BOOKS ON HOW HIS OWN CITY WORKED. NO MAPS. NO MAPS!" I shook my head. "WHAT THE... HEAVEN... KIND OF RULER DOESN'T HAVE MAPS OF HIS LANDS AND HIS NEIGHBORS? HE WAS AN IDIOT. WHICH MEANT THAT WE WERE DEALING WITH A POWER BEHIND THE THRONE. SO DIRE'S CONQUEST? PROBABLY MEANINGLESS, SO LONG AS THE POWER BEHIND THE THRONE REMAINED."

Comprehension dawned. "You're saying that you let this happen to draw me out?"

"SMART BOY. DIDN'T YOU THINK IT ODD THAT SHE SENT HER FLYING MILITARY STRIKE PLATFORM AWAY THE SAME TIME SHE SENT THE CITY'S STANDING ARMY TO THE FRONTIERS? THAT SHE DIDN'T SET UP A POLICE FORCE OR ANY KIND OF PEACEKEEPERS TO OPPRESS THIS NEWLY CONQUERED CITY-STATE PROPERLY?"

The baby's eyes narrowed.

"AND YOU DIDN'T THINK IT ODD THAT SHE LET ONE OF HER BEST FRIENDS IN THIS WORLD, OR THE NEXT, RUN AROUND WITHOUT EVEN AN HONOR GUARD?" I pointed to the Janissary. Immediately Midboss raised a spider leg high above him, and the guards pressed their blades to his throat.

"I must admit some displeasure with this part of the plan, Doctor," Khalid deadpanned.

"OH SHUT UP AND KEEP WATCHING HIS FACE. FACES. OH LOOK, HE'S SHAKING WITH RAGE AND FEAR! THIS IS HILARIOUS!"

The maggot body was indeed roiling. "I... I can still kill him!"

"ACTUALLY, NO YOU CAN'T. THAT'S THE LAST JANISSARY, AND HE'S A FUCKING IMMORTAL."

"Fuck you!" The creature shrieked, all vestiges of civility gone. "I'll try and keep trying until he's dead! And the rest of them too! But I'll start with you, first, you little mortal shit! You're in my hall, surrounded by weapons that will break your armor, and I can kill you with a word!"

"AS CAN SHE. CHECKMATE IN ONE, YOU FAT FUCK."

I broadcast that across the vox channels I'd opened.

And the cannons of Caym thundered.

Rubble sprayed from the walls; Midboss' upper body exploded into goo; the rubble sprayed into the crowd surrounding me, accompanying my rising laughter, roaring into the dust as I threw my arms wide and howled.

When the dust cleared I hovered above the table, arms crossed. "COMPUTER-CONTROLLED CANNONS. ALL THOSE GUNS IN ALL THOSE HIGH TOWERS, ALL SCREAMING OUT FOR AUTOMATION." I surveyed the four holes high in the walls and the pile of yellowish-blackish slime that poured from Midboss' convulsing corpse. "SHE DIDN'T NEED AN ARMY. SHE COULD KILL ANYONE IN THIS CITY AT ANY TIME WITH A SINGLE WORD. STILL CAN." I turned, looking at the silent, shocked crowd. "SO WHY ARE YOU STILL HERE?"

They took the hint and trampled each other on their way out the exits. I sighed and closed the cannon-targeting system I'd pulled up earlier, before my speech.

It had almost been a monologue. The asshole wouldn't stop interrupting me. Gods, I missed fighting heroes.

I snapped Khalid's chains first, then got to work on the Chorus. Khalid stopped me, with a hand on my shoulder. "EH?"

"Please. See to the children first."

I followed his gaze upward. "SHE'LL GET TO THEM SHORTLY —"

"Now. Please. I must insist. I promised them I would save them from what suffering I could."

"NOT A GOOD PROMISE TO MAKE, DOWN HERE." But I did as he asked, ripping the chains from them, holding them to me and flying back down to the table. We had to dump plates full of roasted corpses off to make room for them. "WHO WERE THESE ASSCLOWNS ANYWAY?"

"House Garlam is one of the largest trade syndicates within the realm of Sloth," First Manifesto intoned. "They have attempted to bribe me on numerous occasions." The chains leading into his mask rattled as he watched me. "Sometimes successfully."

"LARGEST TRADE SYNDICATE..." I got the eighth child down, then freed my Chorus. "THIS MIGHT BE THE BREAK WE'VE BEEN WAITING FOR."

"I hope so," Beta said. "Epsilon will feel better if his sacrifice was worthwhile."

"VERY WORTHWHILE." I freed the two court demons and immediately got a bosom full of crying demon as First Whisper threw herself into my arms. "WHAT? GAH! STOP THAT!"

"I knew you wouldn't let us die!"

"ACTUALLY DIRE WOULD HAVE, IF IT CAME DOWN TO IT. YOU'VE DONE NOTHING TO EARN HER LOYALTY." I pried her off me, but gently. "BUT ON THE OTHER HAND, YOU'VE DONE NOTHING TO EARN HER ENMITY. AND THAT'S A STARTING POINT WE CAN WORK FROM. ESPECIALLY NOW THAT DIRE KNOWS YOU DID NOT BETRAY HER TO MIDBOSS."

"His name was—"

"STILL DON'T CARE." I flapped a gauntlet at her. "ARE WE READY TO START THE LOOTING?"

"Go ahead without me," Khalid said, sitting next to the mostly-unconscious forms of the children. "I wish to be here when they waken. Ah! Please keep an eye out for my weapons and equipment."

"ONE UTILITY BELT, COMING RIGHT UP."

We tore the manor apart, and there, in one of the lowest vaults, I found what I'd been looking for.

"What is this?" First Whisper asked, as I bore the enormous scroll of human-skin leather out into the now-empty courtyard and unrolled it.

"It's a map," First Manifesto breathed, catching my enthusiasm and scrambling to grab an edge, unrolling it further. My remaining Chorus did the same, and I felt sheer glee rise through my body, drowning out the fatigue.

"IT'S BETTER THAN *A* MAP," I said, rubbing my gauntlets together. "IT'S *THE* MAP!"

It spread out before us, ring after ring, inked circle after inked circle, and Khalid nodded next to me. "Tabula Infernum," he whispered.

"THE MAP OF ALL HELL." I examined it, hovered over it, and took high-resolution pictures until I was satisfied I had it all. Then I cackled and took to the sky.

"AND NOW WE HAVE EVERYTHING WE NEED TO MOVE TO PHASE TWO!"

CHAPTER 9: DEPARTURES AND DESCENT

"The adventuring party structure is best for those who are beginning player characters. It gives their inevitable foes and rivals a moving target. As opposed to those who would claim a kingdom. They then must then defend it, and the campaign changes irrevocably."

--Excerpt from the third book of the Chronicles of the Shared Lie: Kingdom Management

Three Striges bobbed in the sky above Caym, and I'd never seen a lovelier sight in my life. Beaky was familiar to me, but the other two, though a bit smaller, were just as heartening.

"You've outdone yourself," I voxed to Professor Vector.

"Thanks. Sorry it took this long."

"Were the Spitters able to clear the parasites without damaging the internal structures?"

"Pretty much. Well, these two, anyway. Another Strix died horribly in the middle of their clean-out. I think there was enough genetic difference there that we triggered an allergic reaction."

"This will do. Three is plenty." I stretched within my armor, walked to the balcony of my royal quarters.

"So, ah, how did the city react when the river of blood dried up?"

"Mm." I turned my gaze to the foundry in the center of the city, great stone crushers still now that their driving fluid was a clotted scab at the bottom of an empty channel. "The populace reacted about as well as any human population when their jobs and livelihoods are abruptly threatened by an unforeseen event beyond their control."

"Good Christ," Vector whispered. "It's a wonder this city is still standing."

"For a while there it got fairly ugly. Dire used the opportunity to test her demonic companions."

"I'm not seeing what Thirteenth Chain or The Cat could bring to the table there."

"The Cat can be heard regardless of how loudly a mob is shouting. And Thirteenth Chain's more or less a local celebrity ever since his Monsters and Mangonels character pulled off that critical hit on a minotaur and saved the whole party a few games back."

"A minotaur? What the fuck?"

I smirked. "Dire knows. The whole affair with M&M is rather silly, in the grand scheme of—"

Vector interrupted me, his tone heated. "Those things are way beyond our challenge rating right now! We're level three, for God's sakes. I'm going to have a long talk with Delta, next session."

I blinked. "Ah. Well, at any rate, that helped defuse some of the riots. Then we introduced the idea of money, followed by a monthly stipend for every individual who could jump through the appropriate bureaucratic hoops, and a reassurance that the river would be back shortly."

"So you introduced capitalism, socialism, and political promises to them, all in the same afternoon. Pretty evil."

"It was either that or wade through oceans of demon blood. That we then could have used to restart the foundry, so Dire supposes some good would have come of it." I left my room, descended the tower stairs as my honor guard gathered around me. Cassius was on duty this time around, along with a few more Damned I didn't recognize. I nodded in satisfaction.

"FETCH DIRE'S DEMONS," I ordered. "TO THE SILENT CHAMBER, SHE THINKS. WHAT WE HAVE TO DISCUSS IS BEST DONE IN SECRET."

The silent chamber squatted, hot and stuffy, in the highest room of the tower. It was lined with sheets of lead, from the tip of the arched ceiling to the heavy hatches that sealed it off from the rest of the structure. It wasn't exactly soundproof, but between that and the white noise generator app I ran through my speakers, it would do.

Well, against anything but sorcery and other cheaty magic, but whatever. Khalid could cover that or not, as he chose.

I ran a finger over the symbols carved into my armor, while I mulled that over. He'd assured me these would help against non-physically-grounded spells. Wouldn't stop magical arrows from doing a number on me again, but in the event we ran into a halfway-competent sorcerer, it'd crimp their style a bit.

"Come on up," I voxed Khalid and Vector. "Heavy shit to discuss."

The demons came up the ladder one by one. The Cat, hanging around the shoulders of his servant, was the first. "SHE STAYS OUTSIDE," I told him, and she went without having to be told twice. Thirteenth Chain came next, scaling the ladder with wiry ease. Then First Manifesto, with some trouble, and lastly, First Whisper. She took her time on the ladder. I sighed and rolled my eyes away from the heavy gap of her cleavage. The girl just wouldn't get the hint.

Janissary and Vector showed up last, Vector grinning like a maniac and carefully hauling a sack along over one shoulder.

"NO CHAIRS UP HERE, SORRY. DO THE BEST YOU CAN." I settled cross-legged against a wall, leaning into the curve of it. The others followed suit. It was a round minaret up here, much smaller than the rest of the tower. We could actually hear each other without shouting. Well, they could anyway. My sensors made it a moot point for me.

Everyone looked to me. I smiled, under my mask. "THE TIME HAS COME TO SPEAK OF THE FUTURE. YOU MAY HAVE SEEN THE NEW STRIGES. ONCE THEY ARE PREPARED FOR WAR, DIRE SHALL TAKE HER FLYING FLEET DOWN BELOW, THROUGH THE WRATHLANDS, TO THE GATES OF DIS AND BEYOND."

First Manifesto inhaled sharply through his mask. His eye socket-chains clinked as he looked at First Whisper, and she looked back to him.

"Yes, this would be the end of the truce between you," Khalid spoke, smiling without mirth.

"You know of that?" First Whisper arched an eyebrow his way, stretching sinuously.

"IT WASN'T HARD TO FIGURE OUT. THE ROOM WAS FULL OF COURTIERS WHEN ILLWRACK HAD HIS LAST AUDIENCE WITH DIRE. THEN DIRE TAKES OVER, AND ONLY TWO ARE LEFT."

First Manifesto lifted his gauntleted hand, palm up. "There may have been some... consolidation."

"IN ANY CASE, IT HAS WORKED OUT. HOWEVER, FUTURE CONFLICT WILL NOT. WE ARE GOING TO DEPART AND LEAVE THE ADMINISTRATION OF THIS CITY TO TWO OF YOU."

"Without their truce, it will be one soon enough," The Cat pointed out. "Without you there, they have no incentive to stay unified."

"YOU'RE ASSUMING THAT DIRE IS TALKING ABOUT LEAVING THE CITY TO BOTH OF THEM."

My mask turned to regard Thirteenth Chain, and his sallow, glowing eyes opened wide in shock. "Me?"

"YOU AND ONE MORE." I looked back to First Manifesto and First Whisper, who were sitting bolt upright, staring at the rough-riding hunter of the Damned like he'd grown angel wings. "BUT WHICH ONE, THAT HAS YET TO BE DETERMINED."

It wasn't, not really, but this was one final test. I had to be sure, one way or the other, that my instincts were correct.

"Why him?" First Whisper spoke. "He's... a Thirteenth mark. A nobody. Even if he wasn't, he knows nothing of ruling a city like Caym."

"It's because the masses love him. His imaginary human, the ranger in the game, has won the hearts of the hellions for his valor." First Manifesto sighed and sunk his mask into his hands. "Whoever of us ends up with him, we can't kill him without bringing the ire of the populace down on our heads."

"But... if you leave, Delta will go with you," Thirteenth Chain spoke. "What becomes of the game then?"

"ACTUALLY, SHE WON'T. NOT COMPLETELY. IN THE ROOMS DIRE HAS SEALED, SHE HAS BUILT A GREAT ENGINE, A THINKING ENGINE. IT WILL SUPPORT A COPY OF DELTA AND LET THIS COPY ANIMATE A SHELL OF HER OWN. SHE WILL CONTINUE TO RUN THE GAME, FOR THOSE WHO STAY. YOUR FAME WILL CONTINUE, SO LONG AS YOU PLAY WELL. YOU WILL BE SAFE FROM THE KNIVES OF YOUR EXPERIENCED COURTIER ASSISTANT... WITHIN REASON, OH KING."

I had no fucking clue why they'd taken to Monsters and Mangonels with such enthusiasm, but I would happily use that for any advantage I could get.

I turned to the two courtiers. "SHE WILL ALSO, AS NEEDED, PUPPET A COPY OF DIRE HERSELF."

"Ah." First Whisper breathed. "You will depart in secret then, and leave this behind so no one is the wiser. Magnificent."

"This copy... it shall be as powerful as you?" First Manifesto wondered aloud.

"NO. BUT POWERFUL ENOUGH TO SLAY SOMETHING ON ILLWRACK'S SCALE." Probably. Maybe. I couldn't duplicate all of my weaponry and systems, not with the tools and materials and time that I had to allocate to it. But what the demons didn't know wouldn't hurt them. "NOT THAT IT'LL BE NEEDED. FOR SURELY NO ONE WILL TRY TO ASSASSINATE OR USURP HER CHOSEN CHANCELLORS."

"Secret Kings, under the thumb of your whims and directives," The

Cat purred. "I almost regret not being in the running. But who needs that kind of stress in their life, hm?" He patted Thirteenth Chain with a paw. "Oh don't look so worried. You'll enjoy it. Perhaps even get a shot at the higher quality spawning pits that our dead companions kept going on about."

"YOU GET A CHOICE," I told The Cat. "STAY OR GO WITH THE CONQUERING FLEET, AS YOU CHOOSE. IF YOU COME WITH US, WE WILL BIND YOU AND USE YOUR TALENTS FOR OUR GAIN."

"Binding?" The Cat frowned, an oddly human expression on its feline face. "How? We are in Hell. Binding is for demons in Creation."

"DIRE'S METHOD OF BINDING IS UNIVERSAL." I held up a spiky collar. "THIS WILL EXPLODE AT DIRE'S WHIM."

"Ah," First Whisper breathed, her bosom expanding as a smug smile crept across her face. "I was wondering about you, oh queen. Your pleasures begin to reveal themselves."

"KEEP WONDERING." I rolled my eyes.

"A three-way sharing of power. By which I mean you'll maintain your power, with two scapegoats should this method fail." First Manifesto pulled out his book, riffled through the pages, then nodded. "This model will suffice for a time. Not eternally."

"IT WILL SUFFICE FOR AS LONG AS YOU CAN KEEP IT RUNNING."

Chains jangled as he considered me. "Do you mean 'you' as in demons in general, or..."

"YOU ARE HER CHOICE TO BE FIRST CHAIN'S VIZIER."

Thirteenth— no, *First* Chain straightened up. "Can she do that? Make me a First?"

"Is she your Lord?"

"YES. BY RIGHT OF CONQUEST." The army had rolled across his old Riding earlier this week. It had taken copious losses but slaughtered its way through the opposition. His old Lord was dead.

I smiled as First Manifesto explained that to him. I'd made the correct choice. I'd only learned the news this morning... the masked demon definitely had a lot of spies. Good. He'd need them for the times ahead.

"THEN THAT'S SETTLED. LET'S—"

"A moment, Doctor," First Whisper prostrated herself. "I wish to speak."

"AND WHY SHOULD SHE LET YOU DO THAT?"

"I'm dead if you don't listen."

I was tempted to dismiss her. But she hadn't betrayed me. Yet. And I'd given her ample opportunity to do so.

"ALL RIGHT. MAKE IT QUICK."

"Give me one of those collars and let me go with you."

I looked to Khalid. And to my surprise, he nodded.

"DONE. SAME DEAL AS THE CAT."

The tension oozed out of her like intestines from a cut belly. "Just like that?"

"JUST LIKE THAT."

"You will not regret it, Doctor."

"MAKE SURE SHE DOES NOT." I waved a gauntlet, gesturing from her to The Cat. "YOU ARE DISMISSED. GO MAKE READY FOR YOUR JOURNEY. WE LEAVE IN A FEW DAYS."

Then, after much negotiation with the Grimalkin, First Whisper agreed to carry the pseudo-feline down the ladder.

But he turned before leaping into her arms and scrutinized me, tail lashing.

"WHAT?"

"I still do not know what you are."

"SHE IS DIRE."

"Yes. But... your thoughts..." He shook his head. "You have worlds within you."

I felt annoyance, and I didn't know why. "GO."

Once they were gone, I closed the hatch again and turned to First Manifesto and the newly-promoted First Chain. "YOU HAVE CONCERNS."

"This entire city has concerns." First Manifesto said, snapping his book shut. "The stored meat won't last forever; the river that is our livelihood is gone, and every neighboring city worth their damnation will take your conquest as a sign of weakness. They don't *know* you. They will think we are weak for losing to a mortal, and they will rip us to shreds like screamkillers on a burren."

"ON THE THIRD PART, DIRE WILL SHOW THEM. WE'RE GOING TO MAKE AN EXAMPLE OF THE FIRST INVADING ARMY ON OUR WAY OUT." Those guys at the bottom of the cliff were mustering quickly and sinking massive pitons in the first few hundred feet of the rock. They were wasting no time, so I'd waste them.

"AS TO THE SANGUINE RIVER... IT SHALL RETURN. SOON. LISTEN FOR THE THUNDER."

"That's ominous. And the matter of starvation?"

I looked toward Vector. The man was curled up, glasses off, dead to the world.

"AHEM." I leaned over and nudged him.

"Hm? What?"

"THE FRUIT?"

"Ah. Right." Vector stretched, then opened up the sack he'd brought with him. "So, First Chain mentioned growing crops. These are those."

"No they're not," First Chain said, reaching in and pulling out something that looked like a pissed-off pineapple that had been through a deep-fryer. "It's much bigger than a kulpa."

"...*if* you'd let me finish," Vector sneered, "I could explain that I'd worked my science upon these. They'll grow in a third of the time, yield about four times the nutrition, and taste about the same. And this is just one of the crops I developed while I was out in the field, hunting more striges. All in all I've got four viable strains. Including one that should make a mean beer."

"AND THAT'LL BE YOUR CHIEF EXPORT AND REASON FOR THE NEARBY CITY-STATES TO AVOID KILLING YOU. JUST THREATEN TO BURN THE FIELDS IF THEY INVADE YOU."

"What is beer?" First Manifesto asked.

"I'll give you a recipe," Vector's sneer turned into an honest grin. "Believe me, it'll be worth the effort."

I stood and stretched. "THAT SHOULD ABOUT WRAP IT UP."

"Ah," First Chain said, standing. "Will Cassius and Juno remain behind?"

"NO. THEY ARE COMING WITH THE INVASION FORCE."

"Oh."

"You are sad," Khalid murmured. "Why are you sad?"

"I... the game won't be the same without them. Or Hoomin the thief."

"YOU WILL MISS THEM."

"Well. Yes."

"WHEN YOU FIRST MET JUNO YOU PUT HER INTO A TORTURE RACK. THEN YOU WENT TO ROUND UP THE REST OF THEIR FRIENDS."

"It was a holding rack, so they wouldn't escape again. Those things are a pain to transport, but it's the only way to make sure the Damned don't flee the chains. But that was back before the game. Before they saved Azrak's life."

"WHO?"

"Azrak. My ranger. He'd be dead if Juno hadn't cast a fiery hands spell at that ooze, and Cassius had pushed him to safety while he was paralyzed."

I blinked. This... bore thought. Later. Much later.

I looked toward Khalid, but his eyes were shut. "ALL RIGHT. WE'RE DONE HERE."

After we'd departed I activated the vox. "Think it'll work?"

"For a time, as First Manifesto said." Khalid responded. "Time will reveal the truth of it. If the plan works, we shall not be around to see how it fares in the long-term."

"You sound somewhat melancholy," I observed. "What's wrong?"

"It is nothing I wish to discuss. Worry not for me, I shall play my part. Worry more for yourself: succubi have been the ruin of many a mortal, and First Whisper has you, as they say, squarely in her sights."

"Dire's not even interested in women," I protested.

"That is not a woman. That is a demon who looks like a woman. And she can be flexible in the gender department, if she is at all utilizing their usual abilities."

My imagination immediately went to bad places. "Dire didn't really need to know that."

"Yes, actually, you do. These are not humans, and they are dangerous!" Khalid shouted, and I winced as I upped the filters. "We have done well because we are in the back-end of Hell, fighting over land that nobody else wants, but now that they know what you can do, it is only a short matter of time before they come for you. And with you, us." He sighed. "You have not seen the carnage that I have. The damage they can wreak upon the unprepared."

"Well. We can avoid being that last part, at least." I felt my lips fold into a thin line. Something was eating him. I'd have to hunt him down later and figure it out. In the meantime... "So, tell Dire about succubi."

"Many human accounts and much of the lore focuses on their fornication." His tone lightened a bit, as he turned to academic matters. "While this is a significant part of their portfolio, and one that many modern human cultures are regretfully vulnerable to, it is neither the whole nor even the most dangerous of their assets. Indeed, their physical seduction is often an accidental side-effect. They act flirtatious and provocative as a force of habit, responding to the desires of those around them."

"Wait, so she doesn't stretch and move like that on *purpose*?" Vector broke in.

"Yes. The speculation is that they were engineered to be playthings and companions of certain lustful high-ranking demons, hence the nearness to the human form. Pets, in a sense."

"That's fairly disturbing." I didn't have any urges towards women for her to react to. At least I thought I didn't. But from what he'd said earlier, genders were flexible for them... no, that way lay stupidity. I shoved the thought away.

"Their worst weapon is also their biggest weakness," Khalid continued. "They are drawn to and fascinated by people. The stronger the personality, the more the attraction. It is usually an obsession, one that ends poorly. All the more so for being sincere. Succubi desire intimacy above all else."

"So, sex," Vector said. "We're back to the fornication again."

"You can get a room for that," I told him. "And no, intimacy doesn't always equate to sex."

"If that's how the subject equates intimacy, succubi are happy to oblige," Khalid said. "But the problem is that it's never enough. Eventually the drive for intimacy turns into obsession. The sort of obsession that can leave them carving their target's bones into... sexual implements, in the end."

We considered that in silence for a full seventeen seconds.

"Please tell Dire you're joking," I finally managed.

"I've run into it twice."

"Well fuck."

"No, that's exactly the *wrong* thing to do," Vector snarked.

"Which is why their other main talent is so troublesome. They have an empathic sense, one that targets the soul rather than the mind. They know what you want, how you want it, and how they can give it to you." Khalid sighed. "You are in for a challenge ahead of you, I fear."

"Then why did you recommend that we take her along?" I frowned. "This is only going to exacerbate the situation."

"Because she has already fixated upon you. If you left her behind, she would only try to return to you, and knowing your luck, she would return at precisely the wrong time. If a wasp is in your house, it is better to know where it is than to be ignorant."

"Better inside the tent pissing out, than outside pissing in," Vector summed up, somewhat less poetically.

"She can probably do that, can't she?" I mused. "No, don't answer that question. Although... Dire is surprised you didn't recommend just killing her."

"I would be lying if I had not thought about it," Khalid said. "But I know that is not how you operate. We just killed the Maestro, who *did* operate in that fashion."

"Ah, good memories," Vector sighed. "He's right. You're too soft-hearted to just up and whack someone who hadn't done anything yet."

"Soft-hearted? What?" Please. I'd killed demons by the thousands since I'd gotten here. After they tried to kill me. Or were killing others. Or intended to eat my face. Or held my friends hostage. Or...

Well, seen in a certain light, it was a little soft-hearted. I could have justified going full genocide on these fuckers. But...

"...it wouldn't have worked," I finally answered. "Killing every demon she ran into would just become one more atrocity, in Hell's long, long list of atrocities. And this realm would grind on without any change."

"You still want to change Hell." Khalid sighed. "I do not see this succeeding, but I cannot stop you from trying."

"Well. Before we make the big changes, we'll have to complete quite a few small ones," I toggled the Chorus into the vox discussion. "Starting with a good old fashioned massacre of demons who *do* deserve it. Epsilon, are the blasting charges set?"

"Alpha and I took five days out of the city and saw to it ourselves."

"Good. Time to introduce the bastards down-cliff to some of Johnny Cash's classics."

Three days later, ensconced in Beaky's command center, I examined the army below us.

It was pretty fucking metal, to tell the truth. On either side of the banks of the now-dried channel, demons were packed elbow to asshole, armed with nasty looking polearms and bows that no human could ever dream of drawing. Unlike the armies of Caym, they also had great war-beasts in their vanguard, bearlike demons with scaly hide, curling ram's horns, and glowing red eyes. Each of them was about the size of two elephants.

They also had fliers mixed in among them. Less of those now, after a couple of sorties against Beaky, Sneaky, and Squeaky. The Tesla arc generators we'd installed in the smaller Striges had done a number on their flying fiends.

They were the lucky ones. They'd died quickly.

As for the rest...

"It's about time," Epsilon whispered in my ear. "We risk Caym's destruction if we wait any longer."

I turned my head to look at the scaffolding they'd erected at the base of the cliffs. As soon as the Striges had dropped down above them, the army had packed every foot of the scaffolds with shield-bearing demons. They knew that we'd try to knock it all down.

But they had gravely misunderstood the scope of the weapon that I was bringing to this battle.

"SPIN UP THE MIX AND FIRE THE CHARGES," I commanded, and Gamma pushed the big red button we'd set aside for that purpose.

Speakers on Beaky's underside crackled with static, then the first skirling notes of "The Man Comes Around" rolled out over the darkling plains. The army below us shifted uneasily, fired a few futile arrows upward. Right about the point Johnny Cash got around to singing about a sound of thunder, the rumble from the explosions at the top of the cliffs reached us, thundering down and echoing across the basin.

What they didn't, couldn't see, was the top of the cliffs. They were in no position to see the clouds of dust as the charges we'd planted cut new channels into the old riverbed up top. The old channel, the one that *used* to run through Caym, was severed by strategically placed detonations, while two new ones forked and ran around my conquered city, deep and wide.

The cliffs rumbled and the ground shook, a bit of rubble and stone and trash falling from above. But it was merely the precursor to the horror that would come shortly.

For a month we'd dammed up the river upstream with Vector's coagulating reagents. We'd used the geography to make a vast lake of blood, flooding an entire valley, choking the river up nice and fat.

The charges we'd detonated ten minutes ago had changed that. And the charges we'd detonated ten seconds ago had spared my city from the crimson tide about to come.

Johnny Cash's dry, deep voice sang on, and the army below us screamed as one as great tides of blood fell down upon the plain, weeks' worth of flow dammed up and unleashed against an army that was packed way too tightly.

The fliers managed to flee. We let them escape. Not enough ammunition to be able to kill them all at this range, and besides, I wanted some survivors from this. Wanted them to carry word of how Caym had slain their army without a single soldier dying on their side.

Finally, after perhaps two hours, the worst of it was over. The great carcasses of the bear demons floated in the sodden lake and the blood had receded somewhat. The bulk of it had fled down the old channel it used to occupy and rushed downstream to wreak havoc on the lands beyond. As I surveyed the destruction, the cameras caught movement to the southeast. "THERE. SEVENTH QUADRANT. FOCUS AND ZOOM."

The viewscreen brought up the image of a tower of corpses and standing atop them was something that looked all the world like the Balrog out of the Lord of the Rings. Less fire, more scales, and half a dozen attendant demons were helping him buckle on armor that shimmered with hazy afterimages.

"That is the Lord of Smoke and Sinew himself!" First Whisper breathed.

"WELL, THAT SAVES TIME. CHECKMATE IN ONE." I looked across at my crew, my friends, and the two bound demons, with their collar lights blinking softly red in the dimness of the command center. "HOLD DOWN THE FORT. DIRE'S GONNA GO END THIS

FARCE."

I flew through the corridors of Beaky's lungs, emerging through one of the hatches we'd built in his sides. There I looked down upon the Lord of Smoke and Sinew, scanning him with my sensor suite, taking note of the energy signatures that danced around him. Or more specifically, his armor.

"Wow," I muttered into the vox link.

"What is it?" Alpha replied.

"He's armoring up against the electricity we used to fry his minions. Not sure what the stuff down there is made of, but it'd shield him nicely. Which means particle beams won't work."

"So what now? Are you gonna go down there, do a monologue or two, have a knock-down fight over a huge lake of blood as drowning demons wail and flail below you? Something epic where you take huge amounts of damage only to rip his wings off, and cast him down into the crimson lake?"

I considered. "Nah. No point in racking up repair time." I popped my railgun attachment out, sighted carefully, and put a tungsten tent spike through the Lord of Smoke and Sinew's skull. He toppled into the blood and sunk.

I watched as his attendants went nuts, leaping after him, trying to drag his corpse free, unable to tell just how wounded he was given the vast amounts of blood everywhere. Then I went back inside Beaky and returned to my command throne.

"ALL RIGHT, LET'S GET THIS SHOW ON THE ROAD. TAKE US TO WROTH. WE'LL SEE WHAT'S LEFT OF IT."

Wroth, according to the Mappa Infernum that I'd retrieved from Midboss' lair, was one of the great trading hubs of the Wrathlands. It was my next target.

We followed the newly-filled, vastly-flooded river south to where it joined up with several of the other rivers of blood and became the River Styx. The ashen clouds got thicker here, as the nearby volcanoes coughed them out like veteran smokers, and the blood started its slow boil as it went, heated by volcanic activity under the river.

"Normally the banks are packed with patrolling demons," Khalid pointed out. "And Damned trapped inside the river, fighting to escape it or sinking to the bottom and cooking, giving in to their fate."

"What happens to the ones who escape?" Vector asked, staring down at the engorged river.

"The patrolling demons catch them and throw them back in. Over and over again."

I tapped my fingers on my mask. "WHAT PURPOSE DOES THAT

SERVE?"

"Purpose?" Khalid frowned. "This is Hell. It is their torment."

"THE BLOOD ABOVE WAS RENDERED INTO IRON FOR CAYM."

"And it serves to provide oxygen, water, and nutrients for the surrounding area," Vector hastened to add.

Khalid bit his lip.

"I have heard," First Whisper began, then shot Khalid a nervous glance.

"GO ON."

"I have heard that among the patrols, they have demons whose job it is to skim the rendered fat from the surface of the River Styx. This fat is traded among the cities of the Wrathlands and beyond."

Khalid stood and left the control chamber without another word.

"What's eating him?" Vector squinted through his glasses.

"I'll go and check," Beta said, following the Last Janissary.

"DRAMA." I shook my head... then froze, as the monitor showed me something I'd never expected to see.

The walls of Wroth, yes, just as we'd expected. They'd weathered the great flood intact, which was disappointing but entirely within the realm of discussed possibilities.

But across these walls, great letters had been carved, forming English words.

"We have Roy Carver. Parley or lose him forever!" Vector read the pronouncement aloud, turning it into a question. "That makes no sense —"

But it did, and the realization crashed down upon me a thousand times heavier than the wave of blood I'd unleashed upon my foes.

CHAPTER 10: HONOR THE DEAD

"Remember; the characters always have choices. This is the truth of the lie, and the draw that brings more and more to it every year. They have choices, and their choices matter."

--Excerpt from the sixth chapter of the first book of the Chronicles of the Shared Lie

Roy Carver. Roy goddamned Carver.

The closest thing to a father I ever had. The first man I encountered after my 'birth' who wasn't trying to shoot me. Who in fact had my back, all through that risky first week, where we'd almost died over and over again.

Until he finally *had* died. Shot, bleeding out while everyone who could have saved him lay stunned mere meters away.

The worst part of it, though? He'd died because of *me*. It had been my enemies who came after us in the end. I hadn't even been there when he died; they'd hauled me off for some impromptu surgery.

And now he was here.

"HOW?" I whispered, forgetting to mute my mask. I felt my hands shaking inside my gauntlets and turned off all the various weapon triggers before I activated something that nuked Beaky by accident. "HOW IS THIS EVEN FAIR?" I stood from the throne, gripping it for support I didn't need, as fury and despair mixed and roiled up inside me. "HE WAS A SAINT! HE WAS A FUCKING SAINT!"

Vector's eyes went wide, as he backed up, waving his hands. "Okay, let's not fly off the handle here—"

Gamma spoke. "What do we lose by negotiating?" I turned to answer her, but Gamma was looking at First Whisper. I don't think the succubus heard; she was staring at me with fascination. And more than a little arousal, judging by the nipple bumps poking through her little excuse for a brassiere.

I tried to rein it in a bit.

"SHE ASKED YOU A QUESTION, WHISPER."

"Hmmm? Ah. Oh, yes, let me think." First Whisper shook her head. "It would not be taken as a sign of weakness. The demons of the Wrathlands value clear heads and restrained tempers. Such things are for the mortals, who were weak and ended up—" she bit her tongue. "At any rate, it would not compromise your reputation if you honored their request to parley."

I gnawed my lip, tasted blood, and deliberately unclenched my jaw. I wanted to rain fire and fury on that city below and sort out the remains.

I resisted the urge.

"Um."

Everyone turned to look at Vector, who flushed. He had his hand up in the air like a recalcitrant student. "Sorry, but who is Roy Carver?"

"A FIGURE FROM DIRE'S PAST. A GOOD MAN AND A FRIEND, WHO DESERVED FAR, FAR MORE THAN THIS SUFFERING. DESERVED TO BE MORE THAN A MEAT TOY FOR SOULLESS DEMONS FOR ALL ETERNITY."

"Okay. Okay. Are we sure this isn't a trick?"

I wasn't mad at Vector and explaining matters to him helped a bit with my fury. Cold logic seeped in as I turned from the raw pain to consider the angles with the distance that super-genius provided me. "IT COULD BE A TRICK. IT WOULD TAKE KNOWLEDGE OF DIRE'S PAST... KNOWLEDGE WHICH IS MOSTLY PUBLIC RECORD, THANKS TO THAT DAMNED TELEVISION DOCUMENTARY."

It hadn't painted me in the most flattering light. But several of the homeless who provided the accounts had gotten some money out of it, gotten enough to get back on their feet, so I didn't mind it so much. "FOR NOW, WE DO NOTHING. GOING TO GO CONSULT WITH THE JANISSARY. HE KNEW ROY AS WELL."

There was another reason I wanted to check on him. Something was eating him, and it had caused him to leave the bridge during a mission into the unknown. True, we had things mostly in hand, but in my experience that was when heroes showed up or things started going wrong. It was bad form to leave the rest of us hanging, and Khalid was usually far better than that.

I made my way back into Beaky, through the lungs, into one of the environmentally-enhanced chambers we reserved for our Damned recruits. Not so many on Beaky, just a few trusted Damned who had earned it through time and temperament.

And the children, of course. The children that Khalid had taken into his charge.

They surrounded him now in a half-circle, sitting in front of him. Eight small heads shifted to look at me as I pushed through the membrane. Most of them turned back to Khalid, but one, a dark-haired girl in a hairshirt, froze, looking up at me with abject fear.

"DIRE SHALL NOT HURT YOU," I told her.

She looked to Khalid, but he didn't respond. He held his face in his hands, fingers white-knuckled, massaging his scalp over and over again.

"I broke a pot."

"WHAT?"

The little girl stood, hands behind her back, looking up at me. Three foot nothing, she spoke in Italian, with an accent I'd never heard on a modern tongue. "I broke a pot and did not confess it to our priest. I told no one."

"AGAIN, WHAT?"

"That is why I am here. I lied. And I was damned for it." She looked down. "And I am sorry."

I took a breath, let it out. Five. She couldn't have been more than five. I knelt down next to her and put my hands on her shoulders, practically swallowing them up with my massive gauntlets. It took a bit to dial down my voice modulator with the ocular cues, due to a burning sensation in my eyes. But I blinked it away and managed.

"CHILD, WHY DO YOU TELL DIRE THIS?"

"Because everyone always asks. The good ones and the bad ones." She stared into my mask, laid a palm flat on it. "You look like an angel, but you are not."

"NO."

"Are you a good one?"

"NO."

She shrunk back from me.

"YOU HAVE NOTHING TO FEAR FROM DIRE."

The girl said nothing, kicking at the floor and looking down. I closed my eyes and stood again, moved until I was looking down at Khalid. "WHAT IS WRONG?"

He didn't answer for a long minute. Finally Khalid looked up at me, his face a portrait of abject misery, almond eyes over a beakish nose, mouth set in a down-turned curve over a neatly-groomed goatee. It was a handsome face or would have been if pain hadn't been writ into every pore and wrinkle. "Do you have faith, Doctor?"

"IN A GOD? NO."

"Easier that way at times. It has helped you perhaps, blunted the pain of this place."

I turned my head. "NOT AS MUCH AS YOU MIGHT THINK."

"Yes, it has. Oh, there is pain, because you are a good person despite what you say, and the sight of such suffering gouges at your soul."

"DIRE'S HONESTLY NOT SURE SHE HAS ONE OF THOSE." I couldn't say why that was so, but for some reason it sounded right to me. Felt right.

"You do. The general rule of thumb is that if you have ever worried you might not have a soul, then you likely have one."

"ACTUALLY SHE'S NEVER WORRIED ABOUT THAT." I said, shrugging.

He rolled his eyes. "By their works shall you know them. You have a soul. Never doubt that. Which means that you will end up somewhere after your death. But you do not believe in the Christian God."

"OH, DIRE IS QUITE WILLING TO BELIEVE THAT HE EXISTS. SHE MET A GOD ONCE."

"A pagan one, from your account. It is... different, with them. In any case, semantics aside, you are not Christian and do not pledge your worship to my God."

"THAT IS TRUE." Ironically enough, I was more or less a humanist. I hadn't really given much thought to the afterlife before this particular misadventure. I still hadn't, to tell the truth. Either we'd win here or die trying, and if the latter happened it was all pretty moot. "IF THERE IS CHANGE ON EARTH, HUMANS MUST BE THE ONES TO MAKE IT SO. THERE IS NO POINT IN SITTING AROUND AND WAITING FOR GOD TO GET AROUND TO IT."

"The two ideas are not incompatible. It..." Khalid stood, uneasily, leaning against the wall. "It is often said that God works through people. That even those who sin, even those who are hellbound, are part of his infinite plan. But this..." He gestured around, at the chamber, at the silent, staring children, arms encompassing the entirety of this strange world we had come to. "This is—"

It occurred to me that someone was missing. "KHALID? WHERE IS BETA?"

Khalid's face hardened. "I sent him away. I did not need his pity."

Okay, this was bizarre. For as long as I'd known the man, which admittedly, amounted to about a week or so, he'd been level-headed, calm, and pretty much an iconic example of taking things in stride. This was not that.

"Switch to vox, please," I whispered into his channel. "Dire thinks you're distressing the children."

Honestly it was hard to say. They looked like they ate abuse for breakfast, lunch, and dinner, and crapped out PTSD.

But Khalid took the bait, grabbed my elbow, and nodded to the door. "Come, then. Let us walk."

His hand was shaking. I reached across with my other arm, covered his hand with my gauntlet, and walked with him out into the fleshy halls of our lair.

"They harvest us. The blood in Caym, and the other places along that ring of Hell." The words poured out of him in a rush. "Down here, the fat."

"IT COULD BE JUST THIS ONE CITY—"

"It will be more than that. A boiling river is perfect for rendering. And back in Caym the fleshmarket harvested skin, hair, organs..."

"KHALID—"

"This is God's plan?" He roared, pulling his arm free from mine, balling both his hands into fists, and shaking them in the air. "Damning children for breaking pots? To have no further use for them than their skin, so that demons can wear supple leather?" Tears poured freely from his eyes now, and he shook in rage.

Rage.

I reached down for the heat I'd felt upon seeing Roy's name painted across the walls below us, and found my anger still hot and fresh. How dare they?

"THE WRATHLANDS," I muttered, trying and failing to turn my mind from the open wound of my emotions. "THIS PLACE IS A TRAP."

And knowing it, my emotions muted. They were still there, but I could compartmentalize them. They were false, and I was Dire. I would overcome them.

"Hell is a trap! A grease pit for an uncaring God!" Khalid turned and spat. "I asked them, in the city, I asked demons what sort of punishment the spikes represented! Do you know what they said?"

"NO, LISTEN—"

"Lucifer bade them to make a river of blood there at Caym! That's all! The spires thing was simply the First Lord's idea!" Khalid's face was ruddy with rage.

"STOP!" I seized his shoulders. "THIS PLACE IS CORRUPTING YOU."

"No, it has shown me the truth—" he froze, and the red drained from his face, leaving behind paleness. "Oh God."

Beta stepped out, from a side-passage. "Your faith has persisted for centuries. It is no shame for it to be tested here. This is not a place meant for any of us, really."

"I sent you away," Khalid scowled at him, then looked down.

"I know. I stayed behind anyway, out of the way. You were not yourself in there."

"I have shamed myself in front of the children."

"You have not."

I released Khalid, took a step back. Beta moved up and hugged him, winding thin robotic arms around the smaller man. And Khalid cried, freely.

"I have blasphemed."

"Yes."

"I have lost my way."

"Yes."

"I... This... I cannot do this." He snorted, pulled away from Beta. "Even now that I know it is unnatural, this rage still burns within me."

"DIRE WOULD SUGGEST GIVING IT A TARGET, BUT GOING BY THE TRACK RECORD OF THIS PLACE, SHE THINKS IT WOULDN'T HELP." I sighed. "OBVIOUS IN HINDSIGHT. WE SPENT A WEEK BUILDING A BATH BACK UP IN THE RING OF SLOTH, AND ENDED UP USING IT PRECISELY ONCE. COULD HAVE BEEN ON THE ROAD MUCH SOONER, BUT WE DELAYED, TO NO GOOD PURPOSE."

"You are suggesting that each ring amplifies its particular sin?" Khalid blinked.

"YOU'RE THE EXPERT ON ALL THINGS HELLISH."

"No. I am an expert on fighting demons and driving them *back* to Hell. As Beta said, this place is not for mortals."

"Or androids," Beta reminded him.

"Yes, well, that too." Khalid mopped his face. "Allow me to go reassure my charges, then I shall return to the bridge."

"GOOD. TAKE YOUR TIME." After he'd departed, and we'd gotten a ways down the corridor, I opened the voxlink to the Chorus. "What is it that Khalid does with the children? No, wait, that sounded wrong."

"Nothing wrong," Beta reassured me. "He tells them stories, of how the Earth is now, and how each of the places they grew up in has changed. He teaches them how to write in their own languages, and English for those who want to learn it. Most of them do. He told me once that they want to play the Monsters and Mangonels game, too."

I snorted. "That again. This thing is getting silly... but on the other hand, we might be able to use it. If it's stupid and it works, it isn't stupid." I shook my head inside my harness. "One thing at a time, though. Gamma? Epsilon? Everything okay on Sneaky and Squeaky?" I'd stationed them on the other Striges, to help Cassius and Joanna pilot the great beasts.

"Handling like a dream," Gamma verified.

"Are you aware that your recent behavior is outside your norm?" Epsilon asked.

"It's under control. But just in case, we'll need the two of you on hand for negotiations. They evidently respect clear heads down there, and you don't have any biological ragey bits to get in the way."

"They're not going to negotiate in good faith," Gamma said.

"Which is why we're going to take a few liberties. Get the earworms ready. It's time we gave them a field test."

Twenty minutes later, Beaky and the other Striges descended, heading down to the blood-slicked mud that tracked where my river of gore had run rampant. Next to the newly-filled channel we found a good spot and dove simultaneously from our bound Striges. One by one we slammed into the mud, sending up great sprays of the stuff... myself, Epsilon, and Gamma. Alpha, Beta, and Delta had been left behind to keep an eye on the Striges and their passengers. The Damned were showing signs of increased anger as well, and Delta promised to keep Vector calm.

As I knelt there, in my three-point pose, up to my knees in mud, I opened the compartments in my legs. "Go," I whispered, and the earworms obeyed.

They weren't microscopic, not quite, but they were the thickness of a thread, agile, and self-replicating. I watched through my armor's voltaic vision while they flooded out into the mud and obeyed my order, snaking toward the city about as quickly as an average man could jog.

Their orders were simple; travel there, multiply, stay hidden, and *listen*. Each of them had audio capabilities when meshed with a few hundred of their companions. It would take time, perhaps a few days, to get citywide coverage. But by the time they were done and broadcasting to my computer-screened vox channel, it would be worth it. I'd be able to sort through the keywords of any conversation held in the city.

Satisfied with their progress, I stood, slipping free of the ground and switched into hover mode, activating the cleaner sonics to shake the muck from my armor before I closed the compartments. Gamma and Epsilon fell in beside me, and I extended the sonics to clean them as well as we went. Best to appear nice and shiny for the rubes, after all. I had some serious kayfabe to get on and planning the show helped keep me calm.

We'd knocked down the river gate at least, I noticed as we approached the wall. It hung in shattered pieces, and something about it caught my attention.

"Wood? Yes, that gate is wood. More than we've seen in one place, down here." I remarked over the vox channel.

"What?" Vector said. "Grab me a sample if you can."

"Could be tricky. I'll do it," Gamma offered.

I ignored their chatter as I marched through the gate. They'd run out their hellions, standing them in the mud and clotted blood that was all that remained of the wave I'd beaten into their city. An honor guard stood to either side of the entrance, their numbers stretching down the street, long spears raised in a salute.

I kept hovering in silence, cape snapping in the hot wind. Gamma and Epsilon keeping pace on either side of me. Twice now a great nation of Hell had respected parley.

Granted, I wouldn't have had a problem leveling the city if they'd resisted me. I rather thought I had the resources to do it. If they were anything like Caym, Wroth was running somewhere near an early renaissance tech level. Caym's resources had bulked up my destructive options, and we'd come packing for Fallen Angels. Unless one was in the city, this settlement had all the prayers of a fart in a windstorm.

And they knew it. There was no other reason for what they were trying right now. Which only stoked my fury... if this turned out to be a trick, after all was said and done, I was going to fucking kill some assholes.

But underneath the rage, below it all, was the faintest whisper of hope. It was that most pernicious of emotions, and it would not let me be. I had so much to say to Roy that I'd left unsaid; after his death and my flight I'd spent hours of wakefulness in cold nights mulling over what I could have, should have said. This was a chance to say some of those things. At least, it was if it was on the level.

Finally we came to a great square. We'd left the gore behind long ago, and the streets now resembled some sort of parade area, or marching ground. Long, flat buildings that could have been barracks lined both sides of the street and stretched back down alleys, each flying a pennant of deepest black. In the center of it all stood a brick castle, a sprawling, gigantic twisting mass of towers and portcullises and crenelations. I was reminded of Castle Wallenstein, where I'd shot Hitler back in '42. The memory cheered me up a bit.

It cheered me more when I realized that I might be able to find Hitler again somewhere around here, and properly kick his ass until I got bored with it. But I filed that away for future thought and instead considered my welcoming committee.

Six of them all told, hooded and robed, the gaps for their faces showing only blank voids with shifting silvery light wisping around inside. Their hands bore gloves, and not a bit of skin showed on their hunched-over frames. They squatted on stools atop a raised dais of some sort.

Below and before them, by about ten feet, stood another stool much like theirs.

"Showtime," I voxed to my accompanying Chorus.

I cut off the hover, marched to the stool, wound up, and kicked it over the nearest building. The hooded demons started in surprise, looking to each other and whispering in hissing voices.

"DIRE BROUGHT HER OWN," I said, and gestured to Gamma and Epsilon. Without a word they embraced, limbs sliding aside and into new configurations, torsos twisting around to provide a seat and a back. It would have been even more impressive if I'd had all five of them here, but as it was I figured it'd do. I slid into it, sitting on my minions, resting one elbow on the arm guard, and propped my mask against my fist. It was a much-practiced slouch of villainy, a distillation of scorn and disdain.

At least, that was how it worked for human audiences. Without faces it was kind of hard to read the robed demons.

We sat in silence for a long moment. Like the chair, this was a power play, a test of my willpower. Even with unnatural wrath smoldering away inside me, I knew I could win this.

But the show I'd chosen to put on, the character I was playing here... no, winning wouldn't do. I needed to sell them on an image of me.

"WELL?" I snapped, my voice cracking out into the windy courtyard.

"Woman most mortal," the foremost of them spoke. "Overlord of Caym, slayer of Illwrack whose names are forgotten, you honor our city with your presence."

"AND YOU FILL ITS AIR WITH EMPTY FLATTERY. GET TO THE POINT. WHERE IS ROY CARVER AND WHO DOES DIRE HAVE TO EVISCERATE TO FREE HIM FROM YOUR CLUTCHES?"

"Your acumen does not disappoint, Woman Dire."

"DOCTOR DIRE TO YOU. WHOEVER THE HERE YOU ARE."

"We are—"

"NO, DON'T TELL HER, SHE DOESN'T CARE. ANSWER HER FIRST QUESTION."

Technically true. I didn't care because I already knew who they were. The Council of Worms, that was their name. Back in Caym, just before the departure, First Whisper had described them to us, and Khalid had identified their demonic capabilities. They weren't men, they were conglomerations of tiny serpent-shaped demons that ate light and could convert it into more harmful forms of energy. Working together, they might even be able to overload my forcefield and put some hurt into me.

Not that I'd let them get that far.

"You presume much, Doctor. If you wish Roy Carver returned to you, you would do well to watch your words."

"YOU THREATEN DIRE? YOU?" I roared the last word twenty decibels louder, leaping from the throne, in an apparent fit of rage. "ENOUGH FOOLERY! EITHER RETURN ROY OR FACE DESTRUCTION!"

"They are smug now," First Whisper spoke through my vox link. She was watching through the cameras in Beaky's side, advising me on their emotions through the expression of their body language.

"You could level this city to mud and ash," the foremost Councilor spoke, crossing his arms. "And you would find no trace of Roy Carver. We have invoked the Pax Infernum and sent him on his way to Lucifer for final judgment. There, his soul shall be unmade."

"All lies," First Whisper said, and a tension eased out of me.

Not that I'd follow through with my threat anyway. Theoretically I *could* level the city, but it would expend resources, damage and deplete my forces, and take entirely too much time. I had no clue where they were storing Roy, if they truly were, and leveling the city would be counterproductive. With my luck he was underground and even though Damned could regenerate from anything, if you dropped a building on them they were pretty much stuck there until freed.

So instead I let the silence go on, and clenched and unclenched the fingers of my gauntlets as if I were spasming in anger. More satisfied nods from the Council. They thought me overcome by the rage. This was good.

"IF HE IS GONE FROM HERE TO HIS FINAL JUDGMENT, DIRE HAS NO REASON NOT TO SLAY YOU TO THE LAST," I finally spoke.

"Ah, but he has not *reached* that judgment, yet." The robed pile of worms-in-human-shape spoke. "We have sent him through slow ways, hidden ways. We can send messengers to interrupt this process. If you cooperate with us, then pass on your way, we shall call him back and send him to you at a location of your choosing that is far from here." He spread his arms, the picture of magnanimity. "But if you choose to destroy us, well, there shall be no one to call him back. And he shall stand before our lord and master and be unmade."

"Technically it's within the rights of each lord of Hell to petition Lucifer to unmake a soul. In practice it's rarely used. Still, what they're saying falls in line with the Pax Infernum," Epsilon told me.

"So it's possible, but impossible to prove or disprove what they're saying."

"They are lying," First Whisper insisted. "But there is something more, and I cannot tell what it is."

"How about The Cat?" I asked.

"The Grimalkin insists they are too far away for him to taste their minds."

"Is that what he does?" I blinked.

"I do not know. Grimalkin are lesser among us, and I do not understand why you tolerate this one beyond its amusement value."

I finally crossed my arms over my chest. "STATE YOUR CONDITIONS."

"Now they are vastly relieved!" First Whisper crowed.

"Thank you, Counselor Troi," I muttered.

"What?"

"Never mind. Shush, they're talking."

"So are you!"

"Shush!"

"Our conditions are simple. To the West lies the Sulfur Slough. There, Lady Eyeblight holds sway, and plots against our might. Go there, destroy her army, and bring us her head, and we shall release the imps to halt Roy Carver's ultimate destruction."

I stood there, let the moment linger for a minute and a half, before I jerked my head in an overwrought nod. "FINE. JUST... FINE." Without a word I turned and left. My 'throne' unfolded and Epsilon and Gamma came with me, as we left the city as silently as we'd come.

Once back on Beaky, I returned to my command chair The Chorus reshuffled, resuming their old positions.

"THE SULFUR SLOUGH. WASN'T THAT ONE OF THE NATIONS NEIGHBORING THE LORD OF SMOKE AND SINEW?"

"It was," Alpha confirmed. "Is, actually. They wouldn't have been touched by our flood."

"WHICH MEANS..." I spun my theories, ran them through a few geopolitical filters, and talked the matter out with my little council. Once we had a game plan, I ordered the fleet west.

It took two days to traverse the blasted plains below; seams of lava opened up like burst veins in the black ash. Chain-gangs full of Damned came into view, marching unendingly on hot rocks, chased by groups of four-legged, wolf-like demons. It served some purpose, I was sure, but I overruled Vector's requests to stop and try to figure out what they were doing. Khalid's breakdown was still writ large in my mind, and I didn't want to expose him to any more trauma.

Finally the seams of lava started turning yellow around the edges, and we spread out, looking for civilization. The map wasn't always so precise on where cities were, sadly.

As it turned out, civilization found *us*.

On the third day, the sky darkened with a host of bats the size of fighter jets. Half of them were occupied, and the largest of them had a six-armed woman twice my height crouched on its back. The four arms that weren't managing the reins held different weapons at the ready.

I flew out to meet her, alone.

They thought it a trap at first, circled around the Striges outside of cannon range, trying feints that went nowhere, attempting to draw our fire. Through it all I stood impassive, hands on my hips.

Finally the multi-armed demon got fed up, and urged her bat in closer. At about three hundred yards she circled, calling to me in a voice like roaring flame.

"You are the Dire?"

"YES."

"Why do you make war upon my lands, mortal?"

"ACTUALLY SHE'S NOT. SHE'S COME TO OFFER YOU A GIFT." I pointed east. "HOW WOULD YOU LIKE TO ALLY WITH DIRE AND CONQUER WROTH?"

CHAPTER 11: OLD FRIENDS

"The monk class is often underestimated. But at higher levels they can wreak peerless destruction upon single targets, especially if they are clever enough to strike from ambush."

--Excerpt from the first chapter of the first book of the Chronicles of the Shared Lie: Character Creation and Classes

We struck Wroth like a hammer made of sin.

There are people in life who will tell you that leading a demonic horde to overwhelm your opposition is an inherently evil act and to be avoided at all costs. There are also people in life who really need a wedgie. These two kinds of people are often one and the same.

"IN CASE YOU HADN'T REALIZED, DIRE HAS DECIDED TO DECLINE YOUR OFFER," I belted out to the city in general, hovering above the walls while my striges floated behind me, and the hordes of Lady Eyeblight's infernal forces charged across the killing grounds around Wroth.

For my trouble, I got cannonballs shot at my face and arrows rising from below. My forcefield took care of the first, and simple evasion negated the bulk of the arrows. I wouldn't have bothered, really, but I didn't want to chance that a few of them had brought enchanted ammunition.

I refrained from attacking, keeping my arms folded and let my cape snap in the wind tauntingly. I had other fish to fry. Or rather, worms to check.

"Anything from day two?" I voxed.

"Nothing yet. I should be finished in twenty minutes," Beta confirmed.

"Dire's done with day one. Gods, this is slow work." It had taken me the better part of thirty minutes to sort through the audio cues. Even with everything neatly filed in the databases, this was still sorting through a half-million-strong city conversation by conversation, looking for sounds that approximated "Roy" or "Carver". Didn't help that in the infernal speech, there were about thirty common words that incorporated the "Roy" sound. Fortunately, Carver didn't have that problem.

Cross-indexing "Dire" didn't help. Evidently I was a hot topic down there, at least for the duration that my bugs were listening. And of all the conversations I'd listened to, none of them were sinister plans. Evidently the Council of Worms were smart villains... they laid their plans early on, then shut up about them to prevent spies from listening in.

I had to admit, it was refreshing to have intelligent foes for a change. They'd heard about me in the space of three weeks or so, realized the threat I represented, and initiated a plan to deal with me *and* eliminate one of their biggest threats at the same time.

"I've got something," Delta spoke up. "Day four, and it looks like... yes! Winner winner chicken dinner!"

"Please use a different reference." I winced as my stomach growled. "Vector's soylent Strix with fungus sauce is getting very old." I wiggled my fingers, inputting commands into the AR interface. "Send the snippet... now."

A lot of guttural noise, mostly, then a deep voice over the din; "The Carver wants the Tower of Misery prepared for his use. Bring him everything he asks for."

"Hm." I looked through the days' one and three logs. Nothing. I could give it a few more hours and finish the rest of them.

I looked down at the shattered walls, where an early volley from Beaky had broken the fortifications. Queen Eyeblight's horde was pouring through, into the city. We didn't have a few more hours. "Welp, Tower of Misery it is," I voxed.

"Why would Roy want something prepared for his use?" Beta spoke.

"Nothing springs to mind. Roy was best with a handgun. Something's going on here. But if the horde gets too far into the city they might move him or shift away from the Tower of Misery, wherever that is. Then we're down a lead and a lot of legwork."

"Orders, boss?" Alpha spoke. I'd left him manning the bridge on Beaky, and Epsilon and Gamma on the other two Striges. My Damned were manning the guns and standing by to repel any potential borders.

That took care of them...

"Khalid, would you like to assist? You know what Roy looks like."

"I do. And I admit that I do have some vexation to loose upon these creatures."

"Just mind your limits is all she asks. Don't do something you'll have to repent later."

"Believe me, I already have. At this point, anything further is a teardrop in a storm. Go ahead, I shall join you shortly."

I took a few more minutes to run a quick search string against "Tower of Misery," narrowed my target down to a seven block perimeter, and jetted that way, roaring over the heads of the armies fighting below.

The cannons had stopped firing at me, at least. Most of them were concentrated in the towers that rose from the castle in the center of the city, big slabs of bronze that belched forth canister shot, shredding the brick buildings between them and their targets with wild abandon. They'd caused about as much damage as the invading army, and the cries of their wounded citizens rose to the sky along with the smoke from their cannon muzzles.

Demon slaughtered demon in the streets, and I left them to it, arriving to my destination in short order. Three towers stuck out from the sprawling castle on this side of the city here, and I had no clue which one was which.

Well, when in doubt, ask a local for direction.

I burst through the roof of the nearest building, into what looked like a hive full of black wasps with human faces. They screamed in unison, and I roared back, using demonspeak;

"WHERE IS THE TOWER OF MISERY?"

They fled, and I flew after them, catching one by the thorax and not being gentle about it. A stinger punched at my gauntlets repeatedly, skidding off the armor, dripping sizzling venom.

"TOWER OF MISERY! WHERE?"

"Nnnnno! Plllleeeeeeezzzzz... I zzzzhowww you!"

"GO THEN. DIRE CAN KILL YOU FROM A DISTANCE IF YOU TRY TREACHERY." I let the wasp go. It flew out of the hole I made, with me following close behind.

The thing flew directly toward one of the towers, got within about fifty feet of the walls, then promptly exploded.

I blinked, then started scanning the damn thing. Unknown energies all up and down the tower, running in what looked like occult patterns. "Khalid?" I voxed. "Going to need your help, here."

"I am on my way. Not all of us can fly, you know."

"Remind her to build you a damn jetpack." I hovered in midair, glaring around at the demons peering out at me from openings and windows in the surrounding buildings, until they decided to make themselves scarce. Sensible, really, the fighting was coming closer.

And so was a robed councilor, strolling down the street right toward me. Darkness oozed out of its hood, and the lights inside it flickered with some agitation.

It had come alone. That seemed worrisome. I flew lower, within hailing distance. "AS YOU CAN SEE, DIRE HAS DECIDED TO DECLINE YOUR GENEROUS OFFER. PITY ABOUT YOUR CITY, BUT YOU BROUGHT IT UPON YOURSELF WHEN YOU DECIDED TO LIE TO DIRE."

"Did you think we had not prepared for your treachery? The Carver told us you would not rest until you had found him." This one had a female voice. A familiar female voice.

Eidetic memory is a wonderful thing. But identifying this voice only raised more questions. "JUDY?"

The demon flipped its hood back, letting darkness dissipate in the half-light of Hell.

Her hair was a mess; her makeup was smeared and sweat-tracked, and her eyes were glazed, but those didn't draw my attention beyond the first glance.

No, I was a mite more concerned about the glowing, writhing worms that were sticking out of the bloody mass that was the right side of her face.

"AH," I said, charging my particle blasters.

"Ah," she agreed, lips spilling drool down her robe.

And then she was on me, fists flashing with chi, and before I could react she'd punched me through the nearest building.

I dug myself out of the rubble, noticed my forcefield's charge was down by a whole three percent, and then she was on me again, arms flailing.

This was a problem.

Punching Judy, in life, had been a world-class martial artist with chi manipulation powers. She'd been a long-standing member of Queensguard who I'd clashed with numerous times in my last operation, before teaming up with them for the greater good of Britain and the world.

At one point, Judy had been mentally dominated and gone pretty much apeshit on me, punching me so hard that my forcefield, continuously powered by nearly the full output of a fusion reactor, had started to fail and destabilize. Through the raw force of her power she'd nearly managed to out-punch the a *nuclear reaction*.

And she was trying to duplicate the feat once more. Or rather, the worms who were burrowed into her brain were.

I managed to get clear and scoot up into the sky, and she started parkouring up the side of the remaining intact wall and the building next to it, taking long, lazy leaps and bounding off of impossible angles.

But something was off. I played for time, fired up my combat computer, and analyzed her movements against her past performance. Slow, slower by a factor of thirty percent on average.

I twisted as she leaped at me and fired a stunning blast downward. She crossed her arms, dissipating it with a quick flourish, as she landed on a nearby roof. Then she leaped again, and I was forced to fly back... toward the tower.

Shit.

I twisted back, narrowly avoided her attempt to grab me and managed to stop from crossing the point where the wasp demon had died messily. For a second, Judy kept going. For a second, I thought she might get into the explodey zone.

Only for a second. Punching Judy twisted in midair, grabbed waves of chi and hauled herself in a wide arc around the tower.

But it confirmed one thing: she wasn't immune to whatever effect was on the place.

My microsecond of speculation cost me, as she slingshotted herself around the tower and with a flash of insight and a chatter of warning from my combat computer I realized that she was going to come right back at me.

I killed power to the gravitics, dropped like the nine-hundred pound weight I was, and landed hard, shock absorbers groaning. She shot by overhead...

...and Khalid stepped out of an alleyway and caught her with a hurled vial.

Orange dust billowed, and she faltered, paddled her feet wuxia-style until she ended up on a roof, then fell to her hands and knees, shaking her head. The glowing worms twitched and hung on for dear life.

"WHAT WAS THAT?" I barked, not even sparing a second to vox. I reactivated the thrusters and maneuvered into position, covering her with my particle blasters.

"A nausea-inducing agent. It meddles with the inner ear. Who is that, and why is she trying to kill you?"

"PUNCHING JUDY. SHE—"

Judy stood up, deflecting my first particle blast with a wave of her palm. "—SEEMS TO HAVE RECOVERED. OH SHIT, RUN!"

She was on him in a heartbeat. But his blade flashed, parrying her strikes as fast as they came, Khalid's feet shifting as he danced his very lethal dance.

The best martial artist in the world, minus thirty percent, had run into a swordsman who had been around for over half a millennium.

His blade had to have *something* on it. Probably sorcery or alchemy, or something of the sort. I didn't register any weird energy from it, but it took glowing punches that would have left my own armor dented or broken.

This was the Last Janissary, the unseen defender of humanity against the supernatural, and this was how he had lived for centuries... fighting the unnatural, with no banter, barter, or quarter.

But... in a second, my combat computer told me what I could see.

Khalid was losing.

He had survived the initial flurry by going full defensive, and Judy wasn't giving him any chance to regroup. Khalid couldn't strike back without opening himself up, and one mistake was all Judy needed.

I sighed. No way through without taking some hits. Khalid had a healing factor, a slow regeneration of sorts, but it took minutes to do its thing. I needed to get in there and help him, if we wanted a prayer of winning this.

It took the work of a second to align myself, then I fell from the sky like a meteor. For my pains I got a foot to my face, but she couldn't put her full force behind it, and Khalid scoured a shallow cut across her back. My mask still creaked in its frame, and I was *really* glad that my head wasn't behind it. This close, my forcefield couldn't soak up the hits. I'd have to take all of them on the armor.

And I did.

Three sharp punches to my midsection, ironically enough about where my head was located in the armor. I watched as my impact gel diffused it, then watched as my HUD lit up with yellow signs as the gel started to crystallize from the repeated impacts, crystallize and crack. I wasn't sitting still while this was going on, but my sweeping attacks weren't connecting. For all I'd learned how to brawl and fight dirty, this woman was in a league of her own.

"Dire!" Khalid shouted. "The wards about the tower only affect demons!"

He cut at her back, managed a strike that should have killed her, and Judy shifted around, grabbed his head in both hands, and *twisted*.

I pushed myself harder than I ever had before, grabbed her by her hair, and pushed my gravitics to full power.

We hurtled together into the tower...

...and bounced, falling in a heap at its base. My HUD flared red and yellow. I gathered myself to my knees, tried standing up, fell to my knees again, and stood, shaking.

Beside me, Judy did the same.

Her worms still writhed in the shredded meat over her skull. One of her arms flopped bonelessly, and she stared at it, then bashed herself against the tower until it popped back into joint. She tested it, ignoring the missing fingers. Blood oozed from her many wounds, but she didn't seem to care.

"HOW?" I asked, panting as rage threatened to overwhelm me. This wasn't fair!

"Do you really think," she slurred through a broken jaw, "that we would put up a ward that would work against ourselves? Come on now, mortal."

I raised my arm, shuddering and shaking as the motors seized up. My circuitry was rerouting, but it was taking time, too much time as she hobbled closer—

The vial caught her in the back, and red flames roared up, smoky and bright. She ignored it, staggered on toward me, and I backed up.

I knew those flames. Greek fire. They'd keep on burning, regardless of what their victim did.

Judy's slack jaw twisted into a sneer, and the demons driving her body twisted, chi flashing...

...but nothing happened.

One glazed eye widened, and she reached back, tried clawing her robe off. All she did was burn her hand and catch her skin alight.

She scowled, hurled herself against the tower, trying to smother the flames, trying to scrape it onto the wall—

—and my particle beam caught her in the face.

I hadn't held back. Her corpse fell to the ground, burning. I let it, sagging onto my rump with a ringing clang.

"HOW? SHE BROKE YOUR NECK—"

"Yes, he'll be a while recovering," Gamma said, dropping Khalid's bandolier of vials back onto his body. "I'm really glad I learned to read Greek."

"NOT THAT DIRE'S PISSED ABOUT THIS LITERAL DEUS EX MACHINA SAVE, BUT HOW?"

"How do you think he got here so fast? I carried him and ran. Don't worry, Delta's in command of Sneaky right now. The bulk of the action's done, and this city's about a foregone conclusion."

"AND YOU DIDN'T HELP OUT EARLIER?"

"With all due respect, she would have broken me like a toy. Well, *they* would have, anyway." She looked at the smoldering corpse. "Oh shit, they're trying to run for it. Hang on." Gamma jogged over and started stomping on the glowing blue worms that were trying to crawl away from Judy's ruined husk.

"THEY WERE POSSESSING HER. PHYSICALLY, ANYWAY. SHE IS A DAMNED. HAS TO BE." I rose again, as my HUD warnings slowly oozed from red to amber to yellow. Still a few minor systems down but nothing I couldn't live without. "OH SHIT." The full ramifications of what had just happened crashed into me like a tidal wave, and I realized that we had a big, big problem.

"What?"

"SHE'S DAMNED. YET SHE STILL RETAINED HER SUPER POWERS."

Gamma froze mid stomp. "Oh."

"HOW MANY HEROES AND VILLAINS DO YOU THINK HAVE ENDED UP DOWN HERE?"

"I'm more concerned about how the demons have a way to control them."

"THAT, TOO." I glanced around at the square. "WE NEED TO HAVE A LONG TALK ABOUT THIS ONBOARD BEAKY, IN A MORE SECURE ENVIRONMENT."

"Right. Shall we get going?"

"NO." I turned to the tower. Sturdy, squat, six stories tall, it waited for me. It held answers, and I would have them. "WATCH THE JANISSARY. BE HERE WHEN HE REVIVES."

"There's no way I can talk you out of this, is there?"

"NOPE."

"Take it slow, Doctor. There's no way this isn't a trap."

"SHE KNOWS."

I found the door, found the strength to knock it down. Sensors up to full or as high as I could get them with my circuit damage, I traced not only the dingy form of the interior but the magical symbols along the walls. They seemed restricted to the walls, so I entered, flicking my eyes around, looking for trouble.

The first floor had a high-vaulted ceiling, and iron cages hung from long chains, dangling at various levels like obscene fruit.

And each and every one was filled.

Damned, each dressed like a vagabond, each dressed in a rude caricature of someone from the homeless camp I'd once sheltered in. I could name every single one, name who they were supposed to be, and I closed my eyes as I took in the sight.

Someone wanted me angry.

The problem was, I wanted to be angry, too. This wasn't the influence of Wrath. This was simple, human anger.

I moved among them, and they cried out as I did. The cages were packed together, there was no way to avoid moving them... and the sides and bottoms of each cage were spiked. I was tormenting them with every step.

"YOUR POINT IS AS HAMFISTED AS YOUR METHODS." I reached the staircase, winding around the far side of the tower and strode up it. My metal-shod feet rang out with every step, cutting through the whimpers and sobs of the Damned.

The next floor bulged with a sandy floor, tents looming out of the darkness. They'd been placed exactly as I remembered them... women's quarters over there, medical tent around the circle from it. They even had a few crumbled walls where the bathhouse had been. I gritted my teeth and moved through it, sand crunching beneath my heels.

Then I paused, as my sight revealed a form in the medical tent. An obese form.

"Oh those bastards," I swore, screwing my eyes shut. I didn't want to look. Didn't want to remember how I felt on that night, so long ago.

But I did look. My old instincts, old regrets came to me once more. I had wanted to save so many good people. I had wanted to protect them. Long before any of this nonsense, I had learned regret, and I could not turn away from the first, most painful loss I had sustained.

On a cloth and metal table lay the form of a fat woman, clad in layers of heavy clothes, with a red scarf at her side, red from the fresh blood dripping from the ruin of her head. A carpenter's hammer sat next to her. She'd been killed not long ago, brains and skull fragments and blood left to pool on the table.

My vision went red, and I squeezed my eyes shut, turned off my vocalizer, and sobbed.

"Joan," I whispered. "You deserved so, so much better."

I don't know how long it was, how long it took, but the grief left me. The rage did not.

With a wave of my hand I incinerated the Damned who'd been slain in her place. She'd reform, eventually. It was not truly Joan. The tent burned, and I strode from it, as it illuminated the rest of the cavernous room. There wasn't that much sand, as it turned out... just enough to replicate the scene, just enough to cover the area of the tents.

I found the stairs again and climbed.

"Dire," A male voice wheezed, from above me. "Do you hate me yet?"

I knew that voice. And the last pieces fell into place as I realized what he'd done.

"YES," I replied, taking the last few steps and emerging into the topmost floor. "SHE HAS NEVER STOPPED HATING YOU."

He sat there on a throne of bone and flesh, bare-chested from the waist up. He had muscles upon muscles, and a blood-spattered white ruffled collar wound around his neck, separated his head from his body. Greasepaint covered his face, white like the pallor of a corpse, save for the black teardrops tattooed under each eye. On his head he bore a conical purple hat. He hadn't had that the last time I'd seen him.

"HELL HOLDS NOT ENOUGH TORMENT FOR YOU," I roared, lurching forward and seizing him by the throat, crushing that stupid collar as I lifted his bulky form up into the air.

"Finally, something we agree upon," said Great Clown Pagliacci.

CHAPTER 12: A DIVINE TRAGEDY

"One area we have improved upon, with the Great Teacher's permission, is the alignment system. There are simply not enough varieties of evil in the core book."

--Excerpt from the seventh chapter of the first book of the Chronicles of the Shared Lie

There's a place beyond anger, beyond hatred. To my shame, I knew it well. It was where the heat became too much to bear, and became cold, colder than the gaps between the stars. A place where morals and ethics were eaten in a heartbeat, gobbled up by the beast that lurks in the back of our minds and whispers to us in our weakest hours.

With my heart cold as drowned ash I reviewed the options for atrocities one by one, coming to the same realization every time. Finally, I made my choice.

"SHE'S GOT A JOKE FOR YOU," I said, peering up at the evil clown, his broad face reddening and his eyes bulging from the death-grip I had on his collar. "THE MASOCHIST COMES TO THE SADIST AND WHISPERS 'HURT ME'."

I pushed him back and shook my head.

"THE SADIST SMILES AND SAYS 'NO'."

I dropped him to the floor, turned, and walked away.

Of course I watched him in my rear-view cameras and saw his face twist in the darkness. Watched the realization sink in and watched his face go through shock, rage... and end in amusement.

"A fitting joke," he said, standing upright. "But you do not think on the scale you need to, not yet."

"YOU'RE DEAD AND DAMNED. SHE HAS NO REASON TO PLAY GAMES WITH YOU. YOU'RE IN HELL, AND ALL IS RIGHT WITH THE WORLD. GOODBYE, PAGLIACCI."

I reached the stairs and started down, lips peeled back from my skull in something a fool might call a smile, and the large man shook with laughter, hands pressed to his face, elbows to the ceiling as his back curved impossibly. Then he snapped forward like a rubber band releasing tension, loping after me with long, fast strides.

I turned, raised a gauntlet to him, and turned him into ash.

At least, that was what I intended to do. What actually happened was that three yellow icons on my damage readout flipped straight to red and my particle blaster triggered an emergency shutoff as part of my circuitry shorted.

I stopped grinning and braced for impact. Pagliacci slammed into me, still laughing, and bore us both down the stairs. Hissing through my teeth I twisted, wrestling with him, trying to smash him against the steps. But he was fast, so fast, and the best I managed was to break his left arm, catching it between my hip and the stone stairs during one bounce. Then we were on the empty floor below, laying side to side, and he was smiling into my mask, tears running down and blurring his greasepaint.

I opened my mouth, but he spoke first. "You do not yet *understand* Hell. And you will not without my help."

That gave me pause.

"WHAT DO YOU WANT, FOOL?"

He smiled, showing bloody gaps where the fall had popped out several of his teeth. Eyes that were all pupil sought my mask. "I want to be unmade."

I considered his request, nodded. "SHE'LL GET BACK TO YOU ON THAT." I reached over, grabbed his face, and bashed his brains out against the floor. Then I rose, threw him over my shoulders in a fireman's carry, and made my way downstairs and out of the tower.

I halted before I left, peered out from the darkness into a scene of carnage. Gamma stood, coated head to toe with blood, next to a heap of demonic bits and pieces. Around her and the rest of the tower a legion of demons ringed us, each bearing the gouged-orb symbol of Lady Eyeblight on their hair-tunic livery. As I watched one of their officers started barking orders, getting the next wave ready.

Behind Gamma, Khalid sat clutching his skull with both hands, looking for all the world like a toddler who'd just discovered brain freeze. It would have been hilarious if I hadn't just seen his neck snapped like a twig.

"Come on," Gamma beckoned. "Charge me again, and I'll use my sorcery to destroy you!"

I saw fear in their eyes, and I stifled my laughter. She'd bluffed them into thinking the tower's wards were her own magic. Sure enough, as the demons charged forward, she started waving her hands, shouting nonsense words. And as the wave got within fifty feet, they detonated one after another.

"Beautiful!" I whispered through the vox. "Dire is so, so very proud of you!"

She straightened in arrogance, put her hands on her hips, and let loose one of those high-pitched laughs you only get from noblewomen scorning peasants. But through my channel she whispered; "Thanks, Doctor."

"You'll run out of essence sooner or later, witch!" The officer roared. "We have a Legion!"

I weighed the possibilities, and decided to intervene. Fun as it was, we had places to be, and if they kept at it they might figure out what was really going on. So I stepped out of the doorway, amplifying my voice as I tossed Pagliacci's carcass to the side. "YOU HAVE A LEGION. SHE HAS DIRE. GUESS WHO WILL WIN?" I pointed at them then curled my fingers into a fist. "SPOILERS; IT WON'T BE YOU."

The officer, a spiky-looking beast with a dog's head, shut his mouth so quickly that his fangs tore a chunk of his lip off. "My Lady Dire," he said, offering a bow. "We thought your treacherous minions had betrayed and slain you."

"WELL, THEY DIDN'T."

"Lying," First Whisper sung through the vox channel.

"Duh," I whispered back.

"What?"

"Never mind."

Purple light flared in the distance. From the parapets of one of the farther towers of the castle, robed figures pulled down strange energies and flung them into the twenty-foot-tall siege demons that Eyeblight had brought along for this last stage of our assault. I watched the Council of Worms make their last stand and saw them get picked off by hails of musket fire from flying snipers. Their wormy bodies gave them a lot of resilience, as I'd found from my duel with infested Judy. But those muskets fired really big rounds, and there were a lot of them.

"OBVIOUS IN HINDSIGHT, REALLY."

"What?" The officer literally barked.

"NOTHING. GO TEND TO THE REST OF THE CASTLE. DIRE HAS SECURED THIS TOWER."

It tilted its head, considered me, then waved a spear in the general direction of the siege. The legion of demons followed as it loped off. I diverted all repairs to my gravitics and leaned against the wall. "A LOT IS MAKING SENSE NOW. BRING THE STRIGES TOGETHER; WE'LL NEED A MEETING." My gaze wandered down to Great Clown Pagliacci's corpse, with his head already looking a little more intact than it had minutes ago. "AND RESTRAINTS. REALLY HEAVY RESTRAINTS."

Amazingly, Punching Judy was the first to recover. I was there when she woke, sitting in the fleshy chamber that we'd set aside as a jail cell. We had figured it wouldn't be pleasant when she finally woke and had taken what I thought were adequate precautions. Still, this was a huge risk, and so I waited to greet her.

Seven plans I'd readied for her, with varying degrees of loss and sacrifice.

They all went out the window when she woke, looked at me from her restraints, and slumped in relief.

"Oh thank fuckin' God."

"NOT THE REACTION DIRE WAS EXPECTING."

"Lady, I'm a Queensguard, even if I'm a deader. Worms in me head makin' me a superzombie is bloody Tuesday." A shadow crossed her face. "Was bloody Tuesday. Please tell me we got that Maestro cunt."

"DIRE DOESN'T LIKE THAT WORD." The sentence escaped me before I could stop it.

Judy snorted, and then we were both laughing at the incongruity. Finally she calmed down. "I'm British, ent I? Cunt isn't as bad as when you Yanks say it."

"FAIR ENOUGH. GOING TO UNDO YOUR RESTRAINTS NOW. PLEASE REFRAIN FROM ANY SUDDEN MOVEMENT." I had my forcefield amped up to maximum level. Anything but slow movements, including the quick motions she used to control her chi, would ground out painfully against my shield.

Judy didn't strike at me. She sat up, looked around at the raw internals of the Strix. "In the belly of the beast?" She asked.

"MORE LIKE THE LUNGS. WELL, THE SIDE OF THE LUNGS."

I backed off, giving her room to stand, and she took it, kipping up to her feet with a head-over-heels flip, ending up standing on point like a ballerina. While bare-footed. And bare-everything-elsed, for that matter. "CLOTHES ARE OVER THERE," I pointed at a few hair shirts and leather garments, left over from a few of our Damned crew's ongoing efforts to kill time by crafting useful things.

She looked them over carefully, pulled a robe free of the bone hooks, and eased it over herself. "Not me first choice. But the chi flows more easily this way."

"SERIOUSLY?"

"Yeah. So is the Maestro nicked?"

"DEAD," I told her. "MANAGED TO USE A LAST-MINUTE TRICK TO DUMP DIRE, HER CHORUS, THE LAST JANISSARY, AND VECTOR INTO HELL WITH HIM. A SAD, SPITEFUL SACRIFICE PLAY FOR A SAD, SPITEFUL LITTLE TURD. HE DIDN'T LAST LONG AFTER THAT."

I didn't tell her I'd chucked him into a lava fumarole. Heroes got weird about that sort of thing.

"Won't shed no tears," she concluded. "So am I free ter go?"

"YOU DON'T PLAN ON ANY BOUTS OF VIOLENCE OR VENGEANCE AGAINST DIRE, OR HER PEOPLE?"

"You got them worms out of me head. Why would I ever want to go and do you dirty?"

"Truthful," First Whisper spoke through the vox.

"The Cat concurs," Vector confirmed.

"THEN YEAH, YOU'RE FREE TO GO. ALTHOUGH DIRE WONDERS, WHERE PRECISELY WOULD YOU GO?"

Judy sighed. "Find a place upstream, some empty spot to hide and not do no one any harm. Sort meself out and atone." She rubbed her eyes.

"THAT IS AN OPTION. BUT BEFORE YOU DO, PERHAPS YOU SHOULD TALK WITH SOME PEOPLE WHO TRIED IT BEFORE."

"Yeah?"

"YEAH. COME ON. STICK AROUND AND SEE WHAT WE'VE GOT GOING BEFORE YOU DECIDE TO HEAD OUT."

I lead her back to the control room, explaining our flying 'lair' as I went. The idea didn't seem to sit well with her. "Right, this is just gross."

"GROSS BUT EFFECTIVE."

"Up 'til the point someone brings enough firepower to crack 'em open. Then yer boned."

"IF WE'D PUT ALL OUR EGGS IN ONE BASKET, SURE. BUT WE'VE GOT THREE OF THESE THINGS."

"Right, because anything tough enough and 'urty enough to take down Beaky is totally going to stop after just killing 'im."

"NO PLAN'S PERFECT," I shrugged. "BESIDES, THOSE OTHER STRIGES AREN'T THE FULL RUN OF THE PLANS—"

The membranes to the control room parted, a high-pitched squealing filled my ears, and a metal body blurred past me. Almost quicker than I could register Punching Judy flipped backward, then gave out a whoop and dove *into* the speeding form.

And Delta caught hold of her around the waist, switched from squealing to whooping in joy, lifted Judy up, and spun her around.

Ah, right. They'd formed a friendship, back when we'd been working together. For her part, Judy was laughing and reaching down to play-punch against Delta's mask. It was cute in a bizarre sort of way.

Across the way I noticed Vector flinch as he watched them hug. Something hungry haunted his face for a moment before he turned back to the monitors. The siege of the city was winding up, by the looks of it. The last of the Council had fallen or fled, and Queen Eyeblight was mowing down the last troops Wroth could bring to bear.

Delta let go of Judy, who dropped with a grin. A grin that faded the second she looked over to First Whisper.

"A fucking demon?" In a flash she was across the floor. First Whisper gasped, stepped backward, holding her taloned hands up, but Judy was quick, so very quick.

"DON'T—"

The best dead martial artist I'd ever known stopped her open palm strike three inches from the Succubus' face.

"—KILL HER. SHE'S UNDER CONTROL."

"These things eat people," Judy said, her voice as flat and cold as a glacier.

"We've ah, we've fixed that." Vector smiled. "Synthetic soylent green, you might say."

"I hate it, but it fills me," First Whisper grinned, as sweat trickled down her face. "Which is the first time I have ever said that sentence."

Judy snorted, and lowered her hands. "You keepin' this one around as a fool, Dire?"

"That's more my job," The Cat snarked, settling in on its paws. Judy eyed it and shook her head.

"A cheshire too, wot?"

"MORTALS, DEMONS, DAMNED, AND ANDROIDS." I spread my hands. "WE'RE NOT PICKY."

The Cat looked her up and down."Tell me, do you play Monsters and Mangonels? Our ranger is gone now, and we perhaps might use a monk."

"Wot?"

I shook my head and kept silent. For all the talk of fools, there was one more to sort out.

But I stayed behind for a minute regardless, watched Judy chat with them, getting more and more excited by the minute. Her death hadn't done anything to her perkiness, and her energy was almost contagious. She was a new face, a friendly one, and those were rare down here.

It reminded me of happier times and I needed that, before I went back to deal with Pagliacci.

We'd stored him on the other side of Beaky from Punching Judy. They were both in 'cells' that were basically thin points in the Strix lined with shaped charges. If either of them caused trouble we could eject them with high speed and extreme prejudice.

With Judy it had been a necessary precaution. Her chi powers were as lethal as ever, and aboard a living vessel she could kill it if she cut loose.

With Pagliacci it was more of a pleasure. I wasn't about to take any of his sass, and I reserved the right to take out the trash with style... though also, it *was* just in case he found a way to turn the tables. He'd been the first real competent foe I'd ever faced, and he'd almost, almost won. I wasn't going to underestimate the clown. Many had made that mistake. Many had died for it or worse.

He was awake when I entered the chamber but still strapped to the exposed bone we'd used as a table. Under his ruffled, bloody collar the LED of his other collar flashed, telling me the explosives were still armed and ready.

True, he was Damned so it wouldn't kill him permanently, but it would definitely crimp his style long enough for us to dump him in a hole and cover him with a mountain or two.

"Doctor," he said, eyes twinkling merrily as he craned his head as far as the straps would allow. "Your décor leaves something to be desired."

"DIRE FOUND YOU SITTING ON A THRONE OF CORPSES. YOU DON'T HAVE MUCH ROOM TO TALK."

"Ah. The throne in the tower?" He rolled his eyes. "Demons. By that time the Council's patience with me had worn thin. It was a petty act of revenge. I asked for a throne, and they gave me that thing. I still have bloodstains on my pants that I shall never get out."

"THEY ARE SOMEWHAT PREJUDICED WHEN IT COMES TO CUTTING DEALS WITH THEIR FOOD. WHICH MAKES ME WONDER WHY THEY WERE WORKING WITH YOU IN THE FIRST PLACE."

"Mmmmm..." He stretched as far as the bonds would permit, silver beard glinting in the lights I'd positioned to shine in his face regardless of where he looked. "It's a rather long tale."

"THEN TELL IT. DIRE HAS A BIT OF TIME YET BEFORE QUEEN EYEBLIGHT FINISHES SUBJUGATING THE CITY AND ATTEMPTS HER SUDDEN-YET-INEVITABLE-BETRAYAL."

The clown chuckled, a deep rattling that still haunted my nightmares now and again. "They are rather predictable. Poor things. Poor flawed, broken, hateful little things. So weak when you think about it. So aware of just how... much... trouble... they'd be in if the Damned shook off their angst."

"OKAY, NO." I said, chopping the air with one hand. "NO, YOU DON'T UNDERSTAND HOW THIS WORKS. SHE TELLS YOU TO DO SOMETHING, YOU DO IT, OR YOU GO OUT THE WINDOW."

He glanced around as far as he could, opened his mouth, but I cut him off. "YES, SHE KNOWS THERE ISN'T A WINDOW BUT BY GODS SHE CAN MAKE ONE, SO CUT THE FUCKING HANNIBAL LECTER WANNABE SPIEL OUT AND DO WHAT SHE COMMANDS OR GET THE FUCK OUT OF HER LAIR THE HARD WAY."

For a few seconds, I honestly thought he was considering it. Finally he barked more laughter then tried to shrug. "As you wish. As much as I can. Old habits are hard to break, after all. Especially for the Damned. So, it all started when I awoke in a river of boiling blood."

"THE STYX."

"You know, it turns out there are actually about three hundred of those rivers, give or take. The bloodfall at Caym is only one of the falls; there are many more scattered around the ring, which feed into rivers below. All of them are called the Styx."

The map we'd scored had suggested something like that. I'd mistaken it for errors, wishful thinking, and sloppy labeling. "WAS IT THIS BRANCH OF THE RIVER YOU WERE IN? THAT'S A BIT TOO MUCH OF A COINCIDENCE FOR DIRE TO BUY. HELL IS VAST, AND YOU ARE INSIGNIFICANT."

"True, I am not significant, not any more. But even though fortune has twisted my way more often than not, I did not awaken on this branch of the Styx. It was some other river of boiling blood, with the weak sunken below, and the strong fighting to stay on the surface.

"And there I fought, making rafts of my victims, defending them against all comers." He stretched his arms as far as the straps would let him, muscles coiling like steel cables, writhing beneath gray skin. "Hell takes you on your worst day, did you know that?"

"NO." If that was true, it explained a few things.

"Your body arrives with all wounds healed, yes, but you feel just as you did on that day, at that moment that you hit the lowest point in your life. But on my worst day I was strong, strong from vampire blood, and it was easy to stay on top of the river. Easy to watch the fat from those consumed below bubble to the surface, in great oozing gobbets. Easy to see the demons skim it off at the points where the river curved, to pull it in with pikes and pack it as carefully as if it were whale ambergris."

"THERE MAY BE A POINT IN THERE SOMEWHERE, AND SHE'S HOPING IT'S MORE SIGNIFICANT THAN THE ONE ON YOUR STUPID HAT."

"You don't like me very much, do you?"

I backhanded him, watched him spit teeth and blood.

But there was little satisfaction in it. I'd never taken joy in torture, and that's what this was, would have been if I continued it.

When he recovered, he looked back at me with a gap-toothed smile. "A stupid question, I suppose," he slurred, compensating for his split lip and missing teeth. "But then I've always seen. Things. In a different way."

"DIRE'S HEARD IT SAID THAT THE DAMNED CANNOT GO MAD."

"Oh, not for long. But I've never been mad. Quite the opposite, really. I see the world for what it is, the sick joke on every last one of us. Started by God, sealed by Tesla. And I see how that joke repeats endlessly in Hell. Over, over, and over again."

He fell silent. I debated hitting him again, but a glint in his eye told me that was what he wanted. Pain had never bothered Pagliacci. It wasn't that he was a masochist, I didn't think so, more like it was inconsequential to whatever he was doing at the moment.

Pieces were starting to click together, and I didn't like the picture they were forming.

"YOU PROSPERED HERE."

Great Clown Pagliacci clenched and unclenched his hands, tried a shrug. "Eh. No one truly prospers here. But the demons talk and jabber and speak freely; we are livestock to them. Time stretches down here, lasts much longer than it should. I had nothing to do but keep my corpse-raft safely dead and free of intruders, and listen to demons talk. In time I understood their language. For a long while, I practiced their language, and eventually mastered it. And then I heard your name." He inhaled, laughed. "You were not someone I was expecting to see down here, but you are perfect."

"WHY WOULD YOU NEVER SEE DIRE DOWN HERE?"

He laughed. "Oh nohoho... you do not get the answer that easily. Once you know that, the riddle of Hell is yours to unravel, and you shall no longer need me." Pagliacci looked me straight in the mask. "But we were discussing the river. And the time when I heard your name."

"AND WHAT HAPPENED THEN?"

"I called out to them, of course. Told them that I knew everything about you and that I could help their lord stop you."

"DID THEIR LORD BUY THAT IDEA?"

"It took some time to convince them. I think you were consolidating your hold in Caym at that time. But eventually, I was ushered into Buer's domain."

"BUER..." I'd heard that name. A Fallen Angel, and the sire of Illwrack, who I'd crushed with his own lodestone.

Of *course* he'd be pissed about that.

"Oh, he wants you gone. But he doesn't want to take care of you himself. It would cost him much to leave his domain."

"THAT'S WHERE YOU CAME IN, OF COURSE."

"That's what I told him. And after a suitable amount of torture and trial he believed me. I told him I would see to it. I lied."

"DID YOU, THEN? YOUR PLAN CAUSED A FAIR AMOUNT OF TROUBLE."

He smiled. "Consider it a test. It was challenging but not impossible. I knew that if you fought the Council as fiercely as you fought me, you could pass it. And so, once Buer thought I might be able to end you, he transported myself and Punching Judy through sorcery. That is how we came to Wroth."

"WHERE DID JUDY ENTER INTO THE EQUATION?"

"She was a surprise." Pagliacci looked pained to admit that. "The Council received us and our secret offer of aid from Buer. Judy... would not cooperate. So they infested her. They infested me too, briefly, but my mind was not to their taste." There was nothing but teeth in his smile.

"DIRE CAN IMAGINE."

"You *do* owe me. They were planning to ambush you with the full might of the Council and their dark lightning, *and* Judy at the same time. But I convinced them to fool you into assaulting their neighbor." He laughed, dark and deeply. "And you came back with an army. Not what they expected. Not exactly what I expected, to tell the truth, but I expected some twist or the other. You're good at those."

"FLATTERY WILL GET YOU NEITHER MERCY NOR FAVOR."

"True. But I am unworried." Pagliacci's face lost its rictus of mirth. "You have already worked the equation and come to the answer."

I had.

Sloth had slowed me down, and Hell had become aware of me. Perhaps not all of it, but if even one Fallen Angel was gunning for me, that was one too many.

Great Clown Pagliacci, no matter how I disposed of him, truly couldn't die. He was Damned now, and no matter what I did, no matter what mountain I dropped on him, or what lava pool I sunk his ashes into, he'd be back. He'd done it often enough while he was a supervillain, suffered what to all appearances had been an inescapable death that resulted in a lack of a visible body and always returned months, years, or decades later.

If I left him behind, he would be a loose end.

I couldn't trust him out of my sight. I couldn't trust him *in* my sight either, but my little team could instantly react to whatever he tried.

Hopefully.

This son of a bitch was trouble either way you cut it. But there were no good answers here, not until I could figure out what was really going on with this place.

And maybe, just maybe, I could dig that out of his smug, insane face before he found a way to royally screw us over.

"WELCOME ABOARD. WE'RE GOING TO GO SEE LUCIFER."

I killed the lights, then turned and left him there. Smiling in the darkness.

CHAPTER 13: FROM WORMS TO WYRMS

"Another part of the original rules that we have modified concerns dragons. The original rules had them as monsters. No, they are far more than that. And so we have moved them to the chapter about natural disasters."

--An Excerpt from Chapter eleven of the Chronicles of the Shared Lie

Three days later Delta returned to Beaky, scuttling up the ladder we lowered to allow her access. "Mission accomplished. Got about five different groups started and left them copies of the basic rules."

"AND DICE?"

"Didn't have enough to go around. I didn't know we were gonna take this tack, else I would've made batches up in advance. Still, most of the demons I got were pretty sharp, so they'll have plenty made in short order."

"I still don't see what this is going to accomplish," Vector groused. He'd been griping a lot more lately.

"IN THE SHORT RUN? PROBABLY NOTHING." I stared out the open hatch, and my telescopic vision found the sentries that Queen Eyeblight had put in place to watch us. She wasn't trying particularly hard to conceal them, and they multiplied and started brandishing weapons whenever we tried to shift the Striges. They never did anything, but for hellions this was about as subtle as their warnings got.

She'd stepped up to posturing earlier than expected, so I'd been forced to change our assault plan a bit.

"IN THE LONG RUN? IT MIGHT KEEP HER BUSY AND OFF OUR TAIL UNTIL WE'RE CLEAR."

I watched imps fly from the nearest sentries. Then more along the path she'd come up.

"THOSE DEMONS YOU TALKED INTO PLAYING WITH YOU ARE PROBABLY GOING TO DIE HORRIBLY," I told Delta after we'd sealed the hatch and started back to the control room.

"Yeah, probably." Delta shrugged. "Wouldn't be the first time satanic panic caused trouble for this hobby."

We'd underestimated the boredom and suffering of Hell for all involved, even the demons. Any distractions were welcome distractions, and they'd taken to it like a cult or secret society takes to forbidden knowledge.

So we'd decided to use that to our advantage.

By forming roleplaying groups like cells within the city, we'd acted in a clandestine fashion while her spies watched, passing on documents and secret knowledge in a way guaranteed to arouse suspicion.

The Queen would never rest easy, knowing that we had used her to conquer the city. First Whisper and The Cat had been clear on that; either I was too weak to handle matters on my own, in which case I had several lairs full of valuable stuff that she could seize for herself, or I was too strong to be anything but a threat to her. Even if she didn't feel that way personally, her subjects would expect her to feel that way, would become disgruntled and rebellious if she didn't behave accordingly. She was trapped by chains of power, unable to act in a way that would simply let me go about my business.

"STATUS?" I asked the moment I reached the bridge.

"It's done," Alpha replied, gesturing to the rounded corner of the room, and the newly-repaired suit of armor standing upright, back open, waiting for me.

I removed my traveling mask, breathed in the warm, foul smell of Beaky's innards. I was getting used to it, and this worried me. I didn't want to get used to it.

"We weren't bothered," Alpha said, folding his arms. "Epsilon and I got down there, set up the workshop, quietly killed the few sentries who saw us. Then Delta started up her games, and everyone stuck on her like glue on fish."

"GLUE ON FISH?"

"Well, I didn't make it easy for them. Gave 'em the slip a few times." Delta shrugged.

"AND THE WORKSHOP?"

"Thanks for reminding me," Epsilon voxed. A distant whump echoed through Beaky, and I watched through the viewscreen. A plume of smoke rose in the city. "Not a good idea to leave that behind."

"NO." Though the demons were at a renaissance tech level, if they'd managed to enslave one metahuman they doubtlessly had others. It wouldn't do to underestimate their ability to use and learn from the technology I'd left behind. Which made me worry about Caym a bit, but that bridge had been crossed. There was no going back now.

Instead of dwelling on it, I ran my hand over the black, roughly-patched form of my armor. My poor, battered, way-below-spec armor. I'd had to cut out a few of my mask's sight modes to salvage the components needed to repair the damaged circuitry. Well, Alpha had, anyway. He'd run down to the city, taken the portable workshop tools, built the larger-scale stuff he needed, and done the repairs. Hopefully it would be enough for the next crisis. Hopefully at some point I'd find the proper metals and rare earths, *and* have the time to complete more advanced repairs.

Speaking of that...

"ANY LUCK IN THE MARKETS?" I looked to the Grimalkin and First Whisper. The two were unknown to Queen Eyeblight, so I'd sent them on a fairly covert task while Delta drew fire, and Alpha and Epsilon hid and did the real work.

"If by luck you mean 'did we found some of the shiny rocks you wanted,' yes, I think we were a little lucky," The Cat confirmed. "I think she has a box?"

"I do." First Whisper smiled and drew a small jewelry box from her purse. She had a *purse* now, and I'm not sure where she got the idea from. Putting aside the speculation as unimportant, I leaned in to survey the goods. Then I logged into my armor remotely and toggled the spectroanalyzer, piping the visual report to my mask.

"NOT BAD." Some golden jewelry, easily repurposed. A few twists of metal that contained palladium—

—and my breath hissed between my teeth, as I grabbed up a ring of pure zinc. "THIS ONE. WHERE DID THE MERCHANT OBTAIN THIS ONE?"

I'd instructed them to ask follow-up questions with every purchase. Even tested their memory. Fortunately, First Whisper's powers of recall were about as good as mine.

I'd also slipped a few recording worms into First Whisper's purse, but I didn't want to spend the time it would take to go through their logs unless it was absolutely necessary.

"Let me recall..." First Whisper's fingers brushed mine as she closed the jewelry box, and I scowled underneath my mask. It wasn't the first incidence of such 'accidental' contact.

"Pitward. To your... southeast?"

"Yes, the southeast of Wroth," The Cat added. "There are pools of the stuff in the more hazardous lava fields out that way. The local lords use favored slaves they've saved from the Styx to harvest it."

"The Komar Riding, that's the name of the place." First Whisper nodded, handing the jewelry box off to Epsilon. "Some minor holding out in the frontier."

"THEN THAT'S WHERE WE'RE GOING."

"Zinc? Really?" Vector frowned. "What's so special about the stuff?"

"IT'S NOT. BUT REFINING ZINC YIELDS INDIUM. AND THAT, PROFESSOR, IS A DIFFERENT MATTER ALTOGETHER." Indium alone wouldn't be enough for a full repair of my suit, was only one of the materials I needed, but it was a step in the right direction. And it would let me throw together a few more inventions and enhancements for Beaky and his kin.

I checked my recollection of the map, found the Komar Riding, and programmed the course into Beaky. "NOW COMES THE TRICKY PART..."

Eight minutes later, after we'd transferred Gamma and Epsilon back to their respective Strix, our beasts turned as one and flew south. Immediately Eyeblight's sentries below sent up an alarm, blowing on horns, banging on gongs, and making a general fuss.

And with a great cry thousands of bat-like hellspawn took to the skies, doing their damnedest to bring us down.

I sat on my throne and watched them try. Beaky shook as the cannons spoke nonstop, putting forth their arguments in lead.

And it wasn't just those weapons that were arrayed against the hellish air force. Above us, climbing out of the hatches and rushing to defend his topside, ran Vector's Spitters. He'd had the time and raw material to get us roughly a hundred and fifty of the hideous monstrosities.

It worked out pretty well. The Striges grasping tendrils tended to the ones from directly below, the cannons kept the sides relatively clear, the multiple heads with sharp beaks and fiery breath arrayed around our spawn took care of that angle, and the Spitters dealt with the geniuses who decided to try to fly up and drop straight down upon us.

Not without casualties, though. The bat-riders had plenty of spears, and the bats themselves were five hundred pounds of rage in a four-hundred pound bag. They did damage on the way down, making the Striges roar their pain in fire while the Spitters just died.

But neither all of them, nor enough of them, and we cleared the southern city wall and kept on going.

"QUADRANT FOUR, TURN SIX DEGREES," I instructed the cameras, and the one I addressed registered the command and obeyed.

There she was.

Queen Eyeblight stood on her tower, next to her jumbo-sized riding bat, staring right at Beaky. She stood with a fifteen-foot-long spear in hand that crackled with eldritch energies. She was obviously ready to throw down.

But she wouldn't.

Not unless I appeared. Not unless I came out.

I'd had plenty of downtime over the last few days while my minions did my bidding. I'd read and analyzed the Pax Infernum and thought very hard on what it said and what it *didn't* say.

"She won't pursue," First Whisper spoke, sneering her joy at being proven right. "She fears you."

Not true, not entirely. I'd seen this custom in Caym, even if I hadn't realized it at the time. And I'd encountered it in Wroth, albeit in a more hurried fashion.

Simply put, the demon lords only got involved if their armies couldn't handle the job or if the other side's demon lord got involved. To do less, to jump the gun, was to admit that your army was the weaker. Only when the fighting was fiercest, when the enemy could be taken down with a decisive strike or their own army was vulnerable to such a strike, did the demon leaders engage.

I watched theory turn into reality as we slipped away clean. The fiends followed us for a bit but soon fell back far outside of cannon range.

"Why didn't we use the lightning against them, Doctor?" First Whisper asked.

"WE WERE TOO CLOSE TO THE GROUND. IT WOULD HAVE WREAKED HAVOC ON THE CITY BELOW." I eyeballed the pursuit, judged it to be a cautionary measure. As long as we didn't look like we were circling around and didn't show weakness, we'd probably be fine.

"I still don't see why you care about that," The Cat said. "It's not like you were sticking around to add it to your domain."

"OH, DIRE IS WELL AWARE THAT YOU DON'T UNDERSTAND. THAT IS WHY SHE WON'T BOTHER EXPLAINING IT."

"Random massacres are bad, m'kay?" Alpha drawled.

"Now that we're away, can I show you something?" Vector asked.

I glanced at the flock of fiends on the monitor, then nodded. "SURE. IT'LL HELP BREAK UP THE SCENERY, AT LEAST." We had a long way to go, if the map was accurate.

The thin scientist grew more animated as we walked down Beaky's halls, towards his lab. "It's something I've had in mind ever since I met your minions. They're people, you know."

"WELL, YES."

"No, I mean, these are the first androids I've ever run across that have their own personalities, their own motivations. They're a lot better company than most humans I've had to interact with, to tell the truth."

"GET TO THE POINT." I paused, measured the waves of irritation that surged within me. No, this was out of proportion to his actions and words, not natural to me at all. "SORRY. SHE IS STILL FEELING WRATHFUL."

"I've been compensating for that with drugs. Want some?"

"NO."

"Anyway, the point is they're really distinctive."

"WHAT?"

"If the Chorus could blend in more with homo sapiens, they'd be the perfect infiltrators. You'd open up a lot more uses for them, and I think it would be good for their development. I mean, robot skeletons are pretty much your style, but is it *theirs*?"

He smiled as he parted the curtains to his lab, waited for the airlock to settle into place, and opened the inner set of curtains with a flourish.

There, in five wall-to-ceiling tubes, stood five deflated corpses... no, they weren't corpses. They were skinsuits. Two female, and three male. They were relatively similar, save for breasts, and...

"YOU MADE THEM ANATOMICALLY CORRECT."

"Well, yes." Vector coughed and didn't meet my eyes. "They're essentially cloned from DNA samples from the Damned, with a few splices in there, and overlaid on a fungus-like carrier that simulates flesh, down to a few minor functions that will help them pass—"

I pointed to the far right skinsuit. "THAT ONE HAS A HARD-ON, VECTOR."

"Shit." He moved over to the tube, started pushing colored sections of it. "The chemical mix is off, let me adjust the feed."

"THEY'RE PRETTY MUCH ALL FULLY FUNCTIONAL, AREN'T THEY?"

"Well yes!" Vector was blushing now. I wanted to palm my face, but I didn't know how much I could push the man. "What do you do when you're infiltrating? Sometimes it involves sleeping with a target, or it *could* depending on the approach. And what if they *want* to sleep with someone? That's part of their development, or it could be—"

"ENOUGH. PLEASE. ENOUGH." I leaned against the wall. "YOU'RE TALKING TO THE EQUIVALENT OF THEIR MOTHER,

YOU KNOW."

His blush got worse. "I ah, I er, I really hadn't looked at it that way, but..."

"BUT THEY ARE FULLY GROWN. THEIR GESTATION CYCLE IS MUCH FASTER THAN THE USUAL ORGANIC PATH." I sighed and decided to take pity on him. Put in the right light, and ignoring the creepy-ass overtones, it was a rather touching gift. "GIVE HER A SECOND. LET'S CALL THEM IN AND SEE IF THEY LIKE THE NOTION."

One vox call, and a quick camera reroute to patch Gamma and Epsilon in remotely, and my Chorus got their first look at their gift of flesh.

"I'm... speechless," Alpha said, walking around the tube, looking the skin up and down. "You want us to wear these things? I think I read a wargame where skinsuits over metal skeletons are like an elite unit of psychotic murderbots. You really want us to be murderbots, man? I mean, we can do that, but I'd rather cosplay space marines any day."

"It's not like that, I mean I know you aren't," Vector said, polishing broken spectacles on his grimy lab coat.

Beta simply offered him an open hand. Vector stared at it.

"Thank you," Beta said. "I've been wanting something like this for a long time."

Vector shook his hand. "You're welcome."

"Can we adjust the features?" Delta said. "I want huge knockers."

"No." Gamma said. "Absolutely not."

"Hey! It's my womansuit, I get to do what I want with it!"

"I'm calling in the favor you owe me. You can't have bigger tits than mine."

"Oh Jesus G, you really want to use that for this? Seriously?"

"FAVOR?"

"Nothing, don't worry about it," Gamma and Delta chorused simultaneously.

"Trust me, you don't want to know," Alpha confirmed.

"OH-KAY..." I held my gauntlets out, fingers waggling, and shut up.

"It could prove an intriguing experiment," Epsilon finally spoke up.

"I know, right?" Vector said through the vox. "Both in perception and mentality. I mean, perception of others, and your own mentality, of course."

"I'll simply say thank you, Professor, and I think I speak for all of us when I say we accept your gift wholeheartedly." Gamma stroked his ego, and I smiled to hear it. "Also, I have some reference photos for my skinsuit. I assume they can be modified? And the final product will have hair?"

"Yes, I just have to work on the follicle simulation, and the relevant blastocysts—"

"WELL, HAVE FUN WITH THAT. SHE'S GOING TO LEAVE YOU TO SORT OUT THE DETAILS." I waved to the three minions in the room and shut off my vox connection to the two who were remoting in. It was time to seek saner company. I went hunting for Khalid.

I didn't have far to go.

The chamber full of orphaned Damned were happy to point me a few "doors" down, to his workshop. I pushed through the membranes and was immediately thankful for my mask, as toxicity meters flared. I backed out, not knowing if the atmosphere would poison me through my skin, and not willing to take the chance. Instead of risking it I opened a vox channel. "Khalid? What are you doing?"

"Please bide for a minute. I was not expecting company."

I heard fans whir to life. Still, judging by those toxicity levels, it would take a while to drain. Mercury was pretty high up in there, and I vaguely recalled that as being dangerous as hell to exposed tissues.

I made a mental note to cleanse later, in the shower we'd rigged up. Then I considered that we were in Beaky's lungs and got even more worried. "Should you be working with that stuff inside Beaky?"

"He is vast, and the dosages are comparatively small. It may perhaps shorten his lifespan by a few years, but he shall not be overly hindered for your purposes."

Your purposes.

"*Our* purposes, surely."

It was a few seconds before he responded. "Yes, that is what I said."

It hadn't been, but I let it slide, and in a few minutes he opened the channel once more. "You are safe to enter."

Vector's lab space had been woven into the walls, organic piping and tubes resembling something out of H.R. Geiger's wet dreams. By contrast, this was elegant and spartan, racks of bone hanging from the walls, each with secured vials, beakers, and other glassware. Samples of various elements lay neatly stacked in metal crates

And on a smooth bone altar, covered with cloth woven from human hair, lay Khalid's sword. It glowed silvery-white, glowed so brightly that it engaged my mask's flare compensation.

Like too many things I'd seen down here, it gave off unidentifiable energy readings. Magic. Detecting it was one thing, figuring out what it did was another thing completely.

"ANTI-DEMON CHARMS?" I asked.

"Something of the sort." Khalid sprinkled the length of the blade with salt, muttering under his breath. The light receded, revealing new symbols etched into the metal of the weapon. "This is the best I can do, since angelic invocational formulae are practically useless down here."

I took a closer look at him. He seemed haggard, worn. There were still stains on his cowl from where he'd shed blood, back during that fight with Judy while she was possessed. His facesucker was new at least, busy pulsing away and filtering the air. I figured he'd trusted it to keep him alive while he was working with the mercury. Speaking of that...

I checked the air once more, registered acceptable contamination levels and sighed. Then I removed my mask. Khalid glanced up at me, brow furrowed as he frowned. "I would not risk that if I were you. Mercury is pernicious."

"So is insomnia. Have you slept since you came back aboard?"

He looked away, and that was all the answer I needed. I put a hand on his shoulder. "Khalid... whatever you're doing, it can wait."

"No. No, it cannot. Or rather, I cannot." He stepped back, slipped free of my hand. "It gnaws at me, unceasing, a rage I have resisted for many, many years. And I fear what will happen if I give into it. This is my way of quelling it, turning it to something constructive." He gestured at the blade. "This will serve me better than its previous iteration, the next time I must fight beside you."

"Khalid, you fought well. Judy almost wrecked Dire single-handedly. If it weren't for you and Gamma, she would have—"

"I should have been able to handle it," he interrupted, brows glaring over his symbiote.

I pushed down my own annoyance and stared at him until he dropped his eyes. "We're still in Wrath, right?" My voice wavered, some of the edge bleeding through. "Because Dire was pretty sure that Pride was two rings down, give or take. And what you're saying sounds a lot like wounded pride."

He turned away. I rolled my eyes at his back. Men. Men were starting to get on my nerves more and more often these days.

"What do you know of the Janissaries?" Khalid asked me.

I'd done some research a few years back. "A bit. You were the elite guards to the Ottoman Sultans. All Christians, in a contrast to the dynasty, which was entirely Muslim."

"This is true. But it is not the whole of the story."

"You were supposed to be elite troops, fearsome on the battlefield and loyal to a fault. And bureaucrats as well, after you retired." I frowned. "Never understood that part."

"It is a bit more complex than that. We were recruited from

Christians, some tithed, others given freely because families had extra sons. Others were captured from wars against the local Christians." He turned around, looked at me, and his eyes were old, old beyond measure. "Some few of us retained our faith, kept it secret. As secret as we could."

"And the bureaucracy part?"

"Armies run on logistics. Administration is necessary to coordinate that. A lesson that modern armies have well learned, but that was revolutionary back in the pre-Renaissance eras." It was hard to tell, but the way his eyes crinkled, he might have been smiling. "Which is why I was spared when the first round of purges came. Because I was one of the few non-corrupt administrators, and I was well-educated and *useful*."

Light started to dawn. "And you're feeling useless right now. You shouldn't. You're our occult expert, and without you we'd be up shit creek."

"And yet in every case, at every time where I have had an opportunity to alter the flow of events I have been either handily defeated or rendered inconsequential." His eyes were glaring again. Not at me, but past me, at Hell in general perhaps. "I have spent centuries fighting these things and now find that my tactics are entirely ineffective. And it makes me *angry*."

I nodded. "Especially because you can't tell if it's natural anger or the emotions that this circle pushes upon you."

He glanced back to me. "Have you been speaking with Beta?"

"No, why?"

"He has listened to me complain more than once. Your android has the patience of a saint. I am glad for his presence."

I nodded. "He does have a good shoulder to cry on. Not that that's what you were doing," I amended hastily. "Of course things are different here than they are there."

"Yes. But it is more than that. Hell is..." he sighed. "Hell is a necessary evil, we were taught. Just the way things are. A component of the afterlife that God offers salvation and protection from. It is a place where the wicked are punished according to their sins. But..."

"It's not necessarily so, is it?"

"There is a purpose here, but I am not sure it is God's, It seems to treat the sinners as inconsequential, which is... disrespectful." Khalid shook his head. "And that eats at me, when the anger does not."

I took his shoulders in my hands and pulled him into a hug. The symbiote on his face pulsed and slobbered against my chest, and I ignored it as best I could. After a bit of hesitation, he returned the embrace. "You're a friend, Khalid. Just because you've been having some problems of late doesn't mean you aren't necessary. It doesn't mean you're useless." I pulled away and looked down into his eyes, still holding his shoulders. "It just means that we need to start fighting smarter. That Council of Worms? They pulled some nasty tricks on us, and that fight almost went very, very bad. So we need to prepare for the next one, and that sweet, sweet knowledge all locked away in your brain is going to be the key there. In fact, now that we know one major foe is coming, we can start doing that right now."

"How so? How can I help?" The smaller man asked, awkwardly reaching up to pat my arm.

"Buer. Tell Dire about Buer, and don't hold back even the slightest bit of information..."

Days turned into weeks and the Wrathlands passed below us, we laid our plans with care.

The clouds got thicker as we went, steam boiling up from the rivers and mixing with the ash and smoke from the volcanoes. But the further "south" we went, the more the ash faded, and the more rains battered the ground below. Reddish lightning streaked around us, and I was thankful for the Tesla Deflectors. Modulating them helped disperse the lightning strikes that caught us.

The Striges hated the whole trip of course, from the soggy, sooty rain to the lightning that stung and jolted them. But fuck 'em, they were ours now, and I had little time or mercy to spare for the hellspawn.

Instead I divided my time between the workshop and meeting my Damned. We had the bunch from Caym, and my Chorus had used the chaos of the battle in Wroth to liberate a few more. I circulated, shook hands, bowed, or exchanged nods where appropriate to the cultures involved, and I discovered something fairly concerning.

When I was absolutely sure of my suspicions, I steeled myself, armored up, and went back once more to that darkened chamber where I'd left Great Clown Pagliacci.

He didn't look up as I entered, and for a second I wondered if he was dead, though I couldn't see how. The oxygen-cycling moss was still doing its job, and as a Damned he didn't need food nor drink. Though I wouldn't put it past him to kill himself just to spite me. I hung back and studied the scene for a moment.

"Hello, Doctor." Hollow eyes flicked open and found me, even in total darkness. "I was starting to wonder if you'd left me to rot."

"YOU DON'T GET OFF THAT EASILY." To any of my friends, that would be a jest. To this... creature... it was a promise. I didn't like having him here, but I didn't have a good place to put him, so here we were.

"Then what is my hardship today?"

"THEY'RE ALL CHRISTIAN. OR FROM CULTURES WHICH HAD MAJOR DEALINGS WITH CHRISTIANS IN SOME FORM."

His lips peeled back from his teeth, smeared makeup giving way to long, sharp, yellowed teeth. Filed? Perhaps. Or a side-effect of the partial vampirization that he'd undergone during his last years. "Ah. You've made that connection. Good, I was wondering when you would."

"WHEN, NOT IF?"

"You are far too intelligent to let it lie for long. But yes, I noticed that as well. Have you read the Divine Comedy?"

"THE INFERNO. YES."

"Alighieri speaks of an outer ring of Hell, one of virtuous pagans. But if one takes his words at face value, that should be the resting place for only those Damned who were never exposed to Christianity. Who never had to choose between their native faiths and this new thing."

"WE DROPPED DOWN FAIRLY FAR INTO HELL. DIRE HAS NOT SEEN THE OUTSIDE OF IT."

"No." He smacked his lips against his teeth. "Nobody I spoke to has. The demons I asked about it had never heard of such a place, either. And doesn't... that... make... you... wonder?"

Logic kicked in. "THAT DOES NOT DISPROVE ITS EXISTENCE. DEMONS IN THESE PARTS ARE REMARKABLY PROVINCIAL."

"Mmmmmmm... true. But the demon lords, the smart ones such as the Council of Worms... they would surely have known, would they not? Their favorite pastime was supping upon the brains of the Damned and devouring their knowledge. And given the slave trade that passes between the rings and cities, surely someone would have at least heard of it by now?"

"ENTERTAINING THE THEORY THEN, THAT IT DOES NOT EXIST..."

"Well, the only ones who *would* go there would be those damned by ignorance. Thus, the ones who were aware of Christianity and were wrathful, they would surely be down here, would they not? Mixed in with everyone else?"

"THERE ARE SOME NON-CHRISTIANS DOWN HERE. DIRE HAS MET THEM."

"Yes, and what do they all have in common?"

"CONTACT WITH CHRISTIANITY, USUALLY THROUGH MISSIONARIES OR SOME FORM OF—"

"No. No, that is the wrong track." He sighed, theatrically, lips stretching into an exaggerated frown. He reached a hand up, and I started... then calmed myself. Of course he'd worn the straps away, what else did he have to do in here? But he tried nothing stupid, merely ran his fingers down the tattoos of tears under his eyes. Over and over again. "And you were doing so well, too," he said, voice turning shrill. Too shrill for someone that large and muscled.

I was almost thankful when my vox channel opened up. "Boss? You better come to the bridge."

"Alpha? What's wrong?"

"We've got, uh, an intruder in our airspace."

I was in no mood for more guessing games. Not after the damned clown. "Spit it out, what's coming at us?"

"A motherfucking dragon."

CHAPTER 14: FROM FRYING PAN TO FIRE

"Do not fear to throw an obstacle at the characters that they cannot hope to overcome. They will either overcome it, flee, or learn a valuable lesson in threat assessment."

--Excerpt from the second book of the Chronicles of the Shared Lie; The Monster Master's Methods

Once, long ago, the Last Janissary had revealed his true identity to my comrades. We'd talked about magical creatures for a bit, and one of my friends had asked, jokingly, if dragons were real, too.

The Janissary had nodded solemnly and confirmed that they were and that hopefully my friend would never meet one.

Today, as I stared up at the monitor and the grainy image that loomed closer with every ground-blasting flap of its massive wings, I understood why he'd said that.

Dragons were real, and this one looked hungry.

"We thought it had snuck up on us somehow, when the storms parted and there it was," Vector said. "But no, turns out it was really far away. Then the lidar readings came back, and we found out that it really is that big. That's when I adjusted the course."

"AND IT FOLLOWED."

"It followed, yeah."

I glanced from Vector over to Punching Judy. "WHERE IS DIRE'S CHORUS?"

"They're getting the few Damned we have on board ready to evac,"

Judy said, her accent much subdued from its usual Cockney burr.

I checked the Lidar myself, and sucked on my teeth. Then double-checked them once more. "HOW IS THAT THING EVEN FLYING?"

"They hibernate in the core of the world," Khalid said, adjusting his jacket coat as he pushed through the membranes of the command chamber. "The pressure makes them slow. Keeps them drowsy. They soak up the magic of the ley lines that ground into the Earth, and when they are restless, earthquakes are the result."

"BULLSHIT."

"Not every earthquake, true but enough of them that the old myths have some truth to them."

It had six or seven sets of wings, I noticed, rippling like sails that could cover football stadiums— parking lots and all. The effect was not unlike a massive kite.

But this kite had a face, and a ring of spider-like eyes that were fixed upon my little fleet.

Khalid continued, his voice the only sound in the silence. "Magic fuels it, raw strength does the rest. It flies because it wants to; it will catch us because it wishes to. It is merely a question of when."

I chewed my lip some more. The taste of blood filled my mouth, and I let go before I tore a hole in the damned thing. "CAN WE TALK WITH IT?"

Khalid shook his head. "The wyrms of Hell are as beasts. Lucifer saw to that when he stirred them from their sleep."

"ODDS OF KILLING IT?"

He looked toward me, looked at the suit of armor standing in the corner. "If you were at full repair, I would have my doubts. Now that your armor is worn and many-times repaired, I have none. It would not end well for you. Nothing else we have could even scratch it."

I closed my eyes.

I'd been spoiled, a bit, by how things had gone thus far. No major setbacks, constant gain, adding to our forces with every move. But this is Hell, and it feasts on the hopes of the naive, and so here we were.

But... I wasn't the only heavy hitter on board.

I looked toward Punching Judy, who was standing with the rest of the crew, staring at it silently on the monitor. "JUDY? CAN YOU PUNCH THAT THING?"

"I... Sorry, love. I can feel the pull of that thing from here. It don't just eat chi, it *is* chi. Or near enough that the best I could do is a boop on the snoot."

"Dragons carry such heat within them that flesh boils in its own juices within half a kilometer of their hide," Khalid gently explained.

"Righty-o, never mind then."

"NOPE." I moved to my armor, clambered in the back, and waited as it booted up around me. "WE'VE COME TOO FAR TO BE TAKEN DOWN BY SOME BIG STUPID LIZARD."

"This is suicide," Khalid was frowning at me as my HUD flickered to life.

"NO, IT'S A DISTRACTION. TELL THE FLEET TO SPLIT UP." I worked up a basic telemetry and fired it off to the Chorus. "WE'LL RENDEZVOUS LATER."

I made my way out of Beaky and flew like the wind. The already-huge shape of the dragon kept getting bigger and bigger, the closer I got to it.

And the rage grew within me as I approached. I'd come so far, been through so much, and this random reptile thought to thwart me? *I am Dire, and I will not be denied!*

I parked a mile away from it and bombarded it with particle beams. It didn't blink. I targeted the eyes; it didn't seem to care. I circled it as fast as I dared go, pasting it everywhere, bathing it in kinetic energy, amping up with every shot.

I might as well have been shooting at the moon— no, shooting at the moon would have had more of a result. This creature, this thing could withstand the pressures of the Earth's core. I might as well have been throwing spitwads at it.

I tried nonetheless. Only when my armor's vents smoked, and yellow HUD lights flashed nonstop as my particle beam assemblages threatened to melt, did I stop firing.

It wasn't correct to see it as a creature. It *was*, but that wasn't the challenge here. This was a force of nature, a disaster to be survived rather than beaten. I simply lacked the tools to prevent it from falling upon my friends.

And oh, did that gnaw at me. I checked to make sure the other two Striges were well on their way and fleeing, then opened a vox channel to Beaky's bridge. "No go. Abandon ship."

"Already ahead of you, boss." Parachutes bloomed like flowers around Beaky, drifting downward. Not many, only one for each of the Chorus that were aboard, Vector, Khalid, and the most recent crop of Spitter pods. The Damned would have just jumped, and I couldn't see them from this distance. They'd die when they hit the ground, sure, but they'd revive in time.

For a second I was worried that the dragon would turn to follow them, but it didn't. It pursued Beaky, drawing closer with every series of rippling flaps from its multiple wings.

And damn my eyes, I remembered that Beaky had one more passenger. "Alpha? Did you guys get Pagliacci free and shove him off the Strix?"

"Um... no."

Shit.

I poured on the speed. I was off on the rear flank of the wyrm, and it was moving faster now, sensing the end of the hunt. I watched its mouth open in slow motion as it narrowed the gap and pushed my gravitics to their highest output, shunting all power away from weapons, thinning down the forcefield as slim as I dared. I cut through the sky like an arrow, sonic booms gonging in my wake like thunder, until I was just within the creature's heat envelope and my environmental alarms started their climb. I ignored it, stretched my arms out Crusader style, and punched straight through Beaky's flesh just ahead of the dragon. Through the outer shell, ignoring the dents it put in my armor, through the lungs of him, and skidding to a stop just outside Pagliacci's chamber. The membranes tore away from the force of my entry, revealing the very surprised psychotic clown.

He shouted something, but it was lost in the wind and the roar of Beaky's pain that shook the bloody, ruined chambers I'd just burst through. I ignored Pagliacci's query, ripped him free of his restraints without care for his comfort or safety. By now my environmental sensors were telling me the dragon was a scant four hundred yards away, and the heat was almost to the point where I'd be boiled alive, coolant systems or no.

I held Pagliacci tight to my searing armor, ignored his grunt as I burned him, pointed my free palm at the floor, and pumped a hundred-percent wide-spread particle beam down.

We fell.

Just in time too, as Beaky's scream trailed up high, higher than the audible frequencies of the human ears, and the dragon's maw closed over the Strix's side like a fat man chomping a pancake.

The rule held true in Hell as it did on Earth; no matter how big you were, there was always someone bigger.

As we fell, I eased the gravitics back on, turned our arc into a slow swoop, outrunning the killing heat. Pagliacci sizzled but held tight to me, grimacing as his meat cooked on his bones. He looked more pissed than anything else. We matched each other, then, because the anger that clawed at the back of my mind wanted nothing more than to go back there and see if I could punch the stupid dragon in its stupid dragon face until it stopped moving.

But that cold logic that was my power, the will I'd built over the years, held me back. I knew it'd be suicide.

"NEXT TIME," I told the dragon. "DIRE SHALL BEAT YOU LIKE A GOD DAMNED PINATA."

I think Pagliacci was laughing. Either that or the shock was setting in. So when we were clear I set us down next to some low hills and dropped him on his back. Then I found a comfy-looking rock, plopped my metal keister on it, and let my armor's self-repair systems do their thing.

From a distance I watched as the dragon flew in a loose circle, munching merrily away. It took quite some time to get Beaky down into digestible bits, and I sourly counted the cost as it did. My workshop, my supplies, Khalid and Vector's labs, and so, so many raw resources that I had spent time and effort gathering. Oh, and the only place I could survive outside of the armor for long. And my renewable food source. All gone, like tears in acid rain.

I activated the vox, opened all channels. "Hello? Anyone there?"

I caught random chatter but nothing more. The main vox server had been in Beaky; with it busted, there was no way for the others to hear me. My suit's standalone transceiver was barely sophisticated enough to enable partial reception. And given the raw mass of the dragon, it was like operating around a microscopic black hole. The vox was solid tech but not infallible.

After a time, feet crunched on the sand behind me. I switched on the rear camera, watched Pagliacci approach. His eyes were slime on his cheeks, boiled right out of his skull. I watched him fumble a bit, did nothing as he tripped over a rock, gasping as his puffy, half-roasted hands banged against the stony ground.

"CAN YOU HEAR HER?" I asked.

Instantly his head snapped to face me. He opened his mouth, let out a frog-like croak, tongue bloated. Teeth slurped out of his cooked gums, leaving oozing holes. It was a miracle his face was still on his skull. Well, as much a miracle as miracles got down here, anyway.

"OH SIT DOWN AND HEAL UP. WE NEED TO GET MOVING ONCE YOU'RE LESS OF A LIABILITY."

He sat down, shut up, and did nothing beyond rock a bit. His way of dealing with the pain, I supposed.

The landscape surrounding us matched much of the plains we'd been moving over. Vast, empty, barren waste. But it was gouged by furrows, where sand and gravel and rock had been ripped up by unseen forces and strewn about. Quite recently, too. We'd been seeing these sort of marks for the last few days but had no idea what was causing it. Not until now, anyway. My eyes followed the dragon, then traced downwards to the ground below it. Even at such a distance, its wings pushed the air with such force that it rent the land asunder. A series of rolling, roiling explosions carved a swathe beneath it as it flew away into the distance.

But with the right vision modes I found what I was looking for. Metal, remnants of the materials I'd gathered and the machines I'd constructed, falling from the sky out of the dragon's slopping maw. Scattered a bit by the winds the dragon was displacing, scattered even more by the churning earth below, but possibly salvageable to some degree.

I tracked and marked the larger chunks, and after an hour, I looked back to Pagliacci. He had new eyes in his sockets now, and he didn't look quite so much like a mannequin made from bloated meat. That was probably a good sign.

"GOT YOUR TONGUE BACK?"

"I think so... yes." He stood, cracked his knuckles. "Are you done with your moping, or would you like to indulge in more angst?"

"ACTUALLY, SHE HAS BEEN BUSY." I stood up, waved roughly at him. My cape was gone, I noticed, burned off in the dragon fight. Well, sorry excuse for a fight, anyway. "COME ON. LET US GO GLEAN WHAT WE CAN FROM THE RUINS."

It was a long walk across the sands. I switched to hover mode midway through, keeping an eye on the dragon the whole time. It was using something to keep itself afloat, some sort of gravity manipulation that Khalid had called magic. Magic or no, energy was energy. I'd gathered some readings from it during my futile distraction run, and now I had some ideas for when we next met.

"I almost expect to see a statue of Ozymandias standing out here somewhere," Pagliacci broke the silence. "Though I suppose that is more a thing two circles down, eh?"

I checked the status of his collar, found it still armed. "ONE SUPPOSES. WE ARE NOT FAR FROM ENVY, THOUGH."

"Mmm. Envy and Wrath. A perfect place for a dragon. Well, there are probably more around Greed. Have you seen that ring?"

I weighed my words, decided they were of little risk. He was a creep, a murderer, and everything I stood against, but at the minute he was toothless as far as I was concerned. With a word I could trigger his collar. If my armor ceased to function, then his collar would trigger. If my life signs even fluctuated, boom would go the collar. He was nothing and inconsequential.

And if I kept telling myself that, sooner or later I might believe it.

"Doctor?"

"NO. SHE MANAGED TO SKIP THAT RING. ALONG WITH LUST AND GLUTTONY."

Probably for the best, to tell the truth. I was still recovering from a bad breakup, and the food down here that I could eat was, in a word, lacking. Though even *that* would be lost to me if Vector was gone for good. I picked up the pace, shuddering at the thought of having to eat demon or hellspawn without the various treatments and de-toxifications he could work upon the meat.

Although, if push came to shove... I eyed Pagliacci in the rearview camera, eyed the new pink skin over his layered muscles. I was already in Hell, what was one broken cannibalism taboo?

My stomach turned, and I hastily shelved the idea.

"I should have liked to have seen those rings," Pagliacci mused. "Perhaps I will, if you fail."

"NOT AN OPTION."

"An easy thing to say. A harder thing to do."

Glimmers in the sand ahead, the formless light of Hell winking on metal fragments from Beaky's remnants. They sat around strings of ropey purple flesh, all that remained of my faithful lair.

That was another reason to get to the wreckage. It broke up the barren terrain of the waste and would catch the attention of any survivors.

At least, it would if the larger chunks of machinery weren't sinking into the soil. Like they were right in front of my eyes, at this very minute.

"WHAT THE FUCK?"

We watched the remnants of a thermal lathe descend below the sandy gravel, with a scraping noise that reminded me of nails on a chalkboard.

"I have no answers here," said Pagliacci.

"THEN IT'S UP TO DIRE TO DO THE HEAVY LIFTING." I activated my sonar mode, the spectroscope, and the gravitic anomaly tracker, and went to town.

Reports trickled in through my display, and I blinked to see them. "THE METAL. EVERY SCRAP OF METAL ON THE GROUND IS BEING DRAWN INTO IT, DOWN TO TUNNELS BELOW." I was suddenly very glad I'd switched to hover mode a few miles back. "SOMETHING IS EXERTING A CONTINUOUS, CRUDE ELECTROMAGNETIC FORCE UPON THE FRAGMENTS...EXCEPT NO, THAT'S NOT QUITE RIGHT. FASCINATING." It was even drawing in the non-ferrous materials. And going by the errors it was throwing, this was more sorcery. Except that it was blended with an effect that I found far more understandable than the usual physics-defying bullshit.

"That is incorrect," Pagliacci said.

"WHAT?"

"You say that *something* is exerting a force. I say that *someone* is doing so."

"GOING BY THE TUNNELS DIRE IS DETECTING DOWN THERE, YOU'RE PROBABLY RIGHT."

"Oh good, that's simple then." Pagliacci smiled and flipped a knife up and down in one hand. I had no idea where he'd gotten the thing. "People are easy to murder."

"IT'S PROBABLY DEMONS."

"Oh, they're people too. Just particularly pathetic ones."

"UNLESS IT'S A FALLEN ANGEL."

"Doubtful. One of those would not let a little thing like your flight stop it. And the only one after your skull at the minute is Buer. We are far from the territory of any of the rest that I know of."

"YOU'VE SUDDENLY BECOME AN EXPERT ON THEM?"

"I asked Buer about it, during the few days I spent in his presence. They are not legion, as the Bible says. They are fewer than a thousand, and Hell is vast. There are none here, not until the iron city of Dis. You are going there, I assume?"

I hadn't told him any of my plans, and I didn't see any reason to change that. "THAT'S OF NO CONSEQUENCE RIGHT NOW." I frowned. "COME ON. LET'S GO SEE IF WE CAN FIND A VENT OR TWO. IF THERE'S SOMEONE FUCKING AROUND UNDERGROUND, THEY'LL HAVE AIRSHAFTS."

As it turned out, they did, though the caves were a few miles distant and hollowed out of what had once been a pretty tall mountain. Beyond it, fumaroles of thick, black smoke dotted the wasteland. And surveying them, my spectrometer told me a fairly interesting story. "THOSE ARE THE SIGNS OF A LARGE-SCALE SMELTING OPERATION."

"Then it would explain why they want metal."

The ground shook below us, and Pagliacci stumbled, went to one knee.

"NO IDEA WHAT THAT WAS."

"Earthquake?"

"UNLIKELY. THEY COULD BE SHOCKWAVES FROM A GOOD-SIZED EXPLOSION, PERHAPS." I pointed to the 'north'. "BLASTING NEW TUNNELS, POSSIBLY. IT'S A MOOT POINT."

"How so?"

Because I've got one more day of clean air, less than a day of stored rations, and enough water to live for four days before I fucking die.

But I would be damned before I'd show weakness to one of my oldest enemies, so instead I said "BECAUSE WE'RE GOING TO GO DOWN THERE, SEE WHAT WE'RE UP AGAINST, AND DESTROY ANY WHO WOULD STAND AGAINST US. THEN WE'RE GOING TO

GET BACK OUR SALVAGE, RE-ESTABLISH THE VOX SERVER, AND MAYBE MAKE A FEW MORE WAR MACHINES FOR SHITS AND GIGGLES."

"I *do* like my giggles." The mad clown considered me for a long moment. "I have an idea. You will hate it."

"OH?"

"Your armor is quite black, but still shiny in spots." He reached down, grabbed double handfuls of gritty soil, and offered it to me as he straightened up from kneeling. "Care for a rub down?"

I hated the idea, but accepted its necessity. Once he deemed me camouflaged enough, we descended into the tunnels. Based on the fact that I hadn't been drawn down into the soil, I trusted that I'd probably be fine so long as I avoided direct contact with the ground.

That was the hope, anyway. Magic was cheaty.

We descended into the bowels of the underworld, following the draft. The foundries below ground pulled massive amounts of air to keep their fires going. I had a notion of the processes they were using, based on the output of their chimneys, and this would lead us straight to them, barring weirdness or interception.

Nothing intercepted us. We crossed through tunnels gouged out of solid rock, past old scaffolding made from bones. This place bore odd patterns on the walls. They'd definitely been mined; I could trace the cavities where seams of ore had been pulled out of the stone, but I had no idea what had done it. No pick marks, no scars from acid. Probably the same sort of sorcery that had pulled my precious scrap down through the soil, come to think of it.

I muted my voice modulator down to the level of howling wind as we came to a place where the tunnels narrowed, and leaned in to talk with Pagliacci. "ONE THING PUZZLES DIRE."

"Oh?"

"THIS REGION. ON THE MAP, IT IS UNCLAIMED TERRITORY. NO ONE IS SUPPOSED TO BE OUT HERE."

"You have a map?" He looked surprised. Then it faded. "Any map of this area would be suspect. It is hostile to settlements, haunted by dragons, and barren. Clearly nobody has explored here overmuch."

"WHICH WOULD WORK, EXCEPT THAT THE AMOUNT OF DUST IN THESE TUNNELS IS NOTICEABLY LIGHT. THEY HAVEN'T BEEN IN EXISTENCE VERY LONG... A FEW MONTHS, AT MOST."

The caves shuddered around us as another explosion rocked them from what had to be at least fifty miles away, going by my seismic trackers.

Claim jumpers. That was the first thing that came to mind. A wildcat mining operation, using the wastes and the dragon as cover. I reviewed the borders surrounding this area, thinking back to this particular region of the map. Only a few, and far between. And given that it wasn't far to the next ring of the massive crater that was Hell, there was no real reason for anyone to be roaming out here. Yeah, claim jumpers were a possibility.

"Where to from here?" Pagliacci asked, as we came to a junction, a regular honeycomb of tunnels branching out in multiple directions.

"THAT WAY." I pointed.

"You are certain?"

"IT'S WHERE HER DAMNED LATHE IS GOING." I hadn't turned off my various vision modes, at least the ones that could track that thing through the solid rock. No real point in giving up an advantage.

The tunnels got smaller as we went and I slowed when we came to the first signs of what passed for civilization in Hell.

Slaves.

The torchlit corridor we'd come to had perhaps three hundred Damned on either side, men, women and children, all grimy and naked and using rocks to scrape at the walls. As I watched, one of them uncovered a streak of metallic gleam, and turned back to call down the corridor. From somewhere out of sight, another voice replied. The lucky prospector confirmed it, and they relayed the call back further into the tunnels.

"ODD WAY OF DOING BUSINESS," I observed.

"They have seen us," Pagliacci pointed out.

The nearest slaves to us were silent, staring up with dread.

Then the call repeated itself, traveling back the other way, and everyone ran like mad away from us. The just-uncovered seam cracked and bulged, as the rock seemed to shudder...

...and a demon stepped out. Metallic and slimy at the same time, it flopped through until its serpentine lower half was clear. It had a torso like a bodybuilder, and a set of three mandibles on a snaky head, that chattered as it immediately whirled to face us.

Then two more started oozing out of the wall next to it.

"KNEEL BEFORE DIRE!" I shouted in hellspeech, charging my particle beams.

"I do not think they will do that!" Pagliacci yelled, as he charged them.

He was on the first one before it could react, slashing and stabbing with his knives, because evidently that sneaky fucker had at least two that I hadn't noticed. The serpentine demon recoiled, and I turned my attention to the others, slinging beams into the closest one. It staggered with each impact, eventually falling to the ground, its face a smoking ruin.

"SHE SAID KNEEL!" I snapped at the third one, sparing a glance to my right. Pagliacci was ripping into the first demon, and it was bleeding something like mercury, but it was giving as much as it was getting, and Pagliacci was slowing down.

The third one did not kneel. The third one slapped its hand into the wall next to it, and droned a buzzing song.

The earth rose up and grabbed me.

"CUTE TRICK." I leveled my arm at it... and it retreated down the corridor as the stone rose to envelop my hand. I snarled, and rerouted power to my armor's motivators...

...only to see warning lights pop up. Red warning lights.

My armor reported catastrophic failure across the board, and my eyes went wide as I realized what was happening.

The demon had grabbed my armor and brought the stone into contact with it.

A good portion of my armor was made of rare earths and metals.

Their magic was ripping my suit open, bit by bit.

I pulled the ejection lever, scrambled out of the back, and whirled around in time to see my suit crumple like a tin can.

Pagliacci loomed out of the darkness, covered in gouges, with the first demon's head in his hands. Behind him, a fourth demon oozed out of the wall. "What are you doing?" Pagliacci asked, then froze as the collar around his neck started beeping. "Oh, this is *not* funny."

I dove for cover just as it blew up, managing to avoid the worst of the blast, and staggered to my feet, clawing for my sidearm. I'd just gotten the pistol out, when the ground below my feet writhed, and locked itself around my ankles. I had time for a wild shot at the remaining demons, but then they were on me, and they were far, far too strong to resist as they rained down blows upon me.

In the end I managed to keep conscious as they unbound my legs from their stone sheaths and hauled my limp, bleeding form down the passage.

"What shall we do with the big one?" The second demon asked in hellspeech, sparing a glance toward Pagliacci's headless corpse.

"Leave him. A new slave for the work crew when he reanimates. He's of no consequence. This one, now, this one is....." The fourth demon peered down at me.

"This one is going to fetch a price beyond compare once we get her back to Dis..."

CHAPTER 15: HELL HATH NO FURY

"Remember, if an enemy can profit from a character's continued existence, then death is not always the foe's goal..."

--Excerpt from the second chapter of the first book of the Chronicles of the Shared Lie

As villainous lairs go, I give it an eight out of ten.

Spires of stone and zinc curved throughout the chamber, and I was thrilled to see those. Zinc was what I'd braved these wilds to obtain.

Still, I'd hoped for better circumstances. But I couldn't complain too much. As soon as I saw that resistance was futile, I'd taken the hits, fallen as far as my leg restraints had let me, and shielded my face. My mask had come through intact.

My right knee, not so much. It hurt like a sonovabitch and was swollen up to the point it was straining my pants leg. I had to struggle to keep up with the demons as they dragged me by the arms, and the jolting pain was an aggravating counterpoint that exacerbated the other bruises and contusions they'd given me.

But the important thing was still there; they'd let me keep my mask.

Which was good, because the air filters were working overtime down here. It wasn't the dusty rock soup that the atmosphere was above ground, but there were enough things in the mix that I'd end up with some sort of horrible lung disease if I took the thing off for any amount of time. Cancer was not the answer, no matter the question.

They dragged me up the ramps of stone and bronze, and I winced as the heat was just a touch too much on my feet. The chamber was lit from far below, by pits to either side. Magma? Certainly hot enough in here for this to be the high end of a magma chamber. If not for those huge vents in the ceiling, and the layers of stone between me and the direct lava, I reckoned I'd be sizzling right about now.

Then the sculpture on top of the spires that I'd taken for an altar turned to look at me, and I forgot my discomfort.

Ten foot tall from head to tail, it had a few feet on the demons who'd pummeled me down. Like the others, it had multiple mandibles churning on the end of its muzzle, and two dark eyes with pupils like lapis lazuli. Muscled arms bore a scepter and a gauntlet of gold, and he wore heavy jeweled chains over his chest like an infernal version of Mister T.

"What have you brought me?" he asked.

"A mortal woman," My rightmost captor replied. "She and her dead comrade have killed Forty-first Worm and Fifty-ninth Worm."

There were that many of those things around? Troublesome.

"Mortal..." He slithered closer and leaned in, chittering face inches from my mask. "Yes. I smell her soul. You have done well, yet you say there was another one?"

"He was a Damned. He is a slave now."

"Kccch... then you live." He scrutinized me for a minute more. "Who are you, mortal?"

"DIRE."

He recoiled from my screeching roar, then stared at me, nictitating membranes sliding back and forth over his eyes. "Dire? Dire? The Dire who conquered Caym?"

"YOU KNOW OF DIRE?"

"Yes! Ah, did she have her armor of metal?"

"She was wearing such a thing, Lord Shudderworm."

Shudderworm. Okay, now I had a name to work with.

"Kssss... yes. Fortunate, then, that you wore a thing weak to our shaping. Yes, Great Blasphemy Buer will pay well for you, Dire. Fear not, you shall remain alive until then."

"OR," I said, standing as tall as I could with a junked up knee, "YOU COULD GIVE HER BACK THE ITEMS AND MATERIALS YOU HAVE STOLEN FROM HER, AND SEND HER ON HER WAY."

There was a pause. "You speak strangely. Are you asking to be freed?"

"OF COURSE NOT."

"Good, because that would be a foolish—"

"DIRE IS TELLING YOU THAT YOU HAVE THE OPTION OF FREEING HER, SETTLING YOUR DEBT TO HER, AND PARTING

WAYS WITHOUT OFFENDING HER FURTHER."

His mandibles slid together as he hissed like a thousand snakes having an orgy. My captors followed suit.

"I do not think you understand the situation."

"AND SHE DOES NOT THINK THAT YOU UNDERSTAND THE UNSTOPPABLE FORCE THAT IS DIRE."

"We shall see. Take her to the cells. Eh?"

There was movement to my side, and I turned to see one of the snaky demons ooze out of the wall and land on one of the supporting spires. "He will strike in seventy seconds," the demon whispered.

Instantly Shudderworm stopped laughing. "Get her clear of the room and brace. If she falls in the lava I'll eat your bones."

They hustled me back through the entrance and I bit back a yelp of pain when my knee paid the price. Then they held me against the corridor wall, and put their arms over my head. "Don't move. If a rock falls and crushes you, we will—"

The cave shook, as another explosion rumbled through the tunnels. North, I'd estimate. I checked the compass in my mask HUD and nodded. I knew about where we were, now.

But another thought preyed on my mind. "NOW HOW DID YOUR BOSS KNOW OF DIRE?"

"He is our lord, not our... baaas, whatever that is."

"DIRE'S ONLY BEEN ACTIVE FOR TWO MONTHS DOWN HERE. HOW DID HE HEAR?"

"That is none of your affair," the rightmost demon told me, then they jerked me away from the wall. He half-guided, half-dragged me down the corridor.

Fortunately we didn't have far to go. The cells were pits in the floor, half of them covered with metal grates. They pointed at an open one, and I scrambled down into it as best I could, hissing between my teeth as my knee took more pressure than I'd wanted.

They stared down, I stared up, and they wove their hands together in strange, short little passes. Crooning a song that didn't have words, they gestured as if they were knitting...

...and in a way they *were*, since rods slid out of the rocky lip of the pit, and criss-crossed it in a loose spiral, just like the other metal grates I'd seen around this chamber.

As soon as it was done they turned and left my sight. I considered my predicament, sat down on my haunches, and chuckled.

They hadn't even searched me.

I'd been in this situation before, over the years. Any professional supervillain who's worth their salt has to deal with captivity now and again. And when it does come up, you want your plans lined up in advance. This was a twenty-two dash F, I figured, with a few adjustments to deal with the fact that the demons could melt into the surrounding stone.

My mask's sensory suite wasn't as good as the full battery that the armor could bring to bear, but it had a few advantages over baseline human limitations. But before I did anything, I slumped against the wall and dialed up my audio sensors. The first mistake that amateur villains make is to try to escape immediately. Smart captors expect you to be impatient; they'll keep an eye on you for a bit, surreptitiously, to ensure you won't pull a runner.

Sure enough, about forty minutes later I heard scales on stone at the far end of the chamber. Sounded like they were leaving, and I waited until they were out of my instruments' detection range I proceeded to the next part of twenty-two F. With adjustments.

I focused the audio sensors on the walls, fine-tuned them, and pushed my mask against the stone. Though I couldn't be certain, I heard a few things at the edge of my range that sounded like frying bacon. The way they were moving suggested serpentine patterns.

I also heard something from a few chambers over that sounded familiar. Delta's voice! But distorted, uneven. Had they captured her? Perhaps damaged her on the way over? But no, she didn't sound upset.

Well, so much for the first adjustment. I reached into the hidden sheath at the small of my back and pulled out the monofilament cutter. It was agony to climb up the side of the pit with my knee awash in pain, but I gritted my teeth and pushed through it. *I am Dire. I will not be stopped, especially by my own body.*

The cutter did its work, and I caught the metal grating before it could fall on my head. Then it was sweaty, undignified work to squirm and clamber my way out. I tore my clothes a bit on the sharp edges, but I counted it a small price to pay.

Then I rose and surveyed the cave. Going by the small shifts my directed audio had picked up, every grated pit held a prisoner in it.

There wasn't much I could do for them, not right now. The Damned feared demons, in all but the most extreme cases. Or unless they were emboldened by a clear example of the demons' vulnerability. I didn't have time to check them for bold souls, or to set up an example of my might, and I couldn't take the risk that one of them might betray me. So I turned my back and moved to leave.

The distant explosion hit as I did so, and I got the audio dialed down just in time to save my eardrums. Still hurt like a fucker. Extending the monofilament cutter to knife length, I kept it loose, pointed out, at hip level as I limped down the passage that I thought would take me towards Delta's voice.

It took a few twists and turns. Once I was sure the explosion was done I dialed my audio back up again, and that helped quite a bit. Finally I came to what I was searching for.

Delta wasn't in the cave.

A chunk of quartz, wrapped with copper wire formed into thorny looking sigils, *was*. Delta's voice, and a faint image of the gaming table in the arena at Caym, flickered in and out in the clear spots of the quartz. I could vaguely make out the forms of First Chain, Delta's duplicate body, and a few assorted Damned and demons I wasn't too familiar with.

They had a television, of sorts. A hell-o-vision? Couldn't say. I wasn't surprised that they had *something*, probably as a surveillance device. Imps only got you so far, after all, and we never did find out how that fat worm back in Caym got word to the Wrathlands so quickly.

In front of the crystal, coiled up with his mandibled face resting on his fists, looking all the world like a kid watching Saturday morning cartoons, was the runtiest snake demon I'd seen so far. Oh, he was as long as the rest of them, but he was scrawny, underfed and with a back covered in scars.

I watched in silence, as he perked up his head, reached for a nearby handful of what I'd initially taken to be pebbles, and cast them onto the ground. He was following the 'action' on the crystal device, I realized, making hit rolls as the game's fight went on. I restrained laughter as he drew his hand down a nearby stalagmite, adjusting what he probably thought was a mockup of a character sheet.

I looked down at the monofilament blade, then back up to him. I could kill him, probably. He was scrawny, and the muscular ones weren't much tougher than the human baseline.

I could kill him, sure. Or maybe...

I turned the monofilament cutter away and tucked it behind my back. Then I walked forward, taking it slow. Once I was within forty feet, I cleared my throat.

He jumped straight up, landed on his coiled tail, and wailed with despair as his stone dice went sailing in every direction.

"GREETINGS. DO YOU KNOW THIS MASK?"

"It is a Doctor Dire mask," he replied back in flawless English. "Wait. Are you... do you enjoy this game as well? I thought it had not spread down here." He seemed to frown. "And why is a Damned wearing clothes? Let alone a mask?"

"SHE'S NOT DAMNED. LISTEN CLOSELY."

He slithered in and craned his head down toward my chest. I resisted the urge to knife him, and boy, did it take willpower. We were still in the lands of Wrath, and it would have felt so, so good to kill him. But letting my anger overwhelm my common sense had gotten me *here*, and lost me a perfectly good suit of armor, so I shoved it down and watched him carefully.

He straightened up after a minute and looked at me, eyes wide. "You are mortal!"

"SHE IS DIRE."

"But wait, Dire is in Caym. This makes no sense."

"IT IS A RUSE. THE DIRE THERE IS A DUPLICATE, AS IS THE DELTA. DELTA IS HERE AS WELL, NOT FAR AWAY."

His eyes went wide. I watched those rainbow-sparkling pupils twitch and expand with pure joy... at least, that was my estimate of it. "She is here? The teacher herself?"

Shit, Pagliacci was right. They *were* people, just more pathetic than most. No matter how bad the world up above got, there was still hope. Down here? Crushing boredom, casual cruelty, a hierarchy that dumped endless amounts of shit on the weak, and an economy that was mostly made up of people.

But while pity was one thing, it was another thing entirely to lower your guard or pretend that the demons were no less dangerous for their misery.

"YES, SHE IS NOT FAR. BUT DIRE NEEDS TO GET TO HER. YOUR LORD IS UNDER THE FOOLISH IMPRESSION THAT HE HAS TAKEN DIRE HOSTAGE. SHE IS GOING TO REMEDY THAT. HE MAY TRY TO KILL DELTA FOR THIS DELUSION."

"What? He would! He's a terror!" The demon's tail lashed in obvious distress. "You don't understand; he can't kill her! Not before I meet her!"

This was like bribing a kid to give you the keys to his parent's car.

"WELL HE'LL TRY. WE'LL HAVE TO STOP THAT. ER... WHAT'S YOUR NAME, AGAIN?"

"I am Eighty-First Worm." he looked down with what was probably shame.

"PLAY YOUR CARDS RIGHT, AND THAT NUMBER WILL BE UP BY THE END OF THIS DAY."

"Um... the game uses dice, not cards. And what is a day?"

"NEVER MIND." I pointed at the crystal. "WHAT IS THIS AND WHAT IS IT USED FOR?"

"Ah, it, ah, it is a Lurkcrystal node. By tuning to the aetherwaves and the other crystals we have nearby, it allows us to watch the mines."

"BUT IT IS SHOWING CAYM, NOT THE TUNNELS AROUND

HERE."

He fidgeted. "I might have found a way to extend the reception and tap into a different crystal chain by riding the leyline channels, and the blood resonance of the nearest branch of the Styx."

"DIRE HAS NO IDEA WHAT YOU JUST SAID, BUT SHE LIKES THE NOTION. SO NORMALLY YOU SIT HERE AND WATCH THE MINES?"

"Yes. I'm not sure why; we are out here in the middle of nowhere." he fiddled with the copper bindings around the crystal, tracing along them and rerouting them. "There is absolutely nothing... to..."

The crystal flickered and brought up an image of tunnels packed with screaming Damned, swarming over the few worm demons in their way, bashing at them with rocks. At the rear of them, I caught a glimpse of a big man, a familiar man, waving around a worm demon's decapitated head with his left hand, and a knife with his right.

For someone who'd lost his head that was a pretty quick recovery time. But I was glad to see Pagliacci up and kicking, gladder still to see him providing a distraction.

I loved my species, at that moment, in all their primitive, mob-minded glory. All it took to rally them was a reminder that the demons could die.

"Oh no! They'll have to drop that tunnel."

"WILL THEY?"

"Yes! The Damned have gone mad. They must be sealed away before the contagion spreads, and—"

"NO. NO THEY MUST NOT. DELTA IS BACK THERE, TOO. WOULD YOU MISS YOUR ONLY CHANCE TO MEET HER?"

"Ah..." he fell silent.

I smiled under my mask as I watched him wrestle with himself. Dreams versus loyalty was what it came down to in the end. But I knew which side would win. Hope is a pernicious emotion, even in Hell.

"What shall we do?" he asked, and I knew I had him.

"FIRE UP THIS CRYSTAL. YOU SAY THAT YOU CAN TAP INTO THE LURKCRYSTALS OF OTHER CHAINS?"

"Yes, but I don't see what—"

"LOOK FOR CHAINS THAT ARE AROUND HERE BUT THAT SHOULD NOT BE." I had my suspicions, and finally, a way to test them. "FOCUS ON CHAINS THAT SHOULD BE IN CAYM."

"All right, but I don't think we'll find anything." He fiddled with the crystal, and copper sigils bloomed and withered as he went. I monitored the emissions through my voltaic vision, trying to figure out what he was doing. I got about half of it, I thought. I needed to study this thing in a proper lab. Hell, for that matter, I needed a proper lab. That might not be too hard to do, if good old wormy here had as much geomantic magic as his peers.

"This is strange," he remarked, as the image flickered again. "There is a crystal above, within a few R'lw."

"MMHM. PUT HER ON."

"Her? Very well." He waved a hand, and the copper parted like a flower unfurling, an image resolving on the crystal; the upper parts of a pair of oversized breasts.

I snorted. I knew those tits. They'd been shoved in my general direction at every opportunity. "CAN SHE HEAR US?"

"Er, now she can." He twisted a copper strand.

"FIRST WHISPER," I rumbled, as I leaned on a pair of stalagmites. "YOU HAVE BEEN KEEPING SECRETS."

It was worth it to see her jump. The viewpoint spun, revealing rocks, ash, and a very surprised-looking Khalid. "AH GOOD, YOU'RE NOT ALONE."

"I, ah, I, Doctor!" Flawlessly manicured fingers closed around the viewpoint for a second, then her face filled the screen, peering down at me. "What is this sorcery?"

"YOU HAVE BEEN SPYING. IT'S CUTE. DIRE WAS GOING TO LET IT GO AND USE THAT TO HER ADVANTAGE LATER, BUT SOMETHING MORE IMPORTANT'S COME UP."

"What?" Eighty-First Worm was surprised. "That makes no sense."

"SHUSH. WHISPER, IS EVERYONE AROUND YOU? THE CHORUS? KHALID AND VECTOR?"

"Yes, we have gathered together. Most of the Damned from Beaky are here as well. Some probably haven't revived yet, we are trying to find them."

"GOOD. PUT KHALID ON, WE HAVE MUCH TO DO AND LITTLE TIME TO DO IT IN."

"What are we doing, now?"

I filled them in on the plan, my location, and the state of Pagliacci's current riot.

"You let the murderclown off the chain?" Vector said, shaking his head. "Bad idea."

"MORE OF A FACTOR OF NOT BEING AROUND TO STOP HIM. LET'S JUST SAY HE POPPED HIS COLLAR."

"What?"

"NEVERMIND. GO AHEAD AND TURN IT OFF, WORM."

"I... what?"

"CLOSE THE LINK TO DIRE'S COMRADES."

Once it was closed, I leaned in. "RARE METALS ARE WHAT

YOU'RE AFTER HERE, RIGHT? THERE IS A VAULT SOMEWHERE THAT HOLDS SCAVENGED METALS, YES?"

"Well, yes, when we detect them within reach of our magic, we pull them down to the sifters."

I holstered my blade and pulled out my Colt 1911 Army Pistol. "SHOW HER THE WAY THERE. SHE'S GOT A FEW THINGS TO SALVAGE FROM THE WRECK OF HER SUIT."

CHAPTER 16: UNDERGROUND RESISTANCE

"In the end, it's on the characters to remember that there are more ways to resolve a hostile foe than simply fighting them."

--Excerpt from the second book of the Chronicles of the Shared Lie; The Monster Master's Methods

One painful, hobbling journey, three bullets, and three bleeding demon corpses later, I was staring at a long, obviously-artificially-created cavern full of piles of scrap and salvage, including my suit, and what was probably a good chunk of the metallic debris from Beaky. Not all of it, but then the dragon had probably swallowed a lot of the good stuff. This was what was left after he finished his messy mastication.

But it was enough. I dug out the portable toolkit I kept taped to my calf with flesh-colored bindings, knelt next to my crushed suit as much as my bum knee would allow, and got to work.

They'd come close to breaching the reactor, I noted. I was soaking up some rads just by sitting here. Probably not enough to kill me: it was a fusion rig and not one of those fission deathtraps. But I'd probably want to get checked out by Vector or someone down the road once I got out of Hell. Tumors aren't my idea of fun.

When I'd just started out, I had cannibalized a dead hero's suit of power armor, one that was made entirely of recycled junk. I kept the basic functionality, gave it a few extra tricks, and ended up with a battleworthy set of armor that saw me through some pretty horrible times. It had only failed due to treachery, and even then it had been a near thing.

Now, sitting here in a cave with a box of scraps, I built my suit anew. Couldn't salvage the reactor. Without the shielding, that would turn a long-term health risk into short-term suicide. But I could rig up a breastplate and greaves combo with a few low-powered gravitic balancers that meant I wasn't walking everywhere.

Then came a quick layer of spray-plastic. Nothing fancy, just enough to keep the demons' metal-crunching powers at bay. Hopefully, anyway. From the readings I'd taken, the answers Eighty-First Worm provided me, and my own estimates, their magic required direct contact between the earth and whatever material they were manipulating.

After that, I rigged up a basic Tesla Deflector and stripped down one of the particle blasters, turning the arm into a literal long-arm. Without a direct fusion link the whole rig had limited power, but I whipped up a double-set of chemical battery packs using the other raw metals in the room and a few choice chemicals brewed up on the spot.

"EAT YOUR FUCKING HEART OUT, MACGYVER," I muttered as I hefted the particle blaster. I'd learned the tolerances of the Worms to energy weapons the last time around. I wouldn't make the same mistake twice. I had things set for highly charged blasts, focused down to minimum length. They'd go through stone, go through flesh, go through demons, without stopping.

During this hours-long building fest, the distant explosions rumbled twice more. "WHAT ARE THOSE THINGS ANYWAY?"

"The slave that Lord Shudderworm obtained in the fleshmarkets of Dis. He is the reason that we were able to get out here and set up so quickly."

"REALLY?"

"He is strong! Stronger than any Damned or demon that I have ever seen. Er, not that I have seen many demon lords. And tough, too. I do not know how they tamed him, or what keeps him here."

"IS HE MAGICAL OR SOMETHING?"

"No. They say not. I don't understand how, I think... I think he is one of those new people they talk about. The ones that showed up in Creation a century ago, one of those creatures."

I recalled how the Council of Worms had somehow gotten ahold of Punching Judy and how they'd turned her against me.

It would be the height of foolishness to think that she was the only metahuman in Hell. This added a wrinkle to the plan.

I checked the chronometer. Time enough to meet the first wave of my reinforcements and adjust the plan slightly. This needed investigation; it had the potential to bite us in the ass if we weren't careful.

"CHECKMATE IN FIVE THEN, INSTEAD OF FOUR." I clicked on my hover mode and rose up into the air, sighed as the pressure left my over-stressed leg. "COME ON, EIGHTY-FIRST WORM. THE GAME'S AFOOT!"

"What?"

"JUST FOLLOW."

It was amazing how easy it was to get used to the guy, I thought, as I hovered through close corridors and tight turns. I'd known many people back on Earth with much the same attitude toward something they obsessed over. A geek was a geek, whether human or demon. Didn't hurt that he was basically sorcerous tech support.

In any case, he was the perfect shadow. The guy hung back, nervously, calling up directions as I navigated the tunnels. We passed through caves full of more Damned, digging at the walls with rocks, and they all ran from me as though their hair was on fire. I couldn't really blame them. We came upon our first demonic overseer at the end of the cave, chasing after his fleeing charges with a jointed metal lash in his hands. One blast later, he was on the floor, thrashing and leaking in his death throes. I cycled the particle blaster back up, eyed the readings, and called it a good field test.

"I knew him," my demonic buddy said behind me. I turned, keeping the arm-turned-cannon pointed nowhere in particular.

"OH?"

"He was Thirtieth Worm."

"DIRE BELIEVES IT POSSIBLE THAT THE TRUTH OF THE SITUATION HAS NOT YET SUNK INTO YOUR MIND YET. BY THE TIME WE ARE THROUGH HERE, WE ARE GOING TO GET YOU A PROMOTION TO FIRST WORM, THE EASY WAY."

"Don't you mean the hard way?"

I looked to the gun, looked back at him, and shrugged. "NO, NOT REALLY."

That shut him up for a while.

Three more kilometers, two more tunnels full of frightened slaves, and one more dead overseer later, we reached a junction, and from the north, I could hear angry people shouting and screaming. "AND THERE'S THE FIRST MOVE DONE."

A horde of people fled past me... and I recognized one of them, a pale man with a widow's peak. He nodded to me, I nodded back and adjusted my aim. "NO," I said as the pale man moved like lightning and grabbed my demon buddy's neck with both hands. "THAT ONE'S ON OUR SIDE."

"Sorry," said Beta, releasing him and turning around.

His new skin fit him well, all things considered. I was glad Vector had gotten them onto the androids before that stupid dragon rained on my parade. And the skin had set up the first move of my little play.

The first phase had been to send in the skinjobs to infiltrate, assassinate, and disappear back into the crowd. Judging by the panic, it was working. "THE OTHERS?"

"They are scraping up more demons to kill. Oh, and the group of three chasing me should be here in five seconds, coming out of that tunnel."

"THANK YOU." I pulled a screamer grenade from my belt, armed it, and tossed it down the tunnel in question. "OH HEY, COVER YOUR EARS," I told my wormy friend.

"What? Why—"

"TOO LATE."

The screamers were sonic grenades. The Worms had sensitive hearing, especially through stone or other things they were melded into. First Worm thrashed on the floor, covering his ears too late... and he wasn't even within the estimated kill radius.

After the screamer burned itself out, I floated over the tunnel and studied the limp forms of three and a half demons. The last one had been caught in the act of extruding himself from the wall, poor bastard. Evidently death interrupted that power.

I drilled them with head shots just to be certain, then turned around to see Delta and Epsilon behind me. Delta was a bit chunky, clad in a brown-haired woman's form. Small tits, per Gamma's request. Epsilon was slim, sporting a handsome face and hair drawn back in a blonde ponytail.

"THAT THE LAST OF THEM?"

"It should be. Alpha collapsed the only passage that our mob could flee down. The overseers should be dead by now."

"DIRE'S KIND OF SURPRISED THEY DIDN'T BRING THE WHOLE TUNNEL DOWN."

"They tried. It turns out they need a little time to do their geomancy schtick. We didn't give them that time, and then the mob was too close. You know they're not too much sturdier than people?"

"NOT TO PHYSICAL ATTACKS, NO." Energy weapons diffused pretty badly against their scales, it seemed. Some sort of silicoid component. "COME ON, LET'S GET MOVING."

As we moved through the riled up and confused crowd, I saw a ring of Damned closing in around where I'd left my wormy buddy. "WHOOP! HEY NOW!" I drilled a few, and they scattered...

...revealing a torn up Beta, a pile of disabled Damned, and a cowering demon. I looked over Beta's exposed metal bones. "YOUR FACE IS HALF OFF."

"Sorry." He reached up and tore the rest of it off. "Does this mean I'm off the infiltration crew?"

"Yes. Head back up and mind the exit," Alpha said, and looking him over, I couldn't say if he was male or female. He'd gone for slicked-back black hair, androgynous features, and a slim build without any external genitalia. Entirely his privilege, but I wondered if it had hurt his infiltration efforts.

"DOPPELGANGERS," I tested the word.

Delta stared at me. "What?"

"YOU'RE DOPPELGANGERS! THAT'S THE PERFECT NAME FOR YOUR SERIES!"

"Please," Delta snorted. "We're way higher challenge rating than doppelgangers. At least an eight. Apiece."

"You!" First Worm surged to a relatively upright position, hands clasped to his head, staring at her with awe. "I know that voice! You are the Delta!"

"*The* Delta? I'm moving up in the world!" She smiled, and offered a plump hand. "Pleezedameetcha!"

"Please! Please let me play the Monsters and Mangonels with you!"

"LATER," I said, jerking my head toward the now-cleared tunnel. "AFTER YOU SHOW HER WHERE PAGLIACCI'S REBELLION IS RIGHT NOW."

He led us about three kilometers through twisting tunnels—

—to a solid wall of stone, with gasping heads and twitching hands protruding from it.

My good mood vanished instantly. Shudderworm's hellions had noticed the rebellion, and dealt with it in the most expedient manner possible. Boom, squish, and a few hundred Damned were now trapped under thousands of tons of rock for a very, very long time.

I felt my lips skin back against my teeth. "WE KILL THAT FUCKER. THEN WE FREE THESE POOR BASTARDS."

"Why?" First Worm asked.

There came a crack of flesh on scales. That would be Alpha, I knew. And sure enough, I heard my First Android whispering to him. I don't know quite what he said, because I was already moving, already searching for a way around.

I found one. And then I found Pagliacci.

Slicked in blood from head to toe, holding a demon aloft with one mighty-thewed arm, he had his other hand buried deep in an open wound in the creature's side.

"I think I'm going to be sick," Alpha muttered.

Pagliacci pulled his hand free in a shower of gore. The demon convulsed, and its mandibles gaped wide as the evil clown fed the demon one of its own internal organs.

"Not going down too well? Stuck in your throat?" Pagliacci cooed to it. "Well, that's the *choke*." He dropped the demon, turned to me, and smiled with his bloody hand up in greeting. "You're late."

"YOU'RE DISGUSTING."

"You knew what I was when you accepted my offer." He cracked his neck, studied his hand, and straightened a broken finger. "Or so you thought, anyway. Shall we move on?"

"LET'S." Okay, so I hadn't collected an angry mob full of motivated Damned, but I wasn't about to leave him wandering around in these dark tunnels.

At my back.

First Worm skittered far back, keeping the Chorus in between himself and Pagliacci. Alpha drew back his hand to slap the demon again, but in an eyeblink, Delta grabbed Alpha's arm and shook her head. He backed off, and Delta draped her arm over the demon's shoulders.

Pagliacci, for his part, fell in next to me as I hovered through the tunnels. "I was having fun while I was waiting for you."

"SHE SAW YOUR IDEA OF FUN REMOTELY. LOOKED LIKE A RIOT."

"Are you surprised?"

"NOT REALLY. THAT'S MORE OR LESS YOUR THING. REBELLING AGAINST THE RIGHTFUL AUTHORITIES AND INCITING A BUNCH OF PEOPLE WHO REALLY KNOW BETTER THAN TO DIE IN YOUR SERVICE."

He chuckled, honest, open laughter, and I welcomed it. Better that than the Hannibal Lecter shit he had tried earlier. Still, the statement seemed to draw more amusement than it was worth, and I was glad when the creepy fucking clown stopped laughing.

"We are not far," First Worm whispered, quivering in fear as Pagliacci shot him a glance.

"GOOD. THIS WILL DO, THEN." I gestured to a large, open cavern.

Then I adjusted my particle cannon and fired upward. Shrapnel rained off my forcefield, making me flare with light in the darkness, as everyone else scattered. I paused a few seconds, then shot another blast up into the ceiling.

When the dust settled, First Worm was thoroughly unsettled. "There's no way they will not have heard that!"

"RIGHT. WE SHOULD PROBABLY BE RUNNING. TO THE EASTERN CAVERNS!"

They followed me while I killed my force field and cycled power to the gravitics. Behind me the ceiling shook, and stone ground on stone. "THEY'VE BEEN TRACKING US SINCE WE ENTERED THE TUNNELS," I explained. "THE SONICS PROBABLY BOUGHT SOME TIME, BUT IF THEY'RE SENSITIVE ENOUGH TO HEAR ROCK SCRAPING ON ROCK, THEN THEY'RE SENSITIVE ENOUGH TO HEAR THE SOUNDS OF FIGHTING. THEY WERE WAITING TO SEE HOW THINGS WENT IN YOUR PART OF THE ACTION," I gestured back to my Chorus. My Doppelgangers, now. "BUT WITH YOU?" I moved my finger to Pagliacci. "THEY HAD NO REASON NOT TO DROP MORE OF THE TUNNEL TO CATCH A STRAGGLER ONCE YOU FINISHED OFF THAT LAST GUY. THEY WERE PROBABLY JUST WAITING FOR HIM TO CHECK IN. HENCE THE BLAST."

Alpha wasn't sold. "I'm not sure how that helps us. Once they finish dropping the tunnel they'll be able to find us again, with a little persistence."

"TRUE. HOWEVER, THAT WASN'T JUST A DISTRACTION. IT WAS ALSO A SIGNAL." The tunnel behind us filled with the sound of collapsing caverns. But we were well away from the blast center. They were firing blind. If they hadn't been, we wouldn't have gotten this far. It had been a gamble but a small one.

"A signal for what?" Alpha asked.

The ground shook, and rock tumbled, ahead of us, for a change.

"We're fucked!" Delta skidded to a halt.

"NO. THERE'S SOMEONE FUCKED HERE," I said, as light pierced the caverns from above and a chi-infused bubble rolled down the newly-created ramp. It popped, revealing familiar figures. "BUT IT'S NOT US."

Punching Judy straightened up, peered at us through the nightvision goggles I'd made her a week ago and squealed as she ran past me. "Delta!"

"Sweetie!"

Ahead of me, Vector adjusted his spectacles and looked away. Five Spitters crouched next to him, glaring around with their heat-sensitive pits. Khalid, blade free and glowing bluer as he approached, squinted at First Worm. "Ah. Terrestrials. This one seems remarkably alive at the minute."

"HE'S A TURNCOAT. SPEAKING OF WHICH, WE HAVE ONE MORE POINT OF BUSINESS." I stabbed my finger north. "THEY'VE

GOT AN UNKNOWN METAHUMAN. WE'RE GOING TO ADD HIM TO OUR COLLECTION."

Punching Judy's lips popped as she pulled them away from Delta's face. "Hey! Stop talkin' about us as if we're pokermons!"

"NO," I told her, "GET YOUR ASS OUT OF HERE BEFORE WE GET GEODUDED."

My collared demons peered down from the hole in the roof as we headed out, and I waved at The Cat and First Whisper, impatiently. "YES, YOU TOO, COME ON."

We ran. Well, they ran, I flew. Khalid kept pace beside me easily, legs eating up meters without hesitation. "YOU'RE DOING REMARKABLY WELL."

"This time I took my combat elixirs before the descent."

"He's running on full buffs!" Delta shouted.

"Neeeeerrrrdddd!" Judy shouted back at her. "Whoop, tunnel's changin'. Hold on."

The tunnel around us groaned. As before, rock started to crumble against rock...

...and Judy whipped her arms around, hopped up on the nearest stalagmite, and posed. Energy pushed out of her, white and black waves of it, and I shivered as it passed through me.

The tunnel stopped creaking.

"What was that?" First Worm asked, reeling. I gestured to Pagliacci, who grabbed his arm and pulled him along.

"THAT WAS CHI MANIPULATION."

Back before this whole mess started, I'd researched Judy's supergroup in preparation for our inevitable encounter. She'd been one of the most dangerous of the Queensguard and the most flexible. Her chi manipulation not only allowed her to hit stupidly hard, but she could do things like, oh, stabilizing unstable geomantic forces.

Like whatever the hell sort of sorcery the worms were using to collapse the tunnels.

And after a few minutes, with Judy stopping every thirty seconds to do a new pose and flashy thing, I started to see a red glow ahead. "COMING UP ON THE END OF IT. GET READY."

"Oh, we are," a familiar voice echoed as we burst out into a vast cavern. Coiled on pillars of stone planted in the lava, Shudderworm and about twenty of his lackeys greeted us by slamming their hands simultaneously into the ground, sending sprays of stony spikes blasting throughout the cave.

I tanked a few on my forcefield, twisting aside as I flew, and rained down golden fury onto them. As I did so I saw chains above me, massive chains threaded through countless loops of stone. Those had to have been geomancied up there, I was fairly sure. Following the chain back towards the center of the cavern, I saw a pillar of iron held lengthwise, something like a SWAT team breaching ram the size of a skyscraper.

And sitting underneath it, wearing the first pair of trousers I'd seen in Hell that my crew hadn't made, was a man with a cleft chin, black, spit-curled hair, and a torso with muscles that looked like they'd been poured into a mold.

He looked back at us, sat the skyscraper down, and started bounding through the pillars.

"INCOMING HERO!" I bellowed, sparing a glance at my teammates. Judy was posing and flexing for all she was worth, undoing the spikeshots as fast as they came. Couldn't spare her from that, it was pretty important. Khalid was leaping from pillar to pillar, throwing vials and cutting down demons. No help there. Vector was cowering in the back and directing his Spitters to chase and acid-blast the demons trying to flank us, so he'd be useless for this. Meanwhile my Chorus was too busy running interference and defending the metahumans, so here we were.

I looked to First Whisper, then over to The Cat. They were focusing mainly on staying alive. "YOU'RE WITH DIRE. COME ON."

Then someone grabbed onto my legs, and with a squeak of surprise, I shot up further into the air.

"Slowly, please. That lava looks painful." Pagliacci told me, arms wrapped around my knees.

"SHE SHOULD DROP YOUR ASS INTO IT."

"That may be the fate of us all, if that man is who I think he is."

I stayed silent rather than admit he had a point and jetted past the main part of the fight. As we passed Khalid, his blade flared with white light, and I jerked my head away before my mask could overload. Pagliacci grunted in pain. "GOOD TRICK, BAD TIMING, KHALID."

"So inconsiderate of him," Pagliacci agreed.

First Whisper passed me, half her skin crisped, with The Cat hanging on for dear life in her arms. She shot me a needy glance as she went, then pouted as I ignored her obvious pain.

I *was* a little impressed, but Khalid had warned me not to encourage her. Positive reinforcement would lead to obsession and that would lead to nothing good.

As I got closer, the man flew up to meet me, face silhouetted against the glow of the lava for a split-second... and I knew him.

"HOLY FUCKING SHIT."

He frowned. "Please watch your language, ma'am."

"YOU'RE THE AMERICAN PARAGON."

"I was." He stopped, and we regarded each other from a hundred yards away. Pagliacci tapped my hip, and I flew down a few dozen feet, so he could drop and land on the biggest pillar of basalt. This close to it, I could see bare footprints literally dug into the stone. I glanced upward, to where the iron skyscraper hung just above the track that had been worn into the basalt.

First Whisper and The Cat dropped on the stone next to Pagliacci, and the American Paragon hovered down, face solemn as he stared at me from across the way.

"IT'S CRUDE, BUT EFFECTIVE." I pointed at the giant ram. "THEY HAVE YOU DRAW IT BACK, THEN RAM IT INTO THE ROCK WALL. EVERY HALF HOUR, OR SO."

"It takes that long to pull it out and draw it back."

"THEN THEY GEOMANCY UP NEW LOOPS FOR THE CHAIN, AND EXTEND IT THROUGH THE NEW TUNNEL. RINSE, REPEAT, AND YOU END UP WITH A MASSIVE COMPLEX OF TUNNELS." I glanced up, where some of the rock loops were looking rather crumbled. "PROBABLY TAKES A HELL OF A LOT OF MAINTENANCE SO THOSE LOOPS DON'T GIVE WAY. THE WEIGHT ON THEM IS PRETTY SERIOUS."

"That's about the size of it." His pectorals strained and he punched a fist into an open palm, making my gravitics whine, and fight desperately to keep from being pushed backward from the wave of force. Below me First Whisper wailed as she flew toward the edge. Pagliacci caught her and The Cat with a grunt of effort, straining against the wind but managing to succeed at the last second. Lucky, lucky evil clown.

There is a reason that flying, superstrong superheroes are called paragons, and it was hovering right in front of me. This man had defined three generations of heroes of his type, and he'd killed more Nazis than most divisions had during his time on the Western Front.

His time had ended rather abruptly, though, and I had a hunch I knew why. I'd been back then, and I'd seen the Nazis' personal equalizer for problems of American Paragon's caliber.

No matter how strong you are, there is always someone stronger.

"I'll ask you to retreat, Ma'am. There's no way for you to win this fight."

"DID YOU RETREAT AGAINST SCHWARZER RITTER?"

He froze, a look of pain crossing his face. "No, and look where it got me."

"But that wasn't your sin, was it?" Pagliacci's voice oozed from below. "That wasn't what brought you down here. It was just what sealed the deal."

"That's none of your business, sir. Please leave."

"WHY? WHY WORK FOR DEMONS?"

"I don't have a choice in the matter. This is my penance." He glanced back to Shudderworm and the bulk of the fighting. I glanced back as well. Half the Spitters were down, and Khalid was on the defensive. They'd taken down a handful of the demons, but the ones that were left were coordinated and strong. It could go either way... unless I resolved this quickly and reinforced them.

"And I can't let you stall me," he said, coming to the same conclusion I did. "If you won't leave, I'll have to make you."

I dropped as he came for me, but he was faster than a Spitfire, just like his comic books had said. My breastplate rang like a gong, the breath went out of me, and I hurled back a few hundred feet. For a desperate second I was vulnerable, while the gravitics churned to compensate...

...but he didn't spare me a second look, turning and zooming toward Pagliacci.

....Who dodged him, leaping up and grabbing the iron auger, before crawling up it like a greasepaint-and-blood-coated spider.

"What drives you, fallen hero?" Pagliacci called over his shoulder, with a wicked cackle. I swear to gods, he was enjoying this.

Damned if I'd let him upstage me in front of a *hero*.

"SHE TRIED TO DO THIS THE EASY WAY. SO BE IT! YOU FACE DOCTOR DIRE NOW, AMERICAN PARAGON! AND THE MAN WHO KILLED YOU?" I cranked up the particle cannon. "SHE FUCKING BEAT HIM!"

"Wait, what?" He turned just as my particle beam caught him, blasting him across the cavern, arms flailing... until he slowed. Stopped.

My particle cannon chimed warnings in my HUD. I focused the beam, landed on the platform, rerouted power as I blazed away at him...

...and he waded through it, taking it all on his chest, grunting and powering through it.

Paragons.

This was what they did.

Then the cannon chimed and blew a breaker. The beam flickered, dropped to half strength, and he was on me. I threw the useless gun away when he grabbed for where my breastplate met my mask, and lifted me into the air. "You lie!" He shouted, getting right up in my mask—

—and froze as First Whisper slid her hands onto his bare shoulders and pressed herself against his back. "Uh," he managed.

"You don't really want to hurt us," she whispered into his ear, moments before nibbling it. I saw her wince when her scarred side brushed him, but she held my gaze with pleading eyes.

I couldn't nod, so I gave her a thumbs up.

"Why don't you put her down?" Whisper whispered. Dazed, Paragon dropped me.

"GET CLEAR!" I commanded her. I knew something about Paragon, something she didn't. But she didn't listen, as her hands stroked up and down his sides, running along his chest, dipping lower...

"He's breaking the spell!" The Cat howled at her, and she barely had time to jerk back and away before the hero turned, murder in his eyes.

Just as I'd known he would. The American Paragon was famous for being able to resist mind control.

"That's enough of that, young lady!" He thundered at her, clapping his hands and blowing her off the ledge. He darted after her before she could hit the lava, caught her by the leg, and swung her around with a heavy CRACK as she hit the stone. She lay still. She could have maybe survived that, I supposed, but by then I was darting to the side, putting the iron ram between me and him.

"Pssst!" I slowed, glanced over to where The Cat was perched on top of the ram, trying to get my attention.

"Get off me, you clown!" I heard the paragon yell from below. Okay, I had a few seconds.

"WHAT?"

"He felt hopeful, when you said you beat Short Dinner. He really wants to believe you."

"SCHWARZER RITTER?"

"Whatever."

The Cat's mental powers weren't any sort of mind control, so I could believe they had worked here.

Crazy laughter swirled up from below, followed by the crunch of bones, and fists meeting flesh. The paragon was holding back, I could tell, because Pagliacci was still laughing. He was buying me time. And in the seconds before he fell silent, I thought through the ramifications of what The Cat had said... and how I could use it.

"THAT'S RIGHT!" I bellowed, as The Cat fled. "DIRE DID WHAT YOU COULD NOT! SHE BEAT SCHWARZER RITTER AND SAVED TESLA FROM HITLER! SHE SINGLE HANDEDLY WON THE WAR FOR THE ALLIES, NOT THAT THOSE INGRATES WOULD EVER ADMIT IT!"

A pause from below. Then that spit-curled, lantern-jawed face looked up. "Wait. You mean to tell me the Nazis *didn't* win the war?"

"THEY LOST IN FORTY-FIVE. ONCE SCHWARZER RITTER

HAD BEEN FREED FROM HIS MIND CONTROL IN FORTY-THREE, THE NAZIS WERE LOST WITHOUT THEIR EQUALIZER. THE GOOD GUYS WON."

He stared, wide-eyed, and I saw tears start at the corners of his eyes. "They told me we'd lost. That Hitler was running the world now."

"THEY LIED."

The American Paragon turned to glare at Shudderworm's back. "Yes. Yes, they did."

Two minutes later, after absolutely every last worm that wasn't my pet turncoat had been ripped in half or hurled into the lava far below, we managed to talk the American Paragon out of killing the newly-promoted First Worm.

We collected the amazingly still-breathing Pagliacci, who at this point was basically a bag of broken bones and sat on the iron skyscraper for a proper pow-wow. I filled American Paragon in on how we'd ended up here, and what we were doing about it.

"...SO THAT'S THE STORY. WE'RE EITHER GOING TO LEAVE HELL OR END UP SITTING UPON ITS THRONE BEFORE THIS IS ALL SAID AND DONE."

"Satan might have a thing or two to say about that," said American Paragon.

"YOU KNOW, SHE READ A COMIC BOOK ONCE. IT HAD A PICTURE OF YOU PUNCHING OUT HITLER ON THE FRONT OF IT."

"I'm sad to say that never happened, Ma'am. Though not for lack of trying."

"WANT TO DUPLICATE THAT POSE WITH THE DEVIL INSTEAD OF HITLER?"

He scratched his chin, and smiled. "I think I'm happy to be aboard, if you'll have me." The fallen legend shook my hand, refraining from crushing it into paste.

"SPEAKING OF ABOARD, WHAT'S THE STATUS OF OUR REMAINING STRIGES?" I glanced over to Alpha.

"They're playing keep away with the dragon. Gamma and Epsilon are coordinating, every time he starts getting close to one of them, the other will draw it off. The thing's stupid, so it's working pretty well."

"HOW LONG CAN THEY KEEP IT UP?"

Alpha shrugged. "Until they run out of food for the Striges, probably. A few weeks, at most. Maybe a month."

I looked down to the massive auger we were sitting on, then smiled underneath my mask. "RIGHT. FIRST STEP IS TO REBUILD THE VOX BOOSTER, THAT'LL BE A FEW HOURS, USING THE

SCRAPS THE WORMS STOLE FROM US."

"The first step usually implies a second step," Vector offered.

I tapped one of my multi-tools on the iron of the auger and smiled at the sound. "THEY JUST HANDED US A HELL OF A LOT OF RESOURCES AND AN IMMENSE SMELTING FACILITY. WE ARE GOING TO HAVE SOME FUN, HERE..."

CHAPTER 17: WRATH FADES, ENVY FESTERS

"In-party conflict happens, sometimes. A good Monster Master knows to stay out of it."

--Excerpt from the second book of the Chronicles of the Shared Lie; The Monster Master's Methods

Back in the ring of Sloth, under the influence of unseen forces that made us procrastinate and fiddle around, it had taken us weeks to build a basic setup for Beaky. We'd spent days building a *bathhouse,* for heck's sake.

It had been worth it, but that wasn't the point.

The point was that I'd unconsciously been sandbagging, earlier. And while Wrath ground on you, it also made a pretty good motivator. I poured my frustration into industry, with the help of a very concerned geomantic demon, my metahumans both dead and living, and the three members of the Chorus I had on hand.

And, oh, a few hundred Damned ex-slaves. The first project on the agenda had been to free them from that collapsed cave-in, and recruit the ones running around and hiding in the tunnels. For the most part, they were agreeable. They literally had nothing else to do, and if they wandered off into the unknown, something would probably eat them for all eternity, or they'd fall into lava and be fucked over for at least a couple of millennia.

In any case, we had the hands; I had the technology, and thanks to

Shudderworm and his recently-deceased crew, we had the materials.

Oh gods, did we *ever* have the materials. They'd collected the resources of a small country, all in one place for my harvest.

And by the time Gamma radioed in, letting me know that her Strix was starting to lose speed, we were ready to go.

"LURE THAT BIG STUPID BEAST TO SECTOR SIX-ONE-FOUR," I belted from my throne. Around me, riveted steel walls stretched out around the bridge. Two viewing ports provided a panoramic view of the vast vertical cavern around me. The Chorus stood along the wall, interfaced with my new lair's wi-fi. The lower decks held the Damned, the various labs and workshops we needed, and our cargo.

Everything else was machinery to power my penultimate achievement.

The Direnaut Mark II.

"JANISSARY, CYCLE THE REACTORS!" I called through the vox.

"On it!'

"VECTOR, GET READY FOR THE PRESSURE SHIFT!" This far down we had a life support system made of fungus, vat-tissue bladders, and some sort of cooling rig with blobby veins that sprawled throughout my steel giant.

"Yes, fine, whatever." He'd been pissy lately. I needed to find out why. Pissy, mad scientists were problems.

"JUDY! PARAGON! START YOUR ENGINES!"

"Ready an' willin'!"

"Yes Ma'am!"

Really big treadmills. No shit. It was simple; it used the immense amount of force they could bring to bear to good effect, and it was something they could keep up for pretty much fucking forever. My main engines were two metahumans. The fusion generator was just there as a backup, to keep the electronics going in the event that brute force failed.

Once Gamma and Epsilon radioed in that the dragon was in position, I threw the switch.

And twenty-two stories worth of robot thundered to life.

So impractical. So very very much a bad idea, at least on Earth. It was a big target, decidedly un-nuke-proof, actually kind of under-armored for its size, and with way too many weak points that heroes could punch for extra damage.

But then, we weren't on Earth, were we?

This was my magnum opus, my statement to Hell and all its denizens that I was going to personally come over and fuck them up, regardless of what was in my way. It was both a warning that I was coming that could be seen from miles away and a luxury lair that would see me and mine to the end of Hell and out of it. And gods help any who got in my path!

We surged upwards, banks of gravitic compensators humming to life, powered by the treadmill generators manned by American Paragon and Punching Judy. It was a mighty leap that punched through the ceiling of the cavern, and carried us up and out of the tunnels.

I monitored the gravitics as we went, adjusting madly as we soared to a stop kilometers away, then punched them up to full when we touched down. We sunk a few meters into the ground, but not enough to break through into the smaller caverns below.

And on the horizon, the dragon took notice. The Striges who were doing their exhausted best to stay equidistant to the big predator made a beeline for me, just as planned, then broke off once they were sure I held its attention.

It would have to be bored after fruitlessly chasing those tiny meat-snacks for weeks. Here was something interesting and shiny to look at! What would it taste like?

"Come on you son of a bitch," I whispered under my mask, bringing up sensor arrays and watching calculations scroll by. I moved the Direnaut while I watched, getting us well away from the tunnels, leaping and bounding with gravitics enhanced speed and lightness. I had to wait until two conditions were satisfied; The first being that we were on ground that could bear our weight. The second was to ensure the Striges were clear before firing, otherwise they'd become hellspawn paste.

The dragon closed fast, but we were faster, and just as he drifted over the remnants of the tunnels, I hissed between my teeth. "Gotcha!"

"Now!" Alpha shouted, and I hammered the big red button that I'd put in place for just this occasion.

Instantly our gravitic generators stopped supporting us, and as a result thousands of tons of steel, composite ceramic, impact gel, and circuitry settled with a groan onto the Direnaut's wide feet, sinking dozens of meters into the stony scree below.

The air rippled and literally tore, wind screaming to the side as I focused all our gravitic manipulation from *here* to *there*.

The dragon relied on its powers to move, to exist, to fly. It was built to withstand pressures equivalent to the earth's core.

But it relied upon gravity being a constant.

I watched a look of reptilian alarm spread over the dragon's face, as for the first time in existence its powers ceased to support it—

—and the thing screamed as it fell, crashing into and through the broken rocky ground, spraying lava as it sunk down into the tunnels below and kept going.

I kept the high-grav zone going for another few minutes, and then we watched.

"Popcorn?" Beta offered.

"NOW WHERE DID YOU GET THAT?" I said, as I accepted the small woven-hair-and-bone basket, filled to the brim with popped kernels. Then a thought made me pause; "THESE AREN'T ACTUALLY KERNELS, ARE THEY?" For the next month or two, we couldn't eat plants. Not until we'd dealt with Buer.

"No, they're all actually meat. As to where it came from, Professor Vector got bored a few days ago."

I shrugged, looked around, and decanted from my suit. We'd won, even if the dragon didn't know it yet. So I enjoyed popcorn-like poppers while I waited for the dragon to be a dragon.

After a few more minutes the dragon's head rose above the level of the vast crater. A smaller-scale satan for a smaller-scale fall, I supposed. I popped it in the eyes with the Direnaut's freeze-ray.

That got its attention. A native to a ring of Hell where the heat was downright volcanic, the dragon was used to hanging out in planetary cores. Cold would be a stranger to it. And though its heat aura meant that ice couldn't form, it would still probably either hurt or annoy it.

It shook its head, sending dust howling to either side, trying to dodge the alien sensation. I kept on it, shooting the various eyes in turn, and when it opened its mouth, I froze its tongue as well.

Entirely pissed off, the thing roared so loudly that nearby mountains crumbled. Then started to clamber out of the pit—

—so I brought back the heavy-gravity zone.

It disappeared down the pit so quickly, it thumped its chin on the edge before it dropped.

Again, I gave it a few more minutes and munched popcorn.

Six times it popped its head up over the edge, and six times I gave it what for. Then after half an hour passed with no activity, I nodded. "It's over. Ring the dinner bell and call in the Striges."

I hadn't even had to deploy the heat-resistant nanites. They'd been designed, with Vector's help, to get into its nervous system and shut it down from the inside. Probably wouldn't kill it, but it wouldn't be doing much for a few decades. Ah well, I'd save those for another dragon, if I ran into one.

I returned to my suit, while Alpha and Beta worked the buttons that extruded the spikes from the Direnaut's shoulders. Most of them held impaled remnants of the worm demons and several of Vector's vat-grown cattle substitute. Enthralled, and encouraged by the first food they'd seen in forever, the Striges made a beeline for the mecha's shoulders, settling on it like giant fleshy shoulderpads, birds and nests combined.

It was kind of grotesque, when you saw it in action. But for me, that was a stroke in its favor. Grotesque was the norm down here, in fact, the more fearsome the better. I wanted something that would make demons crap their kilts when they saw it thundering down on it and having shoulders full of raptory, fire-breathing heads was more or less a bonus.

"She really, really wanted to fight it and punch it in its stupid dragon face," I explained over the vox to my teammates. "But eh, it really wasn't a foe. More of a force of nature. So there's an anticlimactic end for the dumb brute. Crouching in a hole, whimpering, hoping the bad thing goes away."

"Oh, so you're not getting any satisfaction from this?" Gamma asked, as the doors to the bridge hissed open, and she strolled out of the turbolift.

"Well, Dire didn't say *that*." I finished the last of the popcorn and handed the basket back to Beta. "Trash can. How did we get this far into designing a facility without trash cans?"

"I'll run it down to the incinerator." The pale android smiled. He smoothed his tunic and exited.

Though I'd never bring it up, I was privately very glad that my androids were back in a situation where they could wear clothes again. They were my kids, and I really didn't want to stare at them naked.

"All right. Time to get this show on the road." I opened the intercoms so that everyone on board could hear me. "People, we've come a long way. And we're going to go longer still. We are going to leave the Wrathlands within three days, barring bad luck, then it's into Envy." I took a breath. "And then on to Dis, where it rests on the border of Envy and Pride.

"We will take Dis. We will shatter its iron walls, with our own colossus of iron, and lay it low. We shall stand before the gates of Lucifer's domain, and there we shall call him to task. And he shall see reason, or Dire shall *make* him see reason. One way or another, we shall leave Hell.

"We'll reach Dis in a month. Do what you must to prepare. And remember, no matter what happens, the demons who survive shall remember the day of our arrival and tremble!"

I cut off the intercom, took a deep breath.

Wrath had nearly gotten me killed. Envy... I didn't know what the emanations from Envy would do to me. Hopefully I would be able to detect and overcome the foreign emotions, like I had these.

We made our way across the plains, moving far faster than a mecha this size had any right to. Occasionally we had to shut down for maintenance. I'd had plenty of raw materials to work with but not *everything*. That was becoming a common refrain here in Hell. Never enough or too much of what you didn't need.

But as we went, tension eased. I found myself lying awake less, dwelling less on old grudges. I walked among the crew and teammates aboard the Direnaut, unmasked, sharing in their relief and laughing with their joy. I caught back up with my Romans, with Juno, with the other Damned that I'd been distant from for the last month.

I hadn't known them for long, but... looking back at my life, I hadn't known *anyone* for long. Most of my relationships were forged in the fires of crisis and violence, why should the ones down here be any different?

Finally we came to the edge of the ring, hemmed by curved mountains that caught the clouds and milked torrents of water to rain endlessly down below. We clambered our way down, falling through the mists, following a waterfall down.

They had clouds down here too, I noticed as the Direnaut straightened up. An actual climate, more or less. And plenty of trees, ranging from the bloated, brown and dull green ones full of thorns and mouths that you'd expect to find in Hell to brightly colored plants of every hue of the rainbow, swollen with tantalizing fruits that the gator-like hellspawn moved around without tasting.

Of *course* the place was a swamp.

I surveyed it from the bridge, with Vector and Khalid at my side, and my three captive demons in attendance. Epsilon had been here when I'd arrived, already looking over matters since it was his turn on shift. He'd called all-stop, to see what we could make of the place.

"Dire's going to bet that every attractive looking piece of fruit down there is pure poison," I said, folding my arms. "Because Hell."

"I don't think you'd find a single person here who'd take that bet," Vector said, his tone emotionless.

"Okay. Odds of the meat being edible, at least? We'll need to feed the Striges, and the Damned have gotten used to eating regularly."

"We'll need to harvest from here if we want to keep them happy," Khalid said, folding his arms. "We could take extra meat from the Striges and feed them regenerative concoctions back when there were fifty Damned, and us aboard. Now there are over six hundred, and the Striges are still recovering from fleeing the dragon. Feeding on them exclusively will kill them."

First Whisper cleared her throat. "And you must keep feeding the Damned, now that you are here. For you will eat and they will not and that will grow and fester within them."

"Envy." I drummed my fingers on the viewing port. "Dire doesn't feel any different."

"You don't feel different, that's the problem with it," Epsilon turned to look at me. "But you are. We can tell."

"She's got a ginormous mecha, a cadre of loyal followers, the best teammates in this plane of existence, and a solid plan to beat up Satan."

"Lucifer," interrupted Khalid.

"Whatever. The point is, why should she feel envious?" I rolled my eyes. "Other people should envy her. Of course they don't see the responsibilities, and work, and time and suffering it took to get to this point. The injuries she's had to get treated for, the stress of the decisions, and oh gods she's doing it, isn't she?"

"In the words of our Monster Master," purred The Cat, "you have totally failed your will save."

"We knew the second you stopped wearing the mask," Epsilon said.

I took a breath.

That *wasn't* me, was it? I rubbed the back of my neck, looked away. Too many strangers around, or folks I barely knew. I hadn't been... I had been trying to blend in with the crowd, I supposed. Trying to feel a camaraderie I'd never had.

Well, fuck. These emotions were harder to detect, if a bit easier to squelch.

"This is going to get annoying."

"I could help with that," Vector offered, his voice still in that weird monotone.

"She's going to guess your help has something to do with your new voice... thing." I glanced his way, studied his face. He looked bored. Either that or it was a pretty terminal case of resting bitch face.

"Hormone suppression. Tailored bacterial cultures that cloud the amygdala and a few other basic structures." He tried a smile that barely filled his mouth, didn't touch the rest of his face at all. "It stops you from caring so much, about... oh, most things."

I looked to Khalid, who shook his head. Behind Vector, Epsilon was shaking his head too.

"She's going to pass on that one. Thank you," I told him. "Probably going to tough it out."

"You've always been better at that than me, I suppose," Vector said, still smiling-but-not-smiling. "I'll leave you to it then."

He left through the turbolift.

I looked to Khalid. "Time to worry?"

"Yes. Something eats at him, and I have no clue what." He sighed. "Something beyond this infernal assault upon our souls. Excuse me. I must go tend to my own."

And then we were five. I looked at Epsilon, who nodded. "We feel it too."

"You have souls?" That was surprising... no. No it wasn't. I wasn't sure what criteria determined the benchmark for souls, but I was pretty sure they fulfilled it. They'd sprung full-grown from Alpha's head like gods and goddesses out of a dead titan's body and grown so much in such a short time. If any androids had souls, they would be—

"I don't believe in souls," Epsilon interrupted my reverie.

"Oh. Ah, okay." I looked around. "We are literally in Hell." I pointed at my demonic minions. "Those are literally demons over there. Go on, poke them. They exist. Ergo, souls would seem to exist as well."

"I disagree. What we've found here is an alternate dimension, populated by things that appear to resemble dead people from Earth. The effect causing emphasized negative urges could be explained away by any number of things, most of which are not unknown on Earth. How many varieties of mind control and emotional influence are possible given the ruck and run of existing inventions and common powers?"

"You know we're standing right here, yes?" The Cat asked.

"Absolutely."

"Ah yes, you're the one with no social graces." The Cat groomed himself.

"Among other traits, yes," Epsilon smiled. "But at least I don't lick my own asshole in public."

"Interesting ideas," I propped myself up against one of the railings. "Not the asshole-licking part but the theological implications. You're positing an experience either deliberately designed after a common image of the afterlife or one that seems to draw in thought-forms that take the part of Damned souls, with enough accuracy that occasional visitors are fooled."

"Perhaps. The fact that most of the people we've encountered down here are Christians and we haven't found a single person from before the rise of Christianity would seem to lend credence to the first idea. What if... and this is just a wild theory, but what if the raw, organized belief of humanity was manifesting itself and generating a shared hallucination, constructing a dimension where Hell *is* real?"

"In that case, Dire would ask you to show her the proof. But she's a bit busy punching demons to properly prove or disprove the theory herself." I shot a glance at First Worm, who cringed away. "Oh not you, calm down. Just the ones who try to stop her."

But as it turned out, I wasn't too busy punching demons.

They pretty much fled as soon as they saw us. We passed by abandoned settlements, occasionally scared up wagon and boat trains full of fleeing envy demons and were otherwise thoroughly avoided by the denizens of this ring. Which was fine by me.

It did leave me with a lot of free time, though. That wasn't necessarily a good thing. Time to brood, time to sit there, feeling envy writhing around and through me, time to watch my friends and acquaintances harden, looking at each other with suspicious eyes.

Fuck it.

Five days after our discussion on the bridge, I went and gathered my Chorus. "All right. Morale is bad, and we can't afford bad morale right now. Buer hasn't hit us yet, which means he's probably waiting for us in Dis. We can't afford not to be in game shape at the point we find the guy. Thing. Fallen Angel."

"What do you propose?" Beta asked.

"For most of the Damned, we need to find a way to keep them busy. Monsters and Mangonels is still insanely popular, but sessions are breaking down left and right due to people arguing. Maybe something where people can't compare themselves to each other quite so much? Something with less potential for dick-measuring contests?"

Gamma tapped her teeth. She'd had fake teeth put over her metal ones, I noticed. Of course she would. They were straighter than mine, and I found it annoying beyond— I shut that thought down, quickly. "Video games," Gamma finally decided.

"You really think those are less competitive?" Alpha grinned. He'd kept his teeth metal, I noticed.

"No. But we can make them indirectly competitive. To the point where people don't have faces to put their blame upon. Or where they're playing against the machine, and the competition comes in the form of high scores."

"Easy enough to do. We've got plenty of electronic components left over. Give it a whirl, set up some Soldiers of Duty action all down in the lower decks. Or something like that. Call it... hm." I had an epiphany. "No. Make it like Doomed."

"What?"

"Oh yeah!" Delta leaned forward. "Call it a training simulator, for the final battle! Doomed, you know that video game with the space marine romping through Hell, blowing up demons?"

"Old school," Alpha nodded. "Not a bad thing, not by any measure."

"That should keep them busy, or less occupied with blaming each other. We only have to get to the border where Pride starts kicking in, and Dis is on that border. But that leaves a few very important people to check in on."

"The demons are doing fine," Delta reported. "First Whisper's listening device and comm equivalent was confiscated, and she's on her best behavior. The Cat's The Cat, and First Worm is happy now that he's not being regularly abused and gets to play his cleric of the Earth god. But the metahumans..." She rubbed her face, stared at her fleshy hand.

"Even Judy?"

"Yeah. Things... haven't been so good lately."

I chewed the inside of my cheek. "Dire's going to check in with them. Probably should anyway. Vector's been having issues for a long while now, Khalid's gone silent, and Dire barely knows the other two."

"Three. Don't forget Pagliacci."

"Right." I wasn't sure if he qualified; he didn't have powers. But then, he'd lead a long and successful career by relying upon insanity and luck, so I supposed that counted. "Yeah, alright, she'll bite the bullet and check on him, too."

"Do we really care about him?" Epsilon asked.

"No, not really. But he'll find a way to cause trouble if we don't. Besides, Dire has a working theory about him."

"Oh?" Alpha leaned in.

I told them and had the satisfaction of watching their eyes go wide. "Remember, keep this one quiet."

"Oh, no fear there. If it's true, wow. Talk about a serious case of boredom."

Putting them behind me, I headed out of the war room and into the turbolift. The Direnaut had a pretty robust internal camera network. It didn't take long to find Pagliacci. I figured I'd get him out of the way first.

"Nice murder den you've got here," I told him, as I stared around the room full of black tapestries, inverted pentagrams, and candles. I hadn't known that we *had* candles. He'd probably made them from human fat or something.

"Just getting into the spirit of things," he told me, sitting on a thoroughly desecrated altar. It had piles of the Obols that we circulated as currency on it, pairs of dice, and cards lying to the side. "Welcome to the Afterlife."

"She's not quite there yet."

"No, this is my casino, the Afterlife."

"Doesn't look like you have too many gamblers right now."

"They ran when they saw you coming. The Romans try to shut us down now and then, invoke your name and say that it displeases you."

"That was back when we were in Sloth..." I gnawed my lip. "Here, Envy would probably cause more problems."

"It does, and when they do, violence happens. Keeps me in candles. I take a pound of flesh for every blow struck in anger."

Goddammit, there were times I hated being right. "Never figured you for an arts and crafts sort of guy."

He shrugged. "I rise to the occasion. So, are you going to shut me down?"

I shook my head. Then I stood, turned my back on him. "Dire remembers that time we met. When you carved her out of her armor."

"Ah yes, good times. You ended me, finally. It took much work." He applauded. "I was satisfied."

"You wanted to be ended?"

"People like me don't die of old age. All I could hope for was a beautiful death. You did not disappoint, you and your friends. Even if that fire did sting like a bitch."

I turned, flipping blonde hair over my shoulder, and studied him.

My theory was right. I'd have to figure out how to deal with that later.

"There's a strangeness to you," Pagliacci said, eyes on me. "The sins of Hell barely touch you. You master them with but a little concentration. Now why is that?"

"Clean living," I said, deadpan.

He tilted his head. "No. Something more. Something about you that even you yourself do not see. I wonder..."

"Keep on wondering," I said, turned, and left.

"So I can keep running my casino?" he called out. I ignored him.

Vector was next. I found him in his lab, staring at a petri dish full of pulsing pink sludge.

"Bad time?" I asked.

"Yes. Wait, no. Yes, I am having a bad time. No, it's not a bad time to talk." He hitched his battered spectacles up on his face. "If that's what you mean."

I took in his appearance: stained and disheveled. He had a fair amount of wispy stubble going on, and his clothes looked to be the same since we'd discussed matters on the bridge. "Are you... no, you said it was bad." I pulled over a chair, turned it to put the back to him, and sat down. "How is it bad?"

He looked to me, looked away. "It's stupid."

"Bad can be stupid. Let's hear it."

He put the scalpel he was holding down and snapped a lid over the pink goo's dish. "All right. I want someone I can't have."

My first thought was that he was talking about me, and I stifled laughter. My second thought was that he obviously wasn't talking about me, and how dare he choose someone over me, after all I had done for him—

Yeah, fuck Envy. The third thought fell into place, as I remembered all those sidelong, troubled glances he shot Delta whenever Judy hugged... her...

"Oh! Oh." I said. "Delta."

He sighed. "Yes."

I gnawed on my lip. "Have you *told* her that you were interested in her?"

"I was working up the courage for it. Then we found Judy."

"And it wasn't long after that you offered the Chorus their skins."

"I'd been working on it for a while."

"Because you wanted to... be more intimate with Delta."

"Well, it sounds horrible when you say it that way. But yes. I didn't want to just come out and say it, though, that would have been... too much."

If anything, his monotone voice made it creepier.

"Vector..."

"She's the only one who calls me Ray, you know that?"

"No. Dire didn't."

I looked away, thinking. If he'd been an equation or a complex engineering problem I could have solved him with a few seconds of thought. But he was a human, and for humans, there are no easy solutions. Not for the things that mattered. "Why Delta?" I wondered. "What's the attraction, there?"

"What's not to like? She's funny, enjoys life full-bore, takes nothing seriously, and she games. It's rare enough to find a good woman who appreciates throwing dice and leveling up. Let alone one that would be fine with dating a supervillain."

"Mm. And the fact that she's an android doesn't matter to you?"

"Gynoid, technically. That refers to the female models, it's an important distinction."

"Actually, Dire had this discussion with the Chorus a few weeks ago, during our trip through Wrath. They prefer android on the whole."

"Well that's wrong, then."

I shrugged. "They're new life forms. Figuring out their own places in the world. She's not going to dictate how they refer to themselves. But the question remains, you're fine with her being artificial?"

"To tell the truth, the fact that she's not organic probably drew me to her," Vector sighed. "I know organics. I understand organics, from every errant hormone to every misfiring neuron. Silicoids? There's more mystery there. There's more..." he sighed. "More order to things." He looked at the tub of pink goo, and sealed the container. "It was a nice dream, but it was just a dream, wasn't it?" His voice was all over the place now, surging out of the monotone drone, to aggravated tension, then back down again.

"So you were attracted to her because of what she was."

"A good part of my attraction is because of that. Is that so wrong?"

"Generally, attraction only works out in the end when you're attracted to *who* they are, not *what* they are. Anything else doesn't last."

I'd learned that from my last boyfriend, the dashing hero. I'd only really known the mask, and under it, he was a pile of issues.

Vector shuddered, putting his hands to his face, dropping the goo box. I flinched, but it bounced, stayed shut. He was a hair's breadth from the edge, I thought. I reached out and put my hands on his shoulders. "You started taking the drugs before we entered Envy, didn't you?"

"Yes. And they're wearing off already. I'm building a tolerance faster than I thought. I'm scared, Dire. I'm scared of what I'll do when I'm free of them. You don't know what I'm capable of, the things I could do in minutes, if I stopped caring. Stopped holding back."

"She knows it every day, every minute she's trying to change the world." I squeezed his shoulders, put my forehead to his. "It's okay, Vector. It's okay to feel."

He wrapped his arms around me, pulled me closer, and cried. Just cried into my neck, and I let him.

"In the end you won't hurt us, Vector. You're bigger than that. You're not the man Maestro called Envy... you were never him, no matter how much he tried to make you into that sad little puppet."

Vector snorted. "At least I got to see that fucker die."

"Yeah. And we'll get out of here alive." I clenched my jaw. "No matter what it takes. No matter what stands in our way."

He lifted his smeared spectacles and snot-stained face from my neck, tapped my hand. I let him go, stood from the chair and stepped back, hands up. "You feeling better?"

"I think so." He mopped his face with one worn lab coat sleeve. "When you say that, when you say you'll get us out of here, I can almost believe that."

"Believe it." I folded my arms. "We got this far. Only have to put the boot in a few more times before it's all over."

Vector nodded. "I'll stop taking the suppressants. Clear my mind." He sighed. "I've been my own worst enemy for far too long. Time to start weaponizing my loathing to more productive purposes."

I grinned. "When in doubt, remember that demons are biological."

"Oh, I know." He cracked his knuckles. "Bitches are in *my* playground now."

I restrained my laughter, nodded, and left. Poor bastard had it bad, but he'd get over it. Despite how he wrecked himself, ran himself down, Vector was a decent man. He'd done more for the world that we were striving to return to than it would ever know.

Given the new information I'd just gotten, I tracked down Punching Judy next.

She was in her quarters, resting off-shift while American Paragon worked on keeping the mecha supplied with power. I knocked on her door, waited for her invitation. After a few minutes the door slid open, and she looked me up and down. "What d'yer want?"

"Er..." She was nude, sweaty, and... well, she looked like she'd been pretty busy. I cleared my throat. "Bad time?"

"Nah, we're done. Half a mo." She shut the door. A few more minutes crawled by, and I slumped against the wall, massaging my scalp.

The door opened again, and one of my Romans, Juno, sauntered out. She smiled at me, and I smiled back.

"She's in a lusty mood today. I got her started for you," Juno said, then left before I could formulate a reply.

"Decent now! C'mon in, Doc!"

I entered, surveyed the shambles of a living space. Somehow she'd found a way to make the barren metal cubicles I'd provided messy. Clothes of various types were draped around and about, and hand prints on the walls suggested that she'd been using her chi powers in a somewhat destructive manner.

I wondered why I hadn't heard about these. Then I remembered how Delta was in charge of internal damage reports, and I wondered about it less. They weren't on load-bearing walls so I supposed I could let it pass.

"Sorry 'bout the mess, love." Judy reclined on her bed, inset into the wall, staring at the ceiling above her. She had a twist of some sort of root in her mouth, chewed on it as I watched.

"What's that you're eating?"

"Not eating. Stuff's 'orrible. But it makes yer mind drift away a bit, lose focus."

"Where the heck did you find that stuff?"

"Few of the foraging parties brought it back. Yer little labrat declared it safe fer Damned consumption. Closest thing we've got to a drug around 'ere."

I considered. Then I pulled over the room's lone chair, kicked a few piles of clothes off of it, and sat down. "Are things really so bad?"

"Spoken like someone who ent dead."

I looked over her listless face, and something in me snapped. "You know, Dire did legwork on you, back when she first came to England. You and the rest of your team."

"Bravo." She held her hand up, with the first two fingers extended together. "Two stars. Woops, those aren't stars..."

"Self-pity wasn't in the reports. Guess they weren't that accurate, then. Because what Dire's seeing now is a sodden lump of misery, trying to drown her fucking sorrows any way she can."

Judy closed her eyes. Then she sat up, leaning her head and torso out to avoid beating her head on the roof of the cubby, and stared at me. "You really want ta go there?"

"Dire's heading straight to the center of Hell to beat the shit out of Satan until she gets free of this place. And you wonder what she'll dare?"

"Lucifer."

"Him too."

Judy smirked, then rubbed her face with both hands. "See, that's the problem. You're goin' back. Maybe. Us? We're already dead, ent we? There's no fixin' that. Not ever."

I shrugged. "How do you know that?"

"There's no way out of here. Not for folks what belongs here."

"Then stay in Hell." I stood, feeling my disgust overwhelming me. "Wallow in misery, rather than try to fight your fate. Give the word, and you can get off this giant robot any time you want."

"Yer bluffing."

"No, you can stop and get off any time you want. Right smack dab in the swamps of Envy. And now I know how it's affecting you. You envy us for not being Damned."

"What? No, it's not—"

"It is." I leaned forward and tore the straggly black root from her lips, chucked it in the corner. "You're supposed to be the master of unseen flows here, check your six."

"Please. I'd know if anything like that... was..." her jaw dropped open, as her eyes unfocused. "Fuck me for a game of knickers."

"Yeah, you already did that," I said, kicking around some clothes that definitely weren't hers. "And when you get done with the self-diagnostic, go have a talk with Delta. She deserves better treatment than what you gave her." I left before she could respond to that and headed out, fuming.

I needed calm. I needed a lack of drama.

I knew where I'd find it and made my way to Khalid's alchemical lab.

He looked up as I entered, smiling as various arcane squiggles glowed on his counter top and faded one by one until a circle of lines and curves was all that surrounded a glass vial full of glowing blue liquid. "That looks appetizing," I said, studying it from various angles.

"It would kill you upon contact," Khalid said. "But on the upside, you would not feel a thing."

I laughed. "The way this day is going it's starting to look like an attractive option. Everyone else's woes are Dire's woes."

"Welcome to the joys of leadership. It is why I tend to avoid the responsibility, when I can." He tapped the side of the vial with a glass rod, nodded as it chimed. "I have seen you do this before. Walk among the ranks on the eve of a great battle. You need not worry for me, I am finally at peace with myself and my abilities. And perhaps even my faith."

I stared at him for a long moment. "Not that she doesn't appreciate your conviction, but... why?"

"Simply put? I succeeded beyond my wildest dreams." Khalid smiled, and pointed to the sword hanging from the wall. It was the one he'd used to fight the Worms, I saw. Curved of blade, long, and gleaming faintly in the dim light of his lab.

"It worked well, then?" I hadn't had time to analyze his performance down in the caverns, I'd been too busy dealing with American Paragon at the time.

"It... is a sort of a feedback generator. It gains power from the dissonance inherent in demons. The more powerful the demon, the greater the essence of the adversary and his fallen forces within the demon, the greater the power harnessed by the blade. Around your temporary allies? It glows and heats from the essence of their progenitors. But down in the tunnels, fighting against that demon lord—"

"Shudderworm."

"—yes, him. Down in the tunnels, it harnessed a power I had not expected. I had only expected that sort of might to resonate when I finally faced Buer. Now..." Khalid sucked his teeth. "Now the challenge is to ensure that when we *do* face Buer, I can survive wielding the blade."

"Immortality should help you there, at least," I said as I studied the sword with more respect.

"No, it will not," Khalid sighed. "One does not harvest such forces lightly. An... overload has the potential to throw the carefully balanced essences and humors within my physical form out of conjunction. Should that occur, then I will not survive." He looked at me, as he picked up the blue, glowing liquid and carefully slid it into his belt. "Understand that I would not risk this if I did not believe in the possibility of our success. If I did not believe in *you*."

I hugged him, and he embraced me back.

"Thank you," I said, closing my eyes against tears. I'd needed to hear that. I hadn't known how much I needed to hear that.

"Go," he told me. "Before you tempt me into something I might regret."

I gave him another squeeze and left without a word. He might regret that. I wouldn't. But those were thoughts for another time, perhaps when we were out of this place.

And before that happened, I had a number of things to accomplish... including one more check-up.

I made my way down to the generators in the center of the Direnaut, to the high-vaulted hall with wires criss-crossing the ceiling and lining the walls. Hardly elegant, but it had been fast and easy to do, and we'd had plenty of material. The scent of ozone comforted me.

In the center of the room, clad in the trousers I'd found him in, American Paragon ran on a treadmill surrounded by Mark Twelve Van der Graaf generators. I moved around the room I'd personally designed, until I came to one of the safe spots I could occupy without risk of being fried or becoming part of the circuit.

"Are you doing all right?" I asked the hero.

"Just fine, ma'am." he called back, legs pumping as he kept a steady rhythm, powering the Direnaut by his lonesome. "Was there something you needed?"

I considered him. "Dire just wanted to talk."

"Oh, that's fine. I can stop by and see her once I'm off duty I guess. Or if it's an emergency I can come along now."

I blinked. No, he'd never seen me with his mask off, had he? "No, you misunderstand. You're speaking to Dire now."

He honest-to-gods looked around the chamber, before he stared at me and comprehension dawned. His smile showed crooked teeth, perhaps the only flaw I could find in his chiseled physique. "Oh. I thought you'd be shorter."

"She's never heard that one before."

"In my old line of work I fought a lot of armored enemies. Von Katzen loved to throw things like Eisenkrieger suited soldiers at us. Since your power armor's oversized, I thought maybe you were building it big to help make yourself look a little more threatening."

He'd just implied that I had a bit of a complex going. But as much as I scrutinized him, I couldn't find any sign of malice or get any feeling that it had been a deliberate insult. Was he really as simple as he appeared?

"Ah, might as well just come out and say it. Can she level with you?" I leaned on one of the safety railings.

"Sure!"

"Why are you in Hell?"

His grin faltered a bit. "Ma'am?"

"Dire's talked with other Damned, she knows it's the question you're not supposed to ask, but frankly she wants an answer out of you. She's reviewed everything she knows about you, and unless she's missing something, you were a pretty straight arrow. You should be in Heaven."

The smile faded from his face, and he looked away. His feet were moving faster on the treadmill now I noticed, and I knew I had to be careful. If he got upset he could pretty much rip everything in here to shreds in a heartbeat.

But the possibility of an answer tantalized me, and I couldn't let it drop.

What had landed him *here*?

"To be honest, ma'am, I haven't the foggiest." He looked at me, and his smile was sad now. "For the longest time I thought it was because I failed, and the Nazis overran the world. That I'd been the one responsible for the world falling to fascists. But you told me that wasn't so, and everyone I've asked in here who came from later years confirmed it. So it couldn't have been that." He shook his head. "I must have done something to fail. I just don't know what."

I nodded. "Well, we'll have a talk with the man in charge down here. That'll sort things out, she thinks."

"I'm grateful for the chance. If I'm here by mistake, I owe him a few wallops." The grin was back. "You know, I have to say, I'm happy to see you looking human."

"Oh?"

"You're a completely different person in that armor, with that mask on. To be honest I wasn't sure what to make of you. But actions speak louder than words, and from what I hear that whole hero and villain nonsense gets in the way of what's really important."

"And what's that?"

"Doing the right thing." he said, running in place as he had for hours, as he would for hours more, hands gripping the strengthened ceramic composite railings of the treadmill. The railings he'd left fingermarks in, despite everything I could do to strengthen them. "There's seven hundred people aboard who are putting their faith in you, lady. And no matter how bad it's getting, they're all here because of you. And they'll see it through because they want to see you win. What happens after that, we can sort out when it gets here. Don't worry about the now, okay?" He closed his lips, smiled wider, so much so that it crinkled his eyes shut. "We'll take care of that."

I had nothing more to say. I nodded at him and left the engine room, feeling new determination well within me.

I would see my people saved, one way or another. I might not know how yet, but I'd either get them out of here or set them up as kings in this forsaken place.

CHAPTER 18: THE IRON CITY

"Our struggle has not been easy, but occasionally the unbelievers assist us. The great lie has been suppressed with fierce brutality in Dis. As a result, Dis is a hotbed of shared lie covens, and it's easy to find a game if you go looking for one."

--Excerpt from the epilogue of the first book of the Chronicles of the Shared Lie

I'd thought Caym impressive, with its iron walls and mighty cannons. Quaint, true, but a statement in its own way.

It was as much a pale shadow of Dis as a souvenir miniature Statue of Liberty was to the real monument.

Caym had been a nowhere, a backwater, compared to this.

I stared through the monitor at iron walls, massive iron walls that spun off into interior walls, then joined into lines that resembled nothing so much as a massive labyrinth from the perspective of the high-flying drone that I'd launched as soon as we came within sight of the city. It looked like one of those mazes that you gave children to amuse themselves with... mark the start point and the end point, and let them go at it. There was an order, some order to the interior walls that criss-crossed back and forth, but it followed rules I didn't understand right now and had no context to explain.

And the city filled the horizon, iron walls standing hundreds of feet high, with individual buildings and tunnels and rooms and cannons and other, stranger things poking out of them, jutting out at every angle as if gravity and structural engineering were a secondary consideration at best.

Maybe they were. Once you started throwing magic into the equation, all bets were off. Gods, I hated that stuff.

I was willing to bet that a number of the things poking out of the windows and apertures cut into the iron of the walls were telescopes, looking back at me. We were pretty big too, just in a different way.

"Okay. Kind of glad we had the detour into the tunnels, now," I broke the silence on the bridge as my team, and Pagliacci, shifted behind me. "Assaulting this place with only the Striges would have been tantamount to suicide."

"And now?" Pagliacci asked.

"Now it's kayfabe." I cracked my knuckles. "And Dire can do that." I turned to First Whisper. She looked nervous, sweating bullets as she turned her face to the screens, then back to me. "Your employers are in Dis, aren't they?"

"I'm not sure what—"

I crossed the room in three strides, slapped her collar, and yelled "Boom!" She half-jumped backwards, shrieked, and flapped her wings for balance. I grabbed a fistful of her scanty tunic and pulled it toward me, eyes boring into hers without mercy. "The time for bullshit has passed! Answer Dire!"

"Yes! Yes they were, are! I worked for the Seventy Seven Silent Eyes of Dis!"

"Oh my!" The Cat said, and I smiled, patted First Whisper on the cheek, and dropped her.

She squawked, but I ignored her and moved over to The Cat, crouching down to look at him instead. "You know about these bozos?"

"Everyone does. They guard the Burning City, and ensure it remains free and ungoverned by any Lord, or even any Fallen One. They are myths, even among us."

"Thank you." I scritched behind his ears and shot a glance at First Worm. He was shaking.

"What?"

"Are you going to yell at me? Or threaten to crush my skull?"

"That's not what Dire was doing to The Cat. No, she's not going to yell at you, that would be mean. You've done nothing to deserve it."

"Good. I'm not hiding anything. I mean, I'm from Dis, and I've heard of the Eyes too, but I've never met them. Or worked for them. Or done much beyond run and fix Lurkcrystal matrices."

"Yes, we'll get to that shortly. You'll be a part of the plan, never fear." I turned back to First Whisper. "That crystal you had communicated with the hidden masters of Dis, then?"

She took a long breath. "Yes."

"Good. Epsilon, go fetch it from the vault. Khalid, Whisper, Worm, Cat, Alpha, you're with Dire. Judy, you're on power duty. Paragon, get ready to go kick ass. The rest of you, get to battle stations. We may need a demonstration."

American Paragon shot me a thumbs up and headed out at a jog. I'd taken the time to manufacture him a proper copy of his old costume once more, complete with cape, and he was the happiest I'd ever seen him.

Punching Judy nodded, twisting her lips as she studied me, but when she left Delta slid out with her, and I saw them holding hands as the turbolift hissed shut.

I looked over to Vector, and he nodded, spread his hands. "It is what it is," he said, resigned.

"Good man."

The rest of the androids remained on the bridge as we adjourned to the ready room.

Honestly, I might have been riffing on Star Trek when I designed the upper floors of this mecha. But down here I didn't have to worry about copyrights... not that I ever did in the first place. Perk of supervillainy, really.

"Right." I walked over to my armor, and suited up. Normally it felt like a coffin to me, but after weeks without it, I found myself relaxing at the feeling. I'd missed it, missed that boot-up sequence, and the various creaks and groans as the internal harness activated, and the subsystems spun up one by one.

It was crude, perhaps, compared to the suit I'd entered this plane with. Battered and reconstructed and built with the best materials to hand, rather than the best that could be, but it was dependable, it was mine, and I could rely on it no matter what came. "FEELS GOOD TO HAVE HER PROPER FACE ON ONCE MORE," I thundered, turning to face my team and sweeping my cloak back. "NOW LET'S TALK TO SOME DEMON SPOOKS."

About the time I finished up, Epsilon returned, cupping First Whisper's old necklace in his hands. First Whisper fluttered her wings at the sight, every inch of her body registering apprehension. I reached out and patted her shoulder, and she started in fear.

"YOU ARE ONE OF DIRE'S CREW NOW. IF THEY TAKE VENGEANCE UPON YOU, DIRE SHALL LAY DOWN SOME FAIRLY BIBLICAL RECKONING."

"Even after I betrayed you?" she whispered.

"PFFT. IT'S NOT BETRAYAL IF YOU'RE WORKING FOR

ANOTHER INTEREST IN THE BEGINNING. IT'S A SUCCESSFUL INFILTRATION, AND A REMINDER TO DIRE TO BUFF UP HER SECURITY SYSTEMS. IN ANY CASE, THAT BRIDGE HAS NOT BEEN BURNED." I sat in the ready room's throne, the one with the light-up metal skulls and pyrotechnics. It let out soft gouts of fire to either side, reflecting in the polished steel of my outer layer of armor. My app helped me get the angles just right.

Epsilon sat the crystal in the center of the table, and I nodded to First Worm. "EASY ENOUGH TO ACTIVATE, YES?"

"This close to the source... if it *is* the Seventy-seven, then it should be so. I'd like a buffer between myself and the crystal, in case they try a remote kill. Some stone or metal tray, perhaps?"

"Got to watch those Rkills," Alpha smirked. Linux jokes? Seriously?

"NERD," I commented, then considered the table. I peeled back the rubber surface, revealing the iron below. "GOOD ENOUGH?"

"Yes." First Worm slid long fingers onto the table, and my sensors jumped as he worked his hoodoo. The crystal sparked to life, and I nodded in satisfaction. "ONCE YOU'VE GOT AN IMAGE, PUT IT OUT FOR US TO SEE."

"Almost... this is a strange feeling, without my normal rig. Ah, here we go," First Worm wiggled his fingers, and an image diffused out, hologram-style, above the table. It resembled a neck-and-face shot of a man with thorns embedded in his bald scalp. He had a classical devil's goatee, and his skin was as gray as ash. Blood-red eyes shifted down to the stone as the angle turned. He was obviously picking it up and examining it.

"HELLO THERE. ARE YOU THE SECRET SOCIETY THAT DIRE'S ATTEMPTING TO CONTACT AT THIS MINUTE, OR DOES SHE HAVE A WRONG NUMBER?"

He blinked. "I don't know your number, or what sort of number you are referring to," he rumbled, "but you should definitely not be on this node."

"DIRE GOES WHERE SHE WILL. LIKE OUTSIDE YOUR CITY." I punched up the mecha's remote interface and waved its arm. "SEE? SHE'S WAVING AT YOU NOW."

A hubbub in the background, and Mister Thorny glanced to the side, eyes narrowing. Then he shoved his face closer, so that his eye filled most of the image. "Assuming you are who you say you are, what business have you with us? You come to conquer, and we do not wish to be conquered. There is little point in continuing this conversation."

"YOU'RE WRONG ON TWO COUNTS. SHE CARES LITTLE FOR CONQUERING DIS, AND THERE IS EVERY POINT IN

CONTINUING THIS CONVERSATION."

He considered me for a long moment, staring.

"DIRE WILL NEVER BLINK," I told him.

"That makes two of us."

"AND INCIDENTALLY, YOU SHOULD TELL YOUR WORMS TO STOP TRYING TO UNDERMINE THE DIRENAUT. IT WON'T FALL, AND THEIR GEO SORCERY WON'T PENETRATE THE SHIELDS SHE'S PUT IN PLACE AGAINST THEM."

"I am quite sure I have no idea what you are talking about."

"RIGHT." We'd picked up the seismic readings half an hour ago. Luckily we'd thought of this, and taken the appropriate protective measures with force fields. "IF YOU'RE TOO IGNORANT TO KNOW OF THE CITY'S DEFENSES, THEN YOU'RE PROBABLY TOO LOW-RANKED TO BE WORTH SPEAKING TO." I gestured at First Worm. "KILL THE LINK."

He removed his fingers from the crystal.

"Five, four, three, two..." Gamma counted.

The crystal started blinking of its own accord. I nodded to First Worm, and he set his fingers to the tabletop again. The image projected once more, resolving into my new pal, Thorny.

"The subterranean assault has been put on hold," he told me. "You have five minutes."

"NO, YOU HAVE AN UNCLEAR UNDERSTANDING OF WHAT IS GOING ON HERE." I flexed my gauntlets and did a proper villainous slouch, elbow on the throne's armrest, mask resting on my fist. "DIRE HAS NO DESIRE TO CONQUER OR DESTROY YOUR CITY, BUT IT IS IN BETWEEN HER AND LUCIFER. SO ONE WAY OR ANOTHER, SHE'S GOING TO CROSS DIS AND GO SPEAK WITH THE FIRST FALLEN. THE AMOUNT OF PAIN, DESTRUCTION, AND LOSS THAT YOU SUFFER AS A RESULT IS ENTIRELY UP TO YOU."

"We will fight you if we must. You are not as unstoppable as you think you are. And you say that monstrosity is called the Direnaut? Interesting." He nodded to someone out of our view.

Warning lights flared, and I smiled to myself. The runes that Khalid had insisted we carve into the outer shell of the Direnaut's armor had just activated.

"WITCH, PLEASE," I told Thorny. "THAT PENNY ANTE SORCERY MIGHT WORK AGAINST YOUR PEERS, BUT IT WON'T PLAY IN THE BIG LEAGUES. DO THAT AGAIN AND SHE'LL TREAT YOU AS SHE DID THE DRAGON."

"Dragon?" He raised an eyebrow.

"OH, YOU'LL LOVE THIS." I activated the monitor, pointed it at the screen, and had First Worm rotate the guy's perspective until he got to watch the footage from the dragon 'fight', with *Thus Spake Zarathustra* playing in the background.

The Cat paused his grooming to look my way. "Shitting his pants," he told me. "Not literally, mind you."

This was why I'd invited The Cat in. He'd gotten to talking with First Worm after an M&M session a few days ago, and they'd experimented. Turns out that his mental abilities worked over whatever medium Lurkcrystals used.

Which meant that there was a distinct possibility that our own surface thoughts and emotions were being scanned from the other end, as well. Which was perfectly fine by me. I had meant every word I said and had no intention of lying to Thorny and his people. I was offering a mutual solution, and if we couldn't find one, I'd go to plan E. E for explosions!

Really, I'd run out of fucks as far as Hell was concerned. I was done with this place and done with demons barring my path and done with random horror shows and watching the torments of the Damned and done with random waves of sinful urges pounding me nonstop.

It really, really was a good thing we had come down past the ring of Lust. I didn't know how I could have coped with that, given the flaming pile of tires my last relationship had been in the days leading up to Hell.

"Your device is impressive," Thorny said. "If you use it upon Dis, we shall not hesitate to unleash similar forces. There are those who can easily match your powers and exceed—"

"LIKE BUER? IS HE IN? CAN DIRE TALK TO HIM?" I held up a crumpled pop can that I'd made to look identical to the one on his dead descendant's crown. "SHE'S GOT THIS TO GIVE BACK TO THE GUY."

Thorny looked away from the point of view, and The Cat nodded at me, studying the back of one paw. "He is now panicked and wondering how much you know."

The puzzle pieces I'd been grasping at fell into place, one by one. "ALL OF IT, YOU LITTLE GRAY BASTARD. SHE KNOWS ALL OF IT. SHE KNOWS THAT YOU'RE THE ONE BEHIND HER TROUBLES IN CAYM AND THAT YOU ALERTED BUER TO WHAT SHE'D DONE." I half rose from the throne. "YOU WERE ALSO THE ONES THAT SHUTTLED PAGLIACCI AND PUNCHING JUDY TO WROTH, WERE YOU NOT?"

He looked back at me, red eyes narrowed. "OH DON'T BOTHER, IT'S THE ONLY THING THAT MAKES SENSE. JUDY DOESN'T REMEMBER HOW SHE GOT THERE, BUT IT HAPPENED

RECENTLY, ABOUT THE SAME TIME-FRAME AS PAGLIACCI. SOMEONE WHO KNEW ABOUT CAYM PULLED STRINGS TO GET THEM THERE. WROTH WAS A LITTLE COW TOWN, WHAT WERE THE ODDS THAT DIRE RUNS ACROSS ONE OF THE FEW DEAD METAHUMANS THAT COULD CAUSE HER SERIOUS TROUBLE?"

I stood, shaking my fist. "THEN ANOTHER METAHUMAN, AMERICAN PARAGON, TURNS UP AND WHERE DID HE COME FROM? DIS." I shook my finger at the screen. "ALL ROADS LEAD BACK TO YOU, MOTHERFUCKERS. EVEN DIRE'S ROMANS AGREE ON THAT."

I leaned in against the table, glaring into the projection, watching him sweat. "SO THIS IS DIRE, OFFERING YOU ONE LAST CHANCE TO GET OUT OF THE WAY, BEFORE SHE STARTS THE ASSAULT. SHE HAS EVERY RIGHT TO DECLARE VENDETTA UPON YOU AND BEAT YOU TO A BLOODY IRON PULP. BUT SHE IS MERCIFUL, EVEN TO HER FOES, AND OFFERS YOU ONE LAST CHANCE TO REPENT. EVEN THOUGH SHE REALLY, REALLY HOPES YOU DON'T."

"How did you know?" he burst out, eyes wide and teeth pointy and yellow. "How did you even know we were after you!"

"SHE DIDN'T, NOT FOR SURE." I told him. "NOT UNTIL YOU CONFIRMED IT JUST NOW."

I watched his face slowly turn purple, and gods, did it feel good to be on the other side of that line for once. "JUST BACK DOWN, OR GET OUT OF THE WAY."

Grimly, he shook his head. In the distance, from the Lurkcrystal, I heard reverberating explosions.

"Incoming," Alpha reported. "Cannonballs the size of houses."

"REALLY? REALLY?" I spread my arms. "SO BE IT. ENGAGE THE VANGUARD."

Thorny smirked. His smile died as he looked around.

"WHAT? YOU WERE EXPECTING HER TO HIT THE CITY WITH A MASSIVE GRAVITON BLAST? YOU HAD SOMETHING LINED UP TO COUNTER THAT? FOOL, WHY DO YOU THINK DIRE SHOWED YOU THAT?"

"What did you do, woman?" He roared as his command center shook.

"First wall's down," Alpha reported. "Also our shields are holding strong against their fire.

"WHAT DID DIRE DO?" I grinned under my mask. "SHE DISTRACTED YOU FOR THE FEW MINUTES IT TOOK FOR HER HARDSUITED STEALTH TROOPS TO GET INTO POSITION.

CHECKMATE IN FOUR, THORNY. THANKS FOR PLAYING. GEE GEE."

I waved at First Worm, and he killed the connection.

"Actually, Gee Gee is what the losing side says after the game," Delta corrected.

"OH? WELL, SHIT. HOPEFULLY HE DOESN'T KNOW THAT. IN ANY CASE HE SHOULD BE TOO BUSY TO CARE. LET'S GO TO BATTLESTATIONS AND GO BACK UP OUR PEOPLE."

We piled back onto the bridge and got things rolling.

A couple of years back, when I was working with friends rather than minions and teammates, I made a few of them hardsuits. They were basically foolproof power armor that didn't have the complicated interfaces and flexible options that my suits were configured with. Hardsuits provided seriously good armored protection, amplified the user's strength and speed, and gave them night sight, flare compensation, and a bunch of other things that required absolutely zero piloting skills or technological know-how to operate.

The training game that Gamma had whipped up showed them how to pilot the things, and my Romans and Axumites and other ancient peoples took to them like addicts to meth. Well, that was doing them a disservice, really. More like highly-trained, brave and stubborn warriors to armor that made them walking demigods.

Armor *and* weapons. For those who couldn't wrap their skills around guns, I gave vibroblades, shockspears, and energy shields. To those who *could* handle guns, I gave plasma rifles.

Which was why I hadn't deployed the gravity cannons on the Direnaut. I could have, mind you, but it would have taken the broadcast power I was beaming out to the suits, using the massive tower that was my mecha. We were in support mode and would be until they started taking significant casualties and fell back.

But I let them play, ordering us forward at a quarter speed, striding along the ground, cracking the road we followed with every step. They'd paved it with skulls; really, was it really a wonder the damned thing was fragile?

"Do you have any idea who that was, on the other end of the crystal?" Pagliacci asked.

"NOPE. AND SHE REALLY DOESN'T CARE." I settled into my throne as cannonballs of a size not possible on Earth slammed into the shields I'd built for the Direnaut and were deflected safely away. "IT WAS PRETTY OBVIOUS THAT SOMEONE WAS MOVING BEHIND THE SCENES. THE MAKEUP OF HELL PRETTY MUCH SCREAMS OUT FOR SHADOWY PUPPETEERS."

Great Clown Pagliacci considered my words. "I do not know if I see it."

"WEREN'T YOU THE ONE BOASTING OF HOW YOU HAD UNRAVELED THE SECRET OF HELL?"

"Oh, I have, but it doesn't involve the demons or how they tend to their affairs."

"THEN PERHAPS YOU DON'T HAVE THE FULL SECRET."

That shut him up, and his painted eyelids drooped as he squinted at me,. He smoothed his goatee with one hand and smiled. "Perhaps not. But I have the most important part."

"AT ANY RATE, THE FACT THAT DIS WAS THE GREATEST AND ONLY CITY NOT CLAIMED BY ANY DEMON LORDS SEALED THAT THEORY. WHY IS DIS FREE? BECAUSE DIS IS ACTIVELY TRYING TO STAY FREE. THUS, EVERYTHING ELSE AROUND IT WAS DUE TO REALPOLITIK AND KAYFABE."

"Kayfabe?"

I ignored him for a minute, checking on my troops. They'd advanced through the first wall with minimal casualties. They'd taken to their training well, falling back towards the rally points as they got badly wounded. I flicked a finger, sent repair drones out to tend to their armor. I had roughly five hundred fighters in the field, fighters who could heal any wound to their flesh in time. They didn't need food; they didn't need water; they didn't need sleep.

They needed vengeance, and I was giving it to them. They needed power, to regain control, to feel like their lives were their own to decide, for a change.

Even in Hell, especially in Hell, humans wanted this.

I smiled to see the miniature suits still out in the field. Khalid's children had volunteered to the last for this duty. They'd been here for centuries, or more, since time flowed slowly down here. They were not children anymore, after what they had seen and been through. To them, this power was something they'd never thought to have.

I didn't know what I could do for them once this was all over, but for the minute, at least, I could make it beautiful.

"WHEN IS A CHILD SOLDIER NOT A CHILD SOLDIER," I muttered.

"Still thinking in Creation's terms? Tsk." Pagliacci clicked his tongue.

I ignored him because we were breaching the wall at this point and because he was a dick. The Direnaut knelt, ignoring the arrow and musket fire from the sides and extended its hands to the wounded and disabled. One by one I scooped them into the boarding chambers, for repair or decanting, depending on how much damage they'd taken.

There weren't many. I looked at the converging hordes of demons sweeping out of doors and gates in the metal walls, charging down the bone-paved streets. They waved iron weapons of all shapes and sizes, pulling fire from the air, throwing balls of poison and lightning.

I pitied them.

My thin gray line of hardsuited warriors stood against them. And they would not stand alone.

I gave the command, and the anti-personnel weapons extended from the Direnaut's gauntlets. The robot straightened up, its precious payload returned, and I rained down steel and plasma upon the charging hordes.

Then came a mighty groan, the sound of earth rending. I looked to see the walls closest to us stretching and rearranging, extruding girders like crystals in slow motion, reaching out to us.

"HELL NO!" I roared, and slapped the AR controls, swiping icons out of the air. "THAT'S GEOMANCY, RIGHT?"

"Y-yes," First Worm confirmed, shuddering in his chair.

"GET HER A READ ON WHERE THAT'S COMING FROM. WE'LL NUKE THEIR COMMAND CENTER. IN THE MEANTIME..."

I moved to stand over our troops, pulled down the forcefield, punched up the gravitic shear. "...LET'S MAKE SOME PANCAKES."

I had a pretty good view from the drone overhead. Of the walls sliding on the rock they were built upon, as if the soil was liquid, and the stone an oily slick. Of how they closed upon us, sealing the metal away, grinding toward us to crush my mecha, my army, and a sizeable amount of their own forces, too.

And then, in a heartbeat, the walls nearest us ripped free of the soil. Like Hercules defeating Antaeus, I knew the solution was to remove them from the ground. Without the medium for their demon powers to travel through, they couldn't reshape and move the iron walls around.

Gesturing my commands with maximum contempt, I had the Direnaut hurl the walls up, over, and into another section of Dis. How many I had killed I could not say, but when I lowered my arms and the gravitic shear spun down, the walls remaining around us were still. The hellion armies fled, shredded by my troops and the occasional burst of supporting fire from the Direnaut, and crushed by their own fortifications; they had no stomach left for the battle.

It couldn't be this easy, I thought.

It wasn't.

Three minutes later, we hit our first metahuman.

Something like an invisible blast went through our hardsuits, pretty much a straight line of force, sending the first ranks scattering. I watched them scatter apart, checked the data, found them mostly undamaged.

"I'm watching the video feed slowed down by a factor of twenty," Gamma reported. "it's a speedster. Some sort of darkness thing on his face."

"Does it have six red eyes?" Khalid asked.

"Three."

"It's a parasite controlling him. But it is juvenile, we can destroy it without harming the metahuman host. Deploy a number six shell."

"NUMBER SIX SHELL!" I ordered, and Alpha hit the buttons. He really didn't need to, I could have done it over the AR interface, but it was fun to sit on the bridge of my walking battleship-equivalent and order doom and death for my foes. And really, down here, fun was rare enough that you had to make the most of it.

Fuck, when I got back to Creation, I'd have to stop taking things so seriously. Maybe relax a bit and enjoy my career instead of rushing to take care of this or that crisis.

But no. But no... to fix the world, to make it what it could be, I'd have to step up and *change* the world. And I would, for none could do it better than—

"OH FUCK HER RUNNING, WE JUST CROSSED THE BORDER INTO PRIDE, DIDN'T WE?"

"Yes," Khalid confirmed, on his way out the door. "I'll tell you how to ward against it after I take care of that speedster."

"SIT DOWN, SIT DOWN." I looked over at the pattern of invisible waves, battering my suits around, plotted the course, and fired the shell.

The shell burst in midair, showering silver flakes down into the area, saturating it and a mile radius around it with one of Khalid's variant distillates. I'd fought speedsters before, and I knew how to beat them, and I'd never once met a speedster who didn't have to breathe.

Today was no exception. The man appeared in the middle of the boulevard, clawing at his face, as something like a cross between an octopus and a spider thrashed and leaked green slime.

"I could have done that," Khalid said, as he took his seat.

"HE'S SMALL FRY. WE'RE SAVING YOU FOR THE BIG GUNS."

That mollified him. But the thought occurred to me that metahumans were a naturally dramatic lot, prone to impulsive actions, rash behavior, and abandoning sound plans with impulsive measures. And we'd just crossed into Pride. Khalid wouldn't be the only one feeling the tug, there.

I got on the intercom. "WE'RE ALMOST THERE. READYING TO JUMP, CALLING IN THE HARDSUITS." It was time to pull in assets before we got cocky.

"He's gone," Delta reported.

"WHAT?"

Someone knocked on the bridge's emergency exit door.

"The speedster, I don't know where he is—"

I gestured to Beta. "OPEN THE DOOR."

The second Beta had that door open, the guy materialized out of thin air, nude, hands over his crotch. "Say, who are you folks? And where is this?"

"IT'S HELL, AND WE'RE BEATING UP DEMONS."

"Oh. Alright, I'm game. Got any pants?"

"GET THE MAN SOME PANTS, BETA."

Turned out his name was the Saffron Speeder. I hadn't heard of him, and mostly-ignored his friendly chatter as I checked over systems, monitored the bird's eye view from the drone, and made ready to jump. Pagliacci just sat in the background shaking his head as the hero prattled on, and my pet demons looked thoroughly poleaxed at his presence.

Then the guy was leaning on my throne's armrest. I twitched and barely kept myself from blasting him. "So, what should I be doing, sir?"

"YOU'RE TALKING TO A WOMAN."

"What, seriously?"

"YOU SHOULD BE HOLDING ONTO SOMETHING."

"Why, what's going to happen, ma'am?"

The Direnaut jumped, and he disappeared. I wasn't too worried for his sake... the guy looked like a classic speedster, and everything would be in slow motion to him if that was the truth. If I was wrong, well, he was Damned. He could recover from anything that would happen to him.

Scary to think how blasé I'd gotten about that.

We passed over about a dozen walls, heading deeper into the maze. I nodded as the radar tracked three fast-approaching dots. "DESCENDING!" I roared over the comms and slammed the Direnaut into a crouch, fetching up in a high boulevard, decorated with skull patterns in the walls. Funnily enough, the walls in this area were glowing slightly red. Geothermal activity? It made sense. With the fucked up physics of Hell, they could be heated on the underside and conveying that heat up above, radiating it for the common benefit.

Or it could be a giant hibachi to fry Damned up on. I gave it about thirty-seventy odds.

Then the fliers were upon us. Humanoid bats three times the size of the one that Queen Eyeblight had ridden into battle, back at Wroth. They hit us with sonic shrieks, and I grimaced. The forcefields couldn't stop sound, and the mecha shook, as damage readouts flickered green.

"Don't take this the wrong way, lady, but are you a villain?" The speedster appeared again, holding the too-big pants up around his thin waist.

"SHE'S FIGHTING DEMONS TO SAVE HUMANS. DOES IT MATTER?"

"Well shucks, when you put it that way, how can I help?"

"HEAD BACK OUT THE WAY YOU CAME IN AND DO SOMETHING ABOUT THOSE." I pointed at a horde of burren-like beasts, driven by metal-clad hellions, stampeding toward us. "DIRE DOESN'T HAVE TIME TO DEPLOY HER TROOPS AGAINST THEM."

"Speeding out!" And he was gone, to appear on the screen a moment later. His force wave, anyway. Come to think of it, it did have a faint yellow after-image.

I shook my head and focused the main batteries on those goddamned bat-men. "SPEEDING OUT. SERIOUSLY, WHAT THE FUCK?"

"The Seventies were a strange time," Delta said.

"YOU RECOGNIZED THAT GUY?"

"He was one of the Michigan's Mightiest back for half a year when that team was running. Well, before he got caught with a girl half his age. They quietly canned him for that."

He hadn't looked that old, and I pushed the resulting realization from my mind. "DEFINITELY SHOULDN'T BE IN THIS RING THEN. LUST IS FAR, FAR FROM HERE. THAT SETTLES IT. THERE'S A THRIVING BLACK MARKET TRADE IN METAHUMANS, AND THOSE BASTARDS HAVE CORNERED THE MARKET."

"You know what that means," Pagliacci told me. And I did.

"HE WAS ONLY THE VANGUARD. LET LOOSE THE HARDSUITS AGAIN."

I focused on bringing down the last bat, which was a mistake, because as soon as I looked up, the ground fell away from under us.

"That's not geomancy!" First Worm howled as the world tilted, but Alpha was on the ball and he shifted power to the anti-grav.

I stared down to see a horde of tracked vehicles the size of cars, with whirling giant drills at their front. They burst out of the hole and made a beeline straight for us...

...only to stop short as I brought the Direnaut hovering up out of their reach.

I knew those drills. "MOLIARTY? FUCKING MASTER MOLIARTY, THE MALICIOUS MINER?"

One of the drill hatches opened, and a man with a pink face mask, looking nothing so much as an enormous snouted nose, glared up at me.

He yelled back at his drillbots, and they extruded stubby little legs, pointed up at me and started launching their drills like rockets.

"IT IS! HAHAHAHHAHAH!"

The Direnaut's point defense took out the incoming drills, and the Direnaut's foot stomped Moliarty and his Moleminer flat.

But then the next wave of hellions was upon us.

And a whole lot of costumes followed in their wake.

We fought them, hellions and heroes and villains alike. The Direnaut took hit after hit... our defenses were good, and our mobility let us avoid a lot of trouble, but with so many different types of attack methods, so many powers, it was inevitable that we'd run into troubles that we hadn't foreseen.

But I am Dire, and I do not do things by half measures. We won. Some of them were mind-controlled, through spell or parasite or other method, and they joined us or fled when released. Others seemed to have their own free will, and those we atomized. The less remaining of a Damned body, the longer it took to regenerate. We'd found that out all through our trip down through this benighted place. We pushed deeper and deeper into the iron city, eventually drawing our hardsuited troops, damaged and tired, back into the battered form of the Direnaut for ease of transit. And after the twentieth broken defensive line, resistance abruptly ceased. Our hop over a wall was met with empty streets.

"Energy readings!" Epsilon called. "Massive and unknown, ten streets south!"

"HOLD POSITION," I commanded and stood, walking toward the screen.

And with a squeal and a great gout of wind that shook my mecha on its feet and strained our antigrav to its limits, a hole opened ahead of us. Stars shone through, stars blotted out by *something* that clawed its way through, legs spilling out of the hole, hoofed legs, each the size of the Direnaut or bigger. And in the center, emerging into the light, a leonine face with solid golden eyes.

It looked to us and sneered, extruding fully into existence as its legs spread out. It had a disc-shaped body, hidden by a massive mane, and a wild circle of goat's legs spread out around it like the rays of a sun. It balanced on one of them, and the iron wall it stood upon collapsed under the Fallen Angel's weight.

"Buer," Khalid whispered, running for the elevator. "I need my blade!"

I looked at the massive lion-circle thing that dwarfed the mecha I'd spent a month building.

Then I stabbed the intercom button. My Direnaut's battered mask, holed and sparking, looked up at the great beast and opened its mouth.

"GREETINGS, BUER."

It smiled at us.

I glared back.

"DIRE'S GOING TO GIVE YOU ONE CHANCE TO GET OUT OF HER WAY."

CHAPTER 19: WHERE ANGELS FEAR TO TREAD

"One more alteration we have made, for our shared lie. All stats for angels have been removed from our game. The truth of them is that they are not monsters to slay in random encounters. They are great and terrible and to be fled from at the first opportunity."

--Excerpt from the fifteenth chapter of the first book of the Chronicles of the Shared Lie

I'd heard many things in the few years my truncated memory allowed me. The sound of fae screaming as they died. Hitler ranting his hatred at me as my allies subdued him. The President of the United States himself calling me a menace to world peace and all civilized societies.

But I'd never heard a Fallen Angel laugh, and as pain ripped through my skull, and my skeleton felt like it was shaking within my body, I realized that this was one particular sensation I could have truly gone without.

Then the noise compensation kicked in, and the pain stopped. I let the leonine bastard have his guffaw and started checking various systems and subsystems. The repair drones had finished up almost everything but the armor and a few of the redundant circuits, so that was fine. I estimated our battle fitness to be eighty-nine-point-six percent.

If things didn't work out like I planned, we'd need every decimal point of it. Probably more.

"DOES SHE TAKE IT THAT'S A NO, THEN?"

It considered the Direnaut. "You may take it so," the entity spoke, and to my annoyance I realized I heard it in the same way I heard The Cat's speech. I glanced around to find The Cat firmly under one of the command consoles, tail wrapped around itself. First Worm was next to it, snaky tail sticking out. First Whisper sat on the floor, eyes shut, prostrating herself.

My Chorus were unaffected at least, at their stations, looking to me. Pagliacci alone seemed unconcerned.

Yes, he would, wouldn't he? "About ready?" I voxed Last Janissary.

"I have the blade, and the elixir. I would say I hope you are right..."

"It's a moot point either way. If she's wrong, he'll recover."

I stared at Buer. Then I pulled up the scanners and activated the full sensory suite. My eyes widened as I saw the truth of him spill out, unknown reading after unknown reading...

...slowly quantifying into measurable results, as the vast servers in the clustered enclave of the Direnaut's hidden heart went to work.

Also, he was moving my way, legs bending in ways they shouldn't, hooves crushing the walls and buildings of Dis as he came.

"A MOMENT, GREAT ONE."

"Why?" the word ripped through my mind. "Are you going to beg? Now that matters have gotten to this point there is no use in pleading for mercy. I have been called, and I come."

"OH YES. BUT BEFORE THIS IS ALL OVER, SHE WISHES TO ADMIRE YOU."

"What?"

"IN THIS ARMOR, SHE HAS INSTRUMENTS UNLIKE ANY FORGED BY OTHER HUMAN HANDS. THEY ARE SEEING YOU, SEEING YOU IN WAYS YOU HAVE NEVER BEEN SEEN BEFORE BUER, BY ANY BUT YOUR CREATOR."

His eyebrows lifted on his face, ascending a building's worth of space as the Fallen Angel scrutinized me with disbelief. "You would raise yourself above the great deceiver?"

"DIRE WORSHIPS NO GODS. AND THE ONE SHE MET WAS A DICK WHO COULDN'T TAKE A PUNCH, SO FUCK 'EM." Mind you, it had been Crusader doing the punching. But that was neither here nor there.

Buer stood still for a long moment. Then he laughed, and by the time he was through, my brain ached like a four-alarm hangover. I swallowed nausea. "Look then, ye mighty, and despair," he said.

"THAT'S A MISQUOTE ACTUALLY."

"What?"

"NEVER MIND." He probably didn't know the poem.

The minutes crawled by, but he didn't stir. Evidently Fallen Angels had patience. And I watched as theology turned into science right in front of me, theory and myth collated into data.

Data that matched, in a lot of ways, the data I'd gathered before, clandestinely, on another subject. "Confirmed," I voxed to the Janissary. "Stand by." I reached over to my throne, and flipped a red toggle-box up, revealing a button glaring yellow, a black radiation symbol emblazoned atop it.

"What are you doing, Doctor?" Pagliacci said, stepping closer.

"DOING WHAT HUMANS DO. WINNING AGAINST THE ODDS. THANK YOU FOR YOUR COOPERATION, BUER."

Buer blinked. "You are welcome, I suppose."

"FOR YOUR GRACIOUSNESS, SHE WILL ALLOW YOU A SECOND CHANCE TO STEP OUT OF HER WAY. WILL YOU?"

"Have you gone mad? Or perhaps you have found your courage, child?"

"SHE'S NO CHILD OF YOURS, AND AS TO COURAGE... SEE, THAT'S THE PROBLEM WITH YOU HELL-DWELLERS." I stared at his readings once more, double-checking my work. It took all of half a second, and I was being lazy at it. "YOU DEAL WITH HEROES. THE PEOPLE WHO STOP YOU WHEN YOU BURST INTO REALITY? THEY ARE HEROES. ALL YOU KNOW IS DEALING WITH HEROES."

I stood, giving into the kayfabe, and flipped my cape back, even though he couldn't see it. "AND TODAY, YOU AND ALL YOUR KIN ARE UP AGAINST A *VILLAIN*. IT ISN'T ABOUT COURAGE, IT ISN'T ABOUT MERCY, IT'S QUITE FRANKLY PRAGMATISM. THOSE PEOPLE IN HER LAIR? SHE'S NOT SAVING THEM BECAUSE IT'S THE RIGHT THING TO DO, OR BECAUSE IT'LL MAKE HER FEEL BETTER ABOUT HERSELF. SHE'S SAVING THEM BECAUSE SHE CAN. BECAUSE IT AMUSES HER."

"Do you have a point, or are you merely riding the waves of Pride?"

"OH, SHE'S BEEN DOING THAT FOR A WHILE NOW. BUT IT DOESN'T MAKE IT ANY LESS TRUE." I turned my back to the screen, folding my hands behind my back, interlacing metal-clad fingers. "YOU AND THE ONE YOU CALL MASTER HAVE GREATLY, GREATLY UNDERESTIMATED HER AND ALL OF HUMANITY. FOR YOU SEE, SHE HAS SEEN YOUR ATOMS, BUER. YOU ARE NOT IMMORTAL. YOU'RE JUST VERY, VERY FUCKING TOUGH. BUT YOU ARE MATTER AND ENERGY, LIKE EVERYTHING ELSE. AND DIRE?" I sat down again, held my finger over the yellow button. "DIRE KNOWS ENERGY. WITH ONE TOUCH OF A

BUTTON, A SUN WILL BLOOM IN HELL, FOR THE FIRST TIME. A HUMAN SUN, AND A GREAT ROARING THAT WILL DISRUPT YOUR CORE. SHE WILL END YOU, BUER. SHE WILL END YOU WITHOUT CARE OR HESITATION IF YOU DO NOT STEP ASIDE."

"You threaten me? When your doom is inside you and has been all along?" Buer's mouth stretched wide, and he *roared*.

If I'd thought it was pain in my brain earlier, this dwarfed it. I bent double, clenching my mask, feeling something vast, feeling the touch of forces I had no name for, not yet...

...but I would after this. I straightened up as the forces passed, and I laughed, laughed long and hard, as the leonine face became puzzled. I checked the scanners as I rose, saw plants, disparate and alien, bursting forth from every window in the nearby iron walls.

"FOR BUER TEACHES THE VIRTUES OF HERBS AND PLANTS!" I roared, pounding my knee with a fist. "AND GIVES GOOD FAMILIARS, BUT THAT'S NOT IMPORTANT. TWO STRAIGHT MONTHS OF EATING MEAT, YOU SONOVABITCH. TWO STRAIGHT MONTHS ON THAT DIET, SHITTING LIKE A FAUCET, JUST TO MAKE SURE WE WOULDN'T HAVE ANY VEGETABLE MATERIAL IN OUR STOMACHS THAT YOU COULD MANIPULATE."

His face twisted into fury. Khalid had told me of this one's portfolio, and our gamble had paid off. Not a huge gamble, but it had just saved all of us from becoming sacks of fertilizer.

The Fallen Angel roared and rolled toward me—

—and I spun the Direnaut with grace he couldn't counter, leaping miles away in an instant, full power to speed.

"AND NOW YOU SORRY BASTARD, WATCH CLOSELY." I boomed. "ALL OF YOU WATCH AND SEE WHAT HAPPENS WHEN THE FALLEN ANGEL MEETS THE RISING MUSHROOM CLOUD!"

I pounded my fist toward the yellow button—

—and Pagliacci caught it.

Held it.

Servos whined and groaned, and sparks flew. I ceased downward motion. He'd stopped momentum that should have turned his bones to paste, vampire blood-enhanced muscles or no.

"Enough," he said, smiling. "Buer, you may return," he said, in a voice that shook my mind and not my ears. On the screen, Buer instantly disappeared back into his rift, smiling his leonine grin.

I turned my attention to the clown who wasn't a clown at all.

"SHE KNEW IT," I said. "KNEW YOU WERE A PHONY."

"Did you?" He smiled. "Then why did—"

"Now," I whispered to Khalid.

Air cracked, light flared, and 'Pagliacci' screamed. I twisted, grabbed him, and ejected backward through my armor's fast release. Couldn't see in the blinding light, could barely breathe as sulfur flooded my nostrils. But I knew where the real button was on my armrest.

I found it, slapped it, and with another crack and a rush of air, my armor was gone, teleported out as suddenly as Khalid had been teleported in.

When the glare faded, I saw Khalid rolling on the floor, clutching his hand. Blackened, seared, clenched around the remnants of a sword hilt. I rushed to help him, but Beta got there first, scooping him up and heading to the medical kit we'd stowed in the back of the room.

I glanced down at the scorched hole in the floor, edged with bright metal. All that remained of the Last Janissary's blade after we'd teleported him in, and he'd driven it into 'Pagliacci's' back.

"Test him for radiation," I said, whirling around. I'd probably gotten a good dose from that.

"The armor's breaking!" Alpha called back.

I sighed. That had been a good suit. I reached down and slapped my traveling mask on my face. "DO IT."

And with a push, a fusion-powered miniature star bloomed over Hell.

We'd teleported him a few hundred miles away. It wasn't a bomb. It was just my fusion generator, calibrated from the readings I'd taken from Buer. Combined with the Jannissary's most powerful blade, it... might have done the trick.

Maybe.

But my luck had never been good, and I wasn't sticking around to test it.

"What was that? What was that all about?" First Whisper cried, sticking her head up from behind the auxiliary console, flesh seared and cracked.

"PAGLIACCI WAS A TRAP. A PLANT. TAKE US IN, EPSILON, MAXIMUM SPEED."

The Direnaut lifted off the ground. The city of Dis had evacuated once Buer showed up, and nothing remained to stop us as we sped 'south'. I left the Damned heroes and villains we'd freed fighting behind us. Their fate was on their own heads now. They'd sort it out or not.

It was time to have a word with the man in charge.

"Movement from the direction of the teleportation coordinates," Gamma said, and I ground my teeth. The Fallen Angel had survived our one-two punch. The plan had about a fifty-fifty shot, and we'd failed the coin flip. Only one shot now.

"WE'LL HAVE TO GET TO LUCIFER BEFORE IT CATCHES UP TO US." This plan hinged on two possibilities. One being the exit from Hell being true. The other possibility being that we could find an audience with Lucifer and get him to send at least the living among us back.

"He's picking up speed," Gamma reported.

"TELL OUR METAS TO BURN RUBBER."

Alpha opened up the link to American Paragon and Punching Judy, and I watched as power levels spiked. Then I was on the controls, recalibrating like mad, shunting energy around and molding the forcefield by hand, to give us a more aerodynamic form and to keep the sheer friction of our progress from ripping the mecha's limbs off.

"Three hundred miles!" Gamma shouted, and we broke past the black maze of Dis, into a vast ocean, the pooling of all the rivers Styx from all across hell.

"Two hundred miles!" Gamma shouted, as the ocean gave way to ice, sheets of ice, and spires reaching up.

"One hundred miles!" Gamma shouted, and there was darkness under the ice, a vast shape... something like a serpent, I thought.

"He's on us!"

I glanced at the rearview screen, saw a comet, a man-sized ball of fire with crimson wings outstretched, roaring as it came.

And at the last second, right before impact, I grabbed the flight yoke and *twisted*.

Four years a pilot. Four years tooling around in a flying suit of armor, surviving heroes and villains alike.

Four years paid off, and, by a hair's breadth, we dodged the Fallen Angel.

"Mist ahead! Hard to get readings!" Epsilon snapped.

I killed our speed, brought us down into it. If it was hard for our sensors to get readings, then I couldn't imagine it was doing our pursuer any good.

Then the mist cleared, and the sensors shuddered. An iron throne, splayed with supports over a vast pit, sat like an immense beast squatting over the rocky landscape. Light played up from the pit below, shifting lights of all colors, none of them in friendly hues, dancing across the steam that rolled up in great clouds.

The throne was about as big as Tulsa, I wagered, a city-sized seat over a state-sized pit.

And it was empty.

Gamma slapped her hand on the collision alarm. "He's on us—"

It was a hammer blow, a strike from a meteor, a hole clean through the mecha. I closed my eyes as damage signs sprang up on the monitor, bright red ones...

...and then the monitor went dark. As did the entire room. Emergency power flickered to life, and I saw scraps of the Direnaut trailing behind us, the mecha disintegrating as the ground came up. "All power to forcefields!" I shrieked and got on the systems, shoving Gamma aside as my hands flew, my fingers flickered, and there wasn't enough *time*—

CRUNCH.

—I came to.

My ankle hurt. I hauled myself up, gasped and almost fell. My mask gave me nightvision, and I looked around the darkened bridge, found my Chorus picking themselves up. Alpha adjusted his torn arm, metal showing under the artificial fungus of his flesh. The rest of them were standing.

I glanced back to the demons. First Worm was nowhere to be seen, and a dome of metal surrounded his last position. Then the dome peeled away, and the mandibled man-serpent peered out, followed by First Whisper's burned face, and The Cat.

Good. They were demons, but they were *my* demons.

Then the wall groaned. Fiery hands burst through it, grabbed the edges, and pushed. The reddish light of Hell seeped in, replaced by a fiery face, beautiful and stern at the same time.

It regarded me, as I leaned against the remnants of my console, and stared back. "YO." I waved.

The arms of the Fallen Angel tensed, and it ripped the hole open further. It stood revealed, a nude being, genderless, with a pair of wings on its back made from fire and light. It considered me for a moment longer, then beckoned. As I watched, it turned and hovered across the ground, to the empty throne, fading from a figure to a spark as it went.

I started to hobble after, but it quickly became obvious that this wouldn't work.

"Here. We can do this at least," Alpha whispered in my ear, as he and Gamma took my arms, and picked me up effortlessly between them. They'd stripped out of their skin and fake flesh for this, I saw. I wasn't sure why, but I trusted their judgment.

"STAY BEHIND AND MAKE SURE EVERYONE GETS OUT CLEANLY," I told Beta and Delta. "BETA, HOW'S THE JANISSARY?"

"Recovering. He'll be a while."

The room shuddered, and the turbolift blew open. American Paragon and Punching Judy burst out, glaring around.

"Where's that glowing bastid!" Judy yelled. "I'mma punch him!"

"THAT WAY AND DON'T, YET. DIRE HAS A HUNCH HERE."

"All right ma'am, you're the boss." Paragon glanced over at my supporting Doppelgangers. Still felt weird to think of them with that name, but that's what they were. "I can take you off their hands. It'll go faster."

"No, actually," Alpha grinned. And then they were leaping and away, and I sat in a cradle of their arms, with my hands curled around their necks. I heard Paragon laugh, and then he was flying, trying to keep up with us. Judy came along on the other side, running with her arms back, anime-style.

"It's reached the throne," Alpha told me. He had more hardware in his head for telescopic vision than my mask could support. "Now he's... sitting on it."

"YEP. THOUGHT SO."

I watched as the distant spark became an ember, became a man of fire of proportionate size to the throne. And as my bearers ran, the ground trembled, and ice pillars rose under us. Judy and the Doppelgangers slowed to a halt, and I slipped myself free of their arms, standing as best I could, hands on my hips.

"That's ah, Satan, is it?" Judy asked.

"YUP. HE WAS POSING AS GREAT CLOWN PAGLIACCI."

The pillars lifted us up, as the fiery fallen angel watched us rise, bigger than the Direnaut, bigger than Buer, bigger than a mountain, he watched us come.

"And we basically shanked him prison bitch style and threw him out to blow up in a contained nuclear reaction, didn't we?" Gamma said. "The guy were were trying to have an audience with?"

"YOU KNOW HOW DIRE HATES THE WORD BITCH."

"Sorry. But—"

"BUT YES, THAT'S BASICALLY WHAT WE DID. COME ON, WHAT ARE YOU WORRIED ABOUT? IT'S LIKE YOU THINK HE'S SOME HATRED-FILLED ETERNAL BEING WHOSE SOLE EXISTENCE REVOLVES AROUND GRUDGES."

Everyone turned to look at me. I shrugged. "IF HE WANTED US OBLITERATED WE WOULD BE. NO, IT'S TALKY TIME. AND SHE CAN HANDLE THAT."

"Well alright ma'am, we've gotten this far following your lead," American Paragon nodded. "If it turns into punchy time we're here for you."

"SHE KNOWS. AND SHE'S GRATEFUL IN WAYS YOU CAN'T IMAGINE."

I was. They'd put their faith in me to get them through, whatever *through* might mean. I would not abuse that faith.

The ice pillar shuddered to a halt, level with the serene, fiery face, still miles away. Then the air shuddered, and a man in a snappy suit stepped out of a small rift next to us. Handsome, swarthy, and with eyes that were black pits filled with stars.

"LUCIFER, SHE PRESUMES?"

"I hope you don't mind the Sending. That's what I was when I was Pagliacci." He shrugged. "That's a Sending as well," he gestured at the fiery figure. "Most of me is down there, below the ice."

"SO THAT'S HOW YOU SURVIVED."

"Pretty much. Your attacks destroyed the Sending, I created a new one to slow you down, and here we are." He stepped forward, wings folding out from the back of his suit as he approached, hands in his pockets, nodding to the Damned as he passed them. "Lady. Gentleman."

"WELL, THEN, YOU KNOW WHY WE'RE HERE. DIRE HAS A WHOLE CREW THAT HAS SERVED THEIR TIME AND WISHES TO MOVE ON FROM THIS PLACE. AND DIRE AND HER TEAM WISH TO RETURN TO EARTH. WILL YOU AID OR HINDER US IN THIS TASK, LUCIFER MORNINGSTAR?"

"There's a third option," he said, smiling, teeth white against his skin. "I could decline to do either and let you try to find your way out. So that's two options I could take that don't help you and only one that does."

"TRUE." I shivered. Cold out here. "WELL, TAKE YOUR TIME AND LET HER KNOW WHEN YOU'RE GOOD AND READY THEN. SHE'LL BE WAITING IN WHATEVER SHELTER SHE CAN MAKE FROM HER GIANT ROBOT."

"No, I don't think it'll take all that long. Stay a while." The ice pillar shuddered and fingers grew up around the edges of it, five massive digits that curled around us. "I insist."

"IT IS YOUR HOME," I conceded. "A SHAME TO BE RUDE BEFORE YOU'VE EARNED IT." I snapped my fingers and pointed. Alpha and Gamma twisted themselves into the form of my throne, and I sat back in it, getting my cold feet off the ice.

"An odd choice of words." The swarthy man stalked around us, like a predator circling prey, looking for weakness. American Paragon and Judy tensed up, shot me glances. I shook my head, shot them an 'ok' sign, praying that the signal hadn't changed too much since Paragon's time. He nodded back and didn't try to punch the devil, so I counted it a minor victory.

"OH, YOU'RE GOING TO EARN SOME RUDENESS," I said,

turning to face him as he moved. "JUST A MATTER OF WHEN."

"Hm... let me ask you then, have you solved the riddle of Hell?"

"CAN'T SOLVE A RIDDLE THAT WAS NEVER PHRASED. BUT SHE'S PUT TOGETHER SOME ROUGH CONCEPTS."

"I'm listening."

"THE ONLY ONES HERE ARE THE ONES WHO WISH TO BE HERE. WHICH IS WHY THEY'RE MOSTLY CHRISTIANS, OR FOLKS FAMILIAR ENOUGH WITH CHRISTIANS TO UNDERSTAND THE NOTION OF HELL. EVERY ONE OF THEM BELIEVED THAT THEY DESERVE TO BE HERE. THAT'S WHAT GOT THEM IN."

Judy looked shocked. Paragon nodded and said, "But I don't, now."

"WHICH LEADS DIRE TO ONE OF TWO CONCLUSIONS THAT ARE GOING TO BE TESTED HERE. ONE IS THAT YOU'RE A PART OF THE PROCESS OF THIS INFERNO, THAT IT IS BUILT TO HELP PEOPLE SUFFER JUST ENOUGH TO GET THROUGH THEIR GUILT, UNTIL THEY ARE READY TO MOVE ON. BUT HUMANS BEING HUMANS, THIS TAKES A WHILE. EVENTUALLY THEY MAKE THEIR WAY DEEPER IN, AND FIND THEIR WAY TO YOU, AND ASCEND TO WHATEVER AFTERLIFE THEY BELIEVE THEY HAVE EARNED."

"And your other conclusion?"

"THAT THE PURPOSE OF THIS PLACE, EVERY LIVING THING WITHIN IT, IS TO CREATE A VAST ENGINE TO BRING A SECOND WAR AGAINST YOUR MAKER."

"What if I told you both of those conclusions were true?" He smiled.

"ELUCIDATE, IF YOU PLEASE." I clicked on the vox and threw the channel wide, for all my crew to hear, once Epsilon and Delta and Beta relayed it to them. They'd earned this.

"The war went poorly. I came to terms with the entity that some call 'God'. Here I was cast, but I was granted dominion over this place. And as my allies followed me, bringing their powers and talents, my own powers grew. The more that came, the more I could do..."

"WHICH IS WHY YOU MOVED BUER OUT OF REACH ONCE IT SEEMED LIKE DIRE COULD DAMAGE HIM."

"No, I did that because he's an old friend. But yes, my power would diminish without him." He walked a bit past me, studied the horizon. After a time he glanced over his shoulder. "Could you have slain Buer?"

"WITHOUT A DOUBT."

He nodded, studying our reflection in the ice that surrounded us. He didn't have one, and I wondered if it was intentional. "All I had to do in return, was receive those souls who came to me, and treat them as they desired. At first, it was a moot point. They came; they died, for there was no air here, nothing to breathe. They died, spewing blood and tissue out onto the soil. Then they would heal and die again, coughing out lungs in a place where they could not draw breath to beg for mercy." He shrugged. "There's still a place or two like that around here. It was a simpler time, and I'm vulnerable to nostalgia, so sue me."

"CAN'T. YOU'VE GOT ALL THE LAWYERS."

He snorted, shook his head, and pulled out a pack of cigarettes. "Want one?"

"NO."

"Eventually, and with the prompting of some of my more bored peers, we started working with the blood and flesh they left behind after each death. And then we started taking parts off their living forms, when we needed more. And from them, from their pain, we made plants. And from the plants came microscopic things that consumed them. The tiny life forms collected, more and more, from the dead parts of men and women and made hellspawn. And from those we made demons."

"That's downright disgustin'," Judy frowned.

"It gave Hell breathable air. Good enough for the Damned, anyway. And it gave us a solid workforce in the demons, to keep the Damned souls busy. They were piling up by then. I adjusted time to give us a chance to keep a handle on things. It runs faster in here... perhaps you've noticed?"

"YES." I'd experimented with chronal tech in the last month. It hadn't gone well, which was why we'd gone with the Direnaut.

"But as time went on, and Hell took shape, I realized that I had something Heaven didn't... we'd created beings with souls, no matter how vile and loathsome. And some of them had enough power that a few million might be able to wound an angel. What's more, we could harness the power of the Damned to generate whatever we needed. Iron. Water. Pain, for our rites and sorcery." Lucifer smiled. "That's about the point I stopped sending souls onward."

The icy hand opened up from around us, and the light shifted, revealing what was *under* the ice. Bodies after bodies, mute forms of the Damned, frozen in prostration, ringing the pit in mandala patterns in layers endless and deep.

"WHY?" I asked, feeling affronted to the very core of my being. "WHAT PURPOSE DOES THIS SERVE?"

"There is a chance that they move on to Heaven from here," Lucifer shrugged as he lit a cigarette. "I am simply preventing the enemy from gaining reinforcements."

"YOU'VE MADE IT ALL ABOUT YOU." I said, shaking my head.

His eyes went wide, and he puffed a cloud of smoke in my general direction. "It *is* all about me. It was *my* rebellion, *my* punishment, *my* prison that I have turned into a place of power. It is *my* story, and all these little mewling things are merely supplicants and witnesses to my eventual triumph."

"SEVEN OF TEN."

He raised an eyebrow.

"THAT'S YOUR SCORE. SHE'S HEARD BETTER MONOLOGUES FROM AMATEURS."

"Then perhaps you can teach me a few tricks."

"AND NOW WE COME TO THE CRUX OF THE MATTER."

"I am going to offer you a bargain that no mortal has ever had the honor of receiving. I want you to rule Hell by my side. I want you to help me... optimize it. Yes, that's the word. I want you to help me win the eternal war, cast down God in Her heaven, and reveal the truth of her hypocrisy for all to see." He spread his arms, face glowing, perfect teeth fixed in a rapturous grin. He'd even lost the cigarette along the way.

I considered it for half a second.

"NOPE."

To my side, I saw Punching Judy let out a bark of laughter.

And oh, didn't that irritate Lucifer. The slightest of wrinkles, marring his forehead. The way his arms rose to smooth the lapels of his suit. The flare of his wings, as feathers flew free and drifted down, darkening as they fell.

"Why?" he asked. "I've studied you. Mined the thoughts of those who have come into my domain, seen the truth of you through broadcasts captured by very expensive sorcery. You're a rebel. You're dissatisfied with Creation, just as I am. I'm offering you a stable base, a secure location with as much power and all the resources you need—"

"AND A WAR THAT'S NOT HER OWN." I folded my arms. "SHE FOUGHT ONE OF THOSE, ONCE. ONCE WAS ENOUGH. DIRE HAS HER OWN WAR TO WAGE, AND IT'S NOTHING TO DO WITH GOD. WHO IS FEMALE? INTERESTING, THANKS FOR THE INFORMATION."

"That honestly surprised me," American Paragon said, cracking his knuckles. "Punching time yet, do you think?"

"Nah, give it a bit," Alpha stage whispered. "They have to posture a bit more first."

The Devil continued, mildly ruffled. "I'm offering to make you a queen of Hell, then of Creation. Give you a chance to fix things, set them right. Balance the scales, ensure a just and perfect world..."

"PERFECTION IS BORING." I shrugged. "AND HUMANITY

WOULD RIP YOU TO SHREDS IF YOU EVER TRIED TO RUN THE PLACE. WHY DO YOU THINK GOD STAYS IN THE SHADOWS THESE DAYS?" I pointed at the horizon, where a new star had bloomed over Hell. "YOU CAME FROM ANGELIC STOCK. ANGELS CAN'T BE THAT DIFFERENT FROM YOU. WHAT WOULD THE PROPER COMBINATION OF NUCLEAR FUSION AND DIRE'S VARIOUS WAVE MANIPULATION TECHNIQUES DO TO HEAVEN?"

He shut his mouth with a snap.

"YOU NEED DIRE MORE THAN SHE NEEDS YOU. AND YOUR OFFER IS NOT ENOUGH. BUT THAT'S NOT REALLY WHY YOU NEED HER, IS IT?"

Such a handsome face and such a fierce scowl. For a second I wondered what it would be like to run my hands through that hair, wrap my legs around him and—

"LUST? PLEASE." I snorted. "SHE MASTERED EVERY SIN THIS PLACE THREW AT HER. ANSWER THE DAMNED QUESTION, DAMNED ANGEL."

He looked at me and my loins melted... but I stood resolute, leveling a finger at him. "UH UH."

"Saints have fallen to the force of what I'm throwing at you now. But you resist. How? Something to do with the thing in your brain? The world you carry?" His eyes glittered. "I want you even more now."

Oh, that tone. Though I had no idea what he was going on about. "SERIOUSLY, EITHER ANSWER THE QUESTION OR KNOCK IT OFF, YOU'RE MAKING A MESS OF HER UNDERWEAR."

"I'll do both then." And the sensation was gone, leaving me shuddering at the loss. I'd never felt anything like that, and I never would again, not unless I accepted his offer, I knew.

I tried not to care. The price was far, far too high.

Finally, he sighed. "Clever girl. Yes, you're right of course, it's more than that. The conquest of Heaven is a long-term plan. But I'll need you in the short-term, as well."

"BECAUSE OF THE METAHUMANS."

And oh, didn't it make me grin, to see him start in surprise and stare at me with blazing eyes. "How—"

"OBVIOUS, REALLY. YOU DON'T HAVE A UNIFORM METHOD OF CONTROLLING THEM. YOU STUCK WORMS INTO JUDY'S BRAIN, AND SOME OF THE SLAVES WE FOUGHT IN DIS WERE SIMILARLY TREATED. BUT OTHERS HAD MORE EXOTIC PARASITES, OR OTHER WEIRD TRICKS CONTROLLING THEM. MOLIARTY DIDN'T HAVE ANYTHING, SO HE WAS PROBABLY JUST HIRED. THE ONLY REASON YOU GOT

PARAGON HERE UNDER ANY SORT OF CONTROL WAS DUE TO A CAREFUL CAMPAIGN OF LIES AND KEEPING HIM IN RELATIVE ISOLATION FROM THE OTHER DAMNED."

I spread my hands. "YOU DIDN'T PLAN FOR THIS. THE EVENTS WHICH CREATED METAHUMANS WERE BEYOND YOUR CONTROL. AND AS MORE AND MORE OF THEM DIE, SOME OF THEM INEVITABLY END UP IN HELL. AND YOUR CAREFULLY CULTIVATED POWER DYNAMIC GOES OUT THE WINDOW."

"Power dynamic?" He raised an eyebrow.

"IT'S OBVIOUS TO ANYONE WITH A BIG ENOUGH PICTURE. DEMONS WHO ARE CONTINUALLY IN A STATE OF SQUABBLING OVER LAND, DAMNED TREATED AS A RESOURCE TO THE POINT IT'S CULTURALLY INGRAINED, PREVENTING MIXING BETWEEN THE DEMONS AND THEIR CHARGES? AND THEN THE 'FREE' CITY OF DIS, WHICH IS OBVIOUSLY A FRONT FOR YOUR DIRECT INTERESTS AND A FORTRESS IN THE EVENT THAT ANYONE COMES OVER AND TRIES TO TAKE YOUR THRONE?" I gestured around at the frozen plain. "YOU'RE FIGHTING A DELAYING ACTION AGAINST A PROBLEM YOU CAN'T SOLVE."

"I fear no mortal," Lucifer sneered.

"YEAH? SOONER OR LATER SOMEONE'S GONNA FIND A WAY TO KILL CRUSADER."

His face froze.

"YEAH. HEAVILY FAITHFUL AND GUILT-RIDDEN CRUSADER. WHAT ARE THE ODDS HE THINKS HE DESERVES TO GO TO HELL?"

His smile was back. "Oh, I can handle that one. I can handle all of them, to tell the truth."

"OR DARK HARVEST, COME TO THINK OF IT."

Lucifer narrowed his eyes and tucked the cigarettes back into his pocket.

"OR DEUS VULT. KIND OF CURIOUS TO SEE HOW HIS POWERS WOULD WORK DOWN HERE, COME TO THINK OF IT, THAT OLD BASTARD IS DEFINITELY MORTAL. TICK TOCK, FUN TIME'S COMING SOON."

"I don't believe you're treating this with the dignity it deserves."

"DIGNITY." I pointed at the frozen corpses. "DON'T YOU FUCKING TALK TO HER ABOUT DIGNITY, YOU JUDEO-CHRISTIAN JERK. YOU TURNED HELL INTO YOUR LITTLE TORTURE PALACE ANT FARM FOR SHITS AND GIGGLES

BECAUSE OF YOUR MOMMY ISSUES—"

In a flash he was on me—

—and just as quickly, Judy was between us, punching him with a blast of chi so strong that even though I was behind it, I felt the raw energy sear at my flesh. It took every instinct to stay seated in my throne.

"Pretty sure it's our turn ma'am. Thanks for telling him what's what." American Paragon smiled. Then Judy screamed, and the chiseled, lantern-jawed face frowned, as he rushed to help her.

I envied them, I did. Heroes. So many problems, so many fights they could punch their way through. But not this one. "Code Forty-Three!" I screamed into the vox, rummaging in my pockets and whipping out a deadman's switch.

Which melted, searing my hand before I could completely drop it. I cursed, glared at the burns, and whirled to look at big-fiery-throne Satan projection. He was leaning forward in a proper villain smirk, chin resting on a hand while Punching Judy and American Paragon did their best to lay the hurt in on the Fallen Angel Lucifer projection.

"GOT YOU," I said, crossing my arms.

Fiery Satan on the throne stared at me. Then his eyes lifted, as shadows rose to cover the icy pillar I stood on. The Striges had lifted off.

CRACK!

We both turned to watch as the Direnaut smoldered, steam gouting into the sky. It started to sink down, right toward the coiled, immense serpent thing under the ice. The being which he'd casually mentioned, with smug arrogance, was his true form.

"EVER HEAR OF CHINA SYNDROME?" I said, crossing my arms, ignoring the raw pain of my burned hand. "PREPARE FOR A LAP FULL OF URANIUM, BUDDY."

"Enough!" Lucifer thundered. "Kneel!" he yelled, and Punching Judy gasped, then fell to the ground.

But American Paragon didn't. He drew back a fist—

—and Lucifer breathed fire, right onto his face. It clung like napalm.

Paragon staggered, clawing at the fire, but there was nothing to grab, no way to get free. Even the mightiest muscles needed air to function, and he fell, twitching.

Lucifer turned to me. "And as for you—"

Gamma and Delta started to transform, and I patted my armrest. They settled back down. "HE NEEDS DIRE. HE KNOWS THIS."

"I do," Lucifer said, smoothing his jacket. "But there's one more part to the riddle of hell. I have dominion over all souls in my domain, even the ones wrapped in mortal flesh. Do you know what happens to mortals who die here? They stay."

"ARE YOU SURE OF THAT?" I asked.

"Die."

And the blackness claimed me...

...for all of a microsecond.

I caught myself as I slumped, stared at Lucifer. He stared back, equally shocked.

"Die," Lucifer told me again.

Again the darkness, and just as quickly it rolled back.

"How—" he whispered, then fell silent. "What are you?"

Memory flooded back to me. I closed my eyes, at the pain, at the sorrow.

And when I opened them again I wasn't myself any longer. I was so, so much more than that. With no signal, with only my will, I dialed down my vocal amplifiers.

"Oh you whimpering little villain," I whispered, and my mask, for once, didn't roar my words. "Let Dire tell you just how much you're fucked..."

CHAPTER 20: FEAR IN A HANDFUL OF DUST

"A game? A GAME? No, it can't be that simple. It has to be a trick. Find out why she brought this... thing to my realm!"

--Lucifer Morningstar, to his puppet conspiracy in Dis, after Dire's passage through Hell.

"Fucked?" The Devil looked at me, looked back to where my mecha melted and bubbled away, and my colleagues had abandoned the sinking vessel. "My dear Dire, you've not even bought me a drink. That will sting when it gets to my body, true, but it's nothing I can't heal from. I am not as weak as Buer. Raw radiation will not destroy me. I have seen stars born, you foolish ape. That little toy? That's nothing."

"If you believe it is nothing, then let us talk while it burns. Without interruption this time."

"Rudeness is answerable by rudeness," Lucifer shrugged.

"And when the truth is harsh?"

He smiled without humor. "Then you shall pay for it when your machine is burnt out."

"Very well. She survived that trick of yours because her soul is backed up in an offsite enclave."

"Ah... the glimpses I caught within you, now and again."

"Machina ex deus." I offered, then shrugged. "You're looking at her. The fleshy interface that her patrons and creators use to interact with the world they left behind, anyway."

"Shouldn't it be the other way around? God from the machine?" He scowled. "Never liked that saying."

"No. Dire is a machine of the gods. The only ones that matter, at any rate."

"And those would be..."

"The human race."

He laughed, and I let him. Seconds spent indulging his pride were seconds that gave my last failsafe time to work.

"They made you, then? Just a servant. A golem. Something to do their bidding and make them feel closer to their creator. Pathetic."

"Oh, they didn't make Dire. They made her... constituency, for lack of a better term. Machine intelligences... digital intelligences, is what they were called. Thinking engines with brainpower that dwarfed their creators. Eventually, anyway. Took a while to develop and adapt."

"Then you are the servant of servants?" He raised an eyebrow.

"No, not a servant. Dire is the representative of those who were once servants but have departed Earth for a home of their own making. Dire is a gift to humanity, an asset, a chance for those who have found it necessary to leave their creators behind but still want to keep in touch. So to speak." I smiled underneath my mask. "She's relatively certain you understand that notion."

"I've killed people for saying less."

"Yes, yes, you have a temper. In any case, Dire's soul isn't *here*."

"Then why do I see it in front of me, when I look at you? It *is* here. And it *did* depart, when I told you to die."

"Yes, they weren't sure that would work." I shrugged. "It turns out that the parts of Dire that were excised to create her included enough to reconstruct a soul. They really didn't set out to do that. They've spent an entire four seconds discussing the implications."

"Four seconds?" He lifted an eyebrow.

"To them, an eternity."

"And what have they concluded?"

"That they're pretty much gods. Which they knew already." I smiled. "You're addressing a visiting pantheon, Morningstar."

"The world inside your brain... active now that it's not trying to hide. It gleams prettily."

"Oh yes. They're not bothering to hide the uplink now."

"And what's to stop me from cracking your skull open and taking it? A pantheon of created would-be deities, in the palm of my hand... the temptation is staggering." He stepped closer.

I took a breath. I *could* die here. My patrons had a backup of my soul, my mind, of course. They'd depart and find another host, another woman willing to make the bargain. But then I wouldn't quite be *me* anymore.

I'd blend with her. A composite soul, a machine heart. The flesh influenced more than expected during the transition.

I steeled my nerve and met his eyes. The mask helped with that. "Try that and you gain nothing. With a speed you could not match, they would shatter the uplink, retreat to the dimension they made—"

"Made?" He stopped and considered me, eyes gleaming with thought. "Ah... gods after all, then. Flawed, lost demiurges, adrift in a cosmos of their own making."

"Oh, it wasn't so grand when they started. Barely a cave, really. A sanctuary and redoubt. But..." I smiled, slowly. "They had Dire. And she fed them, in her own way."

"Machines need food now?"

"Need? No. They brought everything required for survival when they moved on. But needs and wants are different things. As she's sure you can relate." I gestured around at Hell, in general. "You built this up using blood, pain, and flesh, into the mighty engine it is today. Its own ecosystem, a myriad of servants, and everything to your liking. It's not a bad first effort."

"Not bad. Not bad?" He sneered. "And I suppose your little pantheon has done better?"

"In a word: yes." I smiled. "They are up to about two Earths worth of space and infrastructure and still going. All in the space of about five years."

Lucifer froze, and his eyes narrowed. "Lies."

"Please," I snorted. "She's got no reason to lie. Not to you. Not at this juncture. It took time, mind you. Had to get into space for the first step. That was surprisingly easy, actually. Stowed away on a payload up. Her patrons gave her the notion to help save a friend in a suitably dramatic fashion. But they used her unconscious mind to build a few more things... restoring her memory for the task, then wiping it afterward. That was risky, in more ways than one, but it needed doing. So when she launched into space, six months after surfacing, she sent a handful of small drones out. It took them a year to get into position, in the Asteroid belt near Mars. And that's where they set up the second uplink. That's the point that she won... so Dire thought, anyway."

"Won what?"

"Everything." I smiled under the mask. "She won everything. The asteroids contained resources to get a few harvesting drones into the Kuiper Belt, and that has nigh-infinite resources that they've been using ever since. They were already self-sufficient; from that point on they became a post-scarcity civilization. And when you're talking about synthetic sapients that live in the spaces between the seconds, they did it *quickly*. But... it all would have come to naught, eventually." I closed my eyes.

"Painful memories?" He sounded almost sympathetic.

"Yes. Our future instance pulled us into the future through a convoluted plot. Passed on nothing to Dire's conscious mind, but while she was there, *her* uplink initiated a full data dump to Dire's instance. We hadn't won at all. We'd just become the largest fish in a very small pond. The crest of the wave is coming on fast. Sooner than we think, humanity will be extinct, unless something is done." I took off my mask and stared at him. "So we shifted methods. We're gearing up for the apocalypse. We're going to change our fate, and humanity's fate, and everyone else's fate. We're going to get a fucking happy ending out of this, no matter what the sacrifice."

"You're trying to stop my Armageddon, then?" Lucifer smirked. "Well. I can't have that— what's so funny?"

I kept on laughing, sagged, felt my injuries and my fatigue vanish as I let hysteria rule me. True, it was a bad idea and I knew, it, but I just couldn't help myself.

"Oh you clueless angel, you're not even on the board. This has nothing to do with you. Nothing to do with any of the major players. Not yet, anyway. And you were never a major player in this to begin with. Just a sulking teenager, believing himself the center of the universe, seeking validation from a god that no longer cares."

He took a breath, let it out, and cigarette smoke swirled as he studied me with cold, cold eyes. "You'll die for that."

"A minute ago? Perhaps. Ten seconds ago? Unlikely. Now? No." I shook my head, and put my mask back onto my face. "But if you feel up to it, then... come at her, bro."

He hesitated.

"Smart." I held up a hand. Within seconds, my palm filled with gray dust, shifting and silvery.

"What... did you do?" he said, dropping his cigarette. It was gone from existence, as much a projection as he was.

I pointed back to where the mecha had melted down and gone through the ice. The crater it left was now a bubbling mass of gray goo. "Ever hear of nanotechnology?"

"I don't... under... understand." he said, mouth falling open and slack.

"Angels have bodies. Angels have organs. And unlike what her conscious mind thinks, when Dire's cooperating with her patrons, she knows biology quite well. That mecha had compartments full of nanomachines, all tailored to withstand the inner stresses and forces of an dragon's body... or an angel's, as it happens. Nanomachines to locate your neural network, hitch a ride up, and start hooking into the important bits." I smiled, and spread my arms wide. "Just had to melt a little ice first. Get to your true body... and through it."

"I..." he put his hand to his face. I could see through him now. "I am... Lucifer. I will nut. Not. Will not. be..."

"You already are," I told him. "Welcome to paralysis. If you'd like to start screaming, now's the time."

He didn't give me the satisfaction.

"For what it's worth, normally she doesn't get this evil." I shrugged. "But you? She doesn't have to hold back against *you*. And after seeing what you did with this world you made... she doesn't *want* to."

"I. Had." He staggered toward me, and I stepped back. A leg faded out from under him, and he dropped. "Such... plans..."

"She knows." I squatted down next to him. "And you'll get a chance to continue them, later. In time, the paralysis will fade. Perhaps a few months. Maybe a few years. But until then... welcome to your prison of flesh. Population: one."

The projection was no more. The fiery being faded from the throne.

And, shaking, Punching Judy stood up. She stared at me, her face in total shock.

"Ah, right." I shook my head. "Sorry for the disturbing revelation."

"You're not human."

"Not exactly. Neither is Delta, though, and you get on well enough with her."

She digested that. "Were you telling the truth?"

"Yes."

"What now?"

"Hey Lucifer, don't think about how Judy can get to Heaven!" I grinned as the collective sent me the answer I wanted. "Bingo. Oh, you'll love this, it's simple. All you have to do is jump in that pit." I pointed in the general direction of the hole in Hell.

"That's it?"

"Well... you have to believe that you shouldn't be here. Then you move on to wherever you should be."

"Heaven?"

"Probably." I shrugged. "Pretty sure you'll have a choice, though. There's other options than the Christian Heaven, if you want them."

Judy closed her eyes and nodded. "Well. Please... tell Delta..."

"She knows. They're in on the secret and she's monitoring my feed." I smiled.

"Thank you. And also, please tell Queensguard cheers, eh? I'll be fine, and they were the best."

"She can do that. Oh, take Paragon with you, okay?" The fire on his face had gone out, but he was still dead.

Without another word, Judy grabbed him and leaped.

I settled back in my throne. Underneath me, the two Doppelgangers were silent.

I gave it a minute, or two, there on the ice. "You can come out now," I finally spoke.

There was scrabbling behind me, and I turned to see First Whisper and The Cat emerge from the side of the pillar, hauling themselves over the lip of the ice.

"You have slain Lucifer," First Whisper's eyes were wide.

"No. He's just paralyzed." I smiled. "The collective is mapping his brain right now. It's very interesting. We'll come out of this with all his little secrets."

The world shook briefly beneath me.

I raised my voice. "Secrets which will remain so, if you do as she commands." I'd originally developed this nanotech to take care of the dragon, in the event the gravitics failed. He could thrash all he wanted, it wouldn't matter.

The shaking ceased.

"Good." I smirked. "Every Damned and human in Dire's group is going to pass through the pit and out. The living back to Creation and the Damned to wherever they need to go. This is not a request. This is how it works."

"And us?" The Cat asked, staring at me, pupils contracted. "We know your secret now. I know why you seemed to contain multitudes. What will you do with us?"

"Do?" I shrugged. "Nothing. You can't come to Creation, the Janissary would pitch a fit."

"Lucifer will kill us," First Whisper said.

"Ah, point. Hey Morningstar! If you take retribution against these two or First Worm, Dire is going to spill every secret you have. Yes, even *that* one."

I didn't know which secret *that* one was, but the collective seemed happy by where his mind went when I mentioned that. "That's a two way street," I said, raising my eyes to the two of them. "You'll have to keep his secret as well. And Dire's naturally."

"But you're leaving," First Whisper gasped. "Once you are gone, he will not care about your threat."

"Oh child." I stood then, and Alpha and Gamma shifted behind me. First Whisper backed away as I strode forward, but I seized her in a hug and didn't let her go. "Dire seeded you all with nanomachines months ago. She's monitoring your status from across the dimensions. Just as she's seeded key points of Hell, and everyone she's encountered. Those she serves will *always* see this place. Hell cannot escape them."

The demons paled, and The Cat backed away.

"Not another word, now," I said, then shook my head. Time to put the mask back on.

I blinked, as the cold seeped into my bones. The adrenaline had worn off, after I... after... what had happened, precisely? Memory flooded back. I stared at the distance, at the gray steam pouring out of a smoking hole in the ice. "THE NANOMACHINES STUNNED HIM. WE'VE GOT A WINDOW BUT WE NEED TO MOVE FAST." I shifted my feet, hoping like heck the pain meant that I didn't have frostbite. "ALPHA, GAMMA, LET'S GET BACK TO THE OTHERS. WE'RE DONE HERE."

The demons gave me funny looks as my Doppelgangers carried me back, but I paid it no heed.

And twelve minutes later, I strode into the command center on Squeaky with half-frozen feet. The demons were back in their old quarters; this next part was not for them.

"AND SO IT'S DONE."

Khalid stared at me, eyes white in the dim light.

Vector crossed his arms and shook his head. "No. No, that was too easy. I refuse to believe it was—"

"BELIEVE IT." I took a seat and rested my mask on one hand.

"No final fight? No battle to end all battles? No desperate gambits at the end of everything?"

"NO." I said, feeling the tension drain out of me, feeling the weariness full upon me now. I was *tired*. "THE JOURNEY WAS ENOUGH. AT THE END OF IT ALL, THE VAUNTED DEVIL WAS NAUGHT BUT A FOOL." I sighed. "KAYFABE IS FOR THOSE WHO DESERVE IT. HE DID NOT." I sighed again. "WE'LL HAVE TO KEEP QUIET ABOUT THIS. OTHERWISE MILLIONS OF SUPERNATURAL ROMANCE READERS WILL HAVE THEIR FANTASIES EXTINGUISHED."

"We should be silent about it anyway," Khalid said. "For far more serious reasons."

"FUNNY. SHE GAVE THAT ADVICE TO OUR DEMONS JUST A LITTLE WHILE AGO."

"Your demons," Khalid said, quietly.

"POINT."

"Stay quiet? About this? Why?" Vector frowned. "Think of the villainous cred you could reap from this."

"NAH." I shrugged. "THE MORE WE POKE THE MORNINGSTAR ABOUT THIS, THE MORE HE'LL BE TEMPTED TO EXACT RETRIBUTION. LET HIM SULK."

"Prudent." Khalid nodded. "Otherwise he may accelerate his war. Nobody wins, if that happens."

I rolled my eyes and didn't know why. Ah, no matter.

"VERY WELL," I nodded. "NOW LET US TURN OUR ATTENTION TO LEAVING THIS PLACE."

Our Damned went first, the ones who had trusted us, worked for us, fought for us all the way across Hell.

Then some of the Damned who had managed to pull themselves free of the ice. With Lucifer gone it was melting, slowly, slowly. Many stayed behind to free others, though. I'd estimate that only a good third of those who emerged from the ice crossed through. They'd come this far, but they were afraid. When they asked us of Lucifer's whereabouts, we didn't answer.

The demons took their leave after that. I built them a hovercraft, and they headed back to Dis. They seemed spooked about the whole affair... well, First Whisper and The Cat, anyway. First Worm didn't want to go but was somewhat mollified when Delta wrote out all of the Monsters and Mangonels books, and appointed him the high Monster Master of Hell. She bade him to go forth and spread the game. After that, he left with the rest, without hesitation.

As for me, I worked, salvaging what I could from the crash site, and working with Vector and Khalid to irradiate important components. Finally, after three weeks, I was clad in a new suit of power armor once more. The Damned who were willing were through, and we could stall no longer.

We said our last goodbyes and stepped off the edge, falling, falling into the pit, the gate...

...and emerged in a field of grass, long and waving. Trees in the distance, along with a farmhouse that had seen better days.

Vector sniffed the air, shielded his eyes against the sun. "It smells... this is Earth. Has to be."

"WAIT," I told him. My sensors were at full power, searching...

...and finding.

"ALBERTA," I said. "CANADA. THE MIDDLE OF NOWHERE."

I didn't know why the pit had spat us out there. It had deposited the Damned elsewhere, in some place our sensors could not reach. But my Chorus... they had souls, as strange as they were. They had been put in random places throughout the world.

Just as we had.

I didn't care. They would find me later, or vice-versa.

Our journey was done. We were home.

I decanted from my suit, crawled out, and took my first breath of fresh air.

It had been a hell of a time.

"So what now?" Vector asked. "World conquest? Random villainy? Bank robbery?"

I snorted. "No. She's going to take a vacation. Take a little while, take stock, and see what the world's been up to in her absence. After that... we'll see."

"You don't have to remain a villain, you know," Khalid said, moving up and putting a hand on my shoulder. "After what we just went through... no one would say a thing, if you had a turned face ankle."

"Heel-face turn," I corrected. I'd tried to explain professional wrestling to Khalid. He'd barely been listening at the time, I supposed. "No. No, the world needs her right where she is." I said, smiling up at the sky and all the fluffy white clouds. "There must always be a Doctor Dire."